Dear Reader,

As the hot sun [...] what better way to be
prepared for a day at the beach than with a Harlequin
Duets? Remember, when you've finished one story, it's
time to check your tan and turn over!

This month offers two wonderful Duets for your
entertainment. Long-time reader favorite Victoria Pade
brings us *Downhome Darlin'*, a charming and
entertaining story of a good girl who's been "good"
for too long. Then Liz Ireland, familiar to readers of
Harlequin Historicals and Harlequin American Romance,
spins a dizzying tale of identical brothers who switch
places at a wedding in *The Best Man Switch*.

Popular Cheryl St.John pens a delightful and captivating
pretend marriage of convenience with *For This Week
I Thee Wed*. Next Alyssa Dean writes our second
Real Men story, *50 Clues He's Mr. Right*, set around the
women who work at *Real Men* magazine.

Once again, enjoy Harlequin Duets—the lighter side of
love. Double the pleasure. Still no calories.

Happy reading!

Malle Vallik

Malle Vallik
Senior Editor

P.S. We'd love to hear what you think about Harlequin
Duets! Drop us a line at:
 Harlequin Duets
 Harlequin Books
 225 Duncan Mill Road
 Don Mills, Ontario
 M3B 3K9 Canada

Downhome Darlin'

Cal hadn't known a lot of wholesome women.

And in spite of the way Abby had dolled herself up the night before, the minute he'd set eyes on her he'd spotted her as a wholesome woman.

One of the few to ever cross his path.

Since he and women had started taking notice of each other he'd abided by a private code. A code that had counted out women like Abby Stanton even when he did encounter them.

Living the life he led, it just seemed smart. Women like Abby Stanton were not women to play around with. And he'd always been a player.

So what was he doing with her in his bed?

"About last night..." Grant began.

Mitzi shook her head frantically. "I know, you're going to apologize. The bride probably told you to. Grant, we both spoke fairly bluntly last night."

Grant remembered his brother's muttering about being a lout and realized Mitzi must have really let him have it. Good.

"But what I've come to realize," Mitzi continued, "is that I got so angry because I didn't want to admit you were correct."

The last thing he wanted was for Mitzi to accept his Neanderthal brother's assessment of her personality! "Listen, Mitzi..."

"No—I have to say this now or I never will." She looked up at him, her face twisted with emotion. Her brow wrinkled adorably.

Something about her earnestness made him smile. He chuckled under his breath. "Okay, shoot. What is it you want me to know?"

"Just that, if your offer still stands, I want to take you up on it."

"My offer?"

She swallowed. "I want us to have that fling."

HARLEQUIN DUETS

ISBN 0-373-44071-5

DOWNHOME DARLIN'
Copyright © 1999 by Victoria Pade

THE BEST MAN SWITCH
Copyright © 1999 by Elizabeth Bass

This edition published by arrangement with Harlequin Books S.A.

Look us up on-line at: http://www.romance.net

Printed in U.S.A.

VICTORIA PADE

Downhome Darlin'

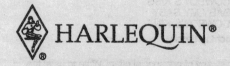

HARLEQUIN®

TORONTO • NEW YORK • LONDON
AMSTERDAM • PARIS • SYDNEY • HAMBURG
STOCKHOLM • ATHENS • TOKYO • MILAN • MADRID
PRAGUE • WARSAW • BUDAPEST • AUCKLAND

Victoria Pade is a bestselling author of both historical and contemporary romance fiction, and mother of two energetic daughters, Cori and Erin. Although she enjoys her chosen career as a novelist, she occasionally laments that she has never traveled farther from her Colorado home than Disneyland, instead spending all her spare time plugging away at her computer. She takes breaks from writing by indulging in her favorite hobby—eating chocolate.

Books by Victoria Pade

SILHOUETTE SPECIAL EDITION
*1159—COWBOY'S LOVE
*1106—COWBOY'S LADY
1057—MOM FOR HIRE
*970—COWBOY'S KISS
*946—BABY MY BABY
*923—COWBOY'S KIN

* A Ranching Family

Don't miss any of our special offers. Write to us at the following address for information on our newest releases.

Harlequin Reader Service
U.S.: 3010 Walden Ave., P.O. Box 1325, Buffalo, NY 14269
Canadian: P.O. Box 609, Fort Erie, Ont. L2A 5X3

1

"I TOLD YOU she couldn't do it."

"Oh, right, like I disagreed."

Abby Stanton made a face at her two sisters. It actually looked as if there were four of them unless she really concentrated on focusing her eyes so she didn't see double.

What was it they had her drinking? She wasn't exactly sure. She recalled Emily and Bree discussing what she should order that would be in keeping with the theme of the night—Abby Stanton Becomes a Wild Woman. They'd mentioned Kamikazes and Slippery Nipples. But she wasn't sure if she'd actually downed either of those. Or both.

Both seemed likely since she was beginning to think this was a suicide mission and every time she caught a glimpse of a certain cowboy over by the bar, she could imagine her nipples being slippery.

"A wild woman would squeeze his buns the next time he walks by," Bree said, goading Abby about that same cowboy, who'd caught her attention. "So that's the deal. You want to prove you can be a wild woman, you squeeze his buns."

A wild woman. Wasn't it enough that she was in a bar and so drunk she could hardly see straight? Because that was pretty wild for a woman who'd grown up in sleepy Clangton, Colorado, a not too large town spread out over a twelve-mile central radius and more outlying farm and ranchland than anyone had bothered to count in the past hundred years.

"I don't think he'd mind too much, Ab," Emily added encouragingly. "He keeps looking over at you, watching you."

"Who is he?" Abby asked as if that would make a difference in accepting or rejecting the challenge.

With a population of 2,032 people in Clangton, it wasn't as if everybody knew everybody else. But Abby, Bree and Emily had been born and raised there and ran the Three Sisters Bakery in the middle of town, so while they might not know every name, it wasn't hard to pick out a new face. Especially one with features that could have been designed by da Vinci—well-defined planes of masculine perfection in a broad brow; a nose that was long, thin and flared slightly at the nostrils; a chin and jawline sharp enough to slice bread; and cheeks that dipped in just enough to make him ruggedly handsome.

"That's Cal Ketchum," Bree said in answer to Abby's question about who the guy was. "He's the new owner of the old Peterson place. Remember, I told you about him. He was friends with Cissy Carlisle's cousin in Denver—the cousin who rotates women like other people rotate their tires. He put Cal Ketchum in touch with Cissy so she could finally use that real-estate license of hers to sell him some property."

Emily picked up where Bree left off. "Cal Ketchum took Cissy out a few times after he moved in. She really liked him but she said that the first time she mentioned that she wanted to get married someday—just in general, not necessarily to him—he said he was not the guy for her, that he wasn't interested in marriage. Cissy says he's an even bigger ladies' man than her cousin is. She called him the original serial dater. A real so-many-women-so-little-time sort of guy, who'll never settle down and take a wife because it would limit him too much.''

"Great. And you want me to goose him and make him think I want to be next on his hit parade of women?''

"A wild woman would do it just because he has the best butt in this place,'' Emily said, not sounding like her usual conservative self. ''Guess you'll just have to admit you aren't a wild woman.''

Which meant admitting that she *was* what Bill Snodgrass had said she was—the reason he'd given for breaking their engagement. He had accused her of being a too shy, too quiet, too predictable, too steady, too provincial bore.

Okay, so he hadn't said she was a bore. At least he hadn't used that particular word. But that's what he'd meant. And tonight Abby had set out to prove she could be as unshy, unquiet, unpredictable, unprovincial and unboring as the best of them. At least to herself. Bill Snodgrass was history.

Just then Bree sat up tall and waved Cal Ketchum over to their table. ''Okay, he's coming. I'm giving you the setup.''

Abby glanced up to find the tall, muscular man headed in their direction, his eyes locked on her the whole way despite the fact that it was her sister who'd summoned him.

Oh, but what eyes they were! An incredible aquamarine color as clear as a spring-fed lake on a blistering summer's day.

Or maybe it was his eyes that were blistering her because they seemed to drill into her with a smoldering heat that made her think all over again about slippery nipples.

"Ladies," he greeted them all while still keeping those gorgeous eyes on Abby alone. His voice was like another drink—a hot toddy of dark whiskey, warm honey and just a hint of lemon to add a tang to it.

Abby was relieved that he stopped across the table from her. Between Bree and Emily. Out of her reach and freeing her from the looming challenge. At least for the moment.

"Somethin' I can do for you?" he asked.

"We just wanted to know if you're who we think you are," Abby answered, sounding overly bright, overly cheerful, overly loud and nothing at all like herself.

Even so, it won her a bad-boy smile that was enough to make her toes twitter.

"Who do you think I am?" he queried with an edge of teasing to his tone.

"Cal Ketchum," Bree said as if it were a quiz show and she needed to be quickest with the answer.

He bowed his head slightly, glancing at her for only a split second before looking back at Abby. "That's me," he said, pausing then as if waiting for them to introduce themselves. But when they didn't, he said, "Are you all celebratin' somethin'?"

"Freedom!" Abby responded too abruptly for it to be true, holding her glass aloft. But the motion was jerky, and she sloshed some of the contents over the rim to spill on the table.

Without considering that it might ruin her wild-woman image, she used a napkin to wipe the outside of the glass clean. Then she set it down and primly mopped up the small puddle.

When she'd finished, she raised her gaze to the man again. His mouth was pale and supple looking with lips that curved gently upward at the corners even when he wasn't smiling. But now he was smiling. A small, secret, knowing smile that drew two deep, curving lines on either side of his mouth and made her think he could see right through her.

"Well, I hope you're enjoyin' yourselves," he said, sounding dubious and slightly confused—probably about why they'd called him over when all the three of them were doing was gawking. "Was that all you wanted?" he asked.

"Pretty much," Bree said airily.

"Okay. Well, now that you know, I hope you have a nice evenin'," he said, being a good sport about things and not at all embarrassed or put off by the fact that clearly they were playing a game with him.

He seemed to catch sight of someone he knew then and stepped around Bree's chair to head for the portion of the saloon behind Abby. Which meant he was going to pass by her after all.

Bree kicked Abby under the table, reminding her of the challenge to prove she really could let loose by pinching the man's backside.

Would she or wouldn't she? she asked herself as time and the handsome cowboy seemed to move in slow motion.

"Do it!" Emily whispered.

And she did. Sort of.

As the back pockets of a pair of tight blue jeans covering a firm, not too round, just right rear end slid by nearly at eye level and close enough for her to reach out an unsteady hand, Abby gave him a tentative little pat.

Still, it stopped him cold and made him turn only enough to look straight down at her with those turquoise eyes.

Abby wanted to crawl into a hole.

Thinking as fast as her liquor-sludged brain would allow, she said, "Bug!" and started stomping her foot on the floor as if to kill what she hoped he'd think she'd just brushed off his backside.

"Bug?" he repeated with just a tinge of facetiousness to his tone, not looking anywhere but at her.

"On you. It might have bitten you," she babbled like a kid compounding a lie to make it more believable. But all the while she could feel the heat that rushed to her face, and no doubt turned it cherry-red to give her away.

"Nice try," he said, winking at her before moving on.

Abby wasn't sure whether he meant that the story about the bug on his backside had been a nice try at covering up or if the pat itself hadn't been any better than a nice try.

She only knew that she needed a quick diversion, so she reached for her glass again and downed its contents in one gulp as if the fiery liquid would wash away the embarrassment she didn't want anyone to see. Then she slammed the glass on the table in a completely false show of bravado and said, "So there."

Bree and Emily laughed.

And a bit of the real Abby emerged to give them a big-sister lecture. "It wasn't very nice of you guys to get him over here and then not at least make conversation so it looked like you called him for a reason."

"We did call him over for a reason—to get you to goose him," Bree answered, sounding pretty drunk herself.

"So how was it? Does it feel as good as it looks?" Emily asked.

Abby drew herself up and pretended indignation. "We wild women don't pat and tell," she claimed loftily. Then to escape further questions, she pushed her empty glass to the center of the table and said, "Order me another drink while I play some music on the jukebox."

She stood for the first time since arriving at the Clangton Saloon and discovered something had melted the starch out of her legs and taken away her equilibrium. As with forcing her eyes not to see double, she had to concentrate to walk in a straight line.

The place was big, all done up like an old Western saloon to put some truth to its name. A carved-walnut bar the full length of an end wall was the centerpiece of the establishment. Behind the bar was a gigantic framed mirror that reflected everything and everybody.

There was floor space enough for dancing and a sea of tables that were all full on this Saturday night as Abby carefully navigated through the crowd. She kept her eyes trained on the bright neon yellow-and-green lights of the jukebox where it stood beside a wide archway with intricate latticework in a fanned wagon-wheel design across the top. The archway led to an adjoining room with four pool tables, a dartboard hung on one wall and checkerboards and chessboards set up on tables in alcoves that jutted out behind velvet tie-back curtains.

"Sorry to hear about you and Bill," someone said as she passed a table.

Someone else added, "Me, too. Keep your chin up."

Abby just raised an acknowledging hand in the general direction of the voices, afraid she'd lose her balance if she looked around to find faces to go with the voices. It didn't matter anyway. Clangton was a small enough town for word to travel fast, and she'd been answering so many sympathetic comments like that since Bill had dumped her three weeks ago that it was beginning to seem like the only way folks could greet her anymore.

The selections on the jukebox were all country-western—most of them the lost-love variety. But Abby managed to choose one of the few lighthearted ditties that was available. Then she decided to make a trip to the rest room before she returned to the table.

The bathrooms were at the end of a small hallway next to the bar where the man whose rear end she'd just patted had been standing most of the night. He wasn't there now, though, and she was grateful for that.

Inside she took care of business and then washed her hands. As she did, she couldn't help catching a glimpse of herself in the mirror, doing a double take because tonight she really didn't look the way she usually did. The wild-woman image she'd adopted had seemed to require different clothes than she ordinarily wore, different makeup. A little shopping that afternoon had netted her the revamped look.

Rather than the loose-fitting blue jeans and tops that made up her wardrobe, she'd purchased a pair of black denims that hugged her every curve like sausage casing. The lowermost point of her V-necked T-shirt dipped into her cleavage—the artificial cleavage the new push-up bra gave her.

And as for her makeup, she had applied a whole lot more than the everyday light mascara and blush. Tonight she had on eye shadow that deepened the already dark brown—almost black—color of her eyes, and even eyeliner to outline them. And lipstick—not her regular bare hint of tint in what was mostly gloss. Tonight she had on something called raisin.

Plus her hair was bigger than she normally ever let it get. As a rule the middle-of-her-back length of dark, dark coffee-bean brown, naturally curly hair was brushed into a tight plait or held in a ponytail or at least kept under control by barrettes. But in anticipation of this evening she'd scrunched and sprayed it to within an inch of its life—all while bending upside down to get the most volume she possibly could. It left her with an untamed riot of curls all around her face and shoulders.

She actually liked the hair, she decided as she assessed the whole picture in the mirror. But the heavier makeup was something else again. It was on the harsh side and very extreme by her normal standards.

But then wild women went to extremes, didn't they? Nope, nothing conservative for her. Not tonight, anyway.

One of the women in the bathroom asked another for the time as Abby dried her hands.

"Eleven thirty-seven," came the answer, and it seemed to echo in Abby's mind.

Eleven thirty-seven...

Where would she have been at eleven thirty-seven if today had gone as planned?

She'd been fighting thoughts like that since waking up this morning, but now she couldn't seem to avoid it.

She had not planned to be in a saloon bathroom—that's for sure.

She and Bill were to have been in downtown Denver by now.

At the Fairmont Hotel.

In the bridal suite.

In the *bed* in the bridal suite...

Except when that image flooded her mind, the man with her wasn't her former fiancé. It was the man whose buns she'd just patted. Shedding his shirt. Stripping off his tight jeans and exposing a body to die for. Long and hard all over. Wanting her. Taking her into his arms—forcefully, but not too forcefully. Kissing her. Touching her. Making mindless, passionate love to her...

It suddenly seemed about thirty degrees too warm in that bathroom.

I really must be drunk, Abby thought, not altogether sure because she'd never been more than tipsy from a glass of wine or a little beer before. Yet what else could account for a fantasy that vivid as she stood at the sink in a public rest room?

But so what if she *was* drunk? This was the night for new things. Maybe she couldn't be in the bridal-suite bed of the Fairmont Hotel, but she could at least be out pretending it didn't matter that she wasn't. If that made any sense at all. Which it probably didn't because the longer she was on her feet the more muzzy her head felt, letting her know that the drinks she'd been chugging one right after another were kicking in with the force of a mule.

"Better get back to the table while the gettin's good," she advised her reflection as she dried her hands.

She turned away from the sink and needed to steady herself until her spinning senses caught up with her. Then she took a deep breath, drew herself up as tall as her five-foot-four-inch height would allow and concentrated on walking without weaving so she could leave the rest room.

But she didn't get beyond the other side of the door before freezing in her tracks. Standing at the open end of the hallway was the rear-end cowboy, his shoulder braced against the wall, facing her dead on as if he'd been waiting for her.

Abby's mouth went suddenly dry, and her courage lagged something fierce. She stared at him as if he were a hallucination she could will away.

But he didn't go away. He just went on standing there in all his glory.

And he was glorious. In fact he was probably the sexiest sight she'd ever laid eyes on with that heart-stoppingly handsome face and that body made for sin. He really was tall—he hadn't just seemed that way because she'd been sitting before. He was probably an inch or two over six feet, depending on the height of the heels of the snakeskin cowboy boots he wore.

His waist was narrow where a crisp white Western

shirt with pearl snaps up the front was tucked into his tight jeans. The sleeves were rolled to midbicep—mid-*muscular*-bicep—also exposing thick forearms that were crossed over a powerful-looking chest, each hand buried under the opposite armpit with only his thumbs insolently poking out. And his shoulders were so broad that Abby had a fleeting image of a mainsail flung wide by the wind.

He had great hair, too, she couldn't help noticing. Wavy hair the rich shade of bittersweet chocolate, just slightly lighter than the color of her own. He wore it a tad too long to be conventional, and it looked as if it got finger combed out of his way when it bothered him, but it didn't seem messy at all. Instead it fell into place and gave him a rakish look that only enhanced his handsome features without any sign that he paid too much attention to his appearance.

Did he even know how great he looked? she wondered. He must. Didn't all gorgeous men know it?

There wasn't any sign of it, though. No arrogance. No indication that he was even aware of the impact he was having on her. But he did keep staring at her as if he was taking stock of her the way she was taking stock of him. Or maybe he was waiting for her to make a move.

But the only move she could think to make was to drop her gaze, wanting to break the connection that seemed to wrap around them and tune out everything else.

The trouble was, her gaze landed on his hips where one of them angled out to brace his weight, and where a big silver belt buckle rested atop the well-endowed zipper of his jeans.

She yanked her eyes upward in a hurry when she realized what she was looking at, poked a nervous thumb over her shoulder and said "Bathroom" as if that explained something.

His oh-so-sensuous lips stretched into a half grin that deepened the crease on that side of his mouth. "I know. How was it?"

He was teasing her. She could tell by the sparkle that lit his eyes even in the dimness of the hallway. And she wished she'd been able to buy some aplomb along with her wild-woman clothes and makeup so she might have a little on hand right at that moment.

As it was, she just felt herself blushing again. "Clean," was all she could think to answer. "They keep a clean rest room here. Most of the establishments in Clangton do. If there's one thing you can say about Clangton, it's that we have clean bathrooms...." Babbling. She was babbling again.

He raised his chin in a little nod. "You got me over to your table for my name...and to brush a *bug* off my backside," he said wryly, as if he'd realized their game, "but you didn't introduce yourself."

"Oh. Um...Abby. Abby Stanton."

"Hello, Abby Abby Stanton."

"Hi," she said, feeling like an idiot. Then she made it even worse by adding, "And bye," as she forced herself to move away from the bathroom door, intending to slip past him and return to her sisters.

This time she made it all the way to his end of the hallway before stalling again. There wasn't space enough for her to get by with him standing the way he was, blocking more than half the entrance back into the barroom. And he didn't seem inclined to move.

Instead he went on staring at her, studying her, this time from the high perch of his height, down his perfectly sculpted nose.

"Excuse me," Abby said, trying not to look straight at him, trying to pretend there wasn't anything sizzling in the air between them. After all, it might just be her imagination.

Still he stayed put for a little while longer before pivoting with his spine against the corner of the wall like a hinge. His eyes never left her as he tossed a nod out toward the table she'd left moments before.

"Looks like your friends have hooked up with more friends."

She couldn't for the life of her have explained why she actually felt heat emanating from his gaze but decided it had to be an alcohol-induced illusion.

Fighting to ignore it, she scanned the barroom until she found her table and discovered what he was talking about. Five other people had joined Bree and Emily.

"Those aren't my friends. Well, the extra five are. And so are the first two, but they're also my sisters," she muttered, referring to his comment about her friends having hooked up with more friends.

"Seems like they're gettin' a pretty good party goin'."

True enough. Everyone at the table was laughing uproariously at something Bernie McGuire, the local dry cleaner, had said.

"Aren't you itchin' to get out there?"

Not really, she thought. In fact not at all. Emily and Bree had been playing along with the put-the-past-behind-her tone for tonight. But Abby knew what would happen when she joined the rest of them. They'd pour on the sympathy, and this would turn into a pity party.

She hadn't realized she hadn't answered Cal Ketchum until his deep, smooth masculine voice came again.

"Why do I have the feelin' you're a fish out of water here?"

"Who, me? No way. I'm a wild woman through and through," she lied.

"Is that so?" He pushed away from the wall and inclined his head in the direction of the bar. "Then how about I buy you a drink, Wild Woman?"

It sounded like a challenge to prove her claim about herself. And this was not the night Abby was going to turn down any challenge.

"Sure. Why not."

"What are you drinkin'?"

"Beats me," she said as he turned to the spot he'd been occupying most of the evening and she stepped up to the bar beside him.

He questioned the bartender, who checked with the waiter who'd been looking after Abby's table, and another drink appeared just like some of those she'd already guzzled tonight.

"What does that mean exactly—wild woman?" Cal Ketchum asked then with that half grin in place again.

"Oh, you know. Devil-may-care. Free spirited. Fly by the seat of my pants. Do just about anything—"

"Really…" he said, drawing the word out as if she'd just given him very intriguing information. Or was that doubt in his tone?

Just in case it might be, Abby lifted the glass and didn't put it down until she'd drained it.

When she looked over at him afterward, she found his expression amused.

"So tell me about yourself, Abby Abby Stanton. Freedom from what?"

"Freedom?"

"You said you were celebratin' your freedom."

"Oh, right. Just freedom. In general."

He nodded but he didn't believe her. She saw it in his eyes. Great eyes. She could get lost in those eyes....

"Freedom to do *anything*," he said suggestively.

She shrugged elaborately.

"Like comin' out tonight, drinkin' and havin' a high old time," he filled in for her.

"Right."

"Are you havin' a high old time?"

"The highest," she said too cheerfully.

He reached over and brushed her hair away from the side of her face. The backs of his fingers barely touched her cheek, but it was enough to start a titillating tidal wave inside her.

"You know what I think?" he said in a soft, conspiratorial whisper that brought his mouth close to her ear.

"What do you think?"

"That you're tryin' too hard and need to relax a little to pull this off believably."

"You're wrong. I'm loose as a goose." But that last word reminded her of the pat on the rear end, and she could feel her face turning red again. To camouflage it, she drained yet another drink that the bartender had replaced the first one with.

Cal laughed—whether at what she'd said or her blush or her drinking display, she wasn't sure. But as rich as his voice was, his laugh was even richer and it sluiced in through her pores and rained glitter all through her veins.

"You're somethin', Abby Abby Stanton," he said appreciatively.

"Why, yes, I am. Thank you very much for noticing," she said, letting the liquor speak for her with a gutsiness she wouldn't have had otherwise.

"I noticed, all right. Been noticin' all night long. Somewhere underneath all that war paint I think you just might be a breath of fresh air."

Take that, Snodgrass!

"I don't know whether or not I *am* a breath of fresh air, but I think I could use one," she said because her head was suddenly spinning drastically more than before and her tongue was starting to feel thick.

"Come on," he said with a nod over his shoulder. "I'll take you outside."

But if all she did was go outside she'd eventually have to come back in and rejoin Bree and Emily and everyone else at the table. And she didn't want to.

"I think I'll walk home instead," she said out of the blue—the same way she'd made the decision.

This time his chuckle was wry. "Honey, I don't think you'd make it."

"Sure, I would. I know the way."

The chuckle came again. "I'll tell you what. Why don't we let your sisters know you're goin', and I'll drive you home?"

"I don't take rides from strangers," she heard herself say as if she were a little kid.

"I'm not a stranger. Well, not completely. In case you didn't already know—and I'm bettin' you did—

I'm Clangton's newest citizen and I've dug roots here buyin' some property outside of town that's gonna keep me here till I'm old and gray.'' He leaned close again, whispering in her ear and letting the warmth of his breath wash over her. ''So if I misbehave with one of this town's sweethearts, I'd have hell to pay, wouldn't I?''

''Yes, you would. Although I don't know who said I was one of the town's sweethearts.''

He just smiled. ''So let me take you home.''

She thought about it.

Actually she thought about a lot of things. Some of them were things she shouldn't have thought about. Like doing more than being driven home by this man.

Like how it might be to have him bending in close to kiss her instead of whisper in her ear.

Like how it might feel to have his big, rawboned hands cupping the sides of her face. Her shoulders. Her slippery nipples...

''You aren't a maniac, are you?'' she asked, not intending for it to sound hopeful.

''I s'pose I could be if you wanted me to,'' he said, laughing once more.

''No, that's okay. Just a ride home'll do.'' And why had that come out with an edge of disappointment? She really was drunk.

''Better let your sisters know you're goin','' he reminded.

''As in, go over to the table and tell them?'' she said, the full flush of her reluctance echoing in her voice.

''You can send them a note if you'd rather.''

''Good idea.''

He reached over the bar for a dry napkin and a pen,

handing them to her. Then he kept an eye on her the whole time she struggled for the coordination to write legibly.

Once she'd accomplished it, he gave the napkin to the bartender with instructions for its delivery and turned his aquamarine eyes on her again.

"Let's go." He held out his arm for her to precede him through the crowd to the door.

This time even concentration couldn't keep Abby from weaving, but she held her head up and hoped everyone in the place saw that she was leaving with the best-looking guy there. Maybe tomorrow they'd all be talking about that instead of her nixed wedding.

Unfortunately she was so busy holding her head up, she didn't see a chair leg that stuck out into the aisle. Her foot caught on it and her tenuous balance disappeared in an ungraceful tumble that threw her back against Cal's hard chest.

And it *was* hard. Hard as a rock.

Long, strong arms came around her to catch her, and she couldn't be sure, but in the process she thought one of his hands might have accidentally brushed her breast.

"Whoa, there," he said into her hair just before he scooped her up into those arms.

Not a soul in the place missed it, and Abby didn't know whether to be glad or embarrassed when he carried her the rest of the way out as if she weighed nothing at all. But even once they were bathed in the clear summer-evening air he didn't set her down.

"I can walk now," she said feebly, even as she clasped him around the neck and let her head fall to his broad shoulder because it was reeling too badly to keep upright.

"Are you always such a pistol, Abby Stanton?"

"No. But could you spread the word around town that I was tonight?"

"Now, that's a request I can't say I've ever had before," he said, chuckling again as if she delighted him. Then he crossed the parking lot to the last space under a beaming streetlight where a black convertible Corvette waited like a sleek panther at rest.

"This yours?" she asked as he gently deposited her in the passenger's seat.

"She's mine."

"Nice wheels," she said, mimicking something she'd heard on television.

He laughed yet again, as if he knew that wasn't the way she usually talked, and she wondered how it was that this man could see right through her.

But all he said was, "Thanks." Then he added, "Buckle up."

But she was already doing that by force of habit. Drunk or not.

By the time he'd rounded the car and climbed into the driver's seat to start the engine, she had to rest her head against the back of the seat and give in to the leaden weight that seemed to have descended on her eyelids.

"So, Abby Stanton," he said as he pulled out of the parking lot. "Now, the question is, do I take you home to your place? Or to mine?"

He was teasing again. At least she thought he was, although it was a little hard to hear him over the buzz that had started in her head. "Mine," she mumbled.

"Okay. Where do you live?"

"Home."

"Okay…" he said, drawing out the word. "But if you don't tell me where home is, I'll have to take you to my place."

Teasing or not, that was getting to be a more and more interesting idea. Especially if going to his place meant getting to be up against his chest again. Or feeling his arms around her again. Or his hands on her breasts for real. On her naked breasts. And his mouth, too…

"Abby?" came Cal Ketchum's voice again.

"Hmm?"

"Which way do I go?"

"Any which way…"

Any which way at all as long as it got her up close and personal with him again…

"You probably should tell me where any which way is," he said patiently, in that conspiratorial way once more.

Yep, she probably should, all right.

And she would, too.

Pretty soon.

Pretty soon after she took a little nap….

2

CAL WONDERED IF ABBY always slept soundly or if all the liquor she'd consumed the night before was contributing to the fact that it was nearly noon and she still wasn't so much as stirring. He'd even gone into his bedroom, rummaged through the closet, opened and closed drawers and taken a shower in the connecting bathroom.

And there she was, still snoozing.

She was lying on her back in his bed, and as he towel dried his hair, he studied her. Even in drunken slumber, with too much makeup clouding her features, she looked like an angel. Her full, curly hair fanned out against the pillow in a coffee-colored halo. Long, thick lashes sealed her eyes closed, resting on high, fine cheekbones that had their own blush of rosy color beneath the too stark smudges she'd painted there.

She also had the damn cutest nose he'd ever seen. Thin, pert. The nose of a girl next door above soft, full, now pale lips that he'd been hankering to kiss since the first time he'd seen her smile from across the bar the previous night.

Even her chin was adorable—and her jawline was smooth, well-defined, with just enough jut to make him think a stubborn streak disguised as a pretty pout had probably gotten her a lot as a little girl.

She must have been dreaming because as he looked

on, she sighed a small, sensuous sigh that lifted perfectly shaped eyebrows aloft and let them float back down—twin feathers on the wind—while the corners of her mouth stayed turned deliciously upward.

The sigh sounded like a response to a lover's caress. And Cal could picture himself as the lover....

After tossing aside the towel he'd been using on his hair, he dropped down on that mattress beside Abby, on top of the sheet and light blanket that covered her. Lying on his side, he propped his head on his right hand and took an even closer look at her face.

She had peaches-and-cream skin without a pore or a line or a mark on it, and he thought that if he were going to bet on it he'd gamble that not only did she not usually wear the artificial stuff she had covering it, but that also it was probably scrubbed clean at least twice a day with some kind of soap that gave it a milky glow and the kind of cool, flawless feel that would be like pressing his cheek to satin.

Appealing thought.

Very appealing.

So appealing, in fact, that he couldn't figure out why she would cover anything that naturally beautiful with goop.

Her ears caught his attention just then, too. Cute ears. Tiny and shell shaped, with only enough of a lobe to nibble. And damn if he didn't want to! It was a struggle to restrain himself, but even so he couldn't help wondering what would happen if he did.

Would she sigh again? Smile that secretly contented smile? Tilt her chin and give him better access?

Because if she did, he'd nibble and kiss his way to the tender spot just behind her jaw, then just underneath it to her neck and on down to the deep hollow of her collarbone. He'd nuzzle her bra strap aside—pretty though it was, there where the V-neck of her T-shirt had gone askew to fall off her shoulder and expose the strap. And he'd drop a kiss or two...or three...to the curve of that shoulder before working his way lower still. Much, much lower...

Feeling ornery—and aroused—he leaned a little closer and blew a soft gust of air onto the side of the white column of her neck.

It caused her to smile again. *That* smile. Which almost made his effort to resist acting out his fantasy worth the trouble.

Maybe it was too bad she wasn't the wild woman she'd claimed to be last night, he thought.

Nah, he didn't mean that.

Sure, it might be nice for a while because then he'd be able to get some relief for the hot desire that was hardening him up right then. But in the long run? That wasn't Abby Stanton's allure.

He'd known his share of wild women—according to her definition and according to his own. He'd known his share of loose women. Feisty women. Women out for nothing but a good time.

But he hadn't known a lot of wholesome women. And in spite of the way Abby had dolled herself up the night before, the minute he'd set eyes on her he'd spotted her as a wholesome woman.

One of the few to ever cross his path.

Since he and women had started taking notice of each other, he'd abided by a private code. A code that had counted out women like Abby Stanton even when he did encounter them.

Living the life he'd led, it just seemed smart. Women

like Abby Stanton were not women to play with. And he'd always been a player.

So what was he doing with her in his bed now?

Enjoying the sight to beat all hell.

And wanting to see even more of her. Wanting to see those big, round, licorice eyes of hers again. To hear her slightly throaty voice. To see what she was going to do when she discovered herself in his bed.

Just the thought of that tickled him and reminded him all over again of the big kick he'd gotten out of her the previous evening. There was something sweet about such a clumsy attempt to be her version of a wild woman. It had been like watching a little girl try to walk in her mama's high heels. A little girl with a sense of humor, who hadn't taken herself or her attempts too seriously. That had put some fun into what might have just been embarrassing to witness of anyone else.

And he had enjoyed it. He'd enjoyed this woman all the way around.

Well, not *all* the way around.

But enough to make him want to know more. Want to go the rest of the way around.

He blew on her neck again. Lightly.

And in her sleep she giggled just a bit.

It made Cal grin.

Oh, yeah, he liked this lady.

"Wake up, Abby," he whispered in her ear.

She wrinkled her nose and turned her head away.

He put his mouth nearer to the earlobe he was wanting to nibble and blew yet again.

"Come on, honey. Wake up," he coaxed.

He knew she was on her way when her delicate features sobered and her brow began to crease into a confused frown.

"Half the day is already gone, and you're missin' it...." he added, trying to tempt her the rest of the way back to consciousness.

The frown deepened. The eyelashes fluttered slightly, but she settled back to sleep anyway.

"I'm not leavin' you alone till I see the whites of your eyes," he warned.

Not that he had any intention of leaving her alone then, either. She'd caught his interest.

And maybe, now that he had a next-door for the first time in his life, he ought to get to know a girl-next-door type for a change. Just to see what made them tick.

"Come on and wake up," he said yet again. Because awake was how he wanted her. Bright eyed. Bushy tailed. Sweet smiling. And making him feel the way he had the night before.

Like a randy buck with a coffee-haired doe.

"Rise and shine," he sang softly. "And make me a happy man..."

ABBY WAS HAVING a great dream.

In it she was lying in a field of wildflowers, the sun was warm on her bare skin and the gentlest of breezes was brushing her neck. From somewhere far away she could hear a voice. A deep, smoky voice. A man's voice.

He said her name like an endearment so sexy that on its own it was enough to make her blood run faster through her veins.

Enticing. Intriguing. Enchanting.

"Wake up.... Rise and shine," he called to her in a tone that was hard to resist.

But harder still was coming out of the deep sleep that

held her wrapped in its heavy cocoon. It felt too good
to lie there. To hear the man beckoning. To feel his big,
hard body so nearby...

So nearby?

She realized suddenly that she wasn't in a field of
flowers. She was in a bed. But it wasn't her bed because
her bed was much softer than this.

And there certainly shouldn't be a man in it.

She struggled to wake up, and the more alert she
became, the worse she felt. Her head was pounding, and
when she managed to open her eyes even just into slits,
daggers seemed to jab into them and force them shut
again.

"That's it," the husky voice urged in more of that
intimate, warm, whiskey tone. "Wake up. You can do
it."

He was definitely nearby. Very nearby. And the voice
was not one she recognized as belonging to anyone she
knew.

Where was she and who was this guy? And how did
she get here? How did she end up with him?

Her brain felt as if it were fogged under, making it
difficult to discern what was real and what was merely
a figment of her imagination or a piece of a dream.

She remembered the previous evening up to a certain
point. The point where she and her sisters were in the
Clangton Saloon. She recalled drinking. A lot. And being challenged to pat some good-looking cowboy's rear
end...

She peeked out of only a bare hint of a crack in one
eye.

That cowboy's rear end.

She clamped the eye closed again and fought harder
to remember.

There'd been a rest room down a hallway. He'd bought her a drink. More than one.

Had he really ended up carrying her out of the place? Putting her into a black sports car?

And what had happened after that?

Total blank. She drew a total blank from there.

But here she was—wherever *here* was—in a bed that wasn't her own.

With the rear-end cowboy.

Oh, my God.

"Abby," he said again. "If you don't come to pretty soon here, honey, I'm gonna start worryin' about you. Are you all right?"

No, she wasn't all right! She felt like an 18-wheeler had driven over her head and she was even more sick about not knowing what had gone on in the past twelve hours.

She steeled herself and opened her eyes all the way, very, very slowly and as she did she wondered what his name was. She couldn't very well call him the rear-end cowboy. She must know his name. She just had to think about it....

Cal. That was it. Cal Ketchum.

"Mornin'," he said when she finally turned her pounding head his way and looked straight at him.

Ingrained courtesy put a weak smile on her face even as it seemed ridiculous to be worrying about manners under the circumstances. "Hi," she said through a throat that was almost too dry to let the word pass.

She swallowed with difficulty, taking some personal stock as she did while still staring up at the man she presumed to be her host.

It felt as if she had on her clothes. Twisted, turned, falling off her shoulder, but at least they were basically where they were supposed to be. And he wasn't under the covers with her.

Neither of those things offered much reassurance, but nevertheless it was better than waking up with both herself and the rear-end cowboy naked under the sheets. A lot better. She didn't know what she would have done if that had been the case. Especially when just the hint of bare chest and stomach showing from the open front of his pale yellow shirt was enough to send her already unstable stomach into flutters.

"I think I drank too much last night," she admitted shakily.

"I *know* you drank too much last night."

"Did I get sick or something?"

"Sick? No, not sick," he said as if that only touched the surface of the whole story.

"Then how do you know I drank too much?"

"You passed out on me, honey."

"Oh." How embarrassing. Mortifying images of herself falling down dead drunk flashed through her mind.

"You didn't actually pass out," he amended as if he could tell what she was thinking about herself. "You just fell asleep. At a pretty inopportune time."

There was an allusion in that. But Abby couldn't even begin to guess what he was alluding to. A whole world of possibilities came to life in her mind, but she didn't think she could handle knowing if any of them had really happened. At least not right away.

So instead she tried to ease into how many ways she might have embarrassed herself by asking, "Did I drool in my sleep?"

He smiled down at her, and she had a sudden memory of the evening before. Of that terrific smile honing in on her as if she were the only person he'd been aware of in the whole bar.

"No drooling, no," he answered.

"Did I snore?"

"No snoring."

"And it was you who put me to bed?" she asked cautiously, edging toward some harder-to-know facts.

"That I did," he said with a slow devilry in his tone.

She couldn't help it. She had to lift the covers and look down at herself just to make sure her clothes really were basically intact.

"No, I didn't undress you," he assured.

"Thank you. I think."

"But you aren't sure."

How could she be sure when she didn't have any idea what had gone on between them, clothes or no clothes?

"Did we…did I ruin your evening?" she ventured.

"Ruin my evening?"

"I'm sure pouring a drunken woman into your bed was not the ending you had in mind. I mean it couldn't have been much…fun…for you," she said, fishing for answers.

"You might be surprised."

His insinuation made her heartbeat speed up. "Did I do something…fun…before you had to put me to bed?"

"Let's just say I had a good time."

Was he teasing her? She couldn't tell. And her fog-shrouded brain was not giving up any memories to help her out.

"I'm afraid I can't recall much about last night."

"Pity."

It took courage to ask "Did I disgrace myself?"

"Disgrace yourself? I didn't think wild women cared about that kind of thing."

Wild women.

Oh, dear.

"How do you know about...that wild-woman thing?"

"You told me that's what you are."

"Ah." She swallowed back her own worst fears and said, "But did I prove it?"

He grinned mischievously from the side of his mouth. "Wild women don't care what happened whether they can remember it or not. They just pick up and go on bein' wild," he said as if he were anticipating the benefits of that.

"Uh...I think I should warn you that I'm not really such a wild woman. I mean, I'm...well...I'm a baker."

"You have *my* ovens lit—that's for sure."

"No, honestly. It's what I do for a living—bake. Cakes. Cookies. Pies. Brownies."

He shrugged one of those broad shoulders she had a vague memory of laying her head against. "Even wild women have to have a day job. It's those off-hours that count," he added with a lascivious arch to one eyebrow.

Without thinking about it, she held the covers in a tight-fisted grip as if it would protect her from what she'd gotten herself into here. This wasn't the kind of run-of-the-mill good ol' boy that Clangton was rife with. This was a man handsome enough to have women throwing themselves at him. Certainly this was a man accustomed to women making good on what they promised. And he didn't seem to be understanding that she hadn't been herself if and when she'd promised anything.

"What I'm trying to say is that I don't know what I

might have led you to believe about me last night...or what I might have led you to believe would happen this morning...but...well—''

''You're just not that kind of girl,'' he finished for her.

''Something like that,'' she admitted reluctantly, feeling like a fool and thinking Bill Snodgrass must have been right about her after all.

''So if you're not that kind of girl, what were you doin' sayin' you were last night?''

She grimaced at the thought. ''It's a long story. I guess you could say I was pretending. To prove a point.'' The admission made her cheeks heat up.

Cal's handsome face erupted in a full-fledged grin. ''So what you're tellin' me is that you aren't a dyed-in-the-wool wild woman? I never would have guessed,'' he said facetiously.

Light finally dawned for her. ''Oh, I get it—you're putting me on.''

''Don't tempt me, honey, I'm tryin' to keep off you.''

''I meant teasing. You were teasing me.''

''Still am,'' he said with a laugh.

She was out of her league with this man in more ways than one and she knew it. But she was still worried about what had gone on the evening before. ''So what really happened last night?''

''*Really?*'' The lascivious tone was back.

''Come on. Give me a break.''

''A break isn't all I'd like to give you.''

She rolled her eyes at him.

Rather than being chagrined, he only laughed at her. Then he said, ''I was takin' you home, but you fell asleep in my car before tellin' me where home is. So I brought you here, carried you up to bed and tucked you in.''

Relief helped her headache. Partial relief, anyway.

"Where did you sleep?"

He arched an insinuative eyebrow at her again, but this time she didn't buy it.

"Not here," she guessed.

"To my everlastin' regret."

"You know what I think? I think you're just a sheep in wolf's clothing."

"Or maybe not," he said with enough of a sexy rumble to his voice to disabuse her of the notion.

"Okay. So you were a gentleman, but it goes against the grain. Thank you anyway."

"You're welcome."

"Now, where exactly am I?"

"In my bed. In my house. If you've lived around these parts for any time at all—"

"I was born and raised here."

"Then you probably know this place better as the old Peterson spread—now in the city registry as the Lucky Seven ranch. I believe it started out as a workin' ranch, got sold off about seventeen years ago and turned into a dude ranch that didn't catch on, and has been left to rot for the past fifteen-plus years. Or have I been misinformed?"

"Ripped off maybe, but not misinformed. I hope you didn't pay too much or buy it blind."

"Eyes wide-open."

But those eyes didn't seem to be seeing anything but her at that moment. The intensity of his gaze reminded her that they were not having a plain conversation on a street corner. They were essentially in bed together.

"Did I hear you say it's nearly noon?" she asked.

"You did."

"I'm surprised my sisters haven't sent the sheriff looking for me. I don't suppose I could impose on you to take me home?"

"Now? When we're just gettin' to know each other?"

The man was a terrible tease.

"Please."

"Do I have another choice?"

"You could make me walk, but it's kind of far for that."

"That wasn't the other option I had in mind."

She didn't think she was up to knowing what he did have in mind.

"Please," she repeated. "I could give you gas money if you wanted."

"Gas money?" he parroted, laughing again, wryly this time. But he pushed himself to a sitting position and then got off the mattress. "I'm gonna want more than gas money."

Abby wasn't up to asking what that "more" might be. She just wanted to get out of there and home to familiar territory.

Since she was dressed, she threw off the covers and got to her feet, too, although not without stabbing pains shooting through her head.

For a moment she had to close her eyes against it. When she opened them again, it was to find Cal Ketchum watching her once more. Standing there in all his glory with big bare feet spread apart, tight jeans zipped but not fastened at the waistband and the tails of that yellow shirt dangling around his hips, leaving a flat, rock-hard stomach and just enough chest showing for her to see the smattering of hair there.

No one should look that good first thing in the morning, barely dressed and clearly without having paid any attention to his appearance. There should be a law, she thought, wondering just how unsightly she was herself.

"How about some breakfast before I take you home? You can call your sisters and let 'em know where you are."

Just the mention of food raised her gorge. "I don't think so. Thanks anyway."

"Coffee? Tea? A little hair of the dog?"

"I don't dare." Eat, drink or stay any longer than necessary with this man whose appeal was so potent. "But I could use the bathroom."

He pointed to a door beside a tall antique bureau. "Through there. Towels and washcloths are in the cupboard. Feel free to shower if you want. I'll even lend you some clothes—just say the word."

No way was she taking off any clothes within ten miles of this man. It would be too tempting to leave them off.

"I might just wash my face." Because it felt as if someone had slathered it with mud. "But then I'll need to go home. Right away."

He made a slight *tsk* sound from the corner of his mouth. "Too bad."

Abby didn't stick around to discuss it. She went into the bathroom, closed and locked the door.

But the lock clicked into place with an inordinately loud noise that seemed to admit that she didn't trust that he would respect her privacy.

"Don't worry, Abby Abby," he reassured through the panel, reminding her of the teasing he'd done the night before, too. "I won't storm the door and ravage you. I like my wild women willing."

Abby groaned to herself and dropped her face in both hands as if someone else could see her grimace at her own follies.

But then it occurred to her that wallowing in embarrassment was only prolonging things and the sooner she got down to business, the sooner she could get home.

She took a look at herself in the mirror, and almost wished she hadn't.

Her hair had been in such an unruly style that it hardly looked different than it had when she'd done it. But her face was something else entirely, and the thought that Cal Ketchum had seen her like this made her groan all over again.

Dark black smudges ringed her eyes in a raccoon effect. The blush she'd applied wasn't her usual pale shade, so it didn't enhance her natural color; it sat on top, adding an orangish tint that clashed. The raisin shade of lipstick was gone except to leave her lips looking bruised. And the foundation she'd applied had cracked and caked into the creases of her chin and nose.

She looked as if she'd barely survived a hard Halloween.

And as much of a hurry as she was in to get home, she couldn't make herself walk back out and face the rear-end cowboy knowing what he'd be seeing. Even if he had already seen it.

The bathroom was large, but showed the decay of the years in peeling paint, chipped and missing tiles and a tub and sink that had seen better days. There were cupboards underneath the sink and what seemed to be a floor-to-ceiling linen closet in one corner.

Since Cal had said towels and washcloths were in the cupboard, she tried under the sink first. But beyond a few cleaning supplies and some spare rolls of toilet paper, the cupboards were bare.

Turning to the linen closet, she finally found what she needed in the way of man-size washcloths. She took two because the only towels were bath sheets and she didn't want to dirty a whole bath sheet just to dry her face. She didn't really want to impose by using anything, but vanity prevailed over her reticence.

The countertop around the sink was clean but cluttered with a straight razor, a can of shaving foam, a bottle of aftershave, deodorant and shampoo. But there was no soap. For that she had to venture inside the black shower curtain that sealed off more than half the tub.

There was a bar resting in a dish on the tub's far edge, and she leaned in to get it. Residual steam from what could only have been Cal's shower wafted around her from inside, smelling the way he did—clean, fresh, masculine.

And although she told herself she'd lost her mind, she actually closed her eyes and breathed deeply, finding herself relishing the thought that not long ago he had been in there. Naked. Glistening wet. Scrubbing that big, hard body with that very soap...

"Findin' everything you need in there?" he asked from outside the door.

The sudden sound of his voice and her own guilty conscience startled Abby into straightening up fast. Without the soap. Which she dived back in for, snatching it like a child stealing candy.

"Fine. I'm fine," she answered too loudly, the sound of her own raised voice erupting yet another memory of the previous evening and her lack of aplomb.

Feeling rotten, she spun around to the sink again and gave herself a fierce stare in the mirror.

"You're just a big, dumb idiot for acting like something you're not," she whispered to herself harshly. "It serves you right to get stuck here now, like this, humiliating yourself all the more. If this doesn't teach you not to pretend to be something you aren't, nothing ever will."

And with that she turned on the hottest water she could stand and proceeded to scrub the life out of her face for punishment.

When the residual makeup was gone and her cheeks were their own color again, she eased up on herself by gently patting her skin dry.

As she did, she became increasingly aware of the bad taste in her mouth. And of how unpleasant her breath must be.

She would never in her life use someone else's toothbrush, but a tube of toothpaste seemed to call to her and she ended up putting some on her index finger and doing a makeshift job on her teeth until every trace of liquor taste was gone.

And then another bit of temptation struck.

Bending over to slurp water from her cupped palm to rinse her mouth, her gaze fell to the bottle of aftershave on the counter. Her attention caught on it like a sweater on a bramble bush, and as she dabbed at her mouth with the dry washcloth she suddenly became obsessed with taking a whiff of the stuff.

The rear-end cowboy had been clean shaved when he'd awakened her, but she hadn't been aware of any cologne smell, so her curiosity about what scent he chose for himself got the better of her.

She reached for the bottle, thinking that the top was screwed on tight.

It wasn't.

The bottle tipped, splashing its contents over her hand, her forearm, her shirtfront and the countertop, filling the whole room with a scent not unlike the soap except with a woodsy undertone.

Groaning yet again, she screwed the top on tight, washed her hand and arm and mopped up the countertop. But there was nothing to be done about the aftershave on her T-shirt to announce that she'd been snooping.

Could this morning get any worse?

There was no way around stepping out of that bathroom reeking of his aftershave, so Abby resigned herself to facing the music, again thinking that the sooner she did that, the sooner she could get home, out of the man's sight and—with a little luck and a lot of hiding for the rest of her life—maybe she'd never have to face him again.

She took a deep breath and sighed it out—as much in self-disgust as to bolster her courage—squared her shoulders and walked out of the bathroom.

"I...uh...accidentally knocked over a bottle of aftershave on the counter. The lid wasn't on tight, and some of it spilled. I'm sorry. I'd be happy to replace it," she said in a hurry.

He was rummaging in a drawer and only when he had a pair of socks in hand did he face her. He leaned near, sniffing as he did. "Smells better on you than on me."

She couldn't imagine that was true but appreciated that he didn't make any bigger deal out of it than that.

Then he straightened up again and studied her face. "Better. Much better."

She self-consciously touched her fingertips to her cheek. "I know I was kind of smeared up."

"This is even better than before that."

Had she looked so bad last night? "Not so clown-ish—is that what you mean?" she asked, embarrassed once more.

"You didn't look like a clown. Just a fresh-faced woman trying to cover it up when she shouldn't have."

"Fresh faced," she repeated. It sounded better than shy, quiet, predictable and provincial. But somehow, in her mind, it went along with those other things and still added up to boring. She was just...*plain.*

And she guessed it was time to give up trying to be anything else and accept it.

"I'd like to go home now."

As if he could tell that she hadn't taken his comment as a compliment, he stepped close in front of her, grasped her chin in a strong hand and tilted her face upward until she was looking right into his aquamarine eyes.

"The makeup just hid how really beautiful you are," he said quietly, as if confiding a secret.

And then he did something that totally and com-pletely surprised her.

He kissed her.

Square on the mouth. A soft, delicate meeting of warm, slightly moist, decidedly expert lips against hers, in a kiss so tender she might never have guessed a man like Cal Ketchum would give it. Except for the added bit of devilry in the tip of his tongue touching ever so lightly to her upper lip just before he ended it.

The kiss was over before she knew it, but still it had wielded power enough to leave her knees weak and her head spinning more than it had been under the effects of alcohol.

And all she could think of was that she wanted more...

Of the kisses, not the alcohol.

"Sure I can't persuade you to stay awhile?"

Awhile? How about forever? As a willing slave to kisses as potent as that one...

"No," she said in a semipanic at her own thoughts, her own weakness—a weakness she'd never known she possessed. "I have to go home. Now."

"Who says?"

"Me," she insisted.

He let out an exaggerated sigh of disappointment. "If your heart is set on it. I guess we'd better go, then."

He began to button his shirt from the top, and a wave of disappointment washed through her. She just wasn't certain over what. Maybe over losing the sexy sight of his bare chest and stomach? Maybe over his agreeing to let her go rather than keeping her captive to kisses like the one before and the silent promise it held of more passionate ones?

She honestly didn't know.

She only knew that she couldn't take her eyes off his hands working their way down that shirtfront and then tucking the tails into his jeans in a way that unwittingly tantalized her imagination with images of what was hidden behind that zipper.

Then, as if he didn't have any idea what he was doing to her insides, he bent over and pulled on the socks he'd taken from the drawer.

Bent over...

Her hand actually itched to reach out and pat that great derriere again.

Maybe she was a wilder woman than she realized.

"Shoes!" she said to snap herself out of her own

reverie as he yanked on a pair of tan snakeskin cowboy boots. "I need my shoes, too."

He nodded toward the side of the mattress. "Those I did take off you. They're over there."

Abby nearly ran for them, grateful for something—anything—to do rather than watch him finish dressing as if they'd shared more intimacy than they had.

"Ready?" he asked when he was.

"Please," she said, knowing it was too polite and kind of a dumb response, but just wanting to escape that room, which seemed to be getting smaller by the minute.

He held his arm out toward the door, and Abby came close to flying out of it, down the stairs and through the front door, all without so much as a glance at anything in the rest of the house.

She was in the passenger's seat of the black convertible parked outside before Cal had made it to the porch steps.

She tried not to watch him finish the trip she'd taken in such a hurry, but even from the corner of her eye she could see long, muscular legs carrying him down the steps. And when he walked around to the driver's side, her gaze seemed to stick like glue to that rear end again.

"Where to?" he asked as he got behind the wheel and started the engine.

This was how I got into trouble last night, she remembered. But this time she didn't hesitate to give him directions to the family home she and her sisters shared.

Then she sank as deeply into the seat as she could so no one in town could readily see her being taken home in the same clothes she'd been wearing the night before, by a gorgeous man who no one would believe had been a gentleman. That kiss notwithstanding.

"Ashamed to be seen with me?" he asked, noticing.

"Ashamed of myself," she answered almost under her breath.

"For cuttin' loose a little?"

"For cutting loose way too much."

"Way too much? Honey, I've seen people cut loose a whole lot more than you did last night. Much to my regret."

"That you've seen other people do worse or that I didn't do more?"

He just grinned over at her and left her guessing.

After a moment he said, "Ask me what I want as payback for behavin' myself."

She was a little afraid to inquire. But she owed him a great deal for not turning the previous evening into the nightmare it might have been had he been another man, so she complied. "What do you want as payback?"

"I want to pick you up tonight about eight and have you show me where around here is the best place to watch the sunset."

An involuntary thrill ran through her at the prospect, even as she told herself she'd be better off never seeing him again as she'd promised herself earlier.

"It looks good from anywhere," she said in an attempt to resist him. And her own desires.

"But there's always a prime place or two to settle in and watch. If you've been here your whole life the way you said, you must know where it is. Or were you lyin' about bein' ashamed to be seen with me?"

"Will you still behave yourself?" she heard herself

ask, hating that she sounded like such a prude. Predictable, provincial and now prudish.

"Can't make any promises," he said. "But I'll try."

"I don't know...." She shouldn't. She really shouldn't give in to this. To him. To herself.

"I'll behave myself better if you do this than if you don't," he threatened with a glint of mischief in the sidelong glance he shot her way.

"What does that mean?"

He only shrugged and grinned.

"My reputation will already be in shreds after you were seen carrying me out of that bar last night."

"Thought that's what you wanted—to show folks you were different than they thought you were."

"Maybe not *that* different."

"What'll they be sayin' if I start showin' up to howl at the moon under your bedroom window every night?"

"That you're a lunatic."

He laughed. "And that all sorts of things must have gone on between us to drive me crazy." He pulled up in front of her house and stopped the car. "So what'll it be? Show me the best place to watch the sunset or have me raisin' a ruckus under your window?"

"This smacks of blackmail, you know."

"Doesn't it, though?" he answered with yet another grin. "Tonight at eight?"

She wasn't sure whether or not he'd actually make good on his threat. And it wasn't really much of a threat to begin with. So she could have refused. Could have and should have.

But she did owe him for driving her home the night before. For not taking advantage of her or of the situation.

"Okay," she said. "Eight o'clock."

His grin turned victorious, and he leaned across the seat as if to kiss her again.

Only she leaned back farther and faster than he leaned forward, avoiding his lips.

"But don't get any ideas," she warned as she got out of the car and closed the door behind her.

"Too late. I already have plenty of 'em."

He pulled away from the curb then, and she could hear him laughing devilishly as he did.

What's gotten into me? she asked herself, watching his car as long as she could see it and knowing she should not have plans to spend any amount of time with the man again. Not when she couldn't hold her own with him. And what did he want with someone like her, anyway, when even the town accountant hadn't found her exciting enough?

So call the man and tell him you won't go after all, she ordered herself.

But she knew she wasn't going to do that. Crazy as it seemed not to.

And it did seem crazy.

Because here she was, shy, quiet, predictable, provincial, prudish Abby Stanton.

Playing with fire.

3

"FINALLY."

"It's about time."

The voices of Abby's sisters came from inside the house as she turned from the curb after watching Cal Ketchum drive off. Bree was apparently on the lookout upstairs at the bay window in one of the four bedrooms—the one they'd used as a guest room since their brother, Lucas, had left. Emily was standing at the window downstairs that opened onto the round turret that wrapped one corner of the two-story white clapboard Victorian house.

Abby just waved without calling any kind of answer back to her sisters because she didn't want to draw any more of their neighbors' attention than she already had.

She headed for the house, struck as she always was by how beautiful the old place was, how much it looked like a dollhouse. Wide porches followed the line of the multicantilevered and gabled front and the turret on both levels, with spindled railings and poles making the turret look like a double-decker, attached gazebo.

A steep roof topped the house, and an octagonal roof finished off the turret, keeping it from being stark. Gingerbread latticework accentuated all the overhangs, and beveled glass surrounded the carved entrance door.

But in spite of how inviting her home was, there was no speed in Abby's climb up the six steps that lifted her into the cool shade where white wicker chairs, a swing and two settees all with flowered cushions waited for someone to while away the early-summer days. She wasn't anxious to face her sisters and so, rather than going right in, she plucked a few wilting leaves from the bright red geraniums that grew in a pot hanging beside the door.

But that only bought her a moment before Emily appeared just inside the wooden screen.

"First—are you all right?" Emily demanded, sounding as if she, not Abby, were the oldest sister when, in fact, she was the middle one.

"I have a splitting headache, but other than that I'm okay," Abby answered as she crossed the threshold into a large entryway with a center table occupying a fair share of the space.

"I can't believe you did this," Bree said from directly overhead. Voices tended to echo slightly in the entryway because it was open to the ceiling of the second floor, surrounded on the upper level by a banistered walkway off which the bedrooms opened. The echo lent power to Bree's disapproval.

"Which part can't you believe?" Abby asked her youngest sister as Bree came around to the oak staircase and descended it to join her and Emily in the entry.

"All of it," Emily said as if the question had been directed at her. "What were you doing letting that guy carry you out of that bar last night? And where did you go with him? And why didn't you call so we didn't have to sit up all night wondering if you were okay or in trouble or sick or who knows what?"

Bree picked up where Emily left off. "We take you out to get your mind off the wedding and Bill, and the next thing we know, some stranger is carting you off like a sack of potatoes. By the time we got through the crowd in that place, all we saw was him driving away with you.''

"And then when you weren't here when we got home and didn't come home *all night*," Emily continued, "we didn't know what to think. Or if we should call the sheriff or if calling the sheriff would end up with him finding you boinking that cowboy somewhere.''

"Bree!" Abby said with an embarrassed laugh.

"Looks to me," Emily contributed, "as if it's a good thing we didn't call the sheriff because boinking that cowboy is just what he'd have caught you doing.''

Emily was as conservative as Abby, so it was an indication of how put out she was that she'd even say a word like *boinking*.

"I was not *boinking* anybody," Abby informed them.

"Oh, no? You spent the whole night with him and here you are now, with your clothes all messed up as if you were wrestling around in them. Your hair has gone crazy. And you're reeking of men's cologne," Bree declared.

"Maybe it isn't only her hair that's gone crazy," Emily pointed out.

They were concerned about her but they were also peeved and goading her, too, to find out what had really gone on in the past twelve hours.

Continuing in that vein, Bree said, "Geez, Abby, this isn't like you.''

"Yeah, we didn't think you'd carry the wild-woman thing *this* far. We've been scared to death that our getting you drunk made you do something dangerous.''

When all else fails, try guilt.

"Okay, okay. I'm sorry," Abby said, finally moving from the entryway.

She was badly in need of an aspirin and something to drink that would remoisten a desert-dry mouth. She could have gone to the kitchen at the back of the house by heading straight down the hallway from the foyer. But her sisters were blocking that path, so it was easier to take a left and go through the formal living room, pass under the yellow-stained-glass-lined archway that connected the dining room and finally to the kitchen from there.

Bree and Emily trailed her like ducklings.

"So what happened?" Bree finally asked outright.

The kitchen was very large, divided in half by a low row of cupboards so the appliances and butcher's block were on one side, and a breakfast nook big enough to seat eight on its U-shaped bench seat was built into the wall on the other.

Abby took a bottle of aspirin from a narrow cupboard beside the sink. "Is there any lemonade left?" she asked rather than answering Bree's question.

Emily poured her a glass from a pitcher in the refrigerator, handed it to her and, with emphasis, repeated, "What happened last night?"

"Nothing," Abby said simply, making a face after swallowing the white tablets with the lemonade Bree always made too sour.

"Nothing, my foot," Bree said, a note of anticipation for a juicy story creeping into her voice.

Abby felt boring again, knowing she was going to disappoint her youngest sister. With all the worrying and waiting up they'd done, they deserved at least a titillating tale. But they weren't going to get it. Unless she lied. Which she considered doing for their sakes. And maybe for her own, too, so she could liven up their image of her.

Only in the end Abby couldn't bring herself to make something up.

"I hate to admit it, but Bill was right about me. I left the bar with Cal Ketchum because I came out of the bathroom and couldn't stand the thought of going back to the table with those other people who had joined you guys." She went on to outline how Cal came to not only carry her from the bar, but also take her to his house, and what had gone on from there.

And when she finished she took a good long look at her sisters, almost hoping they might doubt her bland story and think it was only a cover-up for something deliciously scandalous. That they might say *You don't expect us to believe that's all that happened, do you?*

But they knew her too well.

They both visibly relaxed. Clearly not even entertaining the notion that she and the rear-end cowboy had spent a night of mindless passion because he couldn't resist her and she'd been more than just pretending to be a wild woman. Somehow it was demoralizing to think that her reputation as shy, quiet, steady, provincial, predictable Abby Stanton was so ingrained that even a whole night spent with Cal Ketchum couldn't heat it up.

"It looked like he tried to kiss you in the car just now," Bree said then, proving she had been watching from the upstairs window.

"He did," Abby admitted.

"And you didn't let him," Emily guessed as if that were a given.

It pricked something in Abby and made her decide on the spot to give them a little shock. "Not that time I didn't let him, no."

"There was another time that you did let him kiss you?" Bree asked.

"Just once. Earlier. At his house." And didn't it feel good to let them know that! Almost as good as the kiss itself had felt.

"Then something did happen?" Emily said, perking up hopefully.

But that was as far as Abby could take it. She just couldn't lie. "Only the one kiss. It was next to nothing." To him, anyway. She was certain of that. Sure, it had curled her toes, but to a man like Cal Ketchum? He probably gave away kisses like that every day of the week.

She brought her lemonade to the breakfast nook where both her sisters were sitting and slid in, too.

"So what's up with him anyway? Where did he come from? What's his story?" Emily was anxious now for details.

"I don't know. Unfortunately I slept through most of the time with him and this morning I was too interested in finding out what I couldn't remember about what went on last night. I didn't ask about anything more than that. But maybe I'll find out about him tonight."

"Tonight?" Bree repeated. "What's tonight?"

"He's picking me up at eight so I can show him the best place to watch the sunset," she said matter-of-factly.

"And you're going? With someone you don't even know? Without being drunk?" Emily was finally shocked.

"I owe him. For all he *didn't* do last night," she admitted, not going on to let them know that she was as nervous about it as if it were her first date ever.

"So do you like him?" Emily asked.

Abby shrugged. It wouldn't do to like him. And she wouldn't admit that she did. Not to her sisters. Not to herself.

"He's nice. Nicer than you'd expect for as good-looking as he is. He isn't arrogant or conceited. But it doesn't really matter. I'm just going to pay him back for taking me home last night and not doing anything while I was nearly passed out in his bed and at his mercy. And then that will be that."

"What makes you so sure?" Bree asked, her voice full of possibilities.

"Cal Ketchum isn't interested in someone like me. He acts like he saw through the wild-woman thing, but I'm sure he still thinks that a little of it was real. You know when he realizes the truth he'll be on to someone exciting."

"What are you? Dull as dishwater?" Bree asked.

Abby shrugged again. "Let's be honest, Bill wasn't off the mark when he complained about me. I *am* shy and quiet and steady and predictable and provincial. Even last night I couldn't pull off the wild-woman thing. And this morning I was terrified I might have done something I couldn't face. Or promised something I couldn't follow through on. Maybe I'm not dull as dishwater...I *hope* I'm not. But I'm also not the kind of woman a man like that bothers with. I'm just not the type a world-class ladies' man wastes his time with."

"Oh, Abby," Emily said in a moan. "I'd like to chop Bill Snot-grass into tiny pieces for making you doubt your appeal to anybody."

"Bill Snot-grass?" Abby repeated with a laugh.

"Well, that's what he is. Among other things. I still don't buy his reasons for calling off the wedding. I think he just got cold feet, chickened out and then laid the whole thing on you because he wasn't man enough to admit it.''

"Or worse," Bree said under her breath.

"Or worse?" Abby asked.

"I can't help feeling he had something else up his sleeve. Maybe something he had a guilty conscience over and it made him feel better to pick at you.''

"But I am all the things he said," Abby reminded, wishing she had more than last night and one kiss by the rear-end cowboy to refute it. "Anyway the good news is, being shy, quiet, steady, predictable and provincial isn't fatal. It isn't really bad at all. I'm okay with it. It just won't keep Cal Ketchum coming around. And that's good because I don't want him coming around. I just want to get tonight over with so my debt is paid and I can go on with my own business. *Without* a man to confuse things. I need a break from men for a while. Like maybe the next ten years.''

"It's good to take some time for yourself. Regroup," Emily agreed.

"Besides, rebound relationships never work out," Bree added.

"So let's just not make a big deal out of what isn't a big deal. I did something dumb last night, but luckily I was with a man who didn't take advantage of the situation. Tonight I'll pay him back by showing him the sunset. I'll be home before ten without even a peck on the cheek to say good-night, and that'll be that.''

Both her sisters nodded their heads as if they thought she was absolutely right.

She thought she was absolutely right.

But somehow she couldn't help wishing that she wasn't.

Because for no reason she could begin to understand,

the whole lily-white scenario she'd just laid out for the coming evening made her feel oddly downhearted.

"COME ON OUT, GIRLS," Cal urged. "I have a date and you all can't stay here while I'm gone. Sorry."

It was seven-fifteen that evening, and he was just about ready to leave to pick up Abby to watch the sunset. He only needed to choose a shirt. And get rid of his houseguests.

"Come on, you three little vixens. I'm not kiddin' around. We've had a good time all afternoon, but that's it for now."

He went into his walk-in closet and surveyed his options from among the shirts hanging there, wondering why it was so all-fired important to him to look good. He usually didn't put much consideration into what he wore. Date or no date.

But there was something special about *this* date. About this woman. Something that made him feel there was a higher standard to be met. A level of respectability he hadn't dabbled in before.

Strange to be feeling that way about a woman who'd gotten drunk in a bar and had to be taken home to his house because she couldn't even tell him where she lived.

But he didn't doubt for a minute that had been a fluke for Abby Stanton.

Nope. Watching her reaction to finding herself in his bed this morning, seeing her with her face scrubbed, talking to her, had only served to convince him that she was as wholesome as corn on the cob.

And he'd bet everything he had that he wasn't the kind of man who usually came calling on Miss Abby Stanton.

He finally settled on a fire-engine-red Western-cut shirt. Maybe to warn her.

"Lady beware," he muttered to himself as he slipped it on. "I've been around the block."

He was still standing in the closet, buttoning his shirt, when one of his houseguests attacked him from behind. She landed on his shoulder, lost her footing and tumbled forward. Quick reflexes allowed Cal to catch her, and the furry ball ended up hanging half inside, half outside his shirt.

"Cats are supposed to be surefooted," he told the tiny tabby, holding her up to look her in the eye. "Now, where're your sisters? You all are supposed to be barn cats, not house cats, remember?"

He tucked her against his chest and held her there with one hand while he scanned the shelf from which she'd sprung. Wherever one of them was, the other two were likely not to be too far behind.

Sure enough he spotted the other kittens—one perched atop the hatbox his newest Stetson had come in, and the other peeking at him from around the back of the box.

"Look, girls, I know this has been home since your mama passed on givin' birth to you and you think you can just take over in here. But my turn at playin' mother cat is about up, and you three are old enough to stake out some territory of your own in the barn. Got that?" he lectured as he lifted down the peeking kitten and held her against his chest with the first one, then took the hatbox kitten down, too.

While he cradled the first two in his left hand, he stared eye to eye with the hatbox kitten. "You're the culprit, aren't you?" he said to her. All three were nearly identical silver-gray in color. The two against his

chest were hard to tell apart unless he turned them over
to search for which of them had a white spot on her
belly. But the hatbox kitten had one white ear. She was
the mischief maker.

"You led the troops in here to hide, didn't you?"

The kitten licked his nose.

"Kisses are not gonna cut it, honey."

He stepped out of the closet and set all three cats on
the bed while he finished buttoning his shirt and tucked
it into his jeans.

Good thing none of his brothers knew he was keeping
kittens, he thought as he watched the trio rolling around
on the mattress, playing with each other. There'd be no
end of unmerciful razzing if any of the Ketchums got
wind of it. Especially if they knew that most nights
since he'd found the kittens trying to nuzzle up against
their dead mother in his barn, it had been these females
with him between the sheets instead of any of the two-
legged variety.

Things really were changing.

And that was what he wanted. That was what he'd
set out to do—use his share of their good fortune to
have a life he'd never had before.

"But that doesn't mean you girls can stay in here,"
he told his audience. "I have better things to do in that
bed than share it with pets, you know."

An image of Abby popped into his mind just then.
Of how she'd looked sleeping there. Of how much he'd
wanted to be in it with her. *Not* sleeping...

What would she have done if he'd slipped under the
covers with her?

Kicked him out, probably.

But it might have been fun trying.

On the other hand, if he had pushed things he might

not be about to see her again. And he would have hated that. Because he hadn't looked forward to spending time with any one particular woman this much since he was a boy and being with a woman was a novelty.

So rather than push anything, he was determined to go easy with Abby. Not to scare her away. Get to know her. Let her get to know him before he tried to convince her to try out his mattress again. With him in it.

The trouble was, just the thought of getting her into his bed was enough to set off a whirlwind of responses inside him. Enough to throw his determinations to behave himself right out the window.

"But this one's a lady," he told the kittens. "That makes her worth a little wooin'."

Or maybe a lot of wooing.

He just didn't know if he was up to the challenge.

It had been a long time since he'd denied himself a woman he found attractive. A long time since a woman had denied him.

And he'd never had one hanging on to the sheets with both fists, looking up at him with wide eyes, the way Abby Stanton had.

Just the thought made him smile.

"Turnin' over a new leaf. Startin' a new life. Guess that means learnin' how to treat a new class of woman."

It ought to be interesting.

It was definitely a challenge.

But it was worth it, he decided.

She was worth it.

He could feel it in his bones. And those bones weren't too often wrong.

Hunches. Instincts. Whatever a person wanted to call

them, so far they'd served him well. Made him a rich man. So he wasn't likely to ignore them now.

Especially when they were telling him to go for it with this woman. To reach for that higher standard. That new level of respectability.

Or maybe it was just one bone in particular that was pointing the way to her....

Nah. He wanted more than a tumble with her. First, anyway.

And then, when he did get around to tumbling her?

Even that would probably be different than what he'd known before.

"And you three aren't gonna be here to watch when the time comes—that's for sure," he told the kittens.

Because this was going to be a new experience for him all the way around.

And he didn't want anything messing it up.

ABBY TOOK ONE LAST LOOK in the mirror on the back of her bedroom door. Baggy, pleated-front jeans. White cotton blouse with a covered placket and a collar that reached to her chin. The natural curls of her hair were held back by a denim headband, and her makeup was a bare hint of blush—her usual color—a scant layer of mascara and plain lip gloss.

No false messages tonight.

This was the real Abby Stanton.

When the doorbell rang she headed downstairs, knowing she was alone in the house because Emily and Bree had gone to a friend's home for the evening.

Abby paced herself to hide her anxiousness as she descended the steps. From Cal, at any rate, who was standing on the other side of the screen door. But a leisurely descent of the stairs didn't change the fact that she *was* eager to see him again. No matter how much talking she'd done to herself all day and through the whole process of getting ready for this moment.

Yes, she believed this was a one-time thing.

Yes, she was convinced that when Cal realized what she was really like he wouldn't want to see her again.

Yes, she was certain he would be bored to tears with her tonight.

And yes, that was how she wanted it so whatever was going on between them could end in the next couple of hours.

But deep down she couldn't help the bubble of excited anticipation that kept rising up inside her all on its own anyway.

"Hi," she said as she unlatched the screen door and pushed it open for him, trying not to notice just how terrific he looked. And smelled. He had on cowboy boots and jeans that were just tight enough. A bright shirt. His face was clean shaved. His wavy, wavy hair was combed carelessly. And he was giving off a faint, heady scent of the aftershave she'd spilled that morning, which definitely smelled better on him than it had on her.

He returned her greeting and stepped into the entry, ignoring their surroundings to take a good, long, concentrated look at her.

"No wild woman tonight, huh?" he said with that lopsided grin creeping up one corner of his oh-so-sexy mouth.

"Sorry."

"Don't apologize. I like this better. A lot better."

The funny thing was, he sounded as if he meant it. And Abby felt more pleased than she wanted to be to hear it. Especially since his appreciative gaze stayed on her rather than switching even then to the house, which was usually what happened because the place was an attention grabber all on its own.

But Cal seemed oblivious to everything but Abby.

"Shall we go?" she asked, beginning to feel uneasy beneath his study of her.

He turned on his heels and held the door open for her this time. Abby ducked out in front of him, and he pulled the big door closed behind them as if he were right at home.

"Where to?" he asked as they went to his car.

"I think the best place is out by the lake—Palmer Lake. It's about five miles outside town."

She'd given this a lot of thought today, too. Palmer Lake was undoubtedly the spot for sunset watching, since it was away from town and any artificial lights. But it was also fairly secluded, and she'd debated with herself about whether or not it was safe—or wise—to go out there alone with this man she hardly knew.

In the end she'd decided that if he hadn't done her any harm the night before, he probably wouldn't tonight, either, so she'd discarded the concern for safety.

But was it wise to go to a quiet, romantic spot alone with a man who made her blood boil? Who aroused her every sense and left her nerve endings too close to the surface of her skin for her own good? After all, it wasn't only that she could *see* how attractive he was. She could feel it. Deep inside. In stirrings that shouldn't be happening. Particularly for a stranger.

Yet there she was, wise or unwise, getting into his car, giving directions as he slipped behind the wheel himself and started the engine.

And if someone had asked her at that moment what

had come over her, what had caused her to throw caution to the wind…?

She didn't think she could have given a rational answer.

"How's the head?" he asked, shooting her a sidelong glance once they were on their way.

"Mine? Fine. Now."

"And the stomach?"

"Fine. I'm fine," she answered, a bit uncomfortable at being reminded of her previous evening's antics.

"Did your sisters give you a hard time this morning?"

"They were worried. About last night and tonight."

"They didn't think you should go out with me tonight?"

"They weren't too sure about it." She didn't mention that they'd been less concerned than she was, though. And instead she used the segue to put the evening into perspective. "I told them this was just a friendly payback. Nothing to think twice about. That I'd probably be home by ten."

Cal took his eyes off the road long enough to look straight at her. "Is that your curfew?"

"Curfew? No, I'm too old for a curfew. I just meant that this isn't really a date or anything. It's just sort of a welcome to Clangton, one good turn deserves another."

"Is that all it is?" he asked, sounding amused that she might think so.

"What would you call it?"

"A date. I've been callin' it a date." His eyes were back on the road, but she could see him grinning devilishly, enjoying the fact that he was thwarting her attempts to put a mundane spin on this. Then he added,

"And if I have anything to say about it, we're gonna break that curfew."

Abby didn't know how to answer that. Luckily the turnoff for the lake came into view, and she gave more directions instead of addressing his statement, not certain if she should be glad he wanted to spend more time with her or be troubled by it.

She pointed out the best place to park, deciding to keep the conversation light and impersonal.

"We used to have woodsies out here as kids—teenagers, really."

"Woodsies?"

"That's what we called them. We'd build a big bonfire and stand around it drinking beer and soda. Not a lot of excitement in good old Clangton."

"Guess we'll have to make some of our own, then," he said suggestively as he stopped the engine and got out.

Was he teasing her with innuendos like that? Again? The way he had this morning? Or was he serious?

She wasn't sure.

But then everything about this man left her unsure. Off balance. On edge. He just wasn't the kind of guy she'd had any experience with, and she didn't know how to take him.

Or maybe it was just that she couldn't quite believe he was flirting with someone like her. Choke-collar blouse and all.

He rounded the Corvette to open her door once more, holding out his hand to help her from the low seat.

Should she take his hand or shouldn't she?

It wasn't as if she needed the help. But would she insult him if she refused? Or look even more prudish than she already did?

That thought made her decision for her. She might be shy, quiet and provincial, but she wasn't *that* much of a prude.

She slipped her hand into his much bigger one, feeling the smooth calluses there. But the minute she made the contact of her skin against his, she regretted it.

Not because there was anything wrong with it. But because there wasn't. In the extreme.

It was as if an electrical current sprang from that touch to dance up her arm. The man was like a live wire that set off exquisite sensations upon even small contact. It made her want to curl her fingers around his hand and ease in close to his side so his elbow brushed her breast. So she could feel the heat of his body. So she could tuck her shoulder under his arm. Maybe lay her head against it...

As soon as she was out of the car, she pulled her hand out of his and cleared her throat in an attempt to regain some of the internal composure she'd lost with that sensation and those thoughts.

"That's the east side of the lake, over where that stand of fir trees is. If we sit in front of them, we'll be able to look out to the west and get a clear view of the sunset and see it reflected on the water, too. Sort of a double exposure."

"Sounds perfect," he said, going to the trunk of the car and taking a blanket and a picnic basket from it.

He hoisted the picnic basket and said, "Crackers, cheese, fruit, but no wine. Only some sparkling water and a thermos of coffee. I didn't think you'd be up to more booze after last night."

"You were right." And she was grateful for the consideration.

He tucked the blanket under the same arm carrying

the wicker basket and closed the trunk with his free hand. "Lead the way," he said then, and Abby didn't hesitate, half-afraid he might take her hand again if she waited to walk beside him.

And half-afraid he wouldn't.

They went about a third of the distance around the lake before they were positioned just right. Cal set the basket on the ground while he snapped open the blanket, then he set the basket on one corner and motioned for Abby to sit.

She did, hugging another corner as if the center of the blanket was too risqué.

It didn't matter. Cal still sat close by.

"So," she said to break the silence that had followed them from the car. "Have you always been a big sunset watcher or was this just a come-on?"

"A come-on?" he repeated with a laugh. "That makes me sound so cold and calculating. No, I really am a big sunset watcher. And sunrise, too, if I haven't had too late a night before. Or if the night before is still goin' on about then. It's always been a way of puttin' some continuity into a life that didn't have any. Until just lately."

He didn't seem eager to expand on that because he changed the subject to ask what she wanted to drink as he unloaded the food. He poured sparkling water into two wine goblets and set a plate laden with fruit, cheese and crackers on the closed basket lid within easy reach. Then he stretched out his long legs, crossing them at the ankles, leaned back—braced on his elbows—and stared at the horizon.

"This is a great spot."

Abby looked at him as he watched the sky, studying his sculpted profile and wondering—much the way her sisters had—who he really was, where he'd come from, what made him tick.

He glanced at her and nodded in the direction of mountains, which were only beginning to be outlined in butter-yellow, persimmon-pink and orange the color of a Creamsicle.

"You're missin' it," he warned before turning back.

It wasn't easy to tear her gaze away from him, but she forced herself to. Although she could still see him from the corner of her eye, and in truth watching him as he seemed to lose himself in the view of the setting sun was as intriguing as nature's display itself.

There was something elemental about the man. Primitive and naturally sensual. It went along with his apparent lack of awareness of his own impact on her. It seemed to say that he took for granted his appeal and had no problem stepping outside himself to revel in something like a sunset. And maybe being with her to watch it.

"You know, some of the best colors come from the reflection of the sun's rays through layers of pollution," he said. "I guess that's the good side of a bad thing. But I always wonder what it looked like back when there wasn't junk in the air. If it was spectacular on its own or just a fading glow that no one paid much mind to. Me, I always stop whatever I'm doin', wherever I am, to watch because you just never know what you might see."

"My favorites are when the sun looks like a fireball," Abby offered.

"Does that mean you're a card-carryin' sunset watcher, too?"

"No, I can't say that. I just notice an occasional, exceptional one."

"Then you don't know what you're missin' because even the unexceptional ones have a way of bringin' a peace and calming to the end of the day. I'm not big on stoppin' to smell the flowers, but a sunset, now, that's somethin' else."

They finished to watch in companionable silence, and although she'd never thought of it in his terms before, she came to agree with him. There was something very peaceful, very calming in the spectacle. It helped her relax about being with him.

And then, when the sun's rays disappeared completely and the sky held its last vestige of light before it gave over to the first stars and a nearly full moon, Cal let out a sigh of satisfaction and popped a grape into his mouth.

"Why didn't your life have continuity?" she asked to start conversation up again, referring to what he'd said earlier.

He shrugged a single broad shoulder, angled her way and sat up Indian fashion to face her. "My daddy couldn't grow roots no matter how hard he tried," he said simply before sampling some of the cheese slices on the dish.

"What did he do for a living?"

"You name it, he did it. Trained horses, blacksmithed, rodeoed, was a ranch hand, crop picker, crop duster, barn raiser, and a plain, all-round cowboy. Just never in one place for too long."

"How come?"

"He said he had a restless spirit. Myself, I think it was a way to try outrunnin' responsibilities, but what do I know?"

"Did he outrun his responsibilities?"

"Not for the most part. No way he could draggin' seven kids along with him."

"*Seven* kids? You have six brothers and sisters?"

"Five brothers and one sister."

"Wow. I thought four kids was a big family."

"Yours?"

"Mmm. There's me, Emily, Bree and our brother, Lucas."

"Parents still livin'?"

"South of Denver. They got tired of small-town life. My dad is semiretired, doing some consulting work there and they travel a lot. What about your folks?"

"My mother died givin' birth to baby number seven—Kate. My dad passed on about three years ago—he was kicked in the head by a mule."

"I'm sorry."

"Me, too. He was a good ol' boy, that's for sure. Wanderin' ways and all."

"So you didn't have a home base growing up?"

"No home base. No home. We lived in an old silver-bullet Airstream trailer we pulled behind the truck. Except when a job came with livin' quarters or on rare occasions when we'd stay in a motel or a huntin' camp or something like that. And we did a lot of campin' out."

"Did you go to school?"

"Sure. More of 'em than I could count. Most years we didn't finish in the same one we'd started in. One year we changed schools five different times."

"That must have been awful."

He grinned at her. "Don't go feelin' sorry for me, Abby Abby Stanton. I'm not complainin', just answerin' your questions. With seven kids there was always a bunch of us in a particular school for company.

And there wasn't a time when any one of us went without someone to play with or hang out with. Plus we did a lot of readin'—the old man was big on books. We did just fine. Every single one of us even went to college.''

"And sunsets and sunrises give you a sense of continuity.''

"No matter where we were, it was the same sun comin' up and goin' down. I liked the thought of that. It helped make it so it didn't matter that sometimes I wasn't sure where we were.''

"Didn't you get tired of traveling?''

"Not till just lately.''

"So you even lived that kind of life after you were on your own?''

"Yep. We all have, actually, shootin' off in every direction you can think of.''

"And what have you done for a living?''

"A lot of what my daddy did—cowboyin' in one form or another wherever the wind blew me.''

"Until now.''

"Until now.''

"What made you decide to change?''

"Oh, I was gettin' weary of it, thinkin' more and more about settlin' down. Then a year or so ago my sister and brothers and I were all in the same place, catchin' up with each other. There happened to be a big lottery I'd heard about at the time—called the Lucky Seven Lottery—and I just had a hunch about it. So we pooled our money, bought a bunch of tickets—''

"And won?'' she guessed with a full measure of surprise in her voice.

"And won. We split it up—there was plenty to go around—and all of a sudden my share gave me a lot of choices. I had the chance to use the money to dig some

real roots of my own. Started thinkin' about givin' myself—and maybe my sister and brothers—a home base,
as you put it. A place where I could stay put and so
could they if I could convince 'em to. Maybe it comes
from bein' the oldest, but somehow it seemed like I
could make the home we all never had.''

"So here you are."

"So here I am."

"Rumor around town was that you won the place in
a poker game," Abby informed him.

He laughed at that. "Close, but not quite."

Abby was dying to know exactly how much he'd
won, but it seemed rude to ask. So instead she went
back to what they'd been talking about just before.

"Have your brothers or sister come to see the place
yet?"

"Not yet. But they're due. By the end of the week,
last I heard from my brothers. I haven't been able to
get hold of Kate yet to find out when she's comin'."

"Do you think they'll stay when they do?"

"That's anybody's guess. They know they can. That
I'd like it if they do. Like their help fixin' the house,
startin' up the ranch. But we'll see." He chuckled
lightly, a deep rumble in the cooling night air. "If they
do, we'll be Cal, Cody, Kit, Cabe, Cole, Cray and Kate
Ketchum of Clangton, Colorado—how's that for allit-
eration?"

Abby laughed, suddenly studying him with new eyes.
She would never have guessed he had strong family
ties, a strong sense of responsibility or any desire to
establish a home base for a whole passel of siblings.
Somehow that seemed much more domestic than she
would have ever pictured him.

He stood then and held out his hand to her once more.

"Come on. Let's walk this lake and you can tell me tales of woodsies."

Without thinking about it, she took the hand he offered, remembering only when that electrical current danced up her arm again that that was what happened when he touched her. And how good it felt.

This time when she was on her feet he kept hold of her hand so she couldn't pull it back.

Then, too, she didn't try very hard.

She did tell him about woodsies as they headed off around the lake, though. Nothing she thought was terribly interesting about a bunch of kids building bonfires years and years ago. But he seemed interested nonetheless, listening raptly, laughing where she meant for him to, asking a question here and there that proved he was paying attention.

All the while she was talking, Abby was very aware of Cal. Of the nearness of him. Of her hand in his. Of the warmth and kid-leather toughness of his palm. Of the pressure of each of his long, thick fingers holding her just firmly enough within his grip. Of his thumb rubbing softly back and forth against the tender flesh between her own thumb and forefinger. Of the things that were coming alive in her at being with this man, listening to his deep, quiet voice filling the emptiness around them and to his laugh, so rich it seemed to ripple through her.

And somewhere along the way she started to think that there was more to Cal Ketchum than a gorgeous face and a body to die for. She began to like him. Much, much more than she wanted to.

The lake was a little over five miles around, and slowly strolling it the way they were took a long time.

Ten o'clock was a memory when they reached the blanket again.

"I suppose you're going to say you need to get home now because it's already past your curfew," he said as they neared it.

Going home, ending the evening, was the last thing on Abby's mind. But because he brought it up, she was afraid it was Cal who wanted this over with.

She'd done what she set out to do, she thought—bored him to death.

But there was no satisfaction in a job well done. Instead disappointment washed through her like water through a broken dam.

"I do have an early morning tomorrow. It's my turn to do the first shift baking," she said by way of agreement for him to take her home.

He didn't argue. He just made quick work of packing up the picnic basket and blanket.

And the whole time Abby's spirits and confidence plummeted further and further.

I must really be bad news if a man alone with me late at night, next to the lake, under a sky full of stars, with a blanket spread out and at the ready, doesn't even so much as try to kiss me.

But he didn't try to kiss her.

He just carried the gear back to the car, stashed it in the trunk and handed her into the passenger's seat.

Neither of them said much on the drive to her house. At least not aloud. Abby had plenty to say to herself, reminding herself that it was for the best that he knew the truth about her now. That this was a much better, smarter conclusion to the night than the last one had been. That it was good that she'd turned him off in whatever way she had. That now he'd forget she existed and she could go on with her quiet, reserved life.

There were no lights on inside the house when he pulled up to the curb in front. Emily and Bree had left the porch light on for her, and she suspected they were lurking in a window or two somewhere watching.

There won't be anything to see, guys, she thought, wishing she weren't awash in dejection over that fact.

Still, Cal was gentleman enough to walk her up onto the porch.

"I've been dyin' to know somethin' since pickin' you up tonight," he said as she unlocked the door, pushed it open and then let the screen close as she turned to face him.

"What?" she responded, trying not to notice how good he looked with the pale gold glow of the porch light dusting his features.

He pointed his chin at her clothes. "Are you always this buttoned up or did you just go to the opposite extreme from last night to make a statement?"

"I'm usually this buttoned up."

"Seems to me there ought to be a happy medium."

"Like what?"

He was smiling a small, amused smile that deepened the creases around his mouth and drew lines at the corners of aquamarine eyes that held hers mesmerized.

She was so drawn to that gaze and the sight of his handsome face that she didn't even realize he was raising his hands to her collar until she felt them under her chin.

"How about like this," he said softly, intimately, as he undid the three buttons there.

Oh, my God, he's undressing me on the front porch!

she thought, taking stock of who might be witnessing it.

But he stopped at the second button below the collar—leaving it open a perfectly respectable amount.

"This way you might even be able to breathe," he whispered, bending close to her ear so his own breath was a sweet warmth against her skin.

"I'm breathing all right." Well, except for the difficulty brought on by his being so nearby.

"Not easily, you're not. And I want you breathin' easily."

"Why?"

He didn't answer with words. Instead he slid his hands along the sides of her neck, plunging his fingers up into her hair to guide her head backward so that her face lifted up to his. He lowered his mouth to hers, his lips parting as he did to take hers in a kiss that was nothing like the one he'd given that morning. Nothing like any she'd ever had standing on her front porch.

It was a deep, deep, all-consuming kiss with only a hint of his tongue urging her own lips to relax, to open to him, to let their breaths mix and mingle, to give herself over to the kiss, to the moment, to the man.

Abby's head fell farther back into his cradling hands, feeling lighter than even the liquor had left it the previous evening. Her eyes were closed, and she felt as if she were floating on the pure, sexy intoxication of his mouth on hers, of the liquid movement of his head above her, of the heat and power that seemed to emanate from him, of the scent of that aftershave and the nail-buffer texture of his cheek brushing hers.

So much for assuring her sisters there wouldn't even be a peck on the cheek to say good-night, she thought as she felt her nipples pucker up, her back arch toward him all on its own, her breasts swell toward his chest in an intense longing to be pushed against it.

She parted her lips farther, inviting more. She couldn't quite believe she was actually doing anything that bold, but she was driven by a need she hadn't even been aware of in herself before that moment.

He's a dyed-in-the-wool ladies' man, a tiny voice of caution warned in the back of her mind.

But all she could think about was that it didn't matter, that nothing mattered but the kiss that made it seem as if she'd never really been kissed before....

And then it was over. Leaving her hungering for it not to be. For it to start again and go on and on...

"Night, Abby," he said so softly she wasn't sure she'd heard it.

Or maybe she was just that dazed.

Because it took a moment for her to realize he'd taken his hands away, turned around and was actually leaving, that that most perfect of derrieres was moving down the walkway on a stride that held only a faint swagger.

Not until she saw him get into the Corvette and offer a final wave did it sink in with any clarity that he was gone. That their date was over.

And that he hadn't made any mention of ever getting together again.

But no amount of reminders, no amount of reasoning, no amount of rationalizing or talking to herself could convince her at that moment that that was a good thing.

Because no one could have just been kissed like she had just been kissed and not consider selling her soul for more.

4

"If YOU AREN'T GOING TO TELL us anything about last night, you might as well take off for the day and go by the hardware store on your way home to see about that new faucet we need," Emily said the next day around two in the afternoon.

Abby, Emily and Bree were in the kitchen portion at the rear of the bakery they owned jointly. The Three Sisters Bakery was a fair-size shop in one of the old-fashioned buildings that lined First Street—named because that was what it had been, Clangton's first street. Most of the buildings had been erected during the earliest years of the town and refurbished along the way. The bakery was a two-story structure, with the shop and kitchen on the ground floor and a small apartment on the upper level.

Abby, Emily and Bree also owned the building. Originally it had been a perfect box shape, like a gigantic refrigerator. They'd livened it up by adding a steep Victorian roof to what had only been a flat top before, replacing all the windows with paned glass, painting the whole thing dove-gray and trimming it—including the shutters they'd added to the windows—in crisp white.

Now, from the front at least, it looked more like a quaint turn-of-the-century town house.

"There's nothing to tell about last night," Abby insisted in answer to her sister's comment.

Since Bree and Emily had arrived for work at eight and eleven o'clock respectively, they'd both been on a quest for Abby to talk about the previous evening with Cal. At least they had been every minute they hadn't been putting together pies, cakes, brownies, breads and rolls or waiting on customers.

But even though Abby had said a few things about her date with Cal—giving them a brief outline of watching the sunset, walking around the lake and coming straight home—they weren't satisfied.

"You're holding out on us," Bree declared. "Too much time passed between when we heard the car pull up in front of the house to bring you home, when he drove off again and then when you finally came in. Something went on, and you're being too closemouthed for it not to have been juicy."

"We said good-night," Abby answered simply enough as she measured out the ingredients that would get them started the next morning.

They'd developed a pattern that kept the bakery running smoothly. One of the three of them came in at 5:00 a.m. to start bread dough rising, to make breakfast croissants they filled with jams and cream cheese and to set the wheels into motion for the rest of what they had planned to make for the day.

Another of them came in at eight when they opened up so there would be two of them to attend to the baking and waiting on customers.

The third sister didn't have to be there until eleven when most of the baking was finished for the day. That person would stay to close up at seven, while the first one in left around two o'clock and the second at five o'clock.

They rotated the shifts daily and all shared in the

baking, although each of them had a few specialties that the other two didn't make.

"You said good-night," Emily repeated. "Did he kiss you?"

Abby was glad to know they'd allowed her some privacy and not been peeking out of any windows. "Mm-hmm," she said, hedging and trying to pretend that the kiss hadn't been on her mind ever since it had happened.

"And it must have been a pretty good kiss or else why would you have stayed moony eyed out on the porch watching him drive away?" Bree put in.

"So you were spying. And here I was just thinking I was glad you hadn't been."

Bree smiled victoriously. "Neither one of us was *spying.* I just guessed that was what you were doing out there for a full five minutes after he'd already driven off. Gotcha!"

"Moony eyed?" Abby repeated in a last-ditch effort to regain some of the ground she'd just inadvertently lost.

"Is that what you were doing?" Emily asked.

"I don't get *moony eyed* over anybody," Abby said forcefully. Too forcefully. Her denial gave her away and she knew it. "Okay, so maybe it did take me a little while to come inside after he kissed me good-night and left. That doesn't mean anything."

"Except maybe that the man is some good kisser," Bree mused.

"Is he?" Emily prodded.

"He knows what he's doing, all right."

"Enough to make you go out with him again?" Emily continued.

"He didn't ask me out again," Abby said as if she

didn't care. But she did. That kiss had left her caring a lot. In spite of the fact that she knew she should be hoping she never so much as saw the man again.

"But would you go out with him if he asked?" Bree persisted.

"I don't know. Maybe."

Emily and Bree exchanged knowing looks.

"Definitely a good kisser," Bree said to Emily.

To Abby, Emily said, "Which is why you asked us both if anyone had called at home before we came in today—you were hoping *he* had."

"Not hoping. Just curious." Okay, so maybe she was hoping, too. It stung a little that a kiss that had done so much for her hadn't even prompted him to ask to see her again. Or to call today.

But Abby didn't want to talk about this anymore. Actually she hadn't wanted to talk about it at all. There was something about the pull she felt to Cal Ketchum that seemed almost indecent. Maybe because the heart of her response was so rawly sensual that it embarrassed her to know she was capable of feeling that way.

For what must have been the fiftieth time today, she changed the subject, deciding that leaving her sisters to their own devices was the only way she was going to escape their interest. "Are we decided on the faucet over at the new hardware store or the old one?"

Once more Bree looked at Emily and spoke to her as if Abby couldn't hear. "That's our cue to shut up about this."

"You guys are just making a bigger deal out of it than it is. There isn't that much to talk about. And I've been here long enough today. I'd like to take off. So what about the faucet?"

Her sisters exchanged another glance, but finally gave in.

"Get the one at the new store," Bree said. "Even though I feel disloyal not giving the business to Barry after all these years, he doesn't have one with a high enough spout and we need that for the big pots."

"We'll try to make it up to him later on," Emily concurred.

"Okay, then. I'm going to go," Abby said, washing her hands in the big sink that needed a new faucet to replace what had been leaking for too long already.

"And maybe," Bree added with a sly tone to her voice, "after you finish at the hardware store you ought to take a drive. Like out toward the old Peterson place? Now known as the Lucky Seven ranch…"

Abby sighed elaborately. "I thought we all agreed now was the worst time for me to be even thinking about another man."

"Too late. You're already thinking about him," Bree stated.

"And if you can't help thinking about him—"

"Or getting moony eyed over a kiss from him—"

"—you might as well give in to it all and enjoy yourself."

"Thanks for the blessing. But no thanks."

"Bill Snot-grass never left you moony eyed on the porch for five minutes after he kissed you good-night," Bree reminded as Abby dried her hands and grabbed her purse.

But she didn't answer Bree's remark. She just rolled her eyes, gave her sisters a parting wave and went out the bakery's front door.

There was no sense arguing with the truth.

CLANGTON WAS MORE than a one-horse town. But not much more. The Three Sisters Bakery was midway down First Street. To the east of it were the bank, the post office and the small hospital that had been Clangton's school before more than a half-dozen rooms had been needed and a new school had been built not far from there.

To the west of the bakery was the old family-owned Drug Emporium, which sold everything from foodstuffs to sundries to tennis shoes and sweat suits. There was also a large grocery store that hadn't been around more than a dozen years, and a number of other businesses that served most every need that arose and left the small community fairly self-sufficient.

The weather was still springlike even though June had begun the week before. Since temperatures in the daytime were mild yet, and since the distance to the hardware store wasn't all that great, Abby decided to leave her car at the bakery and walk, enjoying the sights as if she were a tourist.

Clangton proper was a monument to making the best use of what had begun as the foundation of the town, of the buildings built to last and tended over the years so they could. There were no high-rises. The bank was the tallest building at three stories. The rest bobbed up and down from one to two. They were mostly brick of varying shades, mostly square and unadorned, but dignified looking, with an occasional quaint structure sprouting up here and there for flavor.

The old boardwalks hadn't been replaced until 1969 when the city council had voted to replace them with bricks for a cobbled effect, adding tall black Victorian streetlights to jazz things up.

And jazz things up they had. Christmastime found

the poles wrapped in boughs, red ribbons and tiny white lights. They were tied with pastel bows for Easter, wound with red, white and blue banners for the Fourth of July festivities and provided any number of other opportunities for decoration depending on the celebration or time of year. Now, for the onset of summer, the bases were planted with bright pink-and-purple pansies.

Abby enjoyed her stroll, stopping to talk to several people she encountered here and there. Then she turned onto Racine Avenue—which ran north and south to First Street's east and west.

The business district was primarily on First Street but Racine was gaining ground, mainly with the addition of the new, big-city-size center for hardware, building supplies and decorating.

The center had been built between the small shops that had taken over old houses there and the Clangton Saloon, which had previously been slightly disconnected from town.

Abby headed for the hardware center, but even as she did, it wasn't the sprawling new store and lumberyard that caught her eye.

It was the Clangton Saloon just beyond.

The facade was fashioned of rustic wood to look like an old-time saloon, with shutters on nonexistent windows to add effect.

The parking lot was empty at that time of day, but she had a sudden flash of it from Saturday night. Of herself being carried out by Cal. Of her head on his shoulder. Of the feel of his muscular arms holding her as if she weighed nothing at all. Of that big body of his cupped around hers...

She really did need to get back on the straight and narrow from which she'd veered with Saturday night's wild-woman stunt, she told herself firmly as she yanked her wandering thoughts back to reality and tamped down on the tingling sensation that erupted all through her. She shouldn't even be thinking about Cal, because even thinking about him was more of that distraction. The man was not her type. She was not his type. And that's all there was to it.

So with that admonishment under her belt, Abby went into the hardware center and decided to take a look around before buying the faucet she'd come for.

Not much of what she found interested her—lumber, nuts and bolts, tools—until she came upon the remodeling displays where mock bathrooms and kitchens were set up. There was one bathtub in particular that caught her attention and lured her into the secluded alcove where it was displayed.

The tub was a huge, shiny black oval set within three false walls on a pedestal of six tiled steps, with gold tap and handles coming out from the center of the back side rather than at either end, where inward slopes were made for lounging.

Abby liked nothing better than a long soak in a hot bubble bath, but she'd never been in anything but a regulation tub before. She wondered if those sloping ends were as comfortable as they looked. But it was something she'd never know unless she got in and tried it out.

The store wasn't busy. In fact, the way that display was cloistered within the maze of other mock bathrooms and kitchens, she seemed to be all alone.

So with a furtive glance around to make absolutely certain no one was watching, she climbed the tile stairs and stepped into the empty tub.

It really was a decadent device. No one person

needed a bathtub the size of a children's wading pool, with whirlpool jets and a bottom so deep the top edges reached to her chin.

But oh, it was nice!

Abby wiggled around a little until she was sitting just right. Then she leaned back against one of the slanted ends and settled her head in the built-in dip designed for that purpose.

Bliss. It really would be bliss to be soaking in steamy, sweet-scented bubbles like that. Maybe with the lights turned off and only candles burning all around.

She closed her eyes and imagined it, reveling in the picture in her mind, in the feel of the tub cradling her, supporting her back, her head, nearly as comfortable as a bed. Warm water would be swirling over her skin as steam wafted in the air. There might be a little faint music—something slow and lilting. Every muscle would relax. Every nerve ending would slowly awaken to the sensations. The bathroom door would open. In would walk Cal. Naked...

"I don't know if you should be enjoyin' yourself quite so much in public."

Abby's eyes flew open at the sound of the deep male voice coming in low, intimate tones from so nearby she could feel his breath against her ear.

Cal Ketchum had not only just walked into her fantasy. He was there in person.

She didn't know where he'd come from or how he'd managed to get that close without her hearing or even sensing his presence, but he was standing with one booted foot braced on the second step, leaning an arm along the tile that bordered the tub.

"Oh," Abby said, surprised, embarrassed, speechless and sitting up fast.

"Testing out the equipment?"

"I guess you could say that."

"What do you think?"

"About the tub? It's nice. Very nice."

"Good. Because I'm considerin' buyin' it."

Buying it. Filling it nearly to the rim. Getting into it stark, staring naked...

The only thing that would be missing from what she'd just pictured in her mind was her.

She felt her cheeks begin to burn.

Why did this man have the power to make her blush like a schoolgirl over and over again?

Wanting to put herself on a more equal footing, Abby started to stand. But Cal stopped her with a hand on her shoulder. "Don't go anywhere. There isn't anybody I can think of that I'd rather see in it."

She felt ridiculous, but between his hand on her shoulder and his blocking the only side without a wall, she'd have had to force her way out and that would have been even more awkward.

Trying to make the best of the situation and not let him know how uncomfortable this made the prim, prudish part of her feel, she said, "It's a nice tub. Where would you put it?"

"The bathroom off my bedroom. In case you didn't notice the other day, the tub in there is in bad shape."

Abby shot another glance around, afraid someone might have heard the reference to her being in the bathroom off his bedroom.

No one was in sight, but somehow that didn't help her uneasiness. "I just came in for a faucet for the bakery and—"

"And couldn't resist tryin' out the tub."

"Something like that."

"And now that you've been caught in the act, you'd like to run like a rabbit," he guessed with a slow smile.

He was right, of course, but she didn't want to admit it. So she lied instead. "I should get back."

"Humor me first," he said, finally taking his hand off her shoulder in a slow movement that was more a caress than anything.

She didn't know what he meant by humoring him. But she didn't have long to wonder before he climbed into the tub with her.

Abby's legs had been stretched out straight, and she pulled them up in a hurry, looking around yet again. All it would take was one person to see this, and not a soul in Clangton would miss hearing about it.

Again she started to rise. "Let me get out so you can try it yourself," she offered.

Yet not only did Cal not accommodate that idea, but he also motioned her down.

"Come on, Abby, I need your help." He made that sound partly playful, partly sensual.

"I don't know what kind of help you had in mind, but—"

"I just wanted to see if it really is big enough for two," he said, his tone laden with innuendo. "Relax. There isn't a handful of people in this whole place. Nobody'll see."

The thought of security cameras flashed through her mind, but Cal was positioned in such a way—with his back to the side rather than at the opposite end—that she would have had to high-step over his head to get out.

So she had to content herself with hugging her knees to her chest to keep some distance between them.

"You don't look too comfortable," he said with

more amusement in his voice. "I don't think this tub was meant for huddling in the corner. Could you ease up just a little?"

"I don't think so."

"Please?" he asked charmingly, pulling her arms from where they wrapped her shins.

Then he grabbed on to her ankles and eased them under his tunneled legs to stretch out the way they'd been before.

"Now lie back," he instructed.

"I think this is a test you ought to do yourself."

"That would depend on what I was testin' for."

"Which would be…"

"I just want the whole picture before I make up my mind. This is no cheap deal, you know. Now, lie back."

The man was incorrigible. And good-looking. And utterly appealing. And he seemed to be oblivious to so many things that had always been important to her—like the way things looked and what people might think. It all added up to an intriguing package and coaxed Abby out of herself the way a timid child might be tempted to join the fun of a mischievous child when the opportunity presented itself.

She settled her back against the tub's slanted end again.

It made him grin with pleasure. And seeing it gave her a warm rush.

"Rest your head the way you were doin' before," he ordered.

She did that, too.

He must have realized he'd won this round because he leaned back himself, spread his arms along the tub's rim and stretched long legs to cross at the ankles on the opposite ledge.

He looked so comfortable, he really could have been without the restraints of the tight blue jeans and bright yellow shirt he wore, lounging in the bathtub in the privacy of his own home.

"Close your eyes," he added then.

She did, more to escape the all too arousing sight of him than to be accommodating.

"Now tell me what you were thinkin' about when I found you here with that sexy little smile on your face."

So he was teasing her again.

But by then she was willing to play along.

She described the scene she'd been imagining, omitting his nude entrance into the mental picture.

"Are you tellin' me you were all alone?" he asked when she'd finished, his tone suspicious.

"All alone."

"Then you weren't doin' it right."

"Oh, no?" she said with a laugh, forcing the muscles in her face to relax in what she hoped looked like perfect serenity in her solitary imaginings.

"You can't have candlelight and a tub full of bubbles and be by yourself. There has to be a man, too."

"I don't think there *has* to be."

"But it makes for a lot better fantasy."

"Is that so?"

"You bet. A man who happens by and sees you all warm and wet and inviting."

If he could refer to the man in the third person and make this less personal, she could refer to the woman that way, too, and let herself off the hook. "Oh, now she's *inviting*."

"Well, sure. He wouldn't come in if she didn't want him to."

"I don't know about that. He seems to have a mind of his own."

"True enough. But she's still glad to see him," Cal insisted.

Abby just smiled.

"He'd have to strip down, of course," Cal continued as if they were collaborating on the scenario of a novel. "So he could get into the water with her."

"And where would he sit when he did? At her end or at the other one?"

"I think he'd be on his knees to her," Cal said in a voice that was more quiet, more intimate than before. "Straddling her hips so he could bend over and kiss her while he ran his hands along her shoulders. Down her arms."

"Ah. A bath massage," she said, not intending for her own voice to come out almost as a sigh.

"To start with anyway," he said with a devilishly intimate chuckle.

"It would feel great," she said as if she were experiencing it, free to be lost in the vivid scene in her mind because her eyes were still closed against reality.

"Warm. Slippery. Great," he agreed. "So great he'd have to give her the full-body massage."

"The full-body massage?"

"Every inch of her body."

"While he was kissing her?"

"Or watching to see how much she liked it."

"Would she like it?" Abby asked, taunting slightly even though her tone was barely more than a whisper as she drifted deeper and deeper into the images they were conjuring together.

"Oh, yeah, she'd like it, all right. No doubt about that. He'd make sure of it."

"And would he like it, too?"

"So much he'd have a hard time holdin' back."

"And when he couldn't anymore?"

"He wouldn't. He'd start kissin' her again and he'd stop the full-body massage to hone in on a few areas that'd drive her crazy. A few that'd drive him crazy...."

What was she doing? that little voice of caution in the back of Abby's mind shouted at her. This was no way to spend an afternoon. In a public place. With a man she hardly knew. Making up a fantasy that was getting her more turned on by the minute.

Too turned on to stop even though she knew this had gotten way out of hand.

"Then what?" she heard herself say in a bedroom voice that wasn't quite as raspy as his had grown.

"Then he'd point the whirlpool jets at just the right spots and let 'em pulse water while some other pulsin' went on. Long, slow, wet, slippery pulsin'...."

Okay, maybe this had gone far enough.

Abby opened her eyes and fought her way out of the imaginary scene before she embarrassed herself with more than a verbal climax.

"Water would splash all over," she decreed practically.

Cal was watching her with warm aquamarine eyes. He laughed. "Who cares if water splashes all over?"

"They'd care when wood rot ate right through the floor."

He leaned over and spoke directly into her ear again. "It would be worth it."

"You're a wicked man," she said, trying not to smile at the delight that made those turquoise eyes sparkle.

"Who, me? I thought we were talkin' about two other people. Made-up ones."

"Well, those two other, made-up people would have one big mess to clean."

Enunciating each word for emphasis, he repeated, "It would be worth it."

A man dressed in the store's uniform walked by the opening to that section just then, frowning at them but not venturing inside.

Abby knew him. He went to her church. And from the disapproving, impatient expression on his face, it wasn't the first time he'd walked by.

"Oh, boy," she muttered, disregarding awkwardness now to scramble to her feet and out of the tub in a hurry.

Cal glanced over his shoulder in the salesman's direction as if he knew perfectly well that the other man had been periodically looking in on them. Cal didn't move, though. He stayed just the way he was, lounging in the tub.

"So what's the verdict?" he asked her.

"About what?"

"Do I invest in this thing or not?"

There was something in his tone that said he wasn't actually referring to the bathtub.

But if not that, then what?

Abby shot another look at the mock room's opening, finding the salesman no longer in sight. Then she gazed back at Cal. "Are you talking about the tub?"

He just shrugged, and she decided to take that as an affirmative answer because exploring anything else seemed even more dangerous, and certainly more complex.

"If I could afford this bathtub and had the space to put it in, I would," she confided.

"And if I do, will you come over and use it?" he asked with that bad-boy grin.

"I better buy my faucet and get going," was the only answer she could think to give.

"I'll supply the candles," he tempted.

"Really, I have to go now," she insisted, keeping one eye on the room's entrance for her fellow church member.

"You know what I'd like as much as you comin' over to use my tub, if it becomes my tub?"

"What?" she asked, still on the lookout for the salesman.

"I'd like it if you'd stop tryin' so hard to run from me, little rabbit."

"I'm not running. I really have to go," she lied for the third time.

He just stared at her as if he knew it. For a moment, anyway. Then he said, "Okay. Go."

So why wouldn't her feet move?

She stood rooted to the spot, watching him, struck by how terrifically handsome he was, how terrifically appealing, how terrifically sexy, wanting to climb back in the bathtub with him. Fellow church member or no fellow church member lurking just outside.

But in the end she couldn't do it.

"See you around," she said lamely instead.

"Sure."

She finally persuaded her feet to move. But before she'd gotten more than a few steps away, Cal's deep voice stopped her.

"How about we watch the sunrise together sometime soon? I know the perfect place for it."

So maybe she hadn't bored him to death the previous night. Or just now, either.

"I'd like that," she heard herself say before she'd given any thought to the wisdom in it.

Then she wondered if that perfect place to watch the sunrise was from his bed, thinking that perhaps she should add that she'd only like to watch it with him if it was from some respectable spot.

But somehow that seemed presumptuous even if his tone of voice was full of insinuation.

Not to mention that she wasn't altogether sure she wanted to put on that restriction....

"Happy faucet huntin', Abby Abby," he said then, rather than making a firm date.

"Thanks. Enjoy your bathtub."

"Without you? Don't know if that's possible," he said on a sigh.

Incorrigible. He was definitely incorrigible.

And she liked it way too much.

ABBY WAS DREAMING that there was a woodpecker in her room.

Tap, tap, tap.

She could hear it, but no matter how hard she tried, she couldn't see it.

Tap, tap, tap.

She also couldn't figure out how it had gotten into her room.

Tap, tap, tap.

Or maybe it wasn't in her room. Maybe it was pecking from outside. On her window...

She came awake slowly until she realized the pecking wasn't coming from a woodpecker inside or outside her room, that it was someone knocking on her window. Then she bolted the rest of the way out of sleep with a rush of pure adrenaline, sitting up in bed.

Somebody was knocking on her window!

Her bedroom—like all the rest in the house—was on

the second floor. But being in the rear, it had its own outside door onto the wide sunporch that ran the length of the back side. There were a dozen wooden steps that rose up from the yard to the porch, but no one came calling from there. Especially not in the middle of the night. Or even at 4:43 in the morning, which was what her bedside clock said was the time.

The lacy white curtains on her window were pulled but they had a tendency to part about an inch at the center rather than meeting directly. And through that inch she could see that there was a person standing out there, and that was where the soft tapping was coming from and not from the woodpecker of her dream.

She got out of bed and grabbed a bathrobe even though her nightgown, with its high neck and thick cotton fabric, didn't reveal anything. Still, she didn't go to the window until the robe was in place and buttoned from the floor-length hem to the round collar.

She couldn't really see enough of the window knocker to recognize more than that he was a man, but deep down she knew who it was anyway.

Cal.

Who else would have the audacity to come knocking on her bedroom window so early in the morning? No one she knew. And Clangton didn't have any criminal element to be wary of. Besides, burglars didn't patiently stand outside and knock before coming in.

Her heartbeat picked up speed as she finally crossed the room and pulled the curtains open.

It was Cal, all right. Grinning at her and waving as if he were in a parade.

He mouthed, "Open the window," and Abby didn't hesitate to oblige.

"What are you doing out there?" she asked, only

then wondering how she must look—her hair a sleep-ruffled mess, no makeup, probably pillow creases on her face. And all while he didn't seem to have been to bed yet because he was wearing the same clothes he'd had on in the hardware store, his hair carelessly finger combed and his face clean shaved enough to make her think he'd spruced himself up not long before.

"I've been workin' on blueprints of my house all night instead of sleepin'. My eyes were blurrin' but I'm still not tired, so I thought I'd see if you'd come watch the sunrise with me. You said you would, remember?"

"You didn't say when."

"So what about now? I have coffee. And beer nuts—the breakfast of champions," he added as if the coffee and beer nuts were sure lures.

"Beer nuts?"

"Nothin' open around here this time of day, and that's all I could get from the machine outside of the gas station. But the coffee's fresh ground and fresh made."

Abby stared out at him, wondering how he could be so charming, so appealing, so sexy even at that hour, without any sleep. But he was. And just out of a deep slumber of her own, her resistance was low. Not that it was ever too high when it came to this guy.

"You don't have to work, do you?" he asked.

"No, this is my late morning."

"Then what do you say?"

No was what she should say, she told herself. This was crazy. It wasn't even five o'clock in the morning. And sneaking out her bedroom to go off and watch the sunrise with a man who'd just been peeking in her window was not something Abby Stanton did.

But at that moment she didn't really care about anything but the illicit excitement of doing something she wouldn't ordinarily do. With Cal.

"Just give me a few minutes to get dressed."

His grin broadened on only one side. "I'll be waitin' downstairs."

The clock on her nightstand said 5:00 a.m. on the dot when Abby slipped out of the porch door to follow Cal.

She'd applied just a dab of mascara and blush, and brushed her hair but left it free around her face and shoulders rather than waste the time doing more with it.

She'd thrown on a pair of jeans she'd had since high school, and the first blouse she found in the closet—a plain white button-down-collar oxford. Then she'd brushed her teeth as she slipped her feet into a pair of penny loafers, applied a hint of lip gloss and away she went, still surprised at the fact that she was actually doing this.

Cal was sitting on the second step from the bottom and he stood as she went down to him.

Watching her come, he smiled again. "I wasn't sure whether you'd go through with this or just call the sheriff to haul me away."

"There are laws against window peeking, you know," she said just to give him a hard time. "My sisters would shoot you if they knew you'd looked in at them while they were sleeping to figure out which room was mine—that *is* how you figured out which room was mine, isn't it?"

"It is. But yours was the first window I tried." He leaned toward her and confided, "Don't ever underestimate my luck."

Or anything else about him, Abby thought, but she didn't say it.

He held his arm out for her to lead the way around the house to the curb in front where his car was parked, but once they'd reached it he made sure he was there ahead of her to open the passenger's door for her. It struck her that the small courtesy he always performed was something her former fiancé—who would probably be considered the more civilized of the two men—had never shown her.

"So where are we going?" she asked when Cal was behind the wheel and easing the Corvette away from her house.

"It's a surprise," he said.

He drove through town at a leisurely pace, with his right arm stretched across her seat back, seeming to enjoy the sight of a sleeping Clangton.

"What was it like growin' up here?" he asked, almost as if he envied the fact that she had.

"It was nice. Ordinary, though, I guess. We went to school, to the movies on Saturday, to church on Sunday. In the summers we swam in Palmer Lake. In the winters we waited for it to freeze over so we could ice-skate on it. Or we went sledding down Harris Hill. There weren't a lot of restrictions because there weren't a lot of dangers and everybody pretty much knew everybody else, so parents weren't paranoid."

"Were you born here?"

"Mm-hmm. We're the fourth generation in Clangton. My parents are the first not to spend their whole life here."

"Have you ever lived anywhere else?"

"I went to college in Fort Collins. But then I just came back here. I like it."

He nodded his head slowly. "Me, too."

"How did you pick Clangton to finally settle down in?"

"I'd been in and out of Colorado plenty of times. Liked it. Liked the seasons changing. The people—" He shot her a meaningful glance. "So when I decided to buy property I went to Denver and hooked up with an old friend—"

"Cissy Carlisle's cousin." The playboy.

"Word travels fast," he guessed with a sideways glance at her.

"Don't ever doubt it."

"Anyhow, Cissy's cousin set me up with Cissy, who showed me the Peterson place, and there was just somethin' about it and Clangton that said home to me. I told you I trust my instincts. So here I am."

There seemed to be an underlying message in that last part, but Abby didn't know what it was any more than she'd been sure what he might have been alluding to with his question about whether to invest in the tub or something else the previous afternoon in the hardware store. And she didn't have time to find out because just then he turned onto the road that led to his house.

"Your place is the best spot for watching the sunrise?" And what was she going to do if he said watching it from his bed was what he had in mind?

"Yep," was all he answered as he stopped in front of the house and switched off the engine.

"I don't know about this...."

"You gettin' scared on me again?"

"No, I'm not scared. It's just that—"

He pressed a finger to her lips to halt the words. "Just wait and see."

He got out of the car and came around for her, taking

her hand to offer help she didn't need and keeping hold of it once he had.

But rather than guiding her toward his house the way she'd been expecting him to, he veered to the left and headed in the direction of the big white barn that ran at a forty-five-degree angle to the house.

They went through the open great doors that cast what little moonglow lit the way. But darkness didn't seem to bother Cal, who took her confidently to a home-made wooden ladder not far from the barn's entrance.

"Climb up," he said.

"Into the loft?"

"Into the loft."

She hesitated only a split second before doing just that, rising into the scent of freshly cut hay and cool country air.

The hay doors at the far end stood open, too, spilling more moon- and starlight onto a blanket spread over a cushion of hay. A thermos and two mugs were nearby, as was the promised bag of beer nuts.

It could well have been a scene for seduction.

Or nothing more than what he said it was—the perfect place to watch the sunrise since the loft offered a clear view to the east, over the house and the rest of the outbuildings. With Cal it was hard to tell. But by then she was inclined to think that it was all just very sweet. That this man was very sweet, no matter what kind of a reputation had followed him here.

He'd trailed her up the ladder and now pointed toward the blanket to let her know that was their destination.

"When did you do this?" she asked as she crossed to it.

"Just before goin' to kidnap you."

Two hay bales under one end of the blanket made a perfect backrest, and Abby sat in front of them, Indian fashion, looking out the hay doors.

Cal joined her, sitting the same way beside her.

"Coffee?" he offered.

"Not right now, I don't think," she said. She still felt lazy and weighted from sleep, which helped make her more at ease, more comfortable with him. It was nice and she didn't want it disturbed by caffeine.

Instead she surveyed his property beyond the barn.

The main house was the biggest in the county. The center portion was a two-story, redbrick Georgian structure, and on either side were single-story wings that stretched out like welcoming arms.

Behind the house was another barn—smaller than the one they were in, a two-level bunkhouse, a large foreman's house that dated from when there had been a foreman and several smaller cabins that had been built when the place had been turned into a dude ranch.

With the exception of some weather-worn gutters, the main house—because it was brick—didn't show many signs of disrepair on the outside. But since all the outlying buildings were wood, they did. Paint chipped and peeled or was water-stained in a pattern that looked like muddy icicles dripping from beneath the eaves. Window and door screens were torn, glass had broken, shutters were hanging, shingles were in need of replacing, paddock fences had splintered and weeds had overtaken the grounds all around.

Still, though, there was no denying it was a big spread. Especially for a man alone. A man who'd bought the place, Abby recalled, hoping his many brothers and sister might join him. But until that happened, it just felt lonely.

Or maybe he did and she was only sensing it intuitively.

"What're you thinkin'?" he asked, breaking the silence that surrounded them.

"That you have your work cut out for you." She lied, rather than telling him what she'd just been wondering.

"I like a project," he said, once again making it sound as if he were referring to more than what it would take to get the place back in order.

"Is that what I am, a project?" she asked, this time guessing at what else he might mean.

He smiled slightly. "I was thinkin' more of you as a plaything."

"So you're toying with me."

"No, just enjoyin' you," he said slowly, as if contemplating what exactly he was doing with her. Then, in the same way, he added, "Enjoyin' you and thinkin' about you more often than not. Wonderin' about you. Wantin' you..."

"Me?" she asked as if she couldn't believe what he'd just said. Well, actually, she *couldn't* believe it.

He chuckled at her, reaching over to take a strand of her hair and letting it curl around his long, thick finger. "Are you fishin' for compliments or are you a quart low on self-esteem for some reason?"

"It's just that I wouldn't think I'm your type."

"Why is that?" His voice was quiet, but it had a touch of huskiness to it as he stared at her, his eyes caressing her face. And Abby wondered how it was possible for the man to take her from cool porcelain to red-hot flames with just that glance.

"You said you've known a lot of wild women. And from the things I've heard...well, I'd just think wild women were more suited to you," she said as she feebly attempted to fend off her own feelings.

"I've known my fair share of wild women, all right," he conceded.

"*More* than your fair share, is the rumor."

"Is that right? Maybe you ought to fill me in on what's bein' said about me."

"I've been told that you're a ladies' man. A womanizer. A playboy. That you get around…"

"I'm thirty-seven years old and I haven't led a monk's life, if that's what you're gettin' at."

"The insinuation isn't that you date a lot of women. It's that you juggle them. That you're never serious about them—"

He shook his head. "Cissy Carlisle's been doin' a lot of this talkin', I can tell."

"Is she wrong?"

"I don't juggle women. I don't use them. I've never in my life kept company with more than one at a time or cheated in any way. I try to be honorable and honest, and to do everything I can to make sure nobody gets hurt—which is why I didn't ask Cissy Carlisle out again after she made it clear she was husband huntin'. I was not interested in her that way and didn't want to take up time she could be usin' findin' someone who was."

Abby didn't doubt that scenario. Cissy Carlisle was notorious for her hot pursuit of a husband and the fact that no man dated her more than once or twice without her starting to wonder out loud what their kids might look like when they had them.

But Abby was also not losing sight of the fact that Cal was not denying that he was a ladies' man, either.

"So, all the women you don't juggle or use or cheat

on—are they wild women?'' she said, getting back to their original subject.

"Mostly they have been. I guess I have to own up to that. But I seem to have hit a time in my life when that's gotten old.''

"So you thought you'd try out something new—like me?'' she said wryly.

He looked into her eyes. His expression was very serious. "I didn't set out lookin' for a wholesome woman, no. Meetin' up with you just happened. Likin' you just happened. But what I'm findin' in you is that there's one thing wild women have in common that you don't.''

"What's that?''

"They're shallow,'' he confided, leaning near as if someone might overhear him. "No substance. No meat on their bones, so to speak. Over the years I guess I've just been left hungry for somethin' more. Now I'm findin' myself starvin'. And you're lookin' like a feast.''

He held her eyes with his for a long moment before he slipped the hand that was fiddling with her hair behind her head, bracing her for the kiss that came after the slow descent of his handsome face.

It was a gentle, chaste kiss initially. But it didn't stay that way for more than a few moments before his lips parted and his tongue came to urge her lips open, too.

Not that she required much persuasion, especially when she'd been craving this since he'd left her dazed after the sunset kiss.

His other arm went around her, pulling her closer, and for the first time Abby grew brave enough to wrap her arms around him, too. To press her flattened palms to his back—his broad, muscular back—soaking in the feel of the hard hills and valleys that spoke of a healthy, virile, masculine body.

She gave herself over to that kiss, which was even better than the last, as his tongue traced the very tips of her teeth, teasing, taunting, entering only in small darts that enticed her tongue to frolic along with his.

And frolic she did.

Matching him dart for dart, circle for circle, parry for thrust until playing turned more serious, more languid, more sensual, and their kisses became even deeper, their mouths open even wider, their appetite for one another so great neither could seem to get enough.

His hands had been in her hair, or bracketing her face, but now they traveled lower, those firm, strong fingers massaging their way to her shoulders, around to her back where he kneaded away any remnant of tension.

He pulled her shirt free of her jeans and slipped his hands underneath, and Abby couldn't help the groan that escaped her throat when she felt his kid-leather palms against her bare skin.

Wonderful hands! The man had exquisitely wonderful hands that seemed to know just the right time to apply pressure, just the right time to run featherlight strokes along her skin, to set off tingling sensations all through her and leave her wanting more.

His powerful hands found her shoulder blades, working them like clay he could mold to suit whatever form he chose. Warm hands smoothed their way down into the hollow at the base of her spine, low enough to almost reach her derriere but not quite, teasing her with fingertips that barely reached an inch inside her waistband when she yearned for a much deeper dip.

As his mouth continued exploring hers, those magnificent hands slid to the sides of her waist, then trailed a snail's pace upward, to her ribs, and only slightly higher.

Abby's whole body was alive with yearning, with anticipation, with longing for him to rid her of the blouse that seemed to keep her a prim prisoner, of the bra that blocked his path. She wanted to feel his hands on her breasts. Feel them surrounding those oh-so-sensitive mounds that strained for his touch. Feel her already hardened nipples kerneling within his palms...

But he didn't do any of that.

Instead his hands stayed where they were, barely brushing the sides of her breasts, tormenting her with his reserve.

And then she felt something else against her bare back where her shirt was pulled up to accommodate Cal's ministrations beneath it. Something warm. Soft. Furry...

It took her a minute to realize it had nothing to do with what they were involved in, nothing that was coming from Cal at all as it brushed up against her once, twice, three times.

An animal. It was an animal.

Abby gasped and that gasp caused Cal to end the kiss, to pull his hands from under her shirt as if he thought she was letting him know he'd gone too far.

"There's something furry rubbing against me," she said in a hurry, both to let him know what was going on and hopefully to convey that nothing he was doing needed to stop.

He leaned around her, took a quick look, then sat back up, bringing with him a tiny gray kitten with one white ear.

"This is what I get for tryin' to convince them

they're barn cats," he said in a voice raspy with passion as two other fur balls charged into his lap.

"Kittens? You have kittens?" Abby asked, laughing at how funny it seemed for this big, man's man to have pets like that.

"They came with the place. And they think I'm their mama."

"Boy, are they confused," she said, enjoying the sight of Cal with the three tiny cats nuzzling against him as if that was exactly what they thought.

"They also have lousy timing," he muttered.

The sun was just rising on the horizon framed by the edges of the open hayloft door, but Abby was more than willing to set aside the kittens and ignore nature's display to get back to what they'd been doing.

Only for some reason Cal seemed to be drawing into himself and seizing the interruption to let things cool.

He nodded in the direction of the horizon and said, "We're missin' the sunrise." Then he transferred the cats to her lap, clasped her hips to turn her to face the hay door, and maneuvered himself so he was sitting directly behind her, bracing her back with his chest and resting his hands harmlessly on her thighs.

Abby could hear the strain that his determination to end what they'd been sharing put in his voice. And she knew he wasn't stopping for lack of desire because she could feel the proof of that in the iron-hard ridge that pushed against her rear to let her know she hadn't been the only one of them who had been lost in what had just happened.

But he didn't do anything about it.

Instead he was a perfect gentleman as they watched the sunrise, drank coffee, ate beer nuts—even as he drove her home.

Maybe he was *too* much of a gentleman, she thought when he'd left her on her front porch to watch him drive off after nothing but a quick peck of a goodbye kiss.

Because he'd raised a whole slew of yearnings in her.

And a secret part of her couldn't help wishing he'd kept her in that hayloft all day long, satisfying them.

5

"HEY, LADY, IT'S ABOUT TIME," Cal said into the telephone the next afternoon when the call he'd placed was finally answered by a person instead of a machine. "Don't you ever return calls?"

"Don't give me any trouble. I've been calling and calling you, and you're never around. Why don't you get an answering machine yourself so a person could leave *you* a message?" the woman on the other end shot back.

"I have one. I just haven't gotten around to settin' it up."

"Then don't complain."

He softened his tone. "How are you, Katie-my-Kate?"

His sister giggled just slightly, the way she had when she was a little girl and he'd used her name in that same endearment. "I'm fine. How are you?"

"Never better."

"Never better, huh? So Cody was right. By now we know what that *never better* of yours means—there's a new woman on the scene."

"Have you guys been talkin' behind my back?"

"Of course. We all talk behind each other's back. How else would we keep up with things?"

"What'd he tell you?"

"That he thought you were trying to smooth your

rough edges and get gentrified by buying up a bunch of property and getting yourself a small-town girl.''

Cal laughed but pretended to take offense. ''Gettin' gentrified—I'm gonna beat the tar out of 'im when he gets here. And what're you all bettin' on?''

''How long it'll be before the country mouse is out and you're runnin' through the rest of the females in that county.''

''Abby is not a country mouse,'' he said, this time not pretending the offense because he was bristling at the derogatory reference.

''Ooh, do I detect a bit of irritation?''

''She isn't a country mouse,'' he repeated.

''Okay,'' Kate said, drawing the word out. ''What is she?''

''She's beautiful. She's sweet. She's funny. I think she's sort of shy but she's definitely not mousy. She works hard, owns her own business and is a responsible, upstanding member of the community. She's smart. And down-to-earth. She has a body that makes my blood boil. And big, wide, black eyes. And—''

''I get it. I get it. You like her a lot.''

If his sister had been there, she'd have seen him pulling back, surprised at where his own head of steam had taken him. But he didn't admit to Kate's conclusion. Instead he wondered how right she was.

''I don't recall you going for a woman with those attributes before,'' Kate said then, barging into his musings.

''Guess there's a first time for everything,'' he stated noncommittally. ''There's no mistakin' that she's in a class by herself.''

''Then is Cody right—are you trying to smooth your rough edges and get gentrified?''

"Not that I was aware of. Thought I was just havin' a good time."

Kate laughed. "That's more like the brother I know and love. Must've been your rhapsodizing about this woman that threw Cody off."

"Rhapsodizing?" Cal repeated sarcastically.

"Rhapsodizing," Kate insisted. "If I didn't know you better, I'd think you were getting sloppy over her."

"Sloppy! Come on. I told you, I'm just havin' a good time," Cal repeated, although something about this whole conversation rubbed him wrong.

"Are you having more than a ten-day good time with her?" Kate persisted. "Because Cody's betting that this is the person who could make a one-woman man out of you—"

"And you said she isn't and took ten days in the pool for how long my fling with Abby will last," Cal finished for her.

"Too short?"

Cal thought about that and couldn't come up with a genuine answer. He opted for joking instead. "Go out on a limb—take three weeks," he suggested even though he couldn't fathom putting an end to seeing Abby now or in three weeks. Or at all...

"Boy, you must have it bad for this one," Kate marveled facetiously, as if she'd been reading his mind.

But the most he'd admit to was, "She's not like anybody else I've ever been involved with."

"I wouldn't call what you've been in before 'involvement.'"

"What would you call it?"

"Playin' around. Just playin' around."

Cal discovered he didn't like having what he was doing with Abby categorized as just playing around.

Weird. Very weird.

And the only way he could see to escape the weirdness this whole talk was erupting in him was to change the subject. "So are you comin' to see the new digs or not?"

"I'll be there," Kate assured. "But…uh…I'm coming alone."

"You are?"

"Yeah."

"Want to talk about it?"

"Can't. Not right now."

"Okay. Will you be stayin'?"

"No reason not to."

"Are you tellin' me you aren't a one-man woman anymore?" he goaded slightly in return.

"Don't give me a hard time, okay? Times are hard enough all on their own at the moment."

"Okay. Guess I'll see you when you get here, then?"

"It shouldn't take me more than a couple of days."

"Need anything in the meantime?"

"No, thanks, big brother, I don't."

"If you do—"

"I know your number."

"Take care of yourself."

"You, too."

They said goodbye and Cal hung up.

But he went on sitting on the kitchen countertop beside the phone, thinking about the exchange he'd just had with his sister. Thinking about Abby. About what was going on with them. About himself.

No, he hadn't ever been a one-woman man. The best that could be said about him was that he was a one-woman-at-a-time man. And yes, he'd always just played around with the women he'd encountered.

It hadn't mattered. The women had only been playing around with him, too.

But for some reason it struck him that there was something different happening now, with Abby. Something deeper. Something with more substance. Just the way *she* had more substance than those other women.

And as he thought about it, it occurred to him that part of what was happening now that was so different was that he had feelings for her. Strong feelings. Feelings that were more than just wanting her.

The truth was, for the first time in his life, two things were running through him at once. Noble feelings for her—respect, admiration, appreciation of the kind of woman she was—were keeping right up with plain old desire.

Except that it wasn't so plain.

It was all-consuming, red-hot and hard to handle.

Damn, did he want her!

It was an ache inside him. A tight, burning knot that was driving him to distraction.

She was driving him to distraction. Without even trying.

He couldn't sleep for thinking about her, for craving the feel of her small weight on the mattress beside him. The feel of her in his arms. Under him.

As he worked around the house, around the ranch, she kept creeping into his mind's eye, lingering to tease him with that smile of hers, with those eyes that glistened with secret delight, with those lips he wanted to kiss. And kiss. And go on kissing until his own were too numb to even enjoy the warm softness of hers anymore.

She was there with him in the shower every morning as he soaped up his body and imagined her in the stall, too. Naked. Running her hands along every inch of his skin. Closing just one of them around him in a grip that would be surprisingly firm. Lifting her up high enough for her to wrap her legs around his hips so he could guide himself into her and all the while his mouth would be on a tight, kerneled nipple…first the right, then the left…

Oh, yeah, he had it bad. No doubt about it.

Because here he was, sitting on his kitchen counter in the middle of the afternoon, hardening up so much it hurt.

But he could deal with wanting her so much it hurt. What he wasn't sure he could deal with was the rest of it.

Was he turning into a one-woman man? he asked himself. What if this infatuation with her was more than that? What if that other part of what was moving through him—the noble feelings, the respect and admiration for the kind of woman she was—what if that meant there was more to this than he realized?

Hell, it scared him to death, that's what.

Abby was a woman who would take some living up to. He'd never had to do that before. He'd always been able to play things fast and loose because fast and loose was what the women were themselves.

But Abby was different. And if he kept seeing her, he'd have to be different, too. He'd have to be ready for what was between them to be different. And he didn't know if he was. Didn't know exactly what that all meant or where it might lead. Or if he could do it…

What he did know—suddenly, like being struck by a bolt of lightning—was that his feelings for Abby were growing with a will of their own. Feelings that were as new to him as if he were a young boy. Feelings that had him churned up. That had him stewing in his own juices. Worrying about when it would be right to take what was happening between them all the way. Worrying about what Abby might be thinking. About what she might be feeling in return. About what she might be expecting down the road if he did make love to her.

And if he could meet those expectations.

A one-woman man.

Could he be that?

He honestly wasn't sure.

And until he was, he'd just have to keep fighting the desire. Fighting urges he'd always indulged before.

Because she deserved at least that much from him.

The trouble was, noble intentions were great when he wasn't with her.

But when he was...

Well, hell, he was only human.

And damn if he didn't want her in a way that was beginning to need someone superhuman to resist.

ABBY COULDN'T SLEEP that night. No matter how hard she tried, her mind was too agitated, her body too aroused, and she couldn't fall asleep to save her life.

She wasn't scheduled to work the next day until the eleven-o'clock shift, but she'd planned to go in much earlier than that. Every June the mayor sponsored a picnic for the teachers, staff and students to celebrate the completion of the school year. And he ordered a huge batch of Abby's specialty as the crowning glory— brownies with a layer of peanut-butter cheesecake.

But as she watched the hours tick by, it began to seem like a good idea to go into the bakery, make the brownies, then come home to catch a little belated sleep before going back for her regular workday.

So Abby got up, threw on a navy blue tank top, a pair of jeans and some tennis shoes, caught her hair in an elastic ruffle that left a burst of curls atop her head and drove over to the bakery. All the while hoping the quiet, calming act of making brownies would lull her. And chase away thoughts of Cal.

Because thoughts of Cal were what had been keeping her awake. Longings to see him. Longings to do more than see him.

Cal was a little like the brownies, she thought as she measured out the ingredients.

She'd tasted a similar confection on a trip into Denver. They'd been only fair but they'd lit a spark in her. She'd been convinced she could make a much better variation. And until she'd accomplished it, mastering the recipe had been on her mind almost constantly. Every failed experiment had only made her think all the more about what she'd done wrong, how she could alter something to improve it. She'd been obsessed. Until she'd finally perfected them so they were an exquisite blend of rich, fudgy brownies, creamy peanut butter, crackling top.

Cal had lit a spark in her, too. More of a spark than any other man she'd ever known, including the one she'd be married to right at that moment if he hadn't called it off. And like her obsession with this recipe, she just could not stop thinking about Cal. No matter how hard she tried. And she *did* try.

She knew this whole flirtation with him was something she shouldn't be doing. That she was likely headed for trouble…or heartache…if she kept it up. After all, from every account and from his own admission, Cal Ketchum didn't get serious over any one woman. He might be settling down in Clangton to live, but clearly he had no intention of settling down any other way or he might have at least given Cissy Carlisle a chance rather than hightailing it away from her the minute she'd let him know marriage was her eventual goal.

He had no plans to marry, raise a family—which was ultimately the future Abby envisioned for herself. Men like Cal had a good time with whatever woman caught their fancy for a while, then they moved on to the next woman.

But even believing that with all her heart and soul didn't make a difference.

She still couldn't stop thinking about him. Wanting him...

Oh, yeah, she wanted him. Like a chocoholic wanted chocolate.

And that, too, was odd for her.

She'd always considered herself to have a healthy sex drive. But never had she been quite so driven. It was as if the level of desire he roused in her when they were together—and the level was higher each time—stayed with her. Right there. Just under the surface. Sneaking out along with every thought of him at any given moment. Making her skin feel love flushed and her lips hungry to be kissed. By him. Only by him.

And ever since he'd left her off at home after watching the sunrise in the hayloft, she'd felt on the verge of getting into her car, tracking him down and jumping his bones wherever she found him, just to get some relief from the constant yearning for him that he'd left unsatisfied that morning.

She was hot for the man. That's all there was to it.

Well, maybe not *all* there was to it. But she was hot for him; there was no doubt about that. Hot and anxious to feel his naked body against hers. To feel his hands on every inch of her flesh. To feel his mouth on hers. On her breasts. On other parts it embarrassed her to even imagine. She craved the weight of him on top of her, the fullness of him inside her. Curiosity made her wonder if the explosion of ecstasy he'd bring her to could possibly be as incredible as she kept fantasizing it would be....

"So much for baking to take my mind off him," she muttered to herself as she slipped the brownies into the oven.

With time to kill while they baked, she fixed herself a glass of iced tea and sat on one of the tall stools at the worktable in the center of the room, trying consciously to clear the man out of her thoughts.

But it didn't work.

He was still there. Smiling that alluring smile of his. Beckoning to her...

She really did like him on top of everything else. She loved spending time with him. Loved the sound of his voice, the sense of adventure he brought into her life. She loved talking to him, listening to him. She loved his enjoyment of the sunset, the sunrise. She loved that he brought her out of herself, out of the shell of shyness that Bill Snodgrass had complained of.

But all of that notwithstanding, she just plain lusted after him in a way no one—not even her—would believe she could lust after anybody. It was as if she hadn't known real passion until meeting Cal.

And if anything was a recipe for disaster, she thought that was.

Because she was so hot for him and because each time those desires reached a higher level without being satisfied, she was getting more and more ready and willing to throw caution to the wind the way she might have the previous morning if he'd just restarted what the kittens had stopped. She was increasingly tempted to forget all the *shouldn't*s. To ignore all the red flags that common sense kept raising at saner moments. To turn her back on the wiser route of avoidance and just give in to what she craved. To what she lusted after. To Cal.

And if she never found out what it was like to lie naked in his arms, to have him make love to her, she thought it would be something she'd regret the rest of her life. Something she'd wonder about. Dream about. Yearn for with a secret hunger that never quite managed to be sated.

And somehow that possibility seemed as frightening as anything she could think of.

But what if a moment's rapture was all she ever had with him? she asked herself. She knew he wasn't the marrying kind. And it was highly likely that he was just enjoying her company for the time being.

But maybe that moment's rapture would be enough.

Because being with him now felt so good. More than good—it felt great.

And if she couldn't have forever with a man like him, maybe she should grab on to at least that moment's rapture.

It was a thought that terrified her. And set her blood into a rush of excitement at the same time. Just the way he did.

He made her feel alive, she realized. More alive than she had since growing up and becoming responsible, steady, predictable Abby Stanton.

And for once she wanted more than one helping of that feeling. Of all the feelings he raised in her. She wanted to help herself to all the courses right to dessert. And she wanted to gorge on that dessert....

The timer went off to let her know her brownies were baked, startling Abby out of the thoughts of Cal. But not too far out of them.

What was she going to do about the hots she had for him? she asked herself as she tested the brownies, found them done exactly right and took them out of the oven.

"How about getting in your car, tracking him down and jumping his bones," she muttered under her breath.

"They put people away for mumbling to themselves, you know. Or am I missin' somethin' and there's somebody in there with you?"

She really jumped that time, knocking the side of the pan on the edge of the oven with a bang.

Spinning around to the rear door she'd left open so the night air could come in through the screen, she found Cal himself standing just outside in the alley that ran behind the shop, once again making it seem as though mere thoughts of him were enough to conjure him out of thin air.

"You scared me to death," she said, her heart racing so fast it pounded in her ears.

"I'm sorry. I knocked on the front door and then back here, too, about the time that buzzer went off. Guess you didn't hear me."

Abby set her brownies on the rack to cool and then headed in Cal's direction.

"What are you doing out there?" she said, recalling that it was the same thing she'd said to him when she'd discovered him outside her bedroom window the previous night. The man made a habit of showing up at the oddest moments.

"I couldn't sleep again. Decided to take a drive and saw the light on in here when I came by. I know you guys start early, but a quarter to three in the morning? Isn't that a little odd?''

She unlatched the screen so he could come in, seeing the proof that this was an impromptu visit in the shadow of his beard darkening his face and the slight unruliness of hair that looked as if it had been raked through with his fingers once too often.

Not that he didn't still look terrific. A little rumpled, a lot rugged and all the more sexy for it.

"I couldn't sleep, either," she said, explaining her work hours and watching him step into her kitchen.

He was dressed in his usual cowboy boots and tight jeans, but tonight he had on a sky-blue henley T-shirt with the placket open tantalizingly down his chest and the sleeves rolled high enough to show bulging biceps.

To distract herself from the sight of that chest and those biceps she went on to tell him about the mayor's special order, omitting the fact that thoughts of Cal had been what had changed her original plan to fill that order.

"They smell like heaven," Cal said when she'd finished, taking a long whiff of the brownies.

"I think I could probably spare a couple for you to taste, but you'll have to wait for them to cool slightly before I can cut them."

He flashed her one of those smiles that lit her on fire. "Got nowhere pressing to go," he assured her.

"Would you like some iced tea while you wait?"

"Love some."

While Abby filled a glass with ice and the last of the tea she and her sisters kept on hand for themselves, she could see Cal surveying the kitchen.

"So this is your bakery," he said when she'd handed him the glass.

"This is it, all right," she confirmed, sweeping a hand around the big, open space with its worktable, commercial stove and ovens, dishwasher, sinks, cooling racks and the enormous cupboard where they stored their bowls, measuring cups, pots, pans, baking sheets and other utensils.

"What's upstairs?" he asked with a nod toward steps that could barely be seen rising from a corner alcove.

"An apartment. When most of the buildings along First Street were built, folks ran the shops on the ground floor and lived above them."

"Anybody live up there now?"

"No. We keep it clean and furnished because sometimes family will come and stay in it for an extended visit. Or if the weather turns really bad, my sisters and I will use it rather than going home and coming back again in a blizzard. But right now no one's up there."

Which meant they were all alone here.

And realizing that gave Abby visions of taking him upstairs. Of showing him the apartment. Of pausing in the bedroom. Of him leading her to the bed...

"Want to see it?" she heard herself ask, feeling her pulse race all over again, though this time fright had nothing to do with it.

Cal cast a glance at the stairs, and she had the sense that he was debating with himself about going up there, almost as if he knew what she had on her mind.

But in the end he said, "Nah, that's okay. If we leave this kitchen unmanned, somebody might sneak in and steal those brownies."

He took a long pull of his iced tea, set the glass down on the worktable not far from the cooling confections and wandered into the storefront. "This the day-old stuff in the bags on top of the case out here?'' he called back to her.

"Mm-hmm," she answered, watching him. Mostly his derriere. Imagining how it would look without those jeans encasing it. Wondering what kind of underwear he wore. If he wore underwear...

"Aren't you tired?" she asked in a second attempt to distract herself since no matter what she'd decided before he got there, she wasn't altogether sure she really could bring herself to jump his bones. "You were up all night last night. I'd think you'd be beat."

He shrugged a broad shoulder as he came through the connecting doorway again, stopping there to lean against the jamb and look in at her. "I've never needed a lot of sleep. And after seein' you through the window, I perked up as if I'd been drinkin' coffee by the pot. You're a hell of an insomnia inducer."

"Am I?" she said, surprised by the coyness in her own tone.

He grinned at her as if it pleased him. "I know you're what's been keepin' me up nights. But why couldn't you sleep?"

"Why have I been keeping you up?" she asked with more of that coyness.

"Oh, I don't know. Must have somethin' to do with the fact that I can't seem to stop thinkin' about you."

"Maybe thinking about you was what kept me awake."

"Maybe?"

"Maybe," she repeated firmly, unwilling to give him more than that. Then she said, "We can probably cut the brownies now."

"Great."

She went to work, but he stayed standing against the

jamb, watching her. Studying her every movement with a penetrating aquamarine gaze that Abby began to think she could actually feel on her hands as she wielded the knife. On her hair. On her face. On her mouth. On her breasts...

"Is it warm in here?" she asked as she stacked brownies on a tray, feeling more than hot. Steamy, in fact.

"Pretty warm," he agreed, pushing off the jamb and crossing to her on long, confident strides that matched the sound of his boot heels to her heartbeat.

He stopped close beside her at the worktable and took an ice cube from his glass where it still sat waiting for him.

Abby thought he was going to eat the ice to cool himself off but instead he touched it to the uppermost curve of her ear, running it lightly along the outer edge to the lobe, then along the column of her neck to her collarbone and downward, stopping it just above the lowest dip of her tank top, where he let a drop of water fall into her cleavage.

A tiny shiver shook her from the inside out, but it wasn't from the cold. It was from who was applying it and from yearning for him so much she could hardly breathe.

Then Cal followed the path the ice cube had left, blowing softly on the wet trail in a way that was teasing and oh-so-sensual, stopping at the base of her throat rather than following that last droplet.

"Better?" he asked in a whisper against her skin.

Better? She was hotter than ever!

"It's the ovens," she said when she could gather enough voice to speak. "They heat things up a lot."

"And here I thought I might have somethin' to do

with it," he joked with a low rumble of a chuckle, straightening up to look into her eyes. "But if it's the ovens, then maybe we should take our share of the brownies out somewhere cooler."

"Good idea," she said in a hurry because she felt that she might melt if she didn't get out of there. Besides, if she was going for the moment's rapture, she didn't want it to happen in an already overheated kitchen. Or even upstairs in the bedroom that kept flashing through her mind, where the heat had risen to undoubtedly make it overly warm, too. She wanted somewhere more comfortable....

"Know a spot?" he asked.

Lost in her own musings, for a split second she thought he was asking if she knew a spot where they might go to make love. Then she realized he couldn't know what was on her mind, what had been on her mind before he'd arrived tonight.

Reminding herself that he was only asking if she knew a good spot to cool off and eat brownies, she said, "I could deliver these things to the school—I have a key to the cafeteria door so I can leave them inside. Maybe we can come up with a place from there." Like his place...

"Okay."

Abby put a few of the brownies on a paper plate, loosely covered the tray for the picnic with foil so they wouldn't get soggy and did a quick cleanup.

When that was accomplished, Cal carried the tray out to the front while Abby locked the back. By the time she'd followed him through the bakery, he was waiting with the black Corvette's passenger's door open for her.

It occurred to her that if her sisters came into work in the morning and found her car in the alley but her nowhere around, they might be alarmed. Yet it was a brief thought she put aside to deal with later as she slipped into the leather seat and let Cal set the big tray in her lap.

"We won't have a night watchman or a janitor shooting at us for this, will we?" he joked as he started the car and eased away from the curb.

"There isn't a night watchman, and the janitor is only at the school in the day."

"No alarms to set off this time of night?"

"There isn't any alarm at all. This is Clangton, remember. Speeding is the biggest crime we've seen in the last five years. The sheriff doesn't even patrol at night. We're probably the only two people out. And I have a key," she repeated, dangling it at him. "We'll just pop in, leave the brownies, lock up and be out again before you can say boo."

They made it to the school in five minutes flat because it was only two blocks from First Street.

A single-story, blond brick structure, the school was built in a U-shape in order to keep the three levels of education somewhat separate. The youngest kids attended classes in the center section so they could be closest to the gym, cafeteria and main office; the middle-school and high-school kids were put in opposite wings.

Cal pulled into the circular driveway in front, but Abby directed him around the flagpole to another portion of the driveway that took them to the rear where the playground was just behind the building and beyond that was a football field.

One of the football field's eight tall lights was left lit at night—the only concession to security—so it was easy to find the cafeteria door and let themselves in.

Another five minutes and the brownies had been left among other picnic supplies already accumulated, and Abby and Cal were back out in the night air.

But rather than head straight for his car the way she thought they would, Cal paused to look out at the manicured lawn of the football field.

"How 'bout we eat our brownies on the fifty-yard line?" he suggested.

What could she say? *I had a more romantic spot in mind—something along the line of your bedroom maybe....*

"Okay," she answered on a quiet, disappointed sigh that made him frown slightly at her.

But he just went to the car for their share of the brownies and then came to lead her out to the middle of the athletic field, where they sat on the grass.

"Ah, that's nice," he muttered, stretching out long legs to cross at the ankles and leaning on one elbow.

Abby had her legs curved to the side and underneath her, bracing her weight on a single hand, looking down at him.

The gold dusting of that single light didn't reach all the way to the fifty-yard line, so they were in the shadows.

But still she could see his handsome features, not marred by the day's growth of beard that shaded his face. And she had to admit that it was nice to sit there with him, surrounded by the scent of freshly mowed grass and summer leaves, all alone.

Maybe not as nice as being in his bedroom. But nice just the same, with a certain element of privacy in the darkness of night and the fact that all of Clangton was so quiet, so still, they really did seem to be the only two people awake. Certainly the only two people out and about. And it occurred to her that being anywhere with him had a special quality all its own.

"I used to come here to blow off steam when I was a kid," she said as she handed him a still warm brownie and then took one for herself.

"Blow off steam? You? As in temper tantrum?"

"Mmm."

"I never pictured you havin' a temper."

"I don't really. Not now. But you know how kids are. I'd get into trouble or be sure there was some injustice being heaped on me, and then I'd go off in a huff."

"What kind of trouble did you get into?" he asked, as if he didn't believe it was possible.

"I got into my share of mischief," she said defensively.

"Like what?" he challenged her to convince him.

"Like bombarding a birthday party I didn't get invited to with water balloons from over the backyard fence. And booby-trapping a bully's doorstep with open cans I'd filled with paint so when he came out he tripped over them and splattered paint all over himself. And the stoop. And the door. And his mother, who'd followed him out to see who had been calling him names from behind the bushes to get him outside in the first place."

"Abby," Cal admonished. "I never imagined you as an ornery kid."

"Well, I was. But I didn't really start coming here to walk off my mads until I was a teenager. Usually after fighting with my sisters about something and having my parents come down on me for it because I was the oldest and should have known better. Then I'd head over here and sometimes, if I was really peeved, I'd climb up onto the top of the equipment shed and scream at the top of my lungs.''

He sighed. ''Want to do it now? I'd like to see that.''

She wanted to do something right now, but screaming wasn't it.

''Sorry, can't do it without provocation and I'm not provoked.''

''But are you still hot?'' he teased.

She was. Though not in terms of temperature. ''It's nice out here,'' was all she would commit to.

This time it was Cal who just said ''Mmm'' as he took another brownie. ''These have to be the best things I've ever tasted,'' he complimented.

''I'm glad you like them.''

They sat in silence for a few minutes as Abby's gaze caught on that equipment shed she'd just mentioned and her mind wandered.

''What're you thinkin' about?'' he asked.

She laughed and felt her cheeks heat slightly. ''I was thinking about once when I was really, really ticked off at Bree and I came here. I climbed up onto the top of the shed and screamed until my throat was raw. Then I plopped down, flat on my back, spread-eagle like a perfect martyr. I guess lying that way made it hard to see me because a while after my tantrum had worn itself out I heard—and then saw—one of my friends' mothers and the gym teacher sneaking into the shed underneath me. They were both married to other people, so I knew that in itself was bad enough, but then they started... uh...having an affair...inside the shed.''

Actually she'd also been thinking about what it might be like for her and Cal to do just what that other illicit couple had done, but she didn't admit that.

''Ooh, bad timing,'' he groaned and laughed at once.

"You're telling me. I couldn't get down without making a lot of noise and letting them know I was there, so I just stayed, wishing they'd leave. But they didn't. And I could hear everything. I never looked at that shed the same again."

"Funny, but when you were lookin' at it just now, I thought I saw some longing in your expression."

Oh, the man was a devil.

And she loved it.

She met his blue eyes with her own and saw the glimmer in them that said he was enjoying himself.

"Maybe I was longing for a nice pair of shoulder pads," she countered with a barely suppressed smile.

"Were you?"

She straightened her legs, scooted her hips down and lay on her side just the way he was, facing him. "Okay, no, I was not longing for a nice pair of shoulder pads."

He grinned with a single side of his mouth. "What were you longin' for?"

"You're the one who said I was, not me."

"Maybe I was just seein' in you what I was feelin' in myself."

"You were longing for a nice pair of shoulder pads?"

"Not quite," he said so softly she almost couldn't hear him.

He held her eyes with his, and Abby let him, expecting him to reach over to her. To touch her. To kiss her. Wishing he would.

But he didn't. Damn him, he didn't. Now, when she had talked herself into indulging in the feelings, the yearnings he stirred up inside her, when she was ready to give herself to him completely, he only stared into her eyes.

So Abby summoned courage of her own and reached a hand to him, to his hair where it had fallen to his brow, running her fingers through it much the way he did.

Still he only studied her as if delving into the depths of her soul with that gaze.

But Abby didn't retreat. Not when touching him seemed to answer at least one need in her.

She caressed his whisker-stubbled cheek with the tips of her fingers, traced the line of his sharp jaw to his chin, to his mouth, letting them stay there as if to halt words he wasn't even speaking.

He kissed her fingers then, but only barely before parting his lips to flick his tongue teasingly against them. When she still didn't pull away, he drew one of those fingers into the warm, velvety inside of his mouth, sucking slightly.

It didn't take more than that to light sparks in Abby. To awaken the arousal that waited just below the surface and had kept her sleepless tonight. To make her even bolder.

She slid her hand away and leaned forward to replace it with her mouth on his, kissing him tentatively as she trailed her fingertips down his Adam's apple and into the open placket of his shirt, finding a smattering of coarse hair hiding there.

Cal deepened the kiss, finally raising a hand to cup the back of her head, to pull her closer to him as his lips parted farther, as his tongue came to play.

What was it her sister had said? That if she couldn't help thinking about Cal or getting moony eyed over a simple kiss from him, she might as well give in and enjoy herself?

Well, that's exactly what she was doing. And she

didn't care if it was out in the open, in the middle of the football field. With a man who probably wasn't good for her. She didn't care about anything but being with Cal. Kissing him. Touching him. Being touched by him. Quenching the thirst she had for him.

His mouth was open fully, and so was hers, in a kiss that was rapidly turning demanding. He eased her back into the cool grass, laying his big body half on top of her, raising a knee over her thigh in a way that brought them so close together she could feel the hardness lurking behind the zipper of his jeans, straining for her.

Abby reached her arms around him, pressing her palms against the expanse of his broad shoulders, letting them ride the rise and fall of muscles that were like steel, trailing them down to the narrowness where his waistband held his shirt so she could pull it up and slip underneath to feel the warm smoothness of his skin.

Passion made her braver still, and she eased the shirt upward, interrupting their kiss only long enough to bring it off over his head so she could have pure, unadulterated access to at least his magnificent torso, to run her hands across every inch of his back, his shoulders, his hard pectorals and the sides of his flat stomach.

But it wasn't enough.

As wonderful as it all felt, what she needed was to be rid of even the scant barrier of her tank top, to feel her naked breasts flattened to his chest, in his hands, in his mouth....

She arched her back to give him a clue, letting kerneled nipples brush against his skin, hoping it did as much for him as it did for her.

Cal groaned deep in his throat, as if she were torturing him, as if she were tempting him with something he couldn't have.

Then he seemed to lose his power to resist. He nudged his knee between hers and raised it to the juncture of her legs, lighting fire to the sparks within her as he slipped the tank top's straps off her shoulders, then lower still to below her bare breasts.

It was Abby's turn to moan, and her back arched again all on its own, meeting his hand as it covered first one engorged mound and then the other.

The warm kid-leather palm cupped her flesh, kneading, squeezing, teasing in featherlight strokes all in turn.

Strong fingers explored her nipples, circled them, barely brushed the tips, rolled them gently, even pinched but with a tenderness that was anything but painful, driving her almost crazy with the desire that grew more urgent by the moment.

Her hips rose to him; her hands grasped his arms, his shoulders, his sides, his tight, tight derriere. Her tongue met and matched his thrust for thrust in a motion she wished other parts of their bodies were enacting, even if they were out in the open, on the football field. Nothing seemed to matter but the sensations alive in her, the desires he was building within her, the yearnings crying out to be sated. Making love with him was the only thing that was important. Right then. Right there...

But just when she was sure he would go further, go all the way to making love to her, he tore his mouth from hers, his hand from her breast and stopped everything cold.

"If I don't quit now, we'll have to take this to the equipment shed," he said in a raspy, ragged voice.

"I always wondered what it would be like," she heard herself say, the words coming straight from the intensity of her own need.

Cal chuckled wryly but he didn't do anything beyond

dropping the top of his head to her shoulder. "You'd hate me in the mornin'. *I'd* hate me in the mornin'."

Because he'd made love to her in the equipment shed or just because he'd made love to her?

Abby wasn't sure. And her courage came up short of suggesting they take this somewhere else to finish it, just in case he was saying he'd hate himself in the morning if he made love to her at all.

He took a deep breath and held it for a moment before blowing out a long gust of hot air against her skin. Then he raised his head and pulled her tank top back up into place, keeping his eyes closed the whole time when she would have welcomed his looking at her naked breasts.

And Abby had to swallow back desire so sultry she thought it was going to singe her insides.

But swallow it she did while she watched him cover his gloriously masculine torso with the henley shirt again.

Then he raked both hands through his hair with a punishing fierceness, pointed his chin to the sky and again held his breath as if he were fighting as hard as she was to tamp down on all they'd just erupted in each other.

Yet for the life of her she couldn't understand why. Why they weren't on their way to his house, to his bed, right at that moment, if he wanted her the way she wanted him.

But when he stood up and offered her a hand to help her to her feet, too, all he said was, "Come on. Let's get you back to your car so you can go home and get some sleep before this night is through."

She didn't know what to say, so she didn't say anything at all. Not then. Not as they walked across the athletic field. Not in his car on the short drive to the bakery.

He drove up the alley and parked behind her small sedan but he didn't turn off the engine. Instead he left it running as he got out and came around to open her door and take her up to the driver's side of her car.

"What would you say to a real, live date tomorrow night?" he asked only after he'd seen her safely behind the wheel, closed the door and was leaning in through the open window.

"I'd say that sounded good," she managed to answer in a soft voice, confused by this man who never seemed to do or be what she expected.

"How about I pick you up around seven? Cook you dinner?"

"Okay." *And then what?* she wanted to ask. *Will you get me all turned on again only to leave me high and dry?*

But of course she didn't say that.

"Seven it is, then," he said, searching her face and looking somehow confused and frustrated and forlorn himself.

He ducked in for a quick kiss. But only a quick one before ducking out again as if he were afraid of it developing into more than that.

Then he said, "Cut me a little slack if I went over the line tonight, Abby. I haven't had a lot of experience with good girls."

He gave the top of her car a final tap and left her sitting there, watching him go back to his own car through her side mirror.

And unquenched desire notwithstanding, Abby couldn't help smiling.

Was that why he'd stopped short of making love to

her tonight? Because he thought she was a good girl and good girls didn't do that?

And here she'd considered herself to be giving very clear signals to encourage him.

Lord, was she that inept? Or were their wires just crossed?

She honestly didn't know.

But either way she took a deep breath of her own and sighed it out, finding comfort in one thing.

They still had tomorrow night....

6

THE NEXT AFTERNOON when the bell over the bakery's door rang to announce a customer, Abby was alone in the kitchen, bagging up the dinner rolls that hadn't completely sold out. It had been a busy day and with the exception of those buns, there wasn't much of anything else left to sell. She crossed her fingers in hopes that that fact would mean she wouldn't have to spend much time with the customer. She was anxious to head for home, and get ready for her date with Cal.

But one foot through the doorway that connected the kitchen to the storefront and she knew it wasn't any baked goods this particular man had come for.

"Bill," she said in surprise as she found herself face-to-face with her former fiancé on the other side of the counter.

"Hi, Ab," he greeted tentatively.

Abby hadn't had any illusions about never seeing him again. Clangton was too small a town for that. But she hadn't been looking forward to the occasion, either, and it was every bit as awkward as she'd feared. Especially when she knew his plane from the trip that was supposed to have been their honeymoon had only landed a few hours earlier. Certainly she hadn't thought he'd stop by the bakery on his way home. What did he want to do, tell her about the great time he'd had without her?

She wasn't going to help him, if that was the case.

Actually she didn't feel inclined to make anything easier for him. So rather than giving him a conversational opening, she merely stood there, watching him fidget like a shamefaced child.

It was funny, though, because she wasn't thinking that she was glad he was uncomfortable. Instead she was thinking about how different he suddenly looked to her.

Not that anything had changed. Except that now he had a deep tan. He was still slightly under six feet tall. Still lean and lanky. His hair was still a shiny black and so curly he had to keep it cut short in order to have any control over it. He still had swarthy, olive-toned skin and a small ridge on the bridge of his nose. He still had dark eyes that were a little too close together and smallish teeth. He still wore clothes well—white tennis shorts and an equally white polo shirt. He was still attractive enough without being anything remarkable to look at.

But for her he'd lost his appeal. And not only because of what he'd done in calling off their wedding three weeks before it was to have taken place. Not even because he'd done it by attacking her with criticism.

He simply didn't seem to match up when her mind flashed an image of Cal in comparison. Bill Snodgrass just wasn't the man Cal was.

"How are you doing?" Bill finally asked.

"I'm fine," she answered easily. In fact she seemed to be doing better than he was if the lines of strain in his face were any indication.

"Could we talk?"

"About what?"

"A lot of things."

"I'm sort of pressed for time," she said with a glance at the wall clock.

"I was cheating on you," he blurted out in a way that sounded partly as if he thought that would convince her to indulge him and partly as if the weight of carrying the information around with him had suddenly become more than he could bear.

He did manage to shock her. "You were cheating on me?" she parroted as a million questions went through her mind. When? Where? With whom? How could she not have known?

"I met her last fall over in River Run," Bill continued quickly. "She was in that bookkeeping class I taught two nights a week."

Abby had some problems grasping what he was revealing to her. "You cheated on me with one of your students when I thought we were dating exclusively," she said when things began to click. "So why did you ask me to marry you in the middle of it?"

"I was trying not to like Peggy. She wasn't my type. Flashy. Loud. Aggressive. Brash. Brassy. I was afraid if I brought her to Clangton she'd embarrass me. I thought if I committed myself to you formally, it would help get my mind off her. Keep me from doing something stupid, something I'd regret."

He hesitated, shrugged, then admitted, "But next to her you seemed like the same old same old. I mean, we've known each other all our lives. We dated when we were just kids in high school ourselves and then these last two years since I came back to Clangton—where's the excitement in that?"

Oh, yeah, the guy was a charmer.

"So why are you here now, telling me this?"

"I've learned my lesson."

"What does that mean?"

"I took her to Mazatlán with me."

He was having trouble making eye contact with Abby but he accomplished it just then and must have seen the expression of disdain on her face.

"Okay," he said, holding up his hands, palms out, as if warding off an attack even though Abby hadn't moved a muscle or said anything to this last admission. "I know it was tacky to not only go ahead with our honeymoon trip without you but to take Peggy, too. But that's what I did. And it cured me."

"Cured you?"

"She just went berserk down there. Drinking, swearing, doing things I couldn't believe—let's just say it was awful." He smiled halfheartedly, as if he expected Abby to feel sorry for him. To commiserate.

She only went on staring at him, thinking how grateful she was not to be married to him.

He didn't seem to realize it as he went on. "Shy, quiet, predictable, steady and provincial started to look better and better to me," he said, repeating all the reasons he'd originally given for why he'd decided he didn't want to marry her after all, why he didn't love her anymore.

"You have every reason to be furious with me," he went on. "But couldn't we think of this as just a little fling I had before settling down? You know I didn't date a lot—there was you when we were seniors and only one girl in college and one while I was working in Denver before moving back here, and then you again these last two years. I guess I just hadn't gotten it all out of my system. But it *is* out of my system now. Believe me, it's completely out of my system now. And all I could think about on the plane ride back was you.

How much I love you. That marrying you, having kids with you, getting old with you, is really what I want.''

Abby stared at him in disbelief. ''You're kidding, right?''

''I know what I did was lousy. But I'm sorry. And I love you,'' he said as if that wrapped everything up in a neat package.

Abby stared at him, not only in disbelief for all he was saying, but also realizing as she did that somewhere during the time since he'd broken their engagement her feelings for him had changed to such an extent that standing there, facing him, hearing all he'd told her seemed almost as if it were happening to someone else. As if she were that far removed from it. And that distance felt good.

''It's too late, Bill.''

''It can't be. Not after all the years we've known each other. Not after everything—''

''It's too late.''

''You don't mean that. You're just mad. I understand that. But we can work through it. You can have your mad for a while, and I'll jump through some hoops to make amends and we can—''

''No, I'm not just mad. I'm not mad at all. In fact, in a way, I'm glad this happened. Certainly I'm glad it happened before we were married. But I don't want to turn back the clock. Or start over with you.''

''Come on, Ab,'' he wheedled as if she were just playing hard to get and he was losing his patience for it.

She shook her head. ''No, Bill.''

''Then it's true,'' he sneered at her suddenly. ''My brother picked me up at the airport and he said rumor had it that you've been hanging around that shiftless,

no-good, redneck cowboy who won the old Peterson
place in a poker game.''

"Shiftless, no-good, redneck cowboy?" she repeated,
laughing slightly at the derogatory description of Cal.
It was yet another of Bill's categorizations—Cal was
the shiftless, no-good, redneck cowboy and she was shy,
quiet, steady, predictable and provincial. For a fleeting
moment she wondered what tags Bill might put on himself.

Then he broke into her musings. "Do you think he'll
be faithful to you? Because you're kidding yourself if
you do. Love 'em and leave 'em—that's what guys like
him do. That's what he did to Cissy Carlisle and who
knows how many before her—you've heard the talk the
same as I have. And he'll do it to you, too.''

Abby may have contemplated that same thing herself,
but the way her former fiancé said it made her bristle
anyway. "Maybe. But what I've been thinking is that
the love part of it might be worth experiencing anyway.
Which is more than I can say for what I had with you.''

Bill drew himself up in what looked like righteous
indignation, as if that simple statement were more out
of line than anything he'd done or said.

But at that point Abby didn't care one way or another
if she'd made him angry. She just wanted him to leave
so she could get home to dress for her evening with
Cal.

"He'll make you a lot sorrier than I ever did," Bill
shouted.

Abby considered saying that that wasn't possible but
refrained. She wasn't interested in slinging any more
arrows. Instead she said, "I'll take my chances.''

"You weren't enough woman to keep me around.
You'll never keep a guy like him.''

"I think you should just go now, Bill. We've said all we need to."

He didn't budge. "You'll come running back to me. We both know it. Only I might not be waiting."

"Goodbye, Bill."

"He'll ruin you!" her former fiancé shouted again.

Cal had already ruined her for the likes of this man. And she was only glad of that.

But Abby merely said, "Please leave now."

Her former fiancé still stood there, sputtering for a few minutes before he finally turned around and stormed out of the bakery, slamming the door so hard the bell above it clattered even after he was out of sight.

Abby took a deep breath, rounded the corner, turned the Closed sign and locked up.

But as she did, her former fiancé's words haunted her, reinforcing every self-doubt she'd had since meeting Cal. Every concern that he was only toying with her. That there couldn't be any kind of future for them.

But she'd spent the whole day looking forward to this date tonight and she reminded herself that she'd already decided to indulge in the moment's rapture even if that was all she was going to get.

"Don't let Bill Snot-grass wreck it," she advised out loud as she headed for the kitchen to finish what she'd been doing so she could go home.

And since it seemed like good advice, she took it.

AFTER A FAST DRIVE HOME, a shower and a shampoo, Abby scrunched her hair into a mass of full curls, applied a scant touch of mascara, blush and lip gloss and lightly spritzed herself with a perfume that smelled like a field of wildflowers. Then she put on a short-sleeved denim dress that buttoned from a deep-V shawl-collar neckline through body-hugging princess seams to mid-way down a full skirt that ended at her ankles.

The whole time she was getting ready for her date with Cal she tried not to think about Bill Snodgrass or any of what he'd said to her. But the thoughts kept following her around anyway.

It was good to realize that her feelings for Bill were not as strong as she'd thought they were. That the truth was, what she'd felt for Bill was more the kind of love a person had for a brother than for the man she married.

What didn't help was that a big portion of what proved that to her came in comparing not only the way Cal and Bill looked, but also in the way she felt about the two men. It served to open her eyes to the fact that she had never had an overwhelming passion for her former fiancé, the way she did for Cal. That never had she experienced what was running rampant through her now.

In fact it suddenly occurred to her that what she was experiencing now could well be the kind of love she should have had for Bill.

Which made what she was indulging in with Cal all the more dangerous. Because there was the potential to be hurt more by him and by this relationship not working out than she'd been hurt before by Bill's rejection. And that was no laughing matter.

Yet as she heard the Corvette pull up out front and glanced once more in the mirror, her desire to be with Cal couldn't be daunted.

Maybe she was being shortsighted and foolish, but the end of what she and Cal were sharing now seemed like something too far in the future to be concerned with at that moment. And she just couldn't let the possibility of future pain take away the pleasure of the present, any more than she could let the past do it.

"So you really are going to play with fire," she said to her reflection, confirming an earlier thought she'd had about having anything to do with Cal Ketchum.

As if in answer, into her mind flashed the memory of being with him on the football field during the middle of the night. Of his kiss. Of being held by him. Touched by him. Of wanting him to make love to her.

Oh, yeah, she was going to play with fire, she thought. But at least she was doing it with her eyes wide-open.

"Maybe forewarned *is* forearmed," she muttered, hoping that when the end came she'd be bolstered for it.

But whether or not she was, as the doorbell rang she knew it didn't matter.

Ahead of her lay an evening with Cal.

And nothing was going to stop her from enjoying it.

He was standing outside the screen when Abby went down the stairs. He was dressed all in black—black boots, black jeans and a black Western shirt with white pearl snaps forming a line from his narrow waist up the widening grandeur of his chest to the solid column of his neck.

His oh-so-handsome face was clean shaved, his hair shone with freshly washed bittersweet-chocolate highlights and, as she reached the screen, she caught a whiff of that aftershave she'd spilled on herself once upon a time. It made her knees weak. *He* made her knees weak as he let his gaze do a slow roll from the top of her head all the way to her toes and back again.

By the time eyes the color of a clear lake on a summer's day settled on her face, they were glistening with appreciation.

"All this for me?"

All this and honeymoon underwear, too...

"What? This old thing?" she joked of the dress she'd just bought on her lunch hour.

"You'll make my franks-and-beans dinner look shabby," he said, pushing open the screen for her to join him on the front porch.

"Franks and beans?" she asked, not sure if he was teasing or warning her.

He just smiled and swept his arm in the direction of the black car at the curb, leaving her wondering. Not that it mattered. She'd eat just about anything if she could sit across from him to do it.

Once they were on their way to his house, he glanced at her from the corner of his eye. "Get any sleep last night?"

Being turned on and left unsatisfied—again—made for a prickly bed. "Some," Abby answered vaguely. "How about you?"

"Some," he responded just as vaguely but with a half grin that said he'd suffered the same problem and not found much rest himself. Then he said, "So now that I have you on this official date, how about we make another one for Saturday night?" he said as he drove smoothly out of town toward his property.

Abby looked at him curiously. "What if this one turns out badly? It's only just begun, you know. You might not want a second."

"Don't kid yourself," he said with a suggestive undertone to his voice.

"What's Saturday night?"

"My sister and brothers should all be in by then, and

I'd like you to meet everybody. Give 'em a face to go with the name I've been bandyin' about.''

He wanted her to meet his family. *Put that in your pipe and smoke it, Bill!* she thought as a warm wave washed through her. "I'd like that."

"Even if I serve you franks and beans tonight?"

"Even then. And how have you been bandying my name about?"

"Just lettin' 'em know what I'm up to."

"What are you up to?"

With a sly glance at her out of the corner of his eye again, he said, "Enjoyin' myself. I keep tellin' you—and everybody else—that. I'm just up to enjoyin' myself."

He turned onto the private road that led to his house, grinning like a Cheshire cat. But he didn't say any more as he hit the gas hard and went up the driveway fast enough to spew dirt and gravel out from behind them like a dust storm.

He hit the brakes at just the right moment as they drew near the house, spinning the car into a half turn that ended with them stopped as neatly in front of the porch steps as if he'd parked with care. Then he hoisted himself exuberantly out of the car without opening the door and came around to her side.

It all had the feel of someone anxious to get this evening under way, to be alone with her in the privacy of his home.

As anxious as Abby was for those same things.

"Drive like that in town and you'll be the first person in five years to see the inside of Clangton's jail," she cautioned as he opened her door.

"But nobody can touch me on my own land. Unless

I want 'em to,'' he said with a suggestive wiggle of his eyebrows.

He ushered her inside then.

She got as far as the foyer and paused to look around—unlike the last time she was there when she'd been in such a hurry to leave that she hadn't so much as caught a glimpse of what she was running through.

The stairs she'd fled down before were straight across from the front door. To her left were double doors that opened to an empty room no doubt intended to be a den or formal library since all the walls were lined with bookshelves. Beside the staircase was a long, long hall with several other doors opening off it, ending at a swinging door that was ajar enough to see the kitchen beyond that.

To Abby's right was a huge formal living room with a stone fireplace big enough for a grown man to step into and stand erect. That room held dozens of oversize, fluffy pillows on the floor around an overturned egg crate set with two plates, napkins and silverware. On every flat surface that could accommodate them were candles waiting to be lit, and floating up among the rafters of a vaulted ceiling were lustrous black, white, silver and gold metallic balloons like clusters of pearls.

"You don't have any furniture," she said to hide the appeal she found in what was a very inviting, imaginative and sensuous setting in which to eat.

"The house needs so much work I figured it was easier to leave it empty until I get it into shape. Do you mind eatin' your beans and franks on an old crate?"

"Seems appropriate," she answered, beginning to believe him.

"Come on out to the kitchen so I can get things goin' and pour us some wine. Then I'll give you the nickel tour of the place—or maybe you've already seen it in one of its other incarnations.''

"Actually, no, I haven't. It's been vacant, locked up tight as a drum and off-limits except for the two years it was an unsuccessful dude ranch. And I was in college during those two years, so I've never had the chance to go through the house. I'd like to see it.''

"Great.''

He led the way down the hall beside the stairs to an enormous kitchen with outdated appliances, oak cupboards in need of polishing and little else other than a butcher's block in the center of a U-shaped work space. There was room enough for a table and chairs at the other end of the kitchen, but yellowed linoleum was left bare there.

The kitchen had plenty of light, though, from three sets of French doors that all opened onto a back patio where weeds and grass had grown through the cracks between the glazed Mexican flagstones that made up the patio floor.

As promised, Cal poured wine into two crystal goblets, handed one to Abby, then took a tray with three foil-wrapped bundles from the refrigerator and carried it out to a big brick barbecue where hot coals already glowed.

"That doesn't look like franks and beans,'' she observed when he'd set the foil bundles on the grill and returned to the kitchen.

Cal only smiled, picked up his wine and began his tour of the rest of the house.

The place was very large, but not terribly sophisticated. Also on the lower level was a dining room that would probably seat thirty people comfortably, a room Cal used as an office—which explained the floor being strewed with blueprints of the house and outbuildings. The remainder of the main floor featured two bathrooms, a laundry room, a mudroom and a large game room where dartboards hung on the walls and a pool table sat beneath a long, narrow Tiffany lamp hanging from chains from the ceiling—holdovers from the dude-ranch days, Cal informed her.

Upstairs there were five bedrooms, all complete with their own baths and some with smaller rooms connected only to them that could either be sitting rooms or nurseries.

On both levels there were signs of disrepair. Peeling paint. Chipped moldings, sills and door frames. Torn carpets or scuffed hardwood floors. Dangling light fixtures. Drooping drapes or no window coverings at all. Cracked switch plates. Doors off their hinges. Bathroom tiles missing altogether. Torn screens. And any number of other bits and pieces in need of repair or replacement.

There was no doubt about it—the house needed a lot of work. But from what Cal described of his plans as he showed her around, it had the potential to be a beautiful home.

And he had plenty of plans. For the house. For the outbuildings he pointed to through upstairs windows. For adding to the land he already owned so he could turn the place into a working ranch again.

His heart seemed to be in all of it. Exuberance and enthusiasm infused his voice as he talked. His eyes were alight, and even his gestures were more elaborate than anything she'd seen from him before.

She had a vague memory of his telling her on the night they'd met that he was putting down roots here and it occurred to her that he'd been very serious about it. Deep roots that he had no intention of pulling up again.

"Is your family staying with you or in town when they get here?" Abby asked as they finished the tour and returned to the kitchen at the same moment the timer Cal had set went off.

"I suppose you're asking that because there's no furniture, but yeah, they'll be bunkin' here," he answered on his way out to the patio.

Abby watched through the French doors as he removed the foil packages from the grill and brought them inside. "Do they know they'll be roughing it?" she asked.

"We Ketchums have slept in worse," he assured with a laugh. "I have some beds ordered. They'll be delivered tomorrow. As long as my family has those, nobody'll mind that there isn't much in the way of anything else. If they stick around and help with the work to whip things into shape, then we can do some shoppin' to decorate the place and make it their home, too."

"Have any of them said yet if they'll stay for good? I mean don't they have jobs to get back to, families?"

"Not a one of us has planted ourselves for any amount of time. Everybody could pick up without much trouble and move."

"And if they don't stay to help you with the work around here?"

"I'll do it all myself."

He'd piled the wine bottle, his glass, salt and pepper and a dish of lemon wedges on the tray alongside the foil bundles, and nodded toward the living room. "Ready to eat?"

Abby answered by going through the swinging door into the hall, then across the wide foyer into the only

spot in the house other than his bedroom that was actually outfitted for use.

Daylight was dwindling by then, and after setting the
tray on the egg crate, Cal took a book of matches from
his pocket and circled the room to light each of the
candles. When he'd done that, the room was aglow with
soft golden illumination that was multiplied by the
shimmering reflections in each balloon.

"No lamps," he said simply as he rejoined her where
she stood near the egg crate watching him.

"This is a lot better," she said, letting her delight
show this time.

He winked at her, smiling as broadly as a young boy
happy to have pleased a girl he was trying to impress.

Then he bent over and pulled off his cowboy boots.
"If we're gonna eat like we're playin' Arabian Nights,
we'd better do it comfortably," he suggested with a
glimmer of mischief in his eyes.

But so far that mischief was only in his eyes since
he hadn't even held her hand or placed a palm against
her back as he'd guided her through the house. He was
being a perfect gentleman. Damn him anyway...

Still, Abby kicked off her pumps, too, and stepped
with bare feet onto the pillows in front of one place
setting on the crate, sitting Indian fashion within a parachute poof of skirt.

Cal sat the same way, just around the corner of the
crate, and began to open the foil packets. Inside the one
nearest Abby were salmon fillets in a sauce that smelled
of wine, butter and dill. The second held a loaf of
herbed bread. The third offered a variety of steaming
vegetables—tiny new potatoes still in their skins, snow
peas, fresh green beans, julienned carrots, slices of zuc-
chini, artichoke hearts and button mushrooms.

"Franks and beans, huh?" she said as he served her. "Disappointed?"

"Surprised. I expected you to slap a couple of steaks on the grill, not cook like a gourmet chef."

He leaned close to her ear and confided insinuatively, "I'm a man of many talents."

She didn't doubt that. She just wanted the opportunity to experience them all.

As they ate, he explained about working as a dishwasher in a four-star restaurant one winter. He'd been between ranch jobs at the time, and the chef had shown him a few things about cooking.

"But I'm a lousy baker," he added at the end of the story. "So you don't have to worry about any competition for those brownies of yours."

By the time they were finished eating, darkness had descended outside, leaving them in their cocoon of pillows, candlelight and pearly balloons, with only a bit of a summer's breeze coming in through the open front windows that bracketed either side of a center picture window.

Cleanup was easy. At Cal's insistence, Abby stayed where she was while he carried the egg crate—with everything but the wine and their glasses on it—into the kitchen and came right back.

"Out of sight, out of mind," he said with more of that mischief in his eyes.

But it wasn't only his eyes she was feasting on as he returned to her. It was the whole picture. Clean, careless hair, ruggedly masculine face, broad, straight shoulders atop a torso that narrowed sharply to his waist, hips just wide enough, thick, bolelike thighs, naked feet that were slightly flat, slightly wide and seemed to add to the intimacy between them just because they were bare...

How was she going to relay the message that she wanted him and be more clear than she'd been the night before?

Visions of herself crawling like a seductive cat across the pillows and slithering up his body ran through her mind.

Or maybe she could claim she was hot again and casually unfasten several of the buttons of her dress.

But somehow she couldn't bring herself to do either of those things and instead decided on more conversation until she could come up with a better idea.

"So are any of your brothers or your sister married?" she asked as Cal rearranged pillows to fill the gap left by the egg crate. Then he sat very close in front of her.

"Not now, no. There's been a few weddings along the way, but everybody's flyin' solo these days. Unless one of 'em's done somethin' they haven't told the rest of us."

"How about you?"

"Have I done somethin' I haven't told the rest of them? A lot of things," he said with a wry chuckle. "I'm the oldest, remember? I'm supposed to be the role model. What I can keep quiet, I keep quiet."

"No, I mean were any of the weddings along the way yours? Rumor has it that you've never been married, but it's just occurred to me that for all anybody knows you could have been and the grapevine just doesn't have that bit of information."

"No, on that score the grapevine is right. I've never been married. As my sister pointed out yesterday afternoon on the phone, I haven't really been what anybody'd call a one-woman man."

"Well, there's probably no threat to that now since I was just informed today that I'm not woman enough to keep a man like you around,'' she joked, though there was an edge to it as her former fiancé's words rose up on their own.

"I don't know exactly what a man like me is, but whose dumb opinion is it that you aren't woman enough for anyone?"

"A guy named Bill Snodgrass. I was to have married him last Saturday night."

Cal's expression waffled between surprise and what looked like concern for her. "The Saturday night you were celebratin' your freedom?"

"The very same. He'd broken off the engagement three weeks before that." Abby went on to explain what Bill had revealed to her only hours earlier as the real reason for the breakup. But she also made sure to tell Cal all her former fiancé had complained about in her—rattling off his summation of her faults.

Maybe she was warning Cal about her true self, she thought.

Or maybe she was testing him.

Either way, being completely open and honest with him seemed like the best thing to do, in case he'd overlooked the kind of person she was.

"Shy, quiet, steady, provincial and what was the other?"

"Predictable."

Cal smiled at her, his aquamarine eyes warm with delight. "I don't suppose it occurred to anyone that a lot of that is just what I find so appealing about you."

Abby laughed again, wryly this time. "No, that would definitely never occur to anyone."

"Then they haven't walked in my shoes. I've known just about all the other kinds of women there are, and next to them you're like a solid diamond surrounded by yellowed glass.''

Abby tried not to let that statement go to her head. ''Is this part of the wild-women-are-shallow-and-I'm-not stuff?''

''Yep.''

''And is that where the good-girl thing last night came from?'' she asked.

''This is all new to me,'' he admitted. ''I've been tryin' to behave myself. To treat you with the respect you deserve.''

Abby let one eyebrow arch, hoping it looked seductive. ''There's respect. And then there's respect....''

He laughed a full, rich laugh that echoed off the rafters and made the balloons sway. ''Are you tellin' me somethin' here, Abby Abby?''

''I thought maybe you stopped last night because you didn't want me.''

He threw his head back and groaned as if in agony. ''Didn't want you? I've never wanted anyone so much. It's nearly killin' me. I just thought you weren't the kind of woman who would appreciate my givin' in to it.''

''You might be surprised,'' she heard herself say, the words coming directly out of the desire that was again mounting within her just at being so near him, smelling his aftershave, listening to his very masculine voice, looking at him....

''Predictable? Was that one of those things you're supposed to be?'' he said with a laugh. ''Bill Snodgrass is way...*way* off the beam on that score.''

Cal took her glass and his, along with the bottle, and set them all on the mantel. When he came back he lay down on his side in front of her, braced on one elbow, and smiled up at her, raising his free hand to clasp the back of her neck and pull her down to him.

He kissed her. Full on the mouth. Parted lips. Hungry right from the start, as if no time at all had passed since they'd been on the fifty-yard line.

Then he wrapped his arm around her and rolled to his back, bringing her with him so that she was stretched out on her side, half on top of him, half not.

It struck Abby as amusing that they'd both gone along talking and pretending to be civilized and in control when just beneath the surface was that smoldering, primitive passion that needed little encouragement to erupt.

But erupt it did as Cal rolled once more so that Abby was on her back with him above her, to the side, one heavy thigh across hers, the bulging hardness of his desire pressing insistently at her hip.

But he didn't do anything about it. He just went on kissing her, playing circle games with her tongue in a way that seemed as if he were working to keep things from getting out of hand too quickly.

Just don't stop, Abby thought. *Whatever you do, just don't stop this time....*

She had her arms around him, her palms flat against his broad, hard back, and she did what she hoped was a sensual, suggestive massage there, holding tight even as she did. She kissed him in return the whole while, matching each thrust of his tongue with one of her own until he pulled away.

He rained delicate kisses from her chin to the sensitive spot behind her ear, down the side of her neck to follow the V opening of her dress, stopping tantalizingly short of her cleavage, leaving her moaning quietly when he did, afraid he might be stopping for good.

"Tell me what you want, Abby," he whispered in her ear, his breath a hot burst there as he nibbled her lobe.

"I want it all," she whispered in return, feeling very daring to say it.

"You're sure? I want you to be sure."

"I've never been more sure about anything in my life," she said, sounding a little desperate because that's how she felt—desperate to finally make love with this man.

Cal chuckled, a devilishly delighted sound as he recaptured her mouth with his in yet another kiss that was wide-open and hungry.

This time it was his hand that followed the edge of her neckline, only it didn't retreat when he encountered the deepest point of the V. Instead he found the button there and unfastened it. Then the next. And the next.

It was such a great idea that Abby did the same thing with him, pulling her arms from around him to unsnap his shirt. But snaps were easier than buttons, and she managed to have his shirt open and pulled free of his jeans before he'd gotten very far with her dress.

Still, she was too eager for the feel of his skin to wait before sliding her hands inside his shirt, smoothing her way up his solid sides to hard pectorals, where small male nibs were kerneled much the way her own nipples were within the lacy confines of her bra.

But Cal was in no hurry. Even after he'd undone the buttons all the way to below her waist, he didn't reach inside or lay it open. Instead he trailed a hand to her waist outside the dress and only raised that hand at a snail's crawl from there to cover her breast through the fabric.

It felt good anyway, and Abby arched into his big

hand, drawing her head backward, away from his kiss without even thinking about it.

Cal didn't miss a beat, placing tiny kisses on her throat as he finally eased his hand into her dress, even into the cup of her bra, covering her bare nipple with his leathery palm.

A sigh of pure pleasure escaped her, but it was short-lived as he began to work his wonders with a hand that knew just how much to squeeze, how much to knead, how much to tease with the lightest of touches.

Abby yearned to be rid of the confinement of clothing—his and hers—so she slipped her own hands up over Cal's shoulders to ease his shirt completely off, eager to feel her bare breasts against his chest, his whole bare body against hers.

But he wouldn't be hurried. He took his time, exploring one breast, one nipple, then the other. He stopped kissing her to look down at her body, to marvel at her very sheer, very lacy, very sexy underwear before finally reaching around to unhook her bra and push her dress off her shoulders, leaving her only in scant bikini pants.

The denim of his black jeans suddenly seemed like armor against the tender flesh exposed to the cool evening air, and Abby forgot all inhibitions to find the snap of the waistband of those jeans and pop it open.

The zipper nearly spread on its own, so fierce was the pressure of his burgeoning body behind it, so Abby trailed her hands around to the base of his spine, urging his jeans downward from there.

But apparently Cal had lost the will to keep things slow because he shed the jeans himself in a hurry, tossing them aside before settling back beside her where he kissed her as he slipped off her panties, too.

Then he lifted his mouth from hers, braced on one elbow and looked down at her again, letting his eyes travel the length of her naked body.

"You're so beautiful," he said.

But Abby wasn't thinking about how she looked. She was drinking in the sight of him. The glorious, hard, masculine perfection of his honed male body dusted in candlelight.

She wanted to touch him so badly that her hands ached with the need. She wanted to learn the feel of every inch of that sleek skin over exquisite bones, over tight tendons, over steely, bulging muscle....

She reached for him, sliding only one palm from his wide shoulders down his chest to his flat stomach, to his hips and around to that incredible derriere.

But Cal seemed far more enthralled with her body than with anything she was doing to him. He leaned over to kiss her again as he rediscovered her breasts, kneading more firmly now, tormenting her nipples with tiny tugs, rolling the pebbled crests between tender fingertips.

His mouth stayed on hers just briefly, though, before kissing a path to her breasts, before taking her nipple fully in the warm velvet wetness of his mouth. Flicking his tongue against it. Suckling. Nipping. Driving her wild with a whole new wave of desire that was a tight cord stretched from her breasts down through the very center of her to that spot between her legs that cried out for him.

As if he could hear that cry, he finally let one of those miracle hands trail down her rib cage, down her stomach, lower still, finding that spot with the gentlest of touches, teasing, urging her to open like a rosebud to the marvel of his caress until she knew she couldn't last much longer without the fullness of him inside her.

So great was her need that it gave her the courage to reach below herself, to find the long, hard length of him, to explore it, to do a little teasing of her own so he'd know the same urgency she knew.

And he did because only moments passed before he tore his mouth from her breast and finally rose above her, nudging her knees apart with his own, easing his much greater weight onto her, searching, seeking with his body for the opening of hers. That same opening that was craving it so desperately.

He was careful—almost too careful—as he found his way inside her, easing in so cautiously she thought she might scream before he'd completely joined them.

But join them he did, deeply, deeply embedding himself within her.

For a moment that was how he stayed. As if it felt too good to alter.

Yet as good—as glorious—as it felt, neither of them could wait long for more.

At first he only pulsed inside her. Almost as though he were teasing her. Then another. And another. Each slightly stronger than the one before, slightly more forceful, more powerful.

Abby's muscles flexed around him involuntarily, bringing her hips along for the ride to push up into him. And when she drew back, so did he, just before easing in again. Then out. Then in. In what were gentle thrusts. At a measured pace that promised more, that gradually built anticipation, desire, need…

Then it increased as if he couldn't control himself any longer as that desire, that need mounted.

Or maybe that was only how it seemed to Abby because that's how it was for her.

Each drawing out, each plunge back in again, was another flicker of what was to come, each one brighter, sharper than the one before.

Brighter, sharper and more intense until the flicker caught flame and burned in a white-hot explosion that wrenched her upward. She clung to Cal's back as high-pitched groans sounded in her throat with each of his thrusts into her until she couldn't so much as breathe, couldn't so much as make another sound, couldn't do anything but give herself over to wave after wave of pleasure. Pleasure that seemed to lift her up, to leave her suspended in midair as he stiffened above her, exploding within her, driving in so deeply that it was impossible to tell where her body ended and his began, truly becoming one with her in a way that melded more than their flesh; it melded their spirits, maybe even their souls.

And then he relaxed from the rigid power of his own climax, breathing hard into her hair, the weight of him a parachute that helped her float back down to earth very, very slowly....

He held her tightly until taut muscles eased and flesh became pliable again. Then he rolled them both to their sides, their bodies still joined, and pressed her cheek firmly to his chest.

She could feel him relaxing all around her, inside her. She could hear his breathing deepen. She knew he was falling asleep, and she was too spent to stay awake herself.

But even as she was drifting off she couldn't help

thinking about something he'd said earlier—he'd never been a one-woman man.

And she had to wonder suddenly if that had been a warning.

——————

7

No mattress on the floor of anywhere had seemed as much like heaven as the one Cal was lying on when he woke up the next morning just after dawn. There was only one reason for it. Abby was in his arms. Her small body was curved perfectly to his side. One thigh rested over his. He could feel the pillowy warmth of her breast against his rib cage. Hear each even breath she took. And with just the flex of his arm around her, he could press her closer still, hold her firmly enough to give himself the sense that he could keep her.

Yep, heaven.

Especially when it all came after a night full of love-making. Wild, abandoned lovemaking. Soft, slow love-making. Quick, playful lovemaking. Twice downstairs on the pillows in the living room. Again up here in his room, on the mattress. And still he didn't feel as if he'd had his fill of her. As if he would ever get his fill of her...

He didn't understand what Bill Snodgrass had found wrong with her. No one else could hold a candle to Abby, as far as Cal was concerned.

He was crazy about the way she looked—all fresh faced and wholesome. He was crazy about the sound of her voice, her laugh, the way her eyes lit up when she did.

How could that not have been enough for the other guy?

For himself, Cal could talk to her for hours on end, and listen to her for just as long without being bored. She was fun and funny in her own understated way. And she had a smoldering, just-below-the-surface sexiness that was a lot more powerful than any of the upfront, flashy versions he'd encountered. A sexiness that was held in reserve for just one man. Just one man she chose to share it with.

Cal recalled that shy and quiet had also been on her former fiancé's list of flaws. But that seemed like so much bunk to Cal, too. She wasn't shy and quiet once a person got to know her. What had she said that guy had been drawn to? Loud, flashy, brash and brassy?

Cal couldn't fathom the appeal in that. To him those seemed like just the flaws he'd had his fill of. He was glad none of them showed up in Abby. Just as glad as he was that she had pride. And dignity. And self-possession. That she had that substance and respectability that had drawn him to her in the first place. If those things made her seem shy or quiet, then okay. Fine. There wasn't anything about them to find fault in.

What else had Snodgrass called her? Steady. Provincial. Predictable.

Cal thought about all of that, too.

To him steady meant he could trust her. After knowing too many women he couldn't trust as far as he could see them, that was another thing he considered only an attribute.

And what about provincial?

So she was a country girl. Great! To Cal that was like swimming in a clear pond rather than in a murky pool. He couldn't think of anything that was wrong with that. Not a damn thing.

And predictable?

Sure, she lived an ordinary life in a small town where she'd grown up. And yeah, she kept a schedule to work by. Dressed pretty conservatively...on the outside anyway. But predictable?

How predictable had she been when they'd met in that bar? Or when she'd indulged in that fantasy in the tub in the hardware store? Or when she'd sneaked out with him to watch the sunrise? Or on the football field?

Nah, he wouldn't call her predictable. Not when she could surprise him with things like the sexiest, laciest, sheerest underwear in the world hidden beneath a denim dress.

But apparently that other guy hadn't looked beyond the surface. He hadn't bothered to pull back the curtain a little and peek behind it. Because when Cal did, he was never too sure if he was going to find the good girl or a simmering spice of a woman.

For my money I think you just missed out, pal, he thought. *You should have pulled back the curtain a little and taken that peek behind it.*

But Cal didn't want to miss out on anything. Not on a single minute with Abby. He wanted to be able to keep on peeking behind that curtain for as long as he lived.

That thought gave him pause.

Something was going on with him that he didn't quite understand. Something that flooded through him at that moment and left him trying to analyze what it was.

It wasn't mere infatuation. He'd felt infatuation with other women, and this was more than that. He'd experienced schoolboy crushes, and this was definitely more than that. He'd gone through plenty of lust. And lots of like—because he truly did like women. But none of it compared to what he felt for Abby.

This was a deep, all-consuming passion that seemed to saturate every inch of him. That made him hungry for her again within minutes of being satisfied. That made him incapable of thinking about anything but her every time they were apart. That made him so driven to be with her that he couldn't concentrate on anything but plans for how to accomplish it. That made him wonder how he could ever again sleep without her here in his bed, in his arms...

So what the hell did it all mean? he asked himself.

He looked down at Abby's head resting on his chest. The rich mahogany curls of her hair spread out against his skin. Her long, thick eyelashes shadowing high cheekbones. Her pale, pale lips parted just slightly. And he was filled with a rush of something rich and warm. Something he'd never felt before.

Was it love? he asked himself, bowled over by the feeling and by what it might mean.

Was it possible that he'd fallen in love with Abby?

He took a deep breath and watched her beautiful face ride up and down with the rise and fall of his chest.

Hell, a person would think he was a greenhorn when it came to women—that was how het up he felt at that moment.

Het up and confused.

And none too sure what he was going to do about any of it.

CERTAINLY ABBY WAS no stranger to early-morning hours and could ordinarily face them rested and ready to take on the day. But today was no ordinary day. Not when strong male arms tightened around her, when warm lips kissed the top of her head, when Cal's deep voice softly called her name to nudge her out of sleep. Not when she'd spent a long, incredible night of love-making with him. She was not ready to wake up.

She groaned her complaint, snuggled against the exquisite comfort of his big body and drifted back under the wonderfully heavy weight of sex-induced exhaustion.

"Abby... It's mornin'...." Cal called softly into her hair, running a smooth palm up and down her bare arm.

That was all it took to remind her—and her body—of the delights the man could bestow. And sleep suddenly lost its allure.

This time her wiggling against him had nothing to do with getting comfortable to nod off again. She raised the leg she had slung over his thighs to a slightly higher level and rubbed a small circle around his nipple with her cheek, sneaking a kiss to the ridge of rib just below.

"I'll take that as a sign that you're awake," he said with a rumble of a chuckle.

"What time is it?" she asked between more kisses of his broad chest.

"A quarter to seven."

"Mmm. I don't have to be at the bakery for an hour yet."

"I know. It gives us a little time to—"

She'd kissed her way up to his mouth by then and ended his sentence prematurely by meeting his lips with hers to let him know that no more need be said. She was willing. After all, during the night he'd awakened her to joys of lovemaking that she'd never known before, and she had no qualms about having just one more taste of it before leaving him this morning.

"You're not making this easy," he said when she abandoned his mouth to trace his stubbly chin with the tip of her tongue.

"I thought I was making it hard," she joked in return, raising her leg higher still to rest over the object of her intentions.

Cal reached a hand to her thigh to hold it more firmly against himself as he flexed that long, steely thickness and took his turn at groaning.

Abby's nipples turned instantly into two tiny, sensitive knots, straining for the touch they'd come to know so well and making her arch her back so they could press more insistently into his side.

But rather than doing any of the things she thought he might do from there—any of the things he'd done before, the things she wanted him to do—he let go of her leg, jammed his hand through his hair and said, "We need to talk."

There was an ominous undertone to his voice, and she stopped short, dropped her knee, quit kissing his shoulder and opened her eyes to the light of day. In more ways than one.

Cal Ketchum was not a one-woman man—that thought flashed through her mind like a neon road sign. They'd just had a terrific—an incredibly terrific—night of lovemaking. But she'd gone into it knowing it wasn't likely to be more than that. Knowing that she was only indulging in a moment's rapture—and that that moment's rapture was probably going to be all she was ever going to have with him.

And this, she thought, *is where he lets me know the score.*

She ignored the cold, clammy fist of dread that tightened around her stomach, summoned every ounce of

courage she had and swore to herself that she was not
going to let him see how really provincial she was by
waiting around to be told their night of lovemaking,
their few days of seeing each other, had come to its
inevitable end.

"You know what?" she said in a hurry. "I just remembered that I have another special order due out today and I should have been at the bakery an hour ago."

"A few more minutes won't hurt—"

"Oh, but it will." In fact it would hurt her a lot to
hear him tell her he'd had fun but that was all it had
been for him.

Abby bolted out of his arms, out of bed, saying, "No
kidding. I need you to take me home right now!" And
off she went at a jog down the stairs to snatch up her
discarded clothing to take with her into the bathroom.

She was only halfway dressed when the sound of
Cal's voice came from just outside the door. "I had
something important to talk to you about."

"Not as important as this order. It could make or
break the Ladies' League luncheon, and I gave my word
I wouldn't let them down." She pulled on her dress and
buttoned it as quickly as shaking fingers could manage,
slipping her feet into her shoes at the same time. Then
she threw open the door, finding him leaning one shoulder against the jamb, his arms crossed over his bare
chest, a pair of jeans pulled on, zipped but not fastened
at the waistband.

"Honest. I'm in a terrible hurry," she said. "Can we
just go?"

He frowned down at her, his brows drawn so close
together that they met over the bridge of his nose.
"When can we talk?"

"Oh, you know, there'll be time," she said as breezily as if she were well accustomed to leaving a man's bed without a backward glance or a single expectation. Then she made a beeline out the front door and got into his car.

Cal didn't follow her immediately. In fact he kept her waiting there for what seemed like an eternity to Abby. Long enough, at least, for him to put on a shirt and the cowboy boots he'd worn the night before.

And when he finally got into the car behind the wheel, his chiseled features were marred by deep lines that made him look troubled.

She didn't explore it, though. She was too busy keeping up a ridiculous monologue to expand her lie about why she had to rush home, trying at the same time to hide what was really going through her mind—that deep down she was as provincial as she could possibly be and that, after a night like the one they'd spent together, a night during which she'd lost her heart to him, it was killing her not to have any hope for the future.

And then her house came into sight, and he pulled up to the curb in front of it and stopped the car.

"Thanks," she said like a ponytailed high-school girl being dropped off from a sock hop.

And before Cal could so much as answer with a *You're welcome,* she opened the door, got out and nearly ran for the house.

All the while trying not to notice the part of her that was imagining him following her inside to tell her he'd turned over a new leaf and was ready to be a one-woman man after all.

8

IT WASN'T UNTIL almost midnight Sunday night that Emily and Bree got fed up with Abby.

She hadn't been able to sleep. Again. In fact she hadn't been able to sleep since Cal had dropped her off Thursday morning. She knew her nocturnal wandering around the house had bothered her sisters, so tonight she was sitting quietly drinking hot milk in hopes that would eventually help her sleep and not disturb Emily or Bree.

Apparently it didn't matter because there they were, padding into the kitchen in their nightgowns, scowling at her anyway.

"I thought you guys were in bed," she said as each of them slid into a different side of the breakfast nook's bench seat, blocking her with her back against the wall and the only possible escape to crawl under the table.

"We're sick of worrying about you and not knowing what it is that has you upset," Bree said without preamble.

"You aren't eating. You aren't sleeping," Emily added.

"And you aren't talking. Except to bite off our heads whenever we ask what's wrong."

"Or tell you Cal Ketchum called or came looking for you—*again*."

"So bite our heads off if you want to, but we're not leaving until you fill us in."

Abby briefly considered denying for the hundredth time that anything was wrong. But only briefly. She was miserable and maybe it would help to talk about it.

With that in mind, she told her sisters about the night she'd spent with Cal and how she'd been avoiding him so as not to have to be told it was nothing more than fun and games for him.

"But you don't know for sure that that's what he wants to talk about," Bree said when Abby had finished.

"What else could it be? He told me himself that he's not a one-woman man. And I'm certainly not the person who's going to change that."

"Why not?" Emily asked.

Abby rolled her eyes but before she could say anything, Bree answered the question.

"Because Bill Snot-grass trounced on her confidence so completely that she can't believe she can attract—let alone keep—a man. Any man, but especially one who's as big a hunk as Cal Ketchum."

"She's right, isn't she?" Emily said to Abby. "Your self-image, or self-esteem or whatever you want to call it, has just bottomed out. Even worse than we realized before."

"Yeah, and why?" Bree continued. "Because Bill Snot-grass laid all the blame for nixing your wedding on you rather than owning up to his own character flaws and the affair he was having. You weren't at fault. *He* was. But he was so spineless he attacked you."

"And you believed it all," Emily went on. "Hook, line and sinker. That's the worst part of it. And now, instead of Cal's attentions boosting you back up where you belong, here you are, letting Bill's criticisms lock you in a closet rather than even chance hearing what Cal has to say.''

''Just forget all the garbage Bill unloaded on you and hear Cal out,'' Bree advised. ''Besides, even the worst would be better than what you've been doing—hiding from him. If all he wants to do is let you know where he stands, well, then at least you'll end up knowing where he stands.''

Apparently her sisters were satisfied that they'd solved her problems because they both slid out of the breakfast nook the way they'd slid into it.

''And if I were you,'' Bree said as they headed out of the kitchen, ''I'd go over to his place and see what he has to say before missing another night's sleep.''

Abby watched them go, thinking about all they'd said. She *didn't* know what Cal wanted to talk about. She'd just assumed he intended to make it clear that what they'd shared was nothing more than a good time that had reached its conclusion.

But if that was the case, why did he keep calling and coming around to say it? Why hadn't he just accepted that she was dodging him and taken it for granted that that meant she'd had her fill, too?

Her sisters were right; she'd never know unless she heard him out. She just didn't know if she could take another rejection, this one from someone who had touched her more deeply even than Bill Snodgrass had.

But what if Cal wasn't going to reject her? a little voice in the back of her mind asked.

She was afraid to even entertain that thought. Afraid to get her hopes up.

On the other hand, just the thought of getting to see

him again, getting to hear his voice, was almost enough to risk being rejected....

Should she go to him, give him the chance to say whatever it was he wanted to say? she asked herself.

Maybe her sisters were right, too, that even if the worst happened, at least she could get it over with. At least once she knew what he had on his mind, she could stop jumping at every ring of the phone or doorbell or bell above the bakery door and running for cover.

So do it. Get it over and done with, she silently advised herself.

And the sooner the better.

She was still dressed in the blue jeans and plain pink polo shirt she'd had on all day, so she didn't even bother to go upstairs. She just grabbed her keys and went out to her car.

But standing with the driver's door open, she got cold feet.

What if he rejected her as harshly as Bill had?

"Go for it, Ab," Emily called from an upstairs window, like an encouraging guardian angel.

It gave Abby enough impetus to get her into the car, to start the engine, to back out of the driveway and hit the gas.

"It'll be okay. You can do this. It'll be okay. You can do this," she chanted the whole way out of town.

But when she pulled up the driveway to Cal's house, she almost lost her nerve.

There were lights on in nearly every window on the lower level and so many cars and trucks out front that it looked as if he was having a party.

Then she remembered that he'd said his brothers and sister were all due in to see the place, and that helped. But only a little.

Even if his company was his family, they were still strangers to her. Did she really want to do this in front of them?

She didn't.

But she also didn't want to turn back now. She wanted the air cleared. To get the burden of wondering, of worrying, off her back.

And she also wanted to see him just one more time, even if it was to hear that their night together hadn't meant the same thing to him that it had to her. Maybe then she could put it behind her once and for all....

That was when it occurred to her that if the light was on in Cal's room, he might be up there. And if she could get to the window the way he'd gotten to hers before dawn Tuesday morning, then maybe she could see him without having to go through the house or his family to do it.

Or even if he wasn't in his room now, maybe she could wait for him there....

She parked her car behind the others, got out and tiptoed around the side of the house—although she didn't know why she was tiptoeing because no one was likely to hear her footsteps anyway.

Still, she felt inclined to furtiveness and kept to her toes, all the while training her eyes on the house.

And it was a full house. She counted four big, burly, good-looking men in three different windows—one of them shirtless and apparently headed for bed if the yawn he stretched through was any indication. Two of them were playing cards, and another was talking to a woman who hit him playfully with a magazine, apparently over something he'd said.

The Ketchums.

Even if she hadn't known in advance that that's who

they were, she would have guessed because they all shared some feature or another. And each one was as terrific looking as the next. Four gorgeous men and their sister, who would make male jaws drop—wouldn't the singles of Clangton be glad if Cal could get them all to stay?

But even the sight of four masculine, virile, head-turningly handsome men didn't have an effect on Abby. There was only one Ketchum she was interested in. And she hadn't spotted him through any of the downstairs windows she passed by.

The back of the house was darker than the front, and there were no lights coming from Cal's room at all.

But whether or not he was up there, Abby decided to go through with her plan.

There weren't any overhangs or a cover to the flag-stoned patio to aid in her ascent. But there was a trellis that rested between two of the second-floor windows—one of them Cal's, the screen already torn to allow her entry if she could just get up there.

The trellis didn't look very stable. Some of the slats were already broken. But it was Abby's sole option for reaching the upper level, and at that point she was willing to risk that it might not hold her rather than leave or sift through all those Ketchums to get to Cal.

So without another glance around, she grabbed on to the outer edge of the latticework, put her foot inside a diamond-shaped opening and began to climb.

The trellis creaked its complaint, but it held her. The trouble was, she'd assumed the thing was attached to the house and about halfway up she discovered it wasn't. And she discovered it when the trellis started to pull away from the bricks, swaying backward.

The gasp that escaped her throat wasn't silent, but

she didn't expect it to draw a response. She thought she was alone.

Until she heard, "Well, look at this. I think we have ourselves a little lady cat burglar."

The voice was deep and unquestionably male.

But it wasn't Cal's.

Wavering back and forth like a flag in the wind, Abby tried to press herself forward to keep the trellis from falling and all she could manage to say was a weak "Help."

The man stepped up just below and put his weight into pushing the trellis against the wall once more.

Breathing a sigh of relief, Abby could finally look down.

Standing there with his chambray shirt unbuttoned and left untucked to flap around jean-clad hips was a man who looked very much like Cal. The fifth of Cal's brothers, Abby thought, realizing just then that one had been missing from the house.

"Hi," she said feebly, feeling like the biggest idiot in the world.

"Nothin' inside to steal," he informed casually.

"I didn't come to steal. I came to see Cal."

"Was there a problem with the front door?"

"I didn't want to see anybody else," she confessed.

"Want me to leave?" he asked amiably, taking his hands from the trellis long enough for it to sway slightly away from the brick wall again before he pushed it back once more.

"Uh…no. Could you just hold this thing until I can get down?"

"Sure," he agreed. Then he raised his voice to a loud boom and shouted, "Cal! Got somethin' for you. Come on out back."

Abby could hear the message being relayed through the house, one voice after another. Moments later the sound of someone descending the stairs echoed through the place, followed by the noises of more movement than just one man could make. The whole clan was coming for a look.

Abby wished she could dry up and blow away.

Barring that, she had no choice but to climb down.

But as if he thought she might make a run for it, the man waiting on the ground didn't let her get all the way there before scooping her off the latticework to hold her like a baby in his arms. At about the same time Cal led a contingent of other people out the French doors from the kitchen.

"Abby?" he said, sounding confused.

"She was sneakin' up the trellis to see you. Know her?"

"I know her," Cal said, his tone giving no clue as to whether or not he was glad to see her.

"Guess you can have 'er, then." The man who was holding Abby handed her across to Cal as if she were a light sack of grain. And just that quick she was in Cal's arms instead.

"Hi," she repeated, even more feebly to Cal.

"Did you just come window peekin' or did you finally want to talk?" he asked.

"I wanted to talk."

Cal glanced at their very interested audience, then said, "Upstairs," and turned to carry her past them all.

"You can put me down and let me walk," she suggested between clenched teeth and through a forced smile at the onlookers.

But he pretended not to hear her and simply carted her through them into the house and up the steps, not stopping until they were in his dark bedroom and he'd kicked the door shut behind them.

Only then did he set her on her feet, in the center of the room.

"Well, that was embarrassing," she muttered.

Cal went back to the door to flip on the light switch beside it and lean against the wall there. Studying her from a distance, he crossed his arms over his shirtless torso, tucking each hand under the opposite armpit but leaving blunt thumbs poking up toward his muscular shoulders.

He must have been in bed before that because his hair and the sheets were mussed, his feet were bare and his jeans weren't zipped completely or fastened at the waistband—as if he'd pulled them on in a hurry.

But God, he looked sexy!

Abby wished he didn't because if he was going to give her the brush-off it was going to be all the more difficult for her after seeing him like that.

She forced her eyes away from his naked, bulging biceps wrapped over that broad chest and cleared her throat so she could speak.

"I'm sorry. This was all dumb."

"What was?"

"Climbing the trellis. Coming unannounced at this time of night…" She nodded in the direction of his rumpled bed and voiced a fear that had just struck her. "Did I interrupt—?"

He made a sound that was disgusted enough to stop her words midsentence.

"What do you think? That I was in the middle of an orgy? That because you've been playing cat and mouse with me I'd just bring in a couple of other women to horse around with?"

"No, I—" She stopped herself that time. What could she say? That yes, for a fleeting moment she'd been afraid he had found someone else to warm his bed already?

"Why'd you come, Abby?" he demanded then.

"You said you wanted to talk," she said feebly, knowing it sounded ridiculous under the circumstances.

"I wanted to talk four days ago. I wanted to talk every time I called or came by your house or the bakery. Where've you been all those times?"

She shrugged. "Hiding," she admitted.

"Why?"

She told him why, forging headlong into the admission that she'd been trying to be as worldly as he was, not to seem provincial. To take what had gone on between them as lightly as she thought he had and that she hadn't wanted to hear him say just how lightly he had taken it.

"But I guess I need to hear it. Maybe to put some closure to things," she finished fatalistically.

He shook his head, keeping his eyes trained on her. "That's not what I had to say to you."

Abby raised her chin in question, waiting.

"I'm in love with you," he said then. "I realized it the morning I woke up with you in my arms. I realized I wanted to do that every morning for the rest of my life. That I wanted to marry you. To make you mine."

Her breath caught in her throat. "But you sounded so...serious. And you warned me that you're not a one-woman man," she reminded.

"If I sounded serious, it was because it wasn't an easy thing to come to. It's never happened to me before and it didn't quite fit. I had to get used to the idea. And as for the one-woman man thing—I didn't *warn* you. I only said it in passing.''

"I took it as a warning."

"Well, stop it," he ordered in no uncertain terms. "No, I've never been a one-woman man before. But that's because I've never met the right woman. Until you."

"But I'm—"

"Don't give me that stuff about being predictable or provincial or any of the rest of it. I hashed through all that in my head, and it's bull. I don't buy any of it for a minute. Just tell me you love me and that you'll marry me."

To say she was stunned would have been an understatement. Abby just stood there, staring at him, while a hundred things flashed through her mind.

Did she love him?

She'd been terrified to admit it to herself, but now the floodgates opened and out swelled the knowledge that she did. She loved him with all her heart and soul. In a way she'd never loved Bill Snodgrass. With more intensity. More passion. More of everything that made it real and deep and abiding.

But what about all her former fiancé had said about her? What if Cal just wasn't seeing it because things were so new between them? What if she did eventually bore him into another woman's arms?

Her sisters' earlier words came back to support Cal's contention that the other man's accusations were bull, and suddenly Abby gave in to the possibility that they were all right. She wasn't lacking. It was Bill Snodgrass whose character was so weak that he'd trumped up faults in her to justify his own shoddy actions.

She hadn't done anything extraordinary since meeting Cal—well, with the exception of tonight's escapade—yet he'd kept coming around anyway. He'd fallen in love with her anyway. He was asking her to marry him anyway...

And what about the fact that he'd never before been a one-woman man? she asked herself. How risky did that make him?

But she didn't have to consider that for too long, either.

He might not have settled down before this, but he hadn't cheated on anyone, either, which spoke for a stronger character than Bill Snodgrass had, a strong character she'd seen in Cal in other ways, too. In his kindness and consideration. In his care for his family.

And obviously he'd been bent on putting down roots even before he'd met her. His whole purpose of being in Clangton was to do that, and obviously he'd had no problem making a commitment to it.

"Abby?"

His deep voice drew her out of her musings. She looked him square in the eye, giving herself over to the pull of that warm gaze. "I've been really dumb the last couple of days, haven't I?"

"I don't know. Have you?"

"I've been avoiding you when the truth is I love you, too. And marrying you is just what I want."

For a moment he stayed where he was, watching her as if he thought she might change her mind any moment.

But then he shoved off the wall and crossed to her on purposeful strides with a bit of swagger to his step.

He came to a stop close in front of her, slipped his hands around her neck, cupping the sides of her face from the back of her jawbone, his thumbs controlling the angle of her face so he could raise it to look up at him.

She thought he was going to say something. Something very serious from the appearance of the stern frown creasing his brow. But instead he bent to capture her mouth with his in a kiss that was forceful, masterful, possessive. A kiss that claimed her. A kiss that took her only a moment to respond to, to give herself over to, to relax into and enjoy.

But just as she did he ended it, swept her up into his arms again and carried her out of the bedroom, into the bathroom she'd used that first morning there.

Only it didn't look the same by any means.

Where before there had been a grungy old tub and sink, chipped tile and peeled paint, now the walls were freshly whitewashed. A floor-to-ceiling, paned, triple-paneled window had been added and the centerpiece of the newly remodeled room was the bathtub they'd tried out on the showroom floor of the hardware store.

"You've been busy," she said as he set her on her feet alongside the tub.

"And thinkin' about you the whole time. Want to use it?" he asked with a nod at the huge bathtub.

"Do I smell bad?" she joked.

"You smell great," he answered with what was almost a growl.

"A bath might be nice, though...."

That was all the encouragement he needed to turn on the water and the whirlpool jets.

Then it was Abby he turned on, undressing her while the tub filled, shedding his own clothes and pulling her with him into the bubbling water.

He made love to her there. Just the way he'd described when he'd teased her with that fantasy in the hardware store. Wet, slippery love that was playful but poignant, too. He explored every inch of her body, cherished it, teased it, tormented it and finally found his home inside it in a way that melded them together so smoothly, so perfectly that it chased away any lingering uncertainty that they were made for each other.

With every powerful thrust water rose and fell around them like a tidal wave as passion washed through them with a turbulence all its own. Wild, abandoned passion that took them to an explosive, simultaneous climax, bathed in the sensuous silk of warm water and love and the knowledge that they had a whole lifetime of sexy saunas ahead of them.

"I do love you," Cal said as they eased back against one of the tub's slanted ends, holding each other, letting the jets do a little after-magic all their own.

"I love you, too," Abby said in a breathy voice. "But we did make a mess," she added a moment later, glancing at the water that they'd splashed all over the place.

"But it was worth it, wasn't it?"

"It was," she agreed without having to think about it.

"Now tell me you'll marry me," he ordered.

"I'll marry you."

"And be my wife for the rest of our born days, and have my babies and never take a bath alone again."

"And be your wife for the rest of our born days, and have your babies. But I don't know about *never* taking a bath alone again. This tub would be pretty great to lounge in with a good book."

"Are you marryin' me to get hold of my tub?"

"Well, that and one or two other things," she said, getting hold of something much better.

"What was that part about you bein' predictable again?" he said with a low rumble of a chuckle deep in his throat.

"You mean you didn't know I'd come to my senses and give you the chance to propose?"

"You had me worried, Abby. You definitely had me worried that the night we had together had turned you off."

"Turned me *off?*" she said, doing a little further underwater exploration that refuted the notion.

He chuckled deep in his throat at the absurdity of ever having thought such a thing. "Now I'm gonna put more water in this tub before we splash it dry. Then, in a while, I'm gonna take you downstairs and introduce you to your soon-to-be in-laws," he said then.

Abby groaned at that.

"Can't meeting my soon-to-be in-laws wait until tomorrow?"

"I suppose so. Since we'll have a lot of tomorrows," he said, nibbling her earlobe.

A lot of tomorrows...

The words chimed through her heart like joyous church bells.

They'd have a lot of tomorrows together.

The fact that she'd ever doubted it, doubted him, doubted herself, suddenly seemed like something that had happened long ago and far away, to someone who didn't know what she knew.

Because what she knew was that she loved this man in a way she could never love anyone else.

And that he loved her just the same.

And that together they really would have a whole lifetime of tomorrows.

PLAY...

"ROLL A DOUBLE!"

GET 2 BOOKS
AND A
FABULOUS MYSTERY BONUS GIFT

ABSOLUTELY FREE!

SEE INSIDE...

(H-D-07/99)

NO RISK, NO OBLIGATION TO BUY...NOW OR EVER!

GUARANTEED

PLAY "ROLL A DOUBLE"
AND YOU GET FREE GIFTS!
HERE'S HOW TO PLAY:

1. Peel off label from front cover. Place it in space provided at right. With a coin, carefully scratch off the silver dice. Then check the claim chart to see what we have for you – TWO FREE BOOKS and a mystery gift – ALL YOURS! ALL FREE!

2. Send back this card and you'll receive brand-new Harlequin Duets™ novels. These books have a cover price of $5.99 each in the U.S. and $6.99 each in Canada, but they are yours to keep absolutely free.

3. There's no catch. You're under no obligation to buy anything. We charge nothing – ZERO – for your first shipment. And you don't have to make any minimum number of purchases – not even one!

4. The fact is, thousands of readers enjoy receiving books by mail from the Harlequin Reader Service®. They like the convenience of home delivery...they like getting the best new novels BEFORE they're available in stores...and they love our discount prices!

5. We hope that after receiving your free books you'll want to remain a subscriber. But the choice is yours – to continue or cancel any time at all! So why not take us up on our invitation, with no risk of any kind. You'll be glad you did!

THIS MYSTERY BONUS GIFT
WILL BE YOURS <u>FREE</u> WHEN
YOU PLAY "ROLL A DOUBLE"

"ROLL A DOUBLE!"

Place label here

SCRATCH HERE

SEE CLAIM CHART BELOW

311 HDL CQV7

111 HDL CQVR
(H-D-07/99)

YES! I have placed my label from the front cover into the space
provided above and scratched off the silver dice to reveal a double.
Please send me all the gifts for which I qualify. I understand that I am
under no obligation to purchase any books, as explained on the back and
on the opposite page.

Name:
_____
(PLEASE PRINT)

Address: _____ Apt.#: _____

City: _____ State/Prov.: _____ Postal
Zip/ Code: _____

The Harlequin Reader Service® — Here's how it works:

Accepting your 2 free books and mystery gift places you under no obligation to buy anything. You may keep the books and gift and return the shipping statement marked "cancel." If you do not cancel, about a month later we'll send you 2 additional novels and bill you just $5.14 each in the U.S., or $6.14 each in Canada, plus 50¢ delivery per book and applicable taxes if any.* That's the complete price and — compared to the cover price of $5.99 in the U.S. and $6.99 in Canada — it's quite a bargain! You may cancel at any time, but if you choose to continue, every month we'll send you 2 more books, which you may either purchase at the discount price or return to us and cancel your subscription.

*Terms and prices subject to change without notice. Sales tax applicable in N.Y. Canadian residents will be charged applicable provincial taxes and GST.

If offer card is missing write to: Harlequin Reader Service, 3010 Walden Ave., P.O. Box 1867, Buffalo NY 14240-1867

BUSINESS REPLY MAIL
FIRST-CLASS MAIL   PERMIT NO. 717   BUFFALO, NY

POSTAGE WILL BE PAID BY ADDRESSEE

HARLEQUIN READER SERVICE
3010 WALDEN AVE
PO BOX 1867
BUFFALO NY 14240-9952

NO POSTAGE
NECESSARY
IF MAILED
IN THE
UNITED STATES

LIZ
IRELAND

The Best
Man
Switch

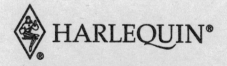

HARLEQUIN®

TORONTO • NEW YORK • LONDON
AMSTERDAM • PARIS • SYDNEY • HAMBURG
STOCKHOLM • ATHENS • TOKYO • MILAN • MADRID
PRAGUE • WARSAW • BUDAPEST • AUCKLAND

Dear Reader,

Several days ago I told a phone buddy that I was writing a scene about two sixteen-year-olds having a calamitous date. Dead air cracked over the telephone wire, then my friend asked, "When you're sixteen, what date *isn't* a calamity?"

Hmm. Come to think of it, there are some (I won't name names) who never seem to graduate beyond the tragic teen pattern—luckily for me and the rest of the Romance Writers of America roster. If the course of true love started running smoothly, what would we write about?

I hope you enjoy *The Best Man Switch*. Stories about identical twins have been a favorite of mine since I saw Hayley Mills in *The Parent Trap*. Growing up I always wanted an identical twin—preferably a math-science whiz!

Liz Ireland

Prologue

"ALL I'M ASKING FOR is a *tiny* favor," Grant Whiting begged his twin brother, Ted. "Just stand in for me at the rehearsal dinner and the wedding ceremony. That's all."

"That's all?" Ted, who had been slouching in the chair on the other side of Grant's desk, suddenly sprang bolt upright. His reaction made him look like a gaping mirror image of his brother. "You call pulling a best man switch *tiny?*"

"It's not like you're standing in for me during an IRS audit or a moon launch. It's just a wedding."

Grant knew what his brother was thinking—that it wasn't like him to cop out on a commitment. Just a glance was enough to tell that Grant was a nose-to-the-grindstone, never-shirk-a-responsibility type. He always dressed for work conservatively—funereally, Ted would say—in dark suits and sensible ties and perfectly polished shoes. Whereas, today Ted had seen fit to show up—late—in a getup more suitable for a beach at Waikiki. White shorts, a floral-print shirt and sandals! All he lacked was a fruity drink with an umbrella.

His secretary was probably whipping up a shaker of those down the hall.

The few times in the past they had pulled switches—an enterprise never embarked on lightly, though they were perfectly identical—it had always been for Ted's benefit. Because he'd had stage fright and couldn't buck up to being George Washington in the third-grade history pageant, or because he never could get the hang of geometry—or Spanish, or botany—or because he just couldn't bring himself to tell Mary Pepperburg that he already had a date. Grant had never needed rescuing before.

"I thought you were looking forward to Kay and Marty's wedding," Ted said.

"Of course. They're my best friends."

"Uh-huh." Ted drummed his fingers and eyeballed him closely. "This isn't about the buyout, is it? Good grief! You can't even leave the store for one measly day!"

Ted thought Grant was a hopeless workaholic. But then, Ted had the work ethic of a house cat.

"It's one night and the next day," Grant corrected him. "I don't think you realize the gravity of our situation." He and his brother were at risk of losing their small chain of family-owned department stores, Whiting's, if they didn't forestall a buyout bid from Moreland's, a larger Midwest chain. "This is the biggest business crisis we've faced since Herman Little from men's suits tried to unionize the salesclerks."

"And what happened?" Ted asked. "We gave everybody a little pay raise."

"A seven percent pay raise!"

His brother shrugged. "Will you relax?"

"You don't have Horace Moreland calling you every ten minutes. And now he's in our territory."

Horace Moreland was a corporate general who devoured local department stores like a kid devours Halloween candy, and he was here this week to munch down on Whiting's. Ted and Grant were against a buyout, naturally, but they weren't in complete control of their destiny. Their uncle Truman, a veteran of Whiting's himself, still had a quarter share in the business. Uncle Truman was a golf nut who seemingly always needed money to keep up with his club dues—a weakness that left him very susceptible to big money talk from Moreland. The other quarter belonged to Mona, Ted and Grant's stepmother. Though their father had passed away seven years ago, his last wife still held considerable sway over their lives in the form of her twenty-five percent, and Mona wasn't just willing to be bought out, she was eager. Champing at the bit, even. Mona was a slave to fashion, and keeping up appearances took money. And wasn't cash better than ownership in a business so subject to the whims of the economy? In other words, if Moreland was the ruthless enemy general, Mona and Truman were the turncoats ready to greet his tanks with welcome signs and confetti.

"I need to be on my toes in order to stave off calamity. I don't have time for weddings."

"You know what I think?" Ted asked. "I think you're going to avoid that wedding because you don't want the reminder."

"Reminder of what?"

"Your divorce."

Grant winced. "You're right. I didn't want the reminder." He was still shocked that he of all people, he who had watched his father remarry three times and always swore he would be different, was divorced.

"You can't avoid women forever, you know. Why not get out and enjoy your new bachelordom? Loosen up!"

"That's what Janice always said." Janice was his exwife.

Ted looked perplexed. "Janice wanted you to go out and meet women?"

"No, she wanted me to loosen up. She called me too stodgy, too rigid."

"Janice was crazy!" Ted had never liked Grant's wife. But he had a natural revulsion against anything that smacked of the domestic.

"Do you think I'm stodgy?"

"Well…" His brother shifted uncomfortably. "Maybe not stodgy exactly…serious. Dignified."

"Stodgy." Grant sighed. "Janice always complained that we never did anything fun or spontaneous, and that I was too responsible. Too responsible! Is there actually such a thing?"

"Janice was a nut."

Was she? Grant had suggested they seek counseling. Really, he meant that Janice needed therapy, but he did want to be present when the psychiatrist pronounced that Janice just didn't appreciate what a sterling husband she had, and that there was positively nothing wrong with their marriage, just as Grant had always claimed.

But before they'd made it to the first session, one morning Grant awakened and discovered his wife had run off with the prince of a thumbnail-size, oil-rich country in the Middle East.

Okay, so maybe there had been something wrong with his marriage…. But needless to say, Janice's bailing out catapulted their relationship way beyond the realm of your average everyday marital dysfunction.

"The truly disturbing thing is, I was completely blind-sided by Janice's defection. While I was the faithful hubby, slaving away at the store by day, and even adding on an extra room to our house on weekends in hopes that we would be starting a family soon, Janice was off having secret afternoon love sessions with Prince Omar.''

"While you were doing the handy-hubby number, she was doing the dance of the seven veils,'' Ted quipped.

"How can I ever find a woman to trust after that kind of deception?''

Ted waved away that concern. "Forget trust. Think legs.''

Grant wished he could be a dyed-in-the-wool bachelor like his brother. "I don't want to get married again.''

"Good!''

"I don't even want to think about it.''

"So don't. Find yourself a babe and have yourself a time.''

Ted's advice was all well and good, but at this wedding he would have to stand through a long ceremony, hearing the words that he'd spoken so solemnly himself to a woman who apparently hadn't given much thought to the "till-death-do-us-part'' part. He just wasn't sure he was up to it. And then there was the small matter of the maid of honor....

"What else is wrong?'' Ted asked.

"It's Kay,'' he said. "The bride.''

"The woman with the mutt!'' Ted exclaimed in disgust.

Kay was one of Grant's friends from business school, and had only met Ted once...but once had been enough. At a backyard cookout at Kay's house, her dachshund, Chester, had earned Ted's enmity by peeing on his prized pair of genuine wallaby-hide boots imported from Australia. Man and beast had been sworn adversaries ever since.

"This has nothing to do with her dog,'' Grant assured him. "It's just...well, Kay is one of these mother-hen types, and now she's getting married, and I'm the best man, and she naturally has been nagging *me* about getting married again."

"Women!" Ted, who loved women—at least, he loved leggy blondes—always became defensive when the subject of matrimony was being discussed. "They'll never be happy until every man on the planet is snagged and strapped down with a wife, a mortgage and kids."

Grant nodded. "That's Kay all over."

Ted tapped a pencil against his thigh in annoyance. "Let me guess… Kay thinks her maid of honor would be just perfect for you." He finished the sentence in a high feminine trill.

Grant grinned. "How'd you guess?" In fact, Kay had mentioned her maid of honor several times. Matchmaking was definitely afoot.

"Oh, they're so predictable." Ted leaned back, parked the pencil behind his ear and shook his head philosophically. "Women engineer these weddings to have their own momentum. First one woman gets married and then another one gets the urge, and before the poor sap she's going out with knows it, he's marching down the aisle, and on and on. The whole wedding thing is like a pep rally for matrimony, whipping females into a bridal frenzy. And unless you're on guard, brother, you'll get sucked into it, too, just like one of those cows getting sucked into a tornado in *Twister*."

Grant smiled ruefully. "If only you'd given me that speech five years ago, I might never have married Princess Janice."

Ted's forehead creased with wrinkles—he did feel guilty for not indoctrinating his brother into staunch bachelorhood earlier. Though Lord knows he'd tried. He'd been on guard against the opposite sex ever since their father married for the fourth time when they were fourteen. He still blamed himself for letting Janice get through the defensive line.

Grant had paid dearly for that lapse. And now look at him—still vulnerable. Easy pickin's for any wily female. It made Ted furious just to think about it.

"Listen, bro, of course I'll do the switch. In fact, I see it as a solemn duty, like pulling my weight here at the store."

Grant choked on a sip of coffee. Ted was essential to Whiting's, especially when it came to entertaining buyers; he could impress executives with his college-football-hero stories. But he weaseled out of the more stressful day-to-day operations of the store in favor of perfecting his tan out on his precious boat. Or, when pressed about his absenteeism, he might show up and play Nerf hoops in his office for a couple hours.

But Ted took pride in being the older brother by twelve minutes, and for being infinitely wiser, at least when it came to women. "Clearly, you're still not equipped to deal with this what's-her-name that Kay has marked you as a target for."

"Mitzi," Grant said, prepping him. "The maid of honor's name is Mitzi Campion, a friend from Kay's high school days."

"Mitzi. Gotcha." Ted narrowed his eyes contemplatively. "Mitzi... You know what that name says to me?"

"No, what?"

"It says perky. It says pushy."

Grant laughed.

"Just think Mitzi Gaynor," Ted explained, all seriousness. "Just think *South Pacific*. That little nurse she played was full of perk—and what happened?"

"She danced a lot?"

Ted rolled his eyes. "She got married! And to some poor French guy who was just sitting on his island, minding his own business before she barreled into him."

"I thought he was a lonely old murderer with two kids..."

His brother sneered. "They just threw that stuff in to make the woman look good."

Grant steered Ted back on topic. "This Mitzi is being flown in and is going to house-sit for Kay next week while Kay and Marty are having their honeymoon, so naturally Kay wants me to squire the girl around and—"

Ted, who'd been absorbed in the briefing, suddenly gestured for Grant to stop right there. "No, no, no. Don't think of this Mitzi character as a 'girl.' In confirmed-bachelor lingo, she's a predator, and before the end of that rehearsal dinner Friday night, I'll let her know what we think about squiring."

Grant chuckled.

"Oh, laugh now, if you want," his brother drawled. "You'll thank me when it's over. Believe me, Grant old boy, after this wedding, perky Mitzi will know better than to fly to strange cities trying to entrap men."

Grant smiled. Overprotective "big" brothers definitely had their good points. For the first time since his marriage fiasco, Grant was beginning to feel in control again. Now he would be able to concentrate all his energies on saving the family store, and with it, his sanity. Best of all, he could forget about weddings and marriage vows and women....

"Sic 'em, tiger," he said to his brother.

1

"YOU'RE GOING to fall in love with Grant Whiting!" Kay gushed from the front seat of the car on the way to the wedding rehearsal. "He's such a dreamboat!"

Mitzi Campion gritted her teeth and smiled at Kay and Marty as if she just couldn't wait to meet this remarkable love god that Kay had talked about nonstop all afternoon. "He sounds great, Kay, really, but right now Chester is my ideal male."

"Oh, Mitzi, you don't mean that."

She sighed, looking forward to a week of leisure and dog-sitting. "You bet. He'll keep my feet warm while I watch videos, and look soulfully into my eyes as I pig out on salty junk food. And it's a cinch that he'll be more faithful than any of my past boyfriends have been."

That was no joke. In the past three years she'd been involved in three relationships, all of which had ended in heartache, not to mention heartburn from the Oreo binges she'd indulged in to make herself feel better. The strange thing was, in all three cases, everything had seemed great—the men had been good-looking, gainfully employed and seemingly well adjusted. But all three of them had run for cover when they'd discovered that Mitzi actually wanted a future that included marriage, kids and mortgage payments. In fact, just mentioning the word *baby* had sent Mike vaulting into the arms of a Sears model, showing Mitzi the softer side of being dumped.

A year later, the vaguest hint of marriage had panicked her boyfriend Jeff, so he abandoned her and galloped off with a female jockey he'd met one weekend at Belmont Park.

Finally, there was Tim. Brother Tim now. *That* was just too humiliating to think about.

Kay shook her head reprovingly, like an elementary-school principal. Which she was. "You can't meet Mr. Right watching videos with Chester."

"I'm through looking for Mr. Right. Apparently nothing makes the urban, workaholic man more jittery than the idea of a woman with marriage on her mind—he's terrified that she's going to have a dozen babies and then abscond with his 401K. No, I'm afraid my Mr. Right is already someone else's happily married hubby."

"You shouldn't be so negative," said Kay.

Easy for her to say, standing with one foot down the church aisle.

"I have to face facts," Mitzi replied. She was nothing if not a realist, except on those occasions when she was a hopeless romantic. "I'm the Typhoid Mary of romance. Three men lost in three years. That means I'm out of the game. If a racehorse had my record, he would have been put out to pasture, or shot in the leg, or whatever they do to the ones who are surefire losers."

Kay, who was so in love she would have been disgusting if Mitzi didn't like her so much, looked over at Marty, her future husband, and winked. "Won't they be perfect?"

Marty laughed.

Mitzi's curiosity flared. "You mean Grant Whiting is among Cupid's casualties?"

Kay turned toward the back seat and put a hand on Mitzi's shoulder. "It's so sad. He's the nicest man, but a little over a year ago his wife left him."

Warning sirens rang out in Mitzi's head. "Okay. What's wrong with him?"

"Nothing! Janice just never appreciated Grant," Kay said with the vehemence of someone defending an old friend. "Anyway, she met this oil sheikh, and...well, you can guess the rest."

Boy, could she. The old dumparoo. Mitzi began to feel a grudging kinship with Mr. Dreamboat.

"The guy was a Middle East oil sheikh," Kay elaborated. "In fact, I think he was actually a prince or something." She shrugged. "Grant's ex-wife might be living in a tent in the desert somewhere, but she could now buy and sell several small countries before lunch and think nothing of it."

"Thrown over for a prince." Mitzi sighed. At least she'd never had to compete with royalty. "That would be a tough thing to get over."

Kay patted her arm. "Janice's folly is your good fortune."

Mitzi screwed up her lips in a patient smile. "Even if I hadn't already decided that love is a delusion, I doubt I could fall head over heels in one short week, Kay."

"Don't be so pessimistic. Just look at Marty and me."

Mitzi stared at her best friend, uncomprehending. In fact, even Marty looked puzzled.

"You two knew each other in college," Mitzi pointed out. "It was thirteen years before you got around to going on a date."

Kay nodded. "That's right—thirteen years, and then *wham!* One day it hit me that I was completely, madly and totally in love. It just goes to show."

Mitzi sank against the velour of the back seat, taking little comfort from her friend's example. If it took thirteen years to fall madly in love at first sight, she was in deep trouble. The only man she'd known for even close to that amount of time was Stanley the doorman at her Manhattan apartment building, and he was seventy-two and had false teeth that clicked like castanets.

Marty turned a corner downtown and pulled into a parking lot next to a large old stone church.

"How pretty," Mitzi exclaimed. With her photographer's eye, she could imagine how the scene would look the next day, with the morning sun beaming bright and shiny through the dappled shade of the sweeping live oaks, a summer breeze blowing at Kay's flowing wedding dress. And the bridesmaids....

Mitzi frowned at the one spectacular blight on the Hallmark-card scene, trying to block the memory of that afternoon's dress fitting from her mind. Tomorrow was Kay's day, she reminded herself. A bride was entitled to make her nearest and dearest friends wear whatever hideously ugly bridesmaid gowns her heart desired.

"Look!" Kay exclaimed, pointing and waving at someone in the parking lot. "There he is! Oh, good. I was worried he wouldn't get here on time."

"Grant practically lives at that store of his," Marty explained.

A workaholic type, Mitzi thought immediately. That didn't bode well. All the men she'd gone out with before were workaholics. She, on the other hand, worked hard at her advertising job but didn't want to make it her entire life. It wasn't as if she could be considered a shooting star of Madison Avenue anyway. So far as a junior ad exec, she'd developed one winning campaign...for canned ham. It wasn't the kind of success that made careers soar. Besides, what she really wanted to be was a professional photographer, but sometimes that seemed as much of a pipe dream as her desire to have a perfect loving husband and her American dream allotment of 2.5 kids.

Still perched forward, looking at the view, she realized her mouth was hanging open in astonishment. Her appreciation wasn't so much for the view of the church anymore as the *dreamboat* just in front of her.

Leaning against a white truck that was practically the size of a semi stood a grade-A Adonis. His casual stance emphasized his impressive height and broad shoulders, his short hair was a mass of sandy curls and his skin was tanned to an Olympian bronze. He had the kind of chiseled jaw and white even teeth that advertisers dream about, and as he saw the bride and groom, his dazzling blue eyes lit up in recognition. Mitzi felt her breath catch, and turned a reproachful glance toward Kay.

"This is a man you refer to as nice? Maybe knowing someone for a decade gives you a different perspective…"

Kay laughed. "Okay, he's gorgeous. Just remember— he's our best friend in the world…and he's completely available."

Mitzi looked back at Mr. Available and actually felt her heart flutter, which hadn't happened in months. Though her heart palpitations did have a rusty creak to them.

Kay and Marty got out and shouted greetings to Grant. Through the car window, Mitzi saw Kay point toward where she was still hovering in the back seat. Grant turned, making eye contact with her. Having all that prime masculinity aimed in her direction caused her heart to do a few more unusual gyrations.

Kay and Marty trotted away in the direction of Kay's mom, leaving Grant with nothing to do but step forward to where Mitzi sat paralyzed with nerves, her hand frozen on the door handle. His walk was sheer male grace, and just the act of opening the car door for her seemed powerful when he performed it. *Maybe the next week would be as pleasurable as Kay had promised....* Suddenly, the realist in her was being badly outraced by the romantic.

Grant stood before her. There was something insouciant about the way his mouth turned up at one corner.

Hmm... Actually, now that she was trapped in its glare, that smile seemed almost a sneer.

He looked her up and down with blue eyes that were almost sharklike in their lack of expression. ''Aren't you ever going to get out of the car?''

Mitzi jumped. She didn't know what she had been waiting for—maybe for Grant to say hello, or help her out? Call her old-fashioned, but when Kay had described him as ''nice,'' Mitzi had expected manners to come along with the package.

Realism started creeping back up on her. Grabbing her handbag that went beyond oversize—it usually carried her entire life, including a camera and a few rolls of film—she hauled herself out of the car, wishing now that she had on something simpler than her long black gauzy skirt and a white sheer shirt. The charm bracelet she always wore, which had belonged to her grandmother, clinked noisily as she unfolded her long limbs and pushed off the seat. Next to Grant, who was so self-possessed-looking in his khakis and conservative button-down shirt, she felt fluttery and fussy.

As she stepped out of the car, her new slick-bottomed sandals slipped against the hard pavement, nearly sending her flying. Before she could fall, she grabbed hold of Grant's arm. His rock-hard arm. The man obviously had a close personal relationship with a Nautilus machine.

Grant pulled her away from the car, let go of her and shut the car door firmly. Then he turned back, arms crossed, and gave her another long up-and-down stare. ''So *you're* Mitzi.''

So you're *the bubonic plague,* Mitzi interpreted. She

tensed, not quite understanding why he was addressing her that way. Then suddenly it dawned on her. "Let me guess. You were expecting Mitzi Gaynor?"

He scratched his chiseled jaw. "Well...yeah."

It never failed—the curse her musicals-loving mother had bestowed on her! Inevitably, people expected a Mitzi to be short and blond and perky, a regular Nurse Nellie Forbush. Perhaps a tap-dancing cutie was what her mother had envisioned, but instead, Mitzi had grown, and grown, to five feet ten, and her body had nowhere near the grace of her nimble namesake.

"Okay, so I'm not a perky movie star. Should that rule me out as maid of honor?"

The gaze he leveled at her was about as mirthful as a peptic ulcer. "Let's just get this over with." He turned and strode toward the church, leaving Mitzi to trail in his wake, astonished.

She had never seen someone react so rudely to her appearance, which, for all her defects, wasn't that terrible! She had even been called a rare willowy beauty once, although, granted, that boyfriend was now ringing prayer bells in a monastery.

Still, Grant's reaction seemed extreme. This was the dreamboat Kay couldn't stop talking about? He seemed more like a battle cruiser, with all guns aimed at her.

Kay's phrase buzzed through her mind. *"Just remember—he's our best friend in the world."*

Had she missed something? Maybe there were extenuating circumstances that momentarily caused Grant Whiting to lose his devastating charm. Maybe he disliked wedding rehearsals, or parking lots. Or her.

Kay bounded out of the church and beckoned them forward, alerting Mitzi to the fact that she and Grant were the last stragglers. The bride-to-be tossed her short blond curls and grinned. "You two need to stop flirting and get with the program—remember, you're the stars of the whole production.''

Grant, with a perfectly affable smile on his face, held the church door open for Kay. ''I thought that privilege belonged to you and Marty.''

He didn't correct her about the flirting business, Mitzi noticed.

Kay laughed. ''That's tomorrow. Tonight, you and Mitzi have to stand in for us.''

He turned and bestowed on Mitzi a look that could only be called sour. Couldn't Kay see it? Mitzi glanced at Kay and saw that, no, the woman was still smiling up at Grant as if he were an overgrown Boy Scout.

''More superstitious wedding nonsense,'' he said with a sigh.

Kay giggled and shooed him inside. ''You'd be superstitious, too, if you were about to march down an aisle in front of two hundred people on heels high enough to bungee-jump off of.''

Grant turned to Mitzi, shrugging helplessly. ''I guess ours is not to reason why, Mitz.''

Mitz? Was he kidding? She watched in awe as Grant, Mr. Charming himself, tweaked Kay's bangs playfully and, handing over control of the door to the bride, ducked past her and disappeared inside.

Kay gestured for Mitzi to hurry. ''What did I tell you?'' she asked. ''Isn't he a doll?''

''He's very…striking,'' Mitzi mumbled.

''And just imagine—he's got a brother who's exactly like him!''

''Two of them,'' Mitzi breathed, awed that nature could make such a tragic mistake twice.

''Only, his brother's not nearly so nice.''

Mitzi wondered idly whether Attila the Hun had a mean little brother.

"Wait'll you get to know him better," Kay assured her. "I couldn't imagine life without a friend like Grant."

Mitzi vowed to be patient. For Kay's sake, she told herself. A bride had a stressful enough time without a fractious wedding party to worry about.

Luckily, all the attendants were inside and the priest was ready to shepherd them through the ceremony. Immediately, the cleric picked out the maid of honor and best man to represent the bride and groom. To Mitzi's surprise, Grant took her arm and went through the rehearsal like an old pro. And when she marched to the front of the aisle where Grant was waiting, hilariously feigning a nail-biting groom, she had to join in the laughter in the church. When the priest got to the part when he would announce that the groom could kiss the bride, Grant vaulted over a pew and planted a kiss on Kay's lips to claps and whoops all around.

He was charming, apparently, to everyone but her. Still, she finished the rehearsal feeling a little more kindly toward him. For Kay's sake.

"Does everybody have a ride to the restaurant?" Marty asked outside the church.

The group was already broken up and headed to their respective cars to drive to the rehearsal dinner. Kay tossed a glance at Mitzi and then tugged on Marty's sleeve and whispered something conspiratorially as she nodded in Grant's direction.

"Oh, Mitzi," Marty piped up, as if Mitzi hadn't noticed them plotting against her. "We've, uh, got some wedding gifts that Kay's mother brought to haul around in the back seat now... I guess you'll have to ride with Grant."

Mitzi stood frozen on the church steps and stared at Grant's gleaming, hulking white truck. "Wouldn't it be better if I rode with your mom? I mean—"

Kay cut her off by hollering for Grant's approval of the plan. "You've got room for Mitzi, don't you, Grant?"

Grant broke into one of his icy smiles. "Maybe you should tell your friend I don't bite."

Kay and Marty laughed as if he'd just tossed off an irresistible witticism. "He doesn't bite," Kay assured Mitzi, practically pushing her down the stairs. As they reached the last step, she added in a whisper, "He likes you—I can tell," and gave Mitzi a final shove that sent her tripping forward.

She clambered up to the passenger seat of Grant's truck and smiled at him. Tentatively. "Well," she said, trying to start out on a friendly note. "That wasn't so painful."

Ted snorted. Oh, it hadn't taken him long to scope out this conspiracy. His hunch had been absolutely right. This whole wedding thing was a marriage setup...and Grant was the target. All of Kay and Mitzi's whispered huddles were strategy sessions. They'd even gotten Marty in on it, had turned the poor sucker against his own species. Or sex, or whatever you called it.

Why couldn't they give a guy a break? After what Grant had been through with Janice, the man deserved some peace and quiet...not some green-eyed woman chasing after him relentlessly. That was just the trouble with women. If you were a little nice to them and gave them an opening, they never gave up until they had you, hook, line and marriage license.

It was Grant's good fortune to have a big brother to run interference for him. And it hadn't taken Ted more than one long look at Mitzi to know what method would send her scurrying back to where she came from. With women as with football, the best defense was a good offense.

And, as Grant had pointed out so often, Ted excelled at offensiveness.

"No, the rehearsal was entertaining," he said. "I especially enjoyed that little performance at the end."

She stared at him blankly. "Performance?"

"The little scene you played out there on the church steps, where you pretended that you wanted to go to the restaurant with Kay's mom. As if you weren't trying to finagle a ride with me to the rehearsal dinner all along."

Mitzi sputtered in astonishment as Grant's monstrous vehicle peeled out of the parking lot. "I would rather have ridden with Kay's mother."

He laughed. "Whatever."

"How far is it to the restaurant?" Mitzi asked, glaring at the road in front of her. She'd never met a man who could send her from annoyed to burning mad in nothing flat!

"Oh, relax. I've never seen anyone so uptight."

"Uptight!" She had to take a deep breath to calm herself. She did feel uptight, but only because he was such a jerk! "Ever since we met, you've been provoking me. I don't get it."

"You don't think it might have something to do with whatever designs you might have cooked up for this wedding?"

"Designs?" It was as if he were speaking a foreign tongue.

"Kay hasn't mentioned me to you before?"

Just constantly, but she wasn't about to tell him that. What an arrogant...! "Well, yes, in passing, but—"

"In passing?"

Mitzi huffed in frustration. "Kay's just in a matchmaking mood. That doesn't mean I was taking her seriously."

A dark blond eyebrow arched skeptically. "Weren't you?"

"Of course not!"

He laughed that husky laugh of his. "Lady, I saw the way you were looking at me when you were sitting in the back seat of that car. Like you were a kid and I was Christmas."

She writhed in humiliation at the memory of how attractive she'd considered him at first glance. Adonis! Adonis with the personality of Hannibal Lecter. "Believe me, my only plan in coming here was to witness my high school buddy's wedding and to have a peaceful week of rest in her house while she's away. Is that so hard to swallow?"

"Frankly, yes."

She tossed her hands in the air. "I give up."

He cast her a sideways glance as if sizing her up. "I've had you pegged from the beginning. You're a single New York woman with a couple of failed relationships under your belt, and now you think you'll come down here and wear your chic black getup and trick some poor soul into thinking you're sophisticated."

Mitzi, huddling in the far corner of the seat, fumed. "If you must know, I received several compliments on my outfit at the rehearsal."

"It's a Southern custom to be polite to strangers."

"Really? You might try it sometime yourself."

Grant pulled into a parking lot in front of an old warehouse building that announced Lou Rae's Bar-B-Q in blue neon. Several people Mitzi recognized from the church were getting out of their cars. She clawed at the door handle and just managed to stop herself from leaping out of the truck before it had stopped moving. The upbeat strains of a western swing band drifted on the warm night air.

"Don't worry," Mitzi assured Grant with a huff. "I'll use all my New York feminine wiles to avoid you like the plague."

He shook his head and looked at her as if she'd said something totally uncalled for. "You know, I think you're just about the most abrasive woman I ever met."

Mitzi gaped at him, speechless. *She* was abrasive? He made it sound as if she were the one who had started the trouble between them. She, who didn't give two hoots about catching a man or even dating one! And as for Grant Whiting, she'd sooner go out with Godzilla!

She trailed a good ten yards behind Grant into the restaurant. Once inside, she was escorted out to a patio that overlooked Lake Austin, which was sparkling with the day's last rays of sun. Several long picnic tables were set up to accommodate Kay's party, which had ballooned in number since the church. The traditional red-and-white-checked tablecloths practically sagged under the weight of heaping platters of barbecued chicken, beef and ribs, and bowls of coleslaw and potato salad. Almost as she walked through the door, a waiter inserted a white plastic cup of beer into her hand.

She took a sip and tapped her toe to the upbeat music, eager to shake off the surly mood the short truck ride had left her in. Mitzi scoped out the lay of the land and chose an empty chair far away from God's Gift to Women.

Sue, one of the other bridesmaids, smiled as Mitzi walked up. "Take a load off," she said.

Mitzi tried to put Grant out of her head and began enjoying herself, eating way too much and drinking...well, more than she'd drunk in a long time. Every time her plastic cup was drained, a waiter bearing a pitcher magically appeared to refill it. Sue's friends were loud but great fun, and Sue herself was as boisterous as

Kay had said she was. She was especially vocal on the subject of the bridesmaid dresses, a topic about which Mitzi was in complete sympathy.

"I mean, I can understand Kay's not wanting the usual pastels," Sue said, "but honestly, the three of us are going to look mighty peculiar standing up there. Lime-green? Fuchsia?" Sue, who was actually wearing a neon-orange dress—"tangerine," Kay called it—laughed lustily at the prospect. "We'll look just like, like—"

"An assortment of Tropical Lifesavers?" Mitzi said.

Sue, cackling, clapped Mitzi on the back hard enough to send her flying forward, spilling the beer in her hand. The magic waiter with the pitcher reappeared, refilling Mitzi's glass before she could even register that it was empty. "I think that man has a psychic connection with the bottom of my cup," she said, sending the table into peals of laughter.

They'd all had far too much to drink.

"Dance time for Mitzi!" Kay yelled suddenly, standing up and pointing at her maid of honor. People began to holler and clap, less in response to what Kay had said than to the volume she had achieved saying it. "C'mon, Mitzi, you haven't danced all night!"

Mitzi shrank back in her metal folding chair. Dance? "I'm not even certain I can stand up."

Amid laughter, her table moved as one to prop her up on her feet and propel her toward the dance floor. "But I don't have anyone to dance with," she protested.

"Yes, you do!" Kay hollered.

Mitzi turned, weaving slightly, and discovered to her horror that Kay was shoving Grant out onto the floor to dance with her. She stood frozen, instantly sober, her gaze darting to the lake, which she considered diving into. Anything to avoid more contact with Grant. And she might have taken that leap, if not for the nagging voice in the back of her head that stopped her.

"Just remember—he's our best friend in the whole world."

Tomorrow was the wedding, she assured herself as Grant weaved in her direction and the band began playing a spirited "Waltz Across Texas." After tomorrow she would never have to see Grant Whiting again for her entire life—a sunny fact that would no doubt comfort her during hard times for years to come.

"Shall we?" He sent her a sarcastic little bow.

She clenched her teeth, determined not to be the one to cause a scene. For Kay's sake.

The easy waltz rhythm might have disguised the stiffness between them to any onlookers, but Mitzi had felt more romance dancing around her apartment with her vacuum cleaner.

"You're stiff as a board," Grant said.

She glared into her partner's blue eyes. "You're not exactly Fred Astaire yourself."

He shook his head. "I thought since you'd managed to get me out on the dance floor—"

Her squeak of dismay only stopped him momentarily.

"—that you might at least make some effort to be pleasant."

She had never met anyone so infuriating. "I did not want to dance with you."

His guffaw made her rage soar. "Right. I could see you were real hard to persuade."

"First you think I'm angling for a ride, now a dance. You are the most outrageous egotist I've ever met in my life!"

To her frustration, her words seemed to have no impact whatsoever. "What I don't understand," he explained, as if he were the most rational person in the world, "is why you just don't go for it."

She squinted in confusion. "Go for what?"

"For me."

"You?"

The man had to be certifiable!

He pulled her a little closer to his hard-muscled torso. Mitzi feared she would throw her neck out leaning away from him. "Just relax, sugar," he purred in his low Texas drawl. "If you just went for what you really wanted every once in a while, you wouldn't be nearly so uptight."

Before she knew what was happening, he twirled her in a spin that sent her reeling toward the largest wood table. Kay, catching her eye, gave her a thumbs-up and a wink. Mitzi shook her head frantically, but soon found herself spinning back into Grant's arms.

"If women like you weren't so focused on marriage all the time, life would be a lot more enjoyable," he finished saying.

She had to give him credit for not missing a beat. "I am not looking to marry anyone, especially you."

He laughed. "You're one of those women always looking for 'serious relationships.'"

"What do you look for—furtive gropes in elevators?"

"Fun."

She rolled her eyes. "How could I doubt it? You're a million laughs."

He tilted his head and fixed her with a philosophical gaze. "Really, I feel sorry for you. You've probably chased away a lot of men with all your scheming and plotting and worrying about how things will come out."

She grew hot with fury. He'd come too close to the truth for her to laugh. Especially about all those elaborate relationships she'd engineered that had come crashing around her.

The dance ended and she pushed away from Grant, glaring. "The only man I've ever wanted to chase away is *you*." She pivoted, heading straight for the pitcher at the waiter's table.

Grant was right on her heels, like old chewing gum. "Have you ever had a successful relationship?"

"Yes." She grabbed a cup and filled it. Then, under his steady, arrogant stare, she amended, "Well, nothing long-term. But I would say definitely successful in the short term."

"They left you," he guessed flatly. "They ran off with women who weren't so serious, that's why."

Then why did they marry them? she wanted to ask. Then she remembered who she was talking to. Grant Whiting wasn't her idea of a couples' counselor. "Not all of them."

Brother Tim, for instance.

He sidled closer to her. She felt a chill run up and down her spine. "You've got that lonely, hungry look about you."

She didn't know how much more she could take. Murdering the best man at her best friend's rehearsal dinner, however, might not be good politics.

"You know what you need, hon?"

She steeled herself for the answer.

"A fling."

She looked into his eyes. How could a man be so good-looking and so infuriating? And why, if he despised her "type" so much, couldn't he leave her alone?

"Maybe a fling with me," he said in a low voice that made her skin crawl. Nothing like being hit on by a misogynist. "What the hell, sugar, we've got a week. Loosen up."

Slowly, she groped her way out of her beer-induced fog enough to focus on his smirking grin. Either he was weaving or she was. Her stomach lurched. But more than that, her temper peaked.

Loosen up? Suddenly, she knew she had to put an end to his insolence once and for all, and she knew just how to do it. As if of its own volition, her arm began to wind, and as it wound, it seemed to gain strength, like Popeye's in those old cartoons.

Grant, oblivious, continued to smile down at her, that shiny white-toothed grin of his giving her a perfect target. "What do you say, sweetie?"

"I say you're an ignorant, egotistical lout!"

And then her arm flew. Suddenly, she felt as if she were half Wonder Woman, half Rocky I, II, III, IV and V. Her hand had enough blood running to it to make her feel as if she were holding a ten-pound weight. She had never thrown a punch in her life, but this felt right. And when her fist made contact with Grant's jawbone, the result was a satisfying *smack!* Just like in the movies.

A stunned Grant grunted and then flew backward. From the tables nearby, a surge of cries went up.

"My God, he's out cold!"

Blushing with the glow of triumph, Mitzi reached down to the keg of beer and pumped the top. "I'll wake him up." She grabbed the spigot, pointed it at Grant's face and sprayed.

For womankind's sake.

2

"BROTHER, did I save you from a fate worse than death!"

As Grant stared at his brother, who he'd hunted down and finally discovered in a semicomatose state on the tiny bed in the cabin of his boat, he was less concerned with Ted's bruised jaw and bad temper than with the bigger problem at hand: Marty's wedding was in thirty minutes, and the best man was hungover!

Ted grunted, then slurred, "That Missstsi packs a bigger punch than George Foreman."

Grant squinted at his brother's jaw with new amazement. "Mitzi hit you? What did you say to her?"

"Nothing," Ted protested. "I was just talking to her and then, pow!, she belted me. She's a psycho."

Starting to panic, Grant glanced at his watch. "Look, Marty's called me three times already. The wedding's half an hour from now. Do you think you can be ready?"

As he stared into his brother's bloodshot eyes, he knew it was like Bob Barker asking Miss America if she was ready to do some quantum physics.

Ted groaned, and Grant wasn't sure if the source of the groan was Ted's jaw or his battered male ego. "She's no Mitzi Gaynor, I can tell you that much. Those parents of hers should have named her after something else, like Big Bertha the Amazon."

"Ted, don't you understand that you have to be at that wedding in thirty minutes?"

Ted weaved along with the motion of the boat for a moment, then collapsed back onto the cushions, one arm flung over his eyes. "Can't. Better stay home today."

Grant stood with his hands on his hips, calculating. Apparently, he had no choice but to serve as best man himself. The idea was even more unappealing now that he knew he had a psychotic bridesmaid to contend with.

"Look, Ted, just tell me quick where in your house the tux is. I have to haul butt."

Ted shook his head. "Not in the house."

Oh, no, he thought with dread. Ted didn't forget to pick up the tux from the cleaners!

Then he noticed that his brother wasn't just shaking his head, he was gesturing with his crooked elbow to the floor. Grant looked down and discovered a rumpled bunch of cleaners' plastic heaped on the blue carpet. Oh, great! Now he would have to appear in public looking as if he'd slept in his clothes. The bowery-bum best man!

"You didn't think I'd forget to bring my tux, did you? You must think I'm really irre—" Ted belched loudly "—irresponsible."

Grant didn't waste time ticking off the many descriptors that would accurately portray his brother's personality. He immediately stripped out of his T-shirt and khaki shorts and threw on the wrinkled tuxedo. He looked like a rumpled penguin.

He never should have sent his brother in his place. What had he been thinking? Ted was notorious for fouling things up. Then again, the task had seemed so simple, all he'd had to do was show up to two social functions. Behaving civilly was nothing Ted couldn't handle under normal circumstances.

That Mitzi woman must really be a number. He glanced at the bruise on Ted's cheek and an idea occurred to him. He rifled through the cupboard in the boat's cabin. "Hey, Ted, where's the first-aid kit?"

"Good thinking, bro, you'll need it if you're heading for round two with that woman."

Grant found the box and got out an adhesive bandage, which he slapped on his cheek approximately where Ted's bruise was.

"Maid of honor," Ted grumbled. "They should have called her the maid of horrors!"

As an heir to a department store, Grant had grown up in a habitat where females ruled the jungle. Anyone who had ever done a behavioral study on a seventy-percent-off handbag sale, or witnessed a lady trying to return a dress which had obviously been worn, knew that all women were not shrinking violets. But weddings were supposed to be where they acted civilized—the watering holes on the savanna of female behavior. What kind of woman started fistfights with men at wedding-rehearsal dinners?

He shoved his feet into Ted's shoes, not even bothering to take off his white tube socks. Naturally, his brother, the Philistine, hadn't thought to bring clean black socks.

Ted, scratching his stubbly cheek, squinted up as Grant was headed out the door. "Hey. Would you say that I'm an ignorant, egotistical lout?"

Grant drew back in mock surprise. "You?"

Satisfied, Ted flopped back against the pillows, shaking his head. "See? I told you she was crazy."

Grant sped back up the dock to where his car was parked, jumped in and raced toward the church, praying that he wasn't too late. Praying Kay and Marty would forgive him for whatever Ted had done at that dinner last night. Praying he could stay out of Mitzi's swinging range.

"OH, THANK GOODNESS—here he comes!"

Mitzi had a much different reaction than Kay as she peeked out the vestry doors and saw Grant Whiting sprinting toward the church. Namely, irritation. "Look at the size of that bandage!" she exclaimed. The tiny adhesive strip on Grant's cheek seemed preposterously inconsequential considering the fact that her entire hand was encased mummy-style in an Ace bandage.

Kay, decked out in her wedding attire, was already jittery as they waited for the wedding march to begin; now she looked positively panic-stricken. "Mitzi, you're not going to pick any more fights, are you?"

Would she ever live this incident down? Last night, after Grant had been propped back on his feet, he and everyone else had looked at her as if she were some kind of monster. She kept having to protest that she had never hit anyone in her entire life, not even a swat or a slap. She'd always been a mild-mannered, almost meek person.

Until she'd met Grant Whiting.

"Don't worry, it's not going to be a Rambo wedding," she assured Kay. "I don't think I could pull it off in lime-green taffeta anyway."

Kay laughed. "I knew there had to be a reason other than bridal insanity that made me choose that color."

Soon after the best man arrived, the processional began, and Mitzi brought up the rear of the Day-Glo bridesmaids as they marched down the aisle in front of Kay and her father. The church, under Kay's mother's guiding hand, had been turned into a floral extravaganza the likes of which she'd never seen. Lilies of every color and variety poured out of sconces, appeared accented with white velvet bows at the end of pews and were arranged in magnificent arrangements near the altar. The effect was stunning. The guests, standing at attention in their bright summer best, seemed like living additions to the decorations. At the front of the church stood a completely besotted and extremely nervous Marty.

But Mitzi's gaze was drawn to the rumpled best man standing to Marty's left, staring at her. The intensity in Grant's blue eyes was nearly blinding, it was as if he couldn't take his eyes off her. Probably scoping her out for damage. She forced herself to keep smiling and flicked glances at the congregation.

Inevitably, however, she had to check out Grant again. He was still scrutinizing her, up and down from head to toe, almost as if he couldn't figure out who she was. As if he'd forgotten the rehearsal dinner altogether. She only wished she could. Just as last night, as she'd lain in bed, she'd wished she could shake Grant's words from her mind. All the things he'd said about her wanting to get married....

Well, hadn't she? For years—before she'd decided that love was a delusion—that had been her goal. But when her old boyfriends did finally choose to get married, it was always with women they'd known for such a short time—a breezy model, or the jockey. Never to her, who had been waiting around for months and months. Like the Old Dog Tray.

No wonder those men tired of her. She needed to loosen up.

Which meant—much as it agonized her to admit it—Grant was right. The odious macho heathen had hit the nail precisely on the head. Yet how could that be? How could a lout like Grant Whiting teach her more in a few insults than she'd learned from years of reading personal-growth bestsellers?

She felt like crying. In fact, she did cry.

Of course, she chalked up the tears to the wedding ceremony. Of their own volition, her feet seemed to have parked her in the right position, and now Kay was standing in front of the altar, her hand locked in Marty's. Kay was so in love, so full of hope, so happy. She and Marty radiated sunbeams, which even managed to poke through the black cloud of eternal singlehood that lurked over Mitzi's head.

A single tear trickled from the corner of her eye, and she tried as discreetly as she could to flick it away. Then, just as her hand began to move, she glanced up and saw Grant, who was still examining her in that weird way. And to make matters worse, his eyes focused directly on that tear making its way down her cheek, hopefully not taking her mascara with it. She stiffened; that lout would probably sneer at her wedding tears of happiness for Marty and Kay.

But instead, a smile came to his lips. A big lumpy grin like one he had given Kay yesterday, a fond, kind smile, with just a hint of teasing in it.

Mitzi felt her lips turning up instinctively; then she blinked, dismayed. Remember, this was Grant! The walking irritant.

Across the aisle, as Kay and Marty began their vows, Grant made his own vow—he was going to clobber that brother of his. Mitzi Campion, a.k.a. the psychotic bridesmaid and Big Bertha the Amazon—was nothing like Ted had described her. Come to find out, she was a willowy creature with dark green soulful eyes. He'd never seen eyes that color. Below them, her wide, expressive lips kept drawing his gaze, too. Her skin was creamy and soft-looking, as fine and flawless as porcelain. She didn't look as if she would swat a fly, much less punch Ted. Of course, the bandage on her hand attested to some sort of set-to, but he couldn't imagine that the scuffle had been unprovoked.

Mitzi. She wasn't at all what Grant had expected. She

was intelligent-looking. Maybe it was her eyes, or the way her mouth seemed perpetually turned up at the corners in a knowing smile. She had great lips, wide and full. Very kiss-worthy.

Ever since his divorce—heck, even before—he'd shunned that part of himself that responded to the opposite sex in favor of less complicated worries like work, survival. His libido had been put on the back burner. But now, long-dormant neurons were suddenly firing again. All systems were go. He was intrigued.

So intrigued that his wedding anxieties were forgotten. Likewise, his stress over the store fell away from him as he concentrated on a whole new problem—what he could do to make up for whatever his knuckleheaded brother had done to Mitzi.

Part of it was his fault, of course. "Sic 'em, tiger," he'd told Ted. But he hadn't meant it literally.

Miraculously, Grant managed to fumble through his pockets and produce the bride's ring at the appropriate moment. Then his heart began to start pumping, because he knew, as best man, his next job was to escort the maid of honor down the aisle.

Mitzi didn't seem to be in a hurry for that part. As the strains of Mendelssohn rang out, Mitzi sidled over to where Grant stood, his elbow proffered eagerly. Those green eyes peered out at him with suspicion, as if she half expected a joy button to be hidden in his sleeve, or water to squirt out of his boutonniere. She gingerly rested her hand against his arm and then surprised him by blasting off down the aisle. Grant jogged along beside her. They would have overtaken Kay and Marty, had not the bride and groom been so eager to get outdoors themselves for a second lingering kiss as husband and wife.

In the sunshine of the June late morning, Grant took a deep breath of clean air and exhaled. Then he looked into

Mitzi's eyes. Those green eyes. Why hadn't Ted warned him about those? They were as lethal as any punch she might swing.

Especially now, when they were shooting daggers at him. But he assumed the reason for her hostile glance was that he had a firm grip on her hand that was looped around his elbow.

He grinned at her. "I wasn't expecting to do the hundred-yard dash this morning. I would have brought my sneakers."

"Well, they would have matched your socks." Her lush pink lips turned down in a thin line. "Do you mind?" she asked, tugging at her hand.

Her voice had a low, smoky quality to it that made him melt. Why hadn't Ted warned him about *that?*

When he just stood there grinning like a love-struck dope, she cleared her throat. "I wouldn't argue, normally, but as you can see, it's the only good hand I have left." She held up her bandaged hand as evidence.

Grant's grin disappeared. "I'm sorry," he said, releasing her. "I hope you found someone to take good care of that. If not, I'd be willing to kiss it and make it feel better."

At that moment, Mitzi looked up at Grant Whiting's eyes and felt her stomach flip suddenly as if she were on the world's loopiest roller coaster. Good heavens, he was sexy! And not just in the superficial way she'd noticed yesterday.

How had she missed it?

Of course, it might have had something to do with the fact that he'd been insulting her nonstop. Now she was amazed. While yesterday, when he'd taken her arm to get out of the car, she'd felt only hostility, today she'd experienced the warm buzz of mutual attraction zipping from his arm to hers. And was that actually an apology his lips had uttered?

She had to remind herself that this was the same man she'd met yesterday. The archenemy. "That won't be necessary," she responded in a clipped tone.

They stood in silence for a moment. Grant was smiling. There was something so different about him today. Something she couldn't quite put her finger on.

"Do you always cry at weddings?" he asked.

She felt her chin lift defensively, waiting for the insult he was sure to tag on. Something like, *"Or was it just sour grapes?"* Or perhaps, *"Or was it just because you're always the bridesmaid and never the bride?"*

Finally, with a creeping flush of embarrassment, she realized that the intended put-down wasn't forthcoming. Grant was just waiting for an answer with—if she wasn't mistaken—a kind smile on his face. What was he, the Dr. Jekyll and Mr. Hyde of the wedding party?

"Have I missed my guess, or have you blacked out everything that happened between us last night?" she asked him.

He cocked his head and threw her a look full of anxiety. "Last night? I guess I was...um...not quite all there."

He kept studying her as if she were an amoeba and he were wearing a lab coat, not a tux. Meanwhile, she stared back, admiring the view. The man was in such good shape he could look rugged even in dress clothes. She could almost imagine doing something impetuous with him, like standing on tiptoe and planting a kiss on those expressive lips of his.

She blinked in surprise at her own bizarre thoughts. Maybe that devilish Grant had planted a dangerous seed in her mind when he'd told her she should loosen up. Because, when she'd been thinking about it last night, she'd decided that he'd made a tiny shred of sense. Since she believed love wasn't in the cards for her, what harm would it be to cut loose for once in her life, as long as she was careful? By the time the sun came up this morning, she'd halfway decided she should have that fling, if and when an attractive, available man crossed her path. But she'd never thought for an instant that man would be Grant!

She couldn't believe it now, either. He was toying with her, hiding the crass misogynist until she let down her guard. What had he said yesterday? *Tell her I don't bite.* Then what had happened? She got in the man's truck, his lair, and he'd bitten her.

She needed to get away from him!

Mitzi plastered a big grin on her face and began backing away. "I haven't congratulated Kay yet. Will you excuse me?"

Not giving him time to answer, she turned and fled from Grant and those eyes and that drawl before she completely lost her grip. She plowed into the mob scene of the wedding party and milling guests, hoping to lose Grant in the hubbub. Naturally, Kay would shun anything so formal as a receiving line in favor of this jumble of humanity. The atmosphere was a joyous mess, like a school yard on the last recess of the year.

Kay spotted Mitzi and ran up to her, enveloping her in a hug. "Have you and Grant kissed and made up, or did you chase him away?"

"He offered to kiss me, but I turned him down."

"I wish you'd give him another chance." Kay clearly heard wedding bells in everyone's future.

"And I wish you'd have let me be your official photographer," Mitzi said, attempting to change the subject.

Kay frowned. "If I'd done that, you'd turn my bathroom into a darkroom and spend the whole week in there.

I want you to have fun, get out and see Austin. Call up Grant…''

Mitzi darted an anxious look at her.

Kay laughed. "Okay, okay. I won't push anymore."

Mitzi crossed her arms and glanced over her shoulder. Through the crowd she could see Grant's gaze zeroed in on her. "You might not, but now Grant, for some mysterious reason, has decided to pester me. I don't want to have any more scenes…"

Kay's eyes widened in horror at the very idea. "Don't worry, Mitz, I promise I'll get Marty and some of the other guys to make sure Grant leaves you alone. We don't want you two turning a rented ballroom into Madison Square Garden."

GRANT HAD TO TALK to Mitzi again.

Unfortunately, getting to her during the reception was proving to be no easy task. Every time she had an empty seat beside her, it would magically become occupied before Grant could make his way over. Every time he headed in her direction for a dance, she would suddenly be on the floor with another partner. The woman was completely unapproachable.

At least to him. And yet she kept watching him. At times, when he was talking and laughing with someone else, he would feel those green eyes on him, studying him.

Even his old buddy Brewster Mewborn was having better luck with Mitzi than he was, and Brewster wasn't exactly considered a lady-killer, unless one counted slaying them with boredom. Brewster was thirty, balding, wore brown horn-rimmed glasses and managed to look square and plump at the same time, even in an expensive tailored suit. And you could bet that his clothes were expensive. Brewster was one of the richest bachelors in

Austin and, because of his devotion to one love—bass fishing—he was one of the least sought-after bachelors, as well.

Grant couldn't talk to Mitzi, but he did at last finally get a word with Brewster, who was hanging out by the groom's cake, grazing. "What have you two been talking about?" Grant said by way of greeting. He and Brewster were friends from college, and so he knew Brewster didn't hold with formalities.

Brewster mopped his forehead with a kerchief and then reached for a plate. "Who? Me and Mitz?"

Mitz, already! Grant nodded, and couldn't say why he felt so jealous.

Brewster hacked off a generous slice of cake and sighed in exhaustion. "We haven't been saying much of anything, really. Tell you the truth, Grant, I haven't danced this much since the day last summer I reeled in that nineteen-pounder."

"Did she say anything about me?"

"Who, Mitz?"

"I didn't mean the nineteen-pounder," Grant replied.

Brewster frowned in thought. "No, I don't believe she did." His thick eyebrows rose. "Oh, except to ask if I knew you."

Grant's heart, stiff from years of neglect, made an almost painful leap. "And what did you say?"

"I said yes, of course."

Elaboration was never Brewster's strong suit. "I don't suppose you thought to add what a wonderful character I possess."

Beady brown eyes squinted in thought again before Brewster shook his head. "No." He took a bite of cake and let out what was, for Brewster, an ecstatic sound. "Mmm, try some?"

"No, thanks." How was he going to talk to Mitzi

when there was a small army of men poised between them?

Brewster leaned in and said in a low voice, "If you're that interested in her, you should talk to Kay. The bride seems to be engineering romantic interference."

Grant patted his old friend on the back and smiled broadly. "Thanks, Brewster. As a matter of fact, I haven't had an opportunity to dance with the bride yet."

Moments later, he and Kay took to the floor during "Unforgettable." "I've seen you watching Mitzi," Kay observed right away. "You seem almost smitten with her."

Smitten! Grant chortled at the ridiculous idea. He'd just met her. He'd hardly talked to her. He couldn't be smitten. He was just...

Smitten. "Am I that transparent?"

Kay couldn't have looked more delighted by his confession. "I knew it! I knew it the moment she punched you in the jaw that there was something going on between you two."

"Oh, well..." He shrugged, unable to confess what a fink he'd been, sending Ted in his place. Kay would never forgive him for almost skipping her big day. "I know this sounds strange, but I honestly don't remember what I did to make her so mad."

"Mitzi said you accused her of being a pathetic husband-hunter. Then you told her she was prickly and uptight."

That would do it.

"Honestly, Grant, what got into you? I'd expect better behavior from that nutty brother of yours."

If he ever got his hands on Ted.... "I'd had a lot to drink," he mumbled, knowing it was a feeble excuse.

Kay's expression suddenly turned somber. "I'm sorry, Grant. This has been difficult for you, hasn't it? I should have remembered that you've tried to avoid weddings since—'' Thankfully, she cut her words off. ''Well, I can only tell you that Marty and I really appreciate your being here. In fact, we couldn't imagine getting married without you.''

Grant felt like a worm. Trying to weasel out of the wedding just because of what had happened to him a year ago seemed silly now. And so unlike him. In fact, for someone who claimed not to have a dishonest bone in his body, it was unspeakable.

Kay laughed. ''Anyway, I was just telling Marty, lashing out last night was probably good for you. Proves you aren't the passionless, overly responsible type you pretend to be.''

Ouch! ''Passionless? Me?''

Kay raised her eyebrows. ''You have to admit, giving your wife a ROTH IRA for your first anniversary isn't typical Casanova conduct.''

''Why should a woman want a Casanova for a husband?''

Kay laughed. ''For that matter, why should she want a tall dark handsome hunk who would sweep her away to the mysterious desert sands?''

Grant frowned at the reference to Janice's prince. ''I was very romantic on our second anniversary. We went on vacation.''

''To a buyer's convention in Dubuque, if I recall.''

''Dubuque's a very nice city,'' he countered.

''But romantic?'' Kay asked. ''I don't think so. Especially, if Janice is to be believed, when you spent the whole night hugging your cell phone in bed because you were afraid Ted would screw up in your absence.''

''Well, he does that sometimes.'' More than Kay would ever know! He looked into her eyes, unable to defend himself anymore. "Okay, so I'm not the kind to fall loopy in love."

"Yet," Kay added, smiling.

He had his doubts about that, but rather than argue the point, he returned to the problem at hand. "I've wanted to apologize to Mitzi, but she's been occupied all afternoon."

Kay tilted her head as if to gauge his sincerity. "I'm so glad, Grant. I would love it if you two became friends...or something."

"Me, too." He was especially intrigued by that "or something."

Mitzi was dancing with Marty, and the two of them were laughing as if they were the best of buddies. Kay shot Grant a sideways glance. "This should be fairly easy to remedy. Ready?"

Knowing exactly what she intended without having to be told, Grant fox-trotted them over to the other couple.

"Well, look who it is," Kay exclaimed, stopping in midtrot and surprising Marty and Mitzi. "Hey, Mitz, you don't mind if I cut in on your man, do you?"

Mitzi graciously stepped back, then glanced around frantically for an escape route. Before she could dart away through the dancing couples, Grant grabbed her arm and pulled her to him. He'd expected resistance, but in response to his firm tug, her lithe body slammed right into his chest. A bolt of awareness struck him. He smiled.

"Can't let good music go to waste, can we?"

She reluctantly followed his shuffling steps. He hadn't danced like this since Ballroom 101 in college, but with Mitzi in his arms he suddenly felt like Fred Astaire, Gene Kelly and John Travolta all wrapped up in one slightly wrinkled tuxedo.

As Grant glided her across the floor, Mitzi couldn't help comparing this graceful dance to the previous night's frantic mauling. Last night she'd been so appalled by what he was saying to her, she hadn't been able to concentrate on how well their bodies fit together. Or how fresh and woodsy her partner smelled. Or how tempted she was to lay her head against Grant's shoulder and sigh like a bobby-soxer of old. How had she overlooked these things? Grant was a dreamboat, just as Kay had said.

Apparently, he was also a dreamboat with a split personality. But right this moment, looking into his blue, blue eyes, and feeling her heart do pirouettes in her chest, she couldn't say she really cared. "Unforgettable" was right! The man was drop-dead gorgeous, and the way he held her and twinkled at her with those baby blues made her want to have that fling he'd suggested.

The realization had been nagging at her throughout the entire reception as she'd been dancing with Marty, and that odd fellow named Brewster, and any number of men that Kay had thrown her way as a safeguard against the one man in the room who made her heart pound like a stampede of rhinos. But all the while, her eyes had kept searching out the man she was trying to avoid, and whenever their gazes met and held, it felt as if a wild electric current were racing through her.

Maybe that same electric current was doing wild things to her brain. She couldn't believe she was going to say what she was about to say. And she sure didn't know how to say it.

Ever since she was a teenager, she'd always aimed for long-term relationships. The idea of having a naughty weekend had never really appealed to her. Now, when she'd about made up her mind that a string of short-term dalliances might be more wise a pursuit than one long-term entanglement that was bound to blow up in her face eventually, she barely knew where to start.

Grant wondered why Mitzi was so silent. She'd

seemed a regular chatterbox with every other partner she'd had that evening. "You're a wonderful dancer," he told her.

As conversation starters went, it was lame, not to mention a lie. Actually, Mitzi dragged her feet and wore an expression that said she'd rather be toiling on a chain gang. But there was the undeniable fact that their bodies fit perfectly together. He could have spent the next fifty years just yanking her around this small dance floor.

One of her dark eyebrows arched up and she peered at him. "You sound surprised."

Had they danced together before? "Look, about last night—"

She shook her head frantically, cutting off his apology before he could even spit it out. "I know, you're going to apologize. Kay probably told you to. She has a habit of treating her friends like recalcitrant fifth-graders."

He laughed, but attempted to refute the idea that Kay had put him up to this. "No, I—"

She interrupted again. "We both spoke fairly bluntly last night."

Grant remembered his brother's muttering about being a lout, and decided that Mitzi must have really let him have it. Good.

"But what I've come to realize," Mitzi continued, "is that I got so angry because I didn't want to admit you were correct."

The last thing he wanted was for Mitzi to accept his Neanderthal brother's assessment of her personality. "Listen, Mitzi, you were right to call me a lout."

"Maybe so, but there's something I didn't speak truthfully about."

"What was that?"

She took a deep breath. "You were right. I am too prickly. Too careful."

She didn't feel prickly in his arms right now. She felt soft and delicate and she smelled like some wonderful flower dreamed up by a love-mad Parisian chemist.

"Listen, Mitzi," he began gingerly, wanting to clear the air.

"No, no, I have to say this now or I never will." She looked up at him, her face twisted with emotion. Her eyebrows knit together adorably.

Something about her earnestness made him smile. He chuckled under his breath. "Okay, shoot. What is it you want me to know?"

"Just that, if your offer still stands, I want to take you up on it."

He cocked his head, uncomprehending. "My offer?"

She swallowed. "I want us to have that fling."

3

FIRST HIS BLUE EYES bugged out in surprise. Then, his feet stopped moving. Finally, his hands let go of her and his arms dropped to his sides. He looked like the victim of a zombie curse.

Mitzi's cheeks blazed. They were standing still in the middle of a dance floor teeming with people, with Grant gawking at her as if she were something out of his worst nightmare. So far, her first attempt at a sexy, spur-of-the-moment proposition didn't seem to be going over so well.

"I..." His voice trailed off in a low broken rasp. "You want to have a fling with me?"

She crossed her arms. "No, I meant with the invisible six-foot kangaroo standing right in front of you."

Her sarcasm barely fazed him. "A fling," he repeated.

And just last night he had practically propositioned her! Now he was staring at her as if she'd lost her mind.

"I believe that's the correct word. At least, it was the one you used."

He blinked again. "You mean I...I asked you to...?"

"Yes, you did."

"Oh, but you see, I don't remember."

He remembered her calling him a lout, but not hitting on her? "Well, you did."

A bronzed eyebrow shot up speculatively. "And now you want to...?"

What could she say now that wouldn't make her look like a fool? "Only because you suggested it."

He nodded. "I see. You would have never thought of it on your own?"

"Well, of course I would have thought it," she snapped. When her statement reached her own ears, she felt more of an idiot than ever. "I mean..."

He grinned. "I know what you mean."

Heat prickled across her skin, making her want to take a step backward, or better yet, run, but her lime-green pumps remained firmly rooted to the floor. Awkwardness and embarrassment began to turn into steamy anger. How could he proposition her one night and then the very next day treat her as if she was about as desirable as a wart?

Thankfully, "Unforgettable" ended, the band took a break and people started milling around, making Mitzi and Grant's standoff a tad less obvious.

"Okay, forget it," she said.

He tilted his head, eyes gleaming. "I'm not sure I want to. It's not every day a virtual stranger propositions me."

"That's what I thought...yesterday." She lifted her chin in an attempt to feign nonchalance. "Besides, I assumed our altercation last night made us closer than strangers. I don't just go around walloping every man I meet, I'll have you know."

He chuckled. "I was wondering about that." Then his smile died. "I'm assuming that you don't ask every man you meet to sleep with you, either."

She scowled, looking for exits out of the corner of her eye. Only great effort kept her from skittering out of the room like a cockroach when the lights came on. "No, and considering the fact that my one attempt at seduction has gone over like a fly in a punch bowl, you might just be the only man I ever ask."

"Good," he said, still grinning. "I mean, I didn't mind being asked for a fling one bit."

She pursed her lips skeptically. "Is that why you looked at me like I had galloping leprosy?"

"You just startled me."

"Horrified you, you mean."

He looked alarmed. "Not at all."

"Are you saying that you want to have a fling now?" She almost was salivating in anticipation of his answer. Because if it was yes, she was going to have the greatest pleasure telling him to go climb a rope. There was something so unbearably smug about this man, maybe because she still, in spite of everything, found him too sexy for her own good.

He looked as if he was about to pick his way through a verbal minefield. "I wouldn't dream of it." Her jaw dropped, and he quickly said, "Not that I don't feel honored."

She would feel honored to punch his lights out. Again. Her jaw clenched tight enough to crack walnuts. What was it about this man that made her—an usually peace-loving person—want to resort to physical violence?

Of course, she wouldn't give him the satisfaction of seeing how much he bothered her. Remembering that she was supposed to be a member of a wedding party, not a potential brawler, she glanced around at the tables decorated with graceful white swags and filled with generous trays of finger food. Sanctuary.

"Excuse me," she said in a frosty voice. Then she pivoted on her heels and marched quickly toward a pickle tray.

Grant watched in amazement as she flounced proudly away, her head high. Had what just happened really happened, he wondered, or was it some sort of subconscious wish fulfillment?

It was too amazing. He hadn't even thought she liked him.

And maybe she didn't. After all, the woman had to think that she was propositioning Ted. That in itself was disturbing, although he comforted himself with the fact that when Ted had suggested he and Mitzi sleep together, she'd belted him. It wasn't until she'd met Grant that she'd changed her mind. And no one need ever know that she'd propositioned the wrong—or, in his opinion, right—man. Especially Ted.

A fling… He couldn't remember the last time he'd contemplated such a thing. That short-term love-'em-and-leave-'em approach was always more his brother's style. Grant valued permanence, responsible behavior, marriage.

On the other hand, he'd married Janice, and look where that had gotten him.

A fling…the idea had definite appeal. And Kay had just been telling him that he was passionless. Maybe this was his cue to cast off the bonds of responsibility and go wild.

A ringing sounded from the general direction of his chest, and it was a few moments before he realized the sound wasn't his heart sounding off, but the cell phone inside his jacket. He turned his back to Mitzi and answered.

It was Ted. "Are you still in one piece?"

"Yes, although you're lucky you are!" Grant whispered into the phone. "Do you realize that you behaved like a complete ass last night?"

"Me?" Ted asked, his tone all innocence. "What did *I* do?"

"I can't go into details here, but let's just say you should be glad you got away with a poke in the jaw. Where are you?"

"Work."

Dread pierced Grant's heart. Ted, at work? On a Saturday? Hungover? "For heaven's sake, get out of there!" He spoke with the urgency of someone instructing a friend to exit a burning building. "What are you doing there to begin with?"

"The boat was making me seasick, and I couldn't find my house keys, so I came here for my spare set. But the minute I walked through the door, I was inundated with work."

"Imagine," Grant quipped. "Work at work."

"There are three phone messages here from Horace Moreland. He's apparently been calling every hour on the dot, trying to set up a dinner on Wednesday. What should I say?"

"I'll take care of that," Grant answered. "Every dinner we have with the man is one less opportunity for him to get to Mona and Truman."

"Good thinking," Ted agreed.

"What else?"

There was a moment of silent confusion on the line. "Nothing. That's all."

Only Ted would label three phone messages an inundation. "Okay, Ted, you've done great. Now, listen closely. Slowly and carefully lock up your office and go home," Grant said, talking him through the process. He was uncomfortable with the idea of Ted wandering around Whiting's unchaperoned. In fact, after last night, he was wondering whether his brother didn't need a permanent keeper. "Don't worry about minding the store, that's what we hire a manager for."

Grant hung up the phone, feeling unnerved. He hated being away from work. What if Ted had agreed to dinner with Moreland? That retail tyrant, an ex-marine, could eat his brother alive, business-wise.

And to think he'd been toying with the idea of having a fling, this of all weeks! He wasn't exactly on vacation here. He had pressing business that screamed for his attention. If he didn't devote this week to the store, his entire future could be in jeopardy. And it wasn't only himself he had to keep in line. He had to ensure that Ted was on his toes, and watch out for Mona and Truman. Just thinking about all that responsibility made sweat break out on his forehead.

A fling? He didn't have time for that kind of nonsense when so much was at stake.

As he stuffed his phone back into his tux pocket, Mitzi turned and darted a glance back at him. Once again Grant felt the powerful allure of those green eyes. Even in a fleeting instant, he read their meaning. She was half checking to make certain he wouldn't join her, and half wondering if he would. When she saw that he was watching her, two splotches of bright red colored her cheeks and she whipped her head back around, focusing her gaze intently on a cauliflower floret.

Of course he couldn't have a fling. He didn't have time, and couldn't spare the emotional energy it would cost him, in any case. He was just getting over Janice. He didn't know what kind of person Mitzi was, or if he could trust her....

But his feet didn't seem to understand any of these arguments. They carried him right over to her. "Mind if I join you?" he asked.

Mitzi felt her pulse leap, then frowned. She didn't want him here, she reminded herself. She looked around, hoping to spot Marty or Brewster, anyone who could be a buffer between her and Grant. "Unfortunately, being maid of honor doesn't give me the privilege of chasing you away from the finger food."

He smiled as if he hadn't heard her caustic tone. "You know, Mitzi, it seems to me that we've gotten off on the wrong foot. I'm really not that bad, you know. I don't bite."

She gaped at him.

"What?" he asked innocently.

Was he kidding?

He stepped back. "Did I say something wrong?"

"Do you really have that short a memory?" she asked.

A look of pure anguish crossed his face as he riveted his eyes on the bandage covering her hand. "Oh, my Lord! Don't tell me I bit you!"

She laughed. "No, you told Kay to tell me that you don't bite. Outside the church? Remember?"

Apparently, he didn't. She stared at him, bewildered. He had either been hitting the bottle earlier than she'd suspected, or he had the memory of a gnat. And either way, she trusted him less and less. Not that she trusted him much to begin with.

He lifted his shoulders and smiled. "I know it seems strange…"

"Uh-huh."

"But really," he said, "I'd like to make up for all my blunders. Say, maybe, coffee sometime?"

This had to be a joke.

She eyed him steadily. He wasn't kidding. "And maybe coffee could lead to…?

His expression was a blank. "Maybe a movie?"

"Right," she said skeptically.

"Good," he said, popping a sweet gherkin into his mouth. "I'll give you a call."

She rolled her eyes. Now she knew he was playing games. "I didn't mean 'right' as in 'sure,' I meant 'right' as in *'forget about it.'*"

"Oh." He looked thunderstruck. "May I ask why?"

He edged closer to her, giving her little elbow room as she tried to pile her plate with raw veggies and little crustless sandwiches. She couldn't wait to get back to a table and talk to someone else, anyone else, besides Grant. The man could curl her toes with just a look, and he made her say outrageous things. A fling, for God's sake! What had she been thinking? She felt so flustered, her shaking hand flipped a paper-thin cucumber slice onto the floor. It hit the high-glossed wood with a muted wet splat.

Mitzi sighed. "I don't know if I can put this clearly enough, but I really don't relish the idea of furthering our relationship, which, in case you haven't noticed, hasn't worked out so well so far."

"That's what I'm trying to remedy." His tone was dead earnest.

She tilted her head. "Right."

He raised a cautionary finger. "There you go using that word again. It's very confusing."

She took a breath for patience. Yesterday the man had wanted nothing to do with her, but today he was as clingy as tumble-dry polyester. Of course, five minutes ago she herself had propositioned him. Now she wished she could retract her words and, while she was dabbling in wishful thinking, she also wouldn't have minded if she could have been magically transported back to New York City.

"Look, for all I know, you might be a perfectly charming person," she told him. "Kay certainly thinks you are.

But at this point, I don't want to have coffee with you, or go to a movie with you, and I certainly don't want to sleep with you."

He raised his eyebrows and sent her what had to be the world's sexiest grin. "You're really stuck on that fling thing, aren't you?"

Mitzi felt a shriek building in her throat and just managed to stifle it. *Don't make a scene. You promised Kay.*

She turned, hunting for an empty spot at a table. As luck would have it, there was an open chair near the bride. She let out a frustrated breath, gripped her overloaded plate and headed toward her friend. She had a bone to pick with Kay, who had, after all, thrown her together with Grant Whiting to begin with.

The bone, however, would go forever unpicked. In the next moment, as Mitzi thrust one leg purposefully forward, the ball of her foot, encased in its green satin pump with a new slick sole, hit the thin, nearly translucent slice of cucumber she had so nervously flung to the floor moments before. The foot flew out from under her, and before she knew what was happening, Mitzi was airborne.

She felt Grant's hand grab her arm firmly, but the gesture was too late to pull her back. Worse, as Grant stepped toward her, he stepped in the residue of oil and spices in which that tasty, pesky cucumber slice had been marinated, and skated after her, wobbling and thrusting his hand out in huge crazy loops to regain his equilibrium.

But it was too late for him, too. Any efforts they made to right themselves were doomed. In fact, *doom* might be a good word to sum up her first twenty-four hours in Austin, Mitzi thought the split second before she and Grant hit the floor in a spectacular crash of well-dressed bodies, broken china and finger food.

"I TOLD YOU she was bad news," Ted lectured.

Grant limped to the other side of the pool table in order to get a better shot. His leg was still stiff from his fall that afternoon. "But you didn't tell me she was gorgeous." He sent Ted's four ball scudding into the corner pocket.

Ted frowned. He had only one ball left, and it was smack in the middle of the table. The eight ball was miles away. He was hosed. Losing didn't make him feel any more kindly toward that Mitzi person. "You call her gorgeous?" he asked in disbelief. "That beast?"

Grant rolled his eyes. Twins they were, but thank heavens their taste in women wasn't identical. To put it kindly, Ted didn't exactly go for the brainy type. To Ted, Susan B. Anthony was right up there with the infamous villains of history.

"She's not a beast, she's a babe, to coin one of your expressions." Grant remembered flowing dark hair, a body to die for and those eyes, and felt a sigh building. It had been a long time since a woman had affected him that way. Mitzi talked so brash and cynical, but her eyes seemed like windows to a sweet, deep soul. And her body...she moved with an intriguing combination of lilting grace and girlish awkwardness that made her seem blithely unaware of her appeal. Boys had probably teased her about her height. But all Grant could think about was how it might feel to be entwined in those arms and legs, looking into those soulful green eyes...

"Earth to Grant!" Ted barked.

Grant shook his head, shook away thoughts of Mitzi. For a moment, at least.

"Good grief! This woman hasn't gotten under your skin, has she?" Ted looked aghast.

Grant wasn't pleased himself. "No," he said, scratching his nose subtly to make sure it wasn't growing. "For heaven's sake, I've only seen her once."

"Once is too much with her."

"She just caught me off guard, is all."

His brother laughed. "Tripped you up, you might say."

Grant grimaced and happily sank Ted's last ball. "You didn't help things," he said. "I thought I could trust you with a simple task of behaving normally at a wedding rehearsal."

"It put an end to the matchmaking, didn't it?"

"Of course! No one wants to be matched with a man who would make Ivan the Terrible seem like a knight-errant."

Ted looked almost proud. "So there. Mission accomplished."

"Did you have to torment the poor woman?"

Ted's breath caught in defense. "Poor woman?" he squeaked, gesturing with his cue to the bruise on his jaw. "Look at this! Look at you," he ranted, pointing to Grant's leg. "We're the victims here."

Though Grant had assured Ted that his own accident hadn't been caused by Mitzi but rather by a marinated cucumber slice, his brother refused to believe him. "You think all women are Eve in disguise."

Ted's eyebrows knit together. "Eve who?"

Grant rolled his eyes. "Eve from Adam and Eve, you dumb cluck."

His brother puffed up in mock offense. "Hey, don't ride me. That's a long book. I never got that far into it."

The trouble was, a year ago, when his marriage had blown up in his face like a trick cigar, Grant wondered whether Ted wasn't right to remain ever-vigilant. Janice had deceived him so thoroughly, he wasn't sure that all women weren't like her. Funny how the minute he'd looked into Mitzi's eyes, his brother's training had flown out the window.

The long-suppressed sigh finally issued from his lips.

"Grant, snap out of it," Ted said, putting away their cues. "It's over. Poor Mitzi will be fine, and at the end of the week she'll fly back to where she belongs and the whole incident will be forgotten."

"It's not the incident I'm worried about."

It was Mitzi. She was going to be at Kay's all alone for a week, in a strange city. Would she call him if she was in trouble? They hadn't parted on the best of terms. Not that he hadn't tried to smooth things over, but after she'd been extracted from the buffet debris, she didn't look eager for his company.

"I forgot to tell her to ask me if she needed anything," he said aloud, taking up the Good Samaritan pose with gusto.

Ted groaned. "You're not going to call her, are you?"

Grant thought about it, then shook his head. She'd probably slam the phone back down the minute she heard his voice.

"Put it behind you," Ted counseled. "You've got enough on your plate with the buyout bid, remember?" He looked worried, as if he didn't feel comfortable having his brother distracted from business, which was understandable. That might mean he would actually have to do some work.

Grant himself was startled that he had forgotten about the store for even a day. Then again, maybe that's why he'd been so taken with Mitzi. He had been so obsessed with staving off Moreland, naturally his brain wanted a rest. She was just a diversion from his troubles. She was just…

Adorable.

He glanced unseeingly at his watch. It could be eight o'clock or one in the morning for all he knew. "I'd better head home," he said quickly. "It's been a long day, what with the wedding and reception and everything."

Surprisingly, Ted followed him out to the parking lot. Usually he would linger at Tom's, one of his favorite haunts, to nurse a beer. "Are you sure you're okay?" he asked, looking genuinely concerned.

Grant stopped at his car. "Sure. Fine." As if to reassure him, he forced a smile and said, "I'll see you at work tomorrow."

Ted appeared more alarmed than ever. "Tomorrow's Sunday. Don't you remember? You were going to have brunch with Mona and Truman tomorrow. To talk to them about the buyout."

"Of course, of course," Grant said. "I'll probably go into work tomorrow, too."

Maybe he should go there right now. Get his thoughts together.

But when he pulled his car out of the parking lot, he knew he wasn't headed for the store, or even home. Without making a conscious decision to, he was driving to Kay's house, where Mitzi was staying. Just to check up on her, he told himself.

He felt strange, out of control. Maybe this was what spontaneity felt like.

A short while later, Grant reached Kay's street. Hers was a corner house, nestled on a dark, quiet street. Grant parked one house down and strolled up the walkway, wondering what the hell he was doing.

But then he came upon the house, so thoroughly and brightly lit that it practically glowed. And when he looked inside the large picture window and saw her, every self-protective reflex he'd developed since Janice left him vanished.

Watching Mitzi, he had to take a deep breath, so deep he nearly became dizzy from the thick night air. She was wearing a slouchy T-shirt and jeans, but somehow he'd never appreciated just what a pair of faded dungarees hugging just the right derriere could do to a man. Her legs looked even longer and more amazing than they had appeared in his imagination. A clip held her hair back loosely, but a strand or two spilled out of its confines, making his fingers fairly twitch to reach across the yard, through the windowpane and across Kay's living room to put them to rights again.

She glanced down and began speaking to the floor. Grant began to consider how charming a woman talking to herself could be, when out of the corner of his consciousness he heard a dog barking. Chester, Kay's dachshund, was who Mitzi was talking to.

Grant smiled. As he did, Mitzi looked up. Instinctively, he ducked toward an oleander bush. He didn't want her to think he was standing outside the window gawking at her. He watched as she scurried briskly around the living room, lowering the blinds. Good thing, he thought, feeling protectiveness swell in him. She shouldn't be alone in a brightly lit house at night with all the windows exposed. Any kind of crackpot could come by.

Grant moved furtively toward the front door, which had a clear glass pane above the doorknob. Chester was going nuts, and Mitzi crossed the house several times. Were they playing? At one point, Grant saw her talking on the telephone and panicked.

He hadn't heard the phone ring. Who would Mitzi be calling?

Kay had said Mitzi didn't know anybody in town, so

he naturally assumed she would be sitting around the house, lonely. But maybe she did know someone here, or was talking to someone she'd met at the wedding. After the buffet incident, he had seen Mitzi talking at surprising length to Brewster Mewborn. Laughing with him, in fact. Maybe she had even been flirting with him.

Something like jealousy flared in him. Brewster Mewborn? No way! And yet, the voice of Ted whispered in his ear, women always liked men with money. The Mewborns hemorrhaged money.

He stepped back and let out a muttered oath. How horrible! First his wife running off with a Saudi oil princeling, and now Mitzi. And Brewster.

At the same time a deep sigh escaped his lips, a thick, beefy hand clamped down on his shoulder.

"Okay, bud, stand back!"

Grant whirled, ready to do battle with anyone who dared to prowl outside Mitzi's house. His eyes squinted tightly against the blinding beam of a flashlight in his face.

"Hold it right there!" the same drawling voice barked. "Hands up!"

Finally able to make out the insignia above the man's left breast pocket, Grant obeyed. The police! Another officer he hadn't seen lunged toward him for a frisk.

Grant scowled. "What's the meaning of this?"

The officer with the flashlight replied. "We had a report of a Peeping Tom."

They thought he was a prowler? Grant gaped at the man. "You can't think I—" He faltered for words that would clear him of suspicion. "I know the woman who lives here! I'm not a peeper!"

The policeman leveled a skeptical gaze at him. "Then what were you doing out here in the bushes?"

"I was just staring at Mitzi through the windows," he explained as rationally as he could.

From the expression on the officer's face, he knew immediately it had been the wrong thing to say.

4

"WE FOUND this man in your oleander, ma'am. Do you recognize him?" When the thickset cop stepped aside, Grant Whiting appeared in the puddle of yellow porch light, managing to look both sheepish and defiant at the same time.

"The bad-news best man!" Mitzi exclaimed in surprise. After their food fiasco of that afternoon, she hadn't expect to see him again. "What are you trying to do, scare me to death?"

She'd been scared enough already. Kay's house was so much bigger than what she was used to, and there were all those windows. And no bars on them, like the ones on her apartment in New York. Just flimsy little locks. She'd thought Chester would make her feel safe and calm, but instead, all evening his droopy ears had pricked up at the slightest sound, and his liquid brown eyes kept a constant fearful watch on all those windows. More times than she could count, those eyes had sent her scurrying to a window to hunt for the ax-wielding madman she was certain lurked outside.

Now Chester, the traitor, ran over to her supposed intruder, whimpering and wagging his tail happily.

Grant lifted his hands innocently, feeling completely ridiculous. This was not the impression he'd hoped to make. "I just came by to see how you were doing. How's your...?" His blue eyes looked furtively at her shapely backside, which had taken the brunt of her fall that afternoon at the wedding.

"Hey, watch it, buddy!" The police, who still thought he was a sicko voyeur, were not pleased by his eyeing her butt. "Would you like to file a complaint, ma'am?"

Mitzi was sorely tempted to treat Mr. Whiting to a night in the slammer, but on the other hand, once he was gone, she would be alone again. And Chester would no doubt start staring again out all those windows. Her gaze flicked to Grant's. He looked so apologetic. More important, with his height and broad shoulders, he appeared so very capable of chasing away predators. And as always, he was sexy as hell, even though he'd traded in his tux for a pair of khakis and a polo shirt just tight enough to accent every pec and ab ripple. The man had a body that would make a nun drool.

Not that that influenced her one teeny bit.

She tried to do her best to appear gracious, not desperate. "I'm sure there won't be any more trouble, Officer." Although Grant Whiting had his own brand of danger, especially around buffet tables, she was fairly certain that he wasn't an ax murderer.

Grant slipped past her into the safety of the house, and gave the policemen a fluttery-fingered goodbye wave. "Nice talking to you gentlemen," he said. "Thanks for stopping by."

Mitzi thanked the cops again—more sincerely than Grant—and closed the door. Chester's nails clicked across the hardwood floors as Grant, limping ever so slightly, led the way to the kitchen.

"Make yourself at home," Mitzi joked to his back as she trailed after them.

"Thanks," he said. "I hope Kay has something to drink in the house. Getting frisked has left me parched."

He gazed into the refrigerator with a familiarity that made her edgy, as if he was ready to settle in for a while. "What brings you here, Grant? Or maybe I should ask you if you've come as friend or foe."

"Friend, definitely."

Grant wondered if now would be the appropriate time to confess to Mitzi that she had been dealing with two very different men who'd had the misfortune to share the same egg. He grabbed a cola, weighing the consequences of coming clean. What if he explained the truth to Mitzi and then she told Kay that he had tried to skip out of the wedding? He didn't want to hurt Kay.

"Actually, I came by to apologize for what happened at the rehearsal dinner...and for this afternoon, too," he explained, putting off a complete confession. "And now I've got peeking in your doorway to add to the list."

She crossed her arms. "So why were you peeking?"

Good question. "I was just checking to see if you were home." Which was as least a fraction of the truth. "It seems that whenever I'm around you, something odd happens."

Mitzi raised an eyebrow and leaned against the counter. "Are you sure it's just around me?"

He took a swig of soda. "Positive. Normally, *I'm* the steady sane one."

"As opposed to...?"

"Everyone else in my family," he replied without hesitation.

"Kay told me you have a brother."

Heat drained out of his face. Could Kay have also told her that they were twins? If so, it might not be difficult for her to put two and two together. "What else did she tell you?"

From his reaction, Mitzi would have guessed that this

brother of Grant's was a lunatic-asylum escapee. "Nothing. Just that you had a brother." She grinned. "And that he's not as nice as you are."

He tilted his head jauntily. "Do I wear my halo well?"

Mitzi chuckled at his attempt at a saintly expression. It was impossible for anyone as sexy as Grant to look goody-goody wholesome. Or maybe it wasn't only his looks, but the memory of their first meeting, when he'd behaved like such a creep, that kept her from buying the altar-boy pose. Which reminded her, given his changeable nature, she couldn't really trust him any further than she could shot-put a Buick.

"Listen," Grant said. "It's a beautiful night. Would you like to go for a stroll? We could exercise our bruises, and let Chester have a walk as well."

Chester, who had a big backyard to play in, nevertheless was overjoyed to hear his name linked so closely with the word *walk*. He bounded out of the room in an ecstatic streak of fur in his hurry to get to the coatrack where his leash was dangling. He planted himself by the door, his fat rump wiggling impatiently.

Mitzi laughed. "Do I have a choice?"

A half hour later, the three of them meandered down a well-lit side street full of houses not unlike Kay's. "This neighborhood's really very safe," Grant informed her. "In fact, I live not far from here."

As if the presence of Austin's Peeping Tom should be reassuring. "Isn't this neighborhood rather downscale for a tycoon like yourself?"

She'd meant the question as a joke, but Grant answered her in dead earnest. "I used to have a bigger place, a lot bigger after all the work I put into it." His mouth turned down. "I couldn't stay there after the divorce."

"Too many memories?"

"Just the opposite. That was the house Janice and I moved into after we were married. I envisioned us being in it for decades, raising a family, having barbecues in a backyard packed with swing sets and trampolines—all that family stuff—with me starring in the role of the perfect dad. I had the role of superdad all figured out. Seems I forgot that I needed to be superhusband first.

"After Janice bailed on me, I was left shambling around that big house, haunted by the future that could have been." He half laughed, half sighed. "So I guess you could say it was the memories that didn't happen there that drove me away."

All Grant's talk about hopes that didn't pan out tugged right at her most sensitive heartstring. How well she understood that feeling. And his wistful dreams of frolicking with children in a big backyard tempted her to leap into his arms right then and there and offer him an egg. How many times had she dreamed of finding a man who wanted to father kids? A man who even gave a second's thought to backyard trampolines and barbecues had to be as rare as a billionaire bachelor. What woman in her right mind would have let this one go?

Of course, she remembered that until thirty minutes ago she'd thought he was an egotistical oaf and would have been almost willing to pay him to leave her alone. Then again, his recent heartbreak over the end of his marriage might have something to do with his slightly erratic behavior. Maybe she'd judged him too quickly, and too harshly. Maybe to get to know Grant, a woman had to do more than scratch the surface.

She looked at his handsome six-foot-plus build as he ambled along behind Chester. But what an enticing surface he had to scratch!

His smile made her heart flip-flop. "So now that I'm

all whined out, how about you? Do you have a boyfriend waiting in the wings?"

That was a laugh. "My last swain rang down the curtain and hoofed it out of the theater quite some time ago. I guess you had me pegged right that first night."

His smile remained plastered on his lips, but his eyes fogged with confusion. "I did?"

"You said that all my efforts at long-term romance are destined to fail. I keep falling in with these workaholic types—you know, men who can't make it through dinner without checking their messages. I, on the other hand, become consumed with engineering the relationships. Then, after all my hard work, they realize marriage is on the horizon and bolt, sometimes with women that had never registered on my radar as rivals."

He nodded his head in recognition. "The unseen enemy."

Was he thinking of his wife's Middle East oil sheikh? Mitzi tried to divert him from unhappy memories by making light of her own amorous misfortunes. "Of course, I shouldn't be surprised when things turn out badly. I've never had a trouble-free relationship with the opposite sex. The first time I was ever kissed was a genuine calamity. Poor Eddie Lumas..."

He looked at her curiously. "What happened to him?"

"Hospitalized," she said flatly. "Broken tailbone."

"What?"

"The porch swing we were kissing on collapsed," she explained. "Actually, for once in my life I was lucky. I walked away with only a neck brace and a chipped tooth."

"That's terrible, like the stories you always hear about kids who get their braces tangled together."

Her hand shot up in the air like a star pupil with the

correct answer. "That happened to me! With Robbie Cooper that time. Unfortunately, when that particular calamity struck, it was the summer my parents sent me away on Outward Bound."

"Good grief!" Grant looked horrified. "Didn't your folks realize you were accident-prone?"

"Maybe they hoped a month roughing it in the wilderness would be a kind of cure. They learned their lesson, though, when Robbie and I had to be airlifted out of the Canadian Rockies and rushed to the nearest orthodontist."

"How awful."

She shrugged. "None of that was as bad as what's happened recently, psyche-wise. Three near misses in three years. But at least I know what kind of man to avoid. The dishonest workaholic type. Or maybe I shouldn't avoid them so much as I should heed your advice and not take these things so seriously."

"Oh, well…you shouldn't listen to me when it comes to romantic advice."

Yesterday, she would have thought that no truer words had ever been spoken. Today, she wasn't so sure. "In my book, any man who dreams about kids and swing sets must have some important thoughts about romance."

As they waited for Chester to pay his respects to a fire hydrant, their gazes met and held. In the moonlight, Grant was even more devastating than ever. But for the first time, she wasn't puzzled by her attraction to him, and she certainly wasn't fighting it. In fact, in her head she was already running across that proverbial field of daisies with arms spread wide.

"Are you doing anything tomorrow?" he asked her suddenly, his voice a sexy, husky rasp in the rich night air.

She snapped out of her Grant-induced trance. "Why?"

He looked surprised. "I...thought we could go out."

"You mean on a date?"

He tilted his head and answered cautiously, "Something like that." Then, as he saw the dismay register on her face, he added quickly, "But I wouldn't call it a date. No, not really."

She breathed a sigh of relief. "I hate to sound defensive, but with my romantic history, even the slightest step toward intimacy is like taking a leap into the arms of doom."

He laughed. "I could tell you were the cautious type when you asked me to have a fling with you."

"That was rash," she said. "And really very uncharacteristic. Actually, I think we should start small."

Grant nodded. Small was fine. Better than all-out fling. Okay, maybe not better. But fine.

"Tomorrow's Sunday," she said. "How about brunch?"

Brunch.

Grant froze in shock and indecision. Brunch! The sinister word jolted him rudely out of Mitzi's magical spell and tossed him back down to planet Earth. He'd already promised Sunday brunch to Mona and Uncle Truman, to try to dissuade them from backing the takeover.

"Did I say something wrong?" Mitzi asked.

Her eyebrows were knit together and her green eyes glittered in concern. The gentle night breeze teased her long, wavy hair. Her funny face was so beautiful in the moonlight that he didn't even notice that her eyes were too far apart, or that her nose had a comical lump in the middle of it, or that an undignified smattering of freckles graced her pale, otherwise flawless cheeks. She was a picture of near perfection, and somehow, against all odds, he had managed to make her forgive him for his blunders of the past two days.

So how could he possibly explain, when she'd just told him that she hated workaholic men, that he already had a business appointment on a Sunday? He might try to pass it off as a family thing, but the fact that he was so embroiled in business even with his family made that seem almost more pathetic. He couldn't cancel brunch with Truman and Mona. But he couldn't stand to turn down Mitzi.

"Brunch sounds great," he lied.

She looked at him doubtfully. "Are you sure you don't already have plans?"

He chortled. "Of course not. What time should I pick you up?"

"How about ten?"

Ten! Good grief, he was supposed to be at Mona's at ten. But then, maybe he could push that up to nine-thirty…

"Ten it is," he said, smiling.

And then, as if he didn't have a care in the world, as if he hadn't just promised to do something that was physically impossible and was bound to bring troubles raining down on him like cats and dogs, he allowed himself to be tugged down the sidewalk by Chester with a light-hearted skip.

"WITHOUT WHITING'S we might as well change our names to Smith or Jones. That store is our lifeblood!"

There! Ted thought proudly. That sounded exactly like something tedious and schoolmarmish Grant might say. Of course, the reason was that Grant himself had written the phrase "store is our lifeblood" across Ted's palm.

But when he looked up, he discovered that all his eloquence in defense of keeping Whiting's in the family had succeeded only in putting Uncle Truman to sleep; and Mona, bored beyond tears, was now on her fifteenth extra-long, extra-nicotine menthol cigarette.

"Grant dear," she explained in her throaty drawl, "you know I never think about business, especially when it comes to that store."

Truman jolted awake. "Poor?" he bellowed. His hearing-aid batteries were running low on juice again. "Of course we're not poor! But no one's rich enough that they should turn their nose up at a gold mine, young man."

Ted shook his head. "But don't you think—"

Truman wagged a thin, knobby finger in his face. "You'd feel differently if you'd suffered through the Great Depression, mark my words!"

Ted rolled his eyes. Truman hadn't exactly suffered through the depression. "It was the store that kept this family well-off during hard times," he reminded his uncle.

Truman frowned. "'Course it was!" he barked. "Don't go lecturing me, you whippersnapper."

Mona exhaled a long plume of minty smoke and shrugged her thin shoulders. "If the second depression hits tomorrow, wouldn't it be just as good to have the security of all that delicious Moreland money as a bunch of troublesome old stores?"

Ted gaped at her, for the first time understanding the frustration Grant must feel trying to save the store. But what he couldn't understand was Grant's abandoning his favorite cause at such a critical juncture, and for what? That bridesmaid!

Ted would never understand that at all. Hadn't Grant's experience with Janice taught him anything? Love must be a terrible thing, to make someone as sensible as Grant behave so irrationally. Not that Grant had mentioned love in relation to that Mitzi character. God forbid! But for him to send Ted in his place to a business discussion...

Well. The man had to be pretty desperate.

Mona's eyebrows, plucked until they were perfect thin black arches above her eyes, crooked even more. "Forgive me, Grant, I know this means a lot to you, but having spent an unhealthy amount of my life asking men if they want one olive or two in their martinis, I always find it difficult to pass up cash."

Ted was surprised. Mona rarely mentioned her history as a cocktail waitress, the position she had held when his father—a two-olive man if there ever was one—had met her. Having never had to wait tables himself, or do anything more arduous than spend a summer as a shoe clerk at Whiting's, he could hardly argue with her logic. He sighed.

"Aren't you going to talk some more?" Mona asked. "You usually don't give up so easily."

Ted thought, but failed to find any more to say. His gaze focused on the heap of melon rinds on his plate. How could he think on a practically empty stomach? Mona had been on a fruit-and-mineral-water diet for ten years. Maybe starving was a leftover habit from her minimum-wage days, too. "How 'bout a bagel?" he asked. "And maybe an omelette, if it's not too much trouble. I'm starved."

Mona laughed. "You sound just like that brother of yours! That man wolfs down enough chow to feed a whole cruise ship."

Again Truman shot out of his semislumber with an undignified snort. "Blue chips!" he cried. "What about blue chips?"

Mona flicked the elderly gentleman an annoyed glance.

Although it was hard to stay annoyed at Truman for long. First, he was the oldest of the Whitings, the head of the old-money Austin clan, and dressed like a Kentucky colonel in elegantly tailored white suits in summer that hung loose over his old thin frame. Though a dyed-in-the-wool curmudgeon and a spendthrift, his irrepressible style endeared him to everyone, especially someone so style- and name-conscious as Mona.

"Not blue chips," Mona corrected him, "cruise ship."

Gray eyebrows rose in wonder. "Is Grant running off on a cruise, at this important juncture in the family's travails?"

Ted grinned. Uncle Truman was the one person in the world who actually thought Grant was the irresponsible one.

Mona sighed in exasperation. "Not Grant—Ted. I was talking about how much Ted eats."

Truman shook his head. "'Course he eats a lot! He's a sportsman, best damn football player I ever saw. You weren't there, Mona, during the state championships back in eighty-four."

To Ted's dismay, Mona waved her hand to stop him. Sports bored her. "Grant, do you think Ted would take out Joy Moreland? I promised Horace Moreland that I would try to show his daughter a good time while she was here."

Ted nearly fainted, and it certainly wasn't just from hunger. She wanted him to squire around that Moreland woman? "What?"

"Well, you said you wouldn't do it."

"Oh, I did, did I?" That stinker Grant—he'd probably planned to foist this Moreland chick off on him as well.

Truman brayed in dismay. "Ted can't be wasted squiring some girl! He's a sportsman! He needs to entertain the male Morelands, on the golf course...maybe take them out on that boat of his. Fine craft!"

Ted grinned, feeling a little crafty himself. "You're absolutely right, Uncle Truman. We shouldn't squander Ted's talents. If anything, we should be encouraging my dear brother to spend less time at the office and more time on the golf greens."

Truman grunted his agreement. "Damn straight."

He was loving this! Ted proceeded to do an imitation of one of Grant's patient, long-suffering sighs. "All right. I suppose I'll take Joy out on the town."

Mona beamed with pleasure. "Will you? Oh, you darling!" She leaned forward, puckered her bow lips and sent him a string of little air kissies. "I know you'll just love Joy. She's the most adorable creature."

"Is she? Good." Maybe the adorable creature would help get Grant's mind off that frightful woman he seemed to be stuck on now. Mitzi, for God's sake.

Ted winked at Mona. "Now that I'm being so cooperative and all, do you think you could persuade your cook to rustle up an omelette?"

Giggling, Mona tossed back her perfectly coiffed head. "Oh, Grant, you kidder. You're getting to be just like Ted!"

"CHURCH LET OUT LATE?" Mitzi quipped when Grant showed up at her door at ten-thirty.

Grant was lucky to get here that early. Wresting Ted out of bed and prepping him for brunch with Mona and Uncle Truman was a feat of Herculean magnitude. It had taken an abundance of begging and wheedling, with a promise of an extra week's paid vacation finally doing the trick. Grant had been so proud of his accomplishment that he hadn't thought to dream up an excuse for his tardiness.

At the moment, Mitzi's suggestion sounded as good as the truth. "Uh, yes, as a matter of fact."

Mitzi blinked in surprise. And appreciation. Grant's Sunday best, apparently, was a pair of well-worn jeans that hugged every contour of his mouthwatering bod. "I guess the dress code's changed since the last time I darkened the doors of Sunday school."

He glanced down at his jeans. "Oh, I always wear casual clothes to church, because nobody sees me."

She narrowed her eyes at him. "No one sees you?"

He nodded, thinking frantically. "Yes, because I'm...in the choir."

That really surprised her. And impressed her, for some odd reason. "I didn't know you could sing."

"Me?" he asked. "I'm a regular Caruso!" To demonstrate, he hummed a few shaky bars of a song.

One of her dark eyebrows arched. "Hmm, Caruso does Blues Traveler," she said. "What kind of church is this?"

"We're a progressive denomination."

Desperate, too, apparently. The Met wouldn't be knocking down Grant's door anytime soon. "You should have told me you had somewhere to go this morning. We could have set the time back."

"I was afraid you wouldn't understand."

"Ridiculous!" How strange, and cute, that he should be nervous about what she would think of him. Of course, what she thought was that he had to be the sexiest choirboy in America, but she left that opinion unspoken as they got into his car and sped to a sprawling restaurant on a hill overlooking Lake Austin.

Because the restaurant was already filling up, they

snagged an inside table and wasted no time ordering coffee and enough food to feed North Dakota for a day. Mitzi had to keep reminding herself not to ogle Grant; just watching his tanned, muscled forearm passing their menus back to the waitress was enough to make her schoolgirl-giddy.

He leaned back in his chair and made a production of stretching out his long, jean-clad legs. "I sure do love to relax. Nothing like a long, leisurely Sunday morning."

"Really." She tilted a glance at him. "I heard you practically live at the store."

"Whoever told you that obviously doesn't know me very well."

"It was Marty." His oldest friend.

His placid expression turned pained. "Well, sure I work—during the week. Nine to five. I do have a work ethic, but I would never let that bleed into my free time. A man has to set his priorities, after all."

His words were more moving than Beethoven's *Seventh*. She leaned forward and told him confidentially, "Would you believe that I went out with a guy once who was so wrapped up in his work that he sent his best friend to fill in during our Valentine's date so he could stay at the office?"

Grant drew back, appalled.

"I guess he thought I wouldn't notice."

"How terrible!"

"Well, it's a story with a happy ending," Mitzi assured him. "I broke up with the boyfriend, and the best friend ended up getting married to the waitress at the restaurant where we had the Valentine's dinner."

As Grant laughed, it occurred to Mitzi that she wasn't the best huckster for her own love life. She did tend to dwell on the disasters. She decided she needed to do a better sell, as they said in her business, or change the subject.

She changed the subject. "Did Kay tell you I was in advertising?"

Grant's eyebrows squished together adorably. "She told me you were a photographer."

"That's what I'd really like to be," she said. "But in this lifetime I have to earn a buck. And I assume you do, too." She reached into her purse and pulled out the paper she'd been reading while waiting for him, and held up a page containing an ad for Whiting's. "If so, this ad won't help you much."

As the waitress served their food, Grant studied the black-and-white layout, which mostly outlined sale items. "Bad?"

"Honestly? If I put this paper by the back door, I don't think Chester would pee on it."

He gave it a closer squint and nodded. "It is kind of flat. I don't know why I didn't see it before." Taken aback, he looked up at her. "I thought you didn't like to talk business."

"I dislike shoddy workmanship more. And of course, if the choice is between business or rambling on about my nonexistent love life, I'd pick business any day."

"Really?" His voice was a husky drawl. "I'd take your love life."

She gazed into those blue eyes of his and felt her heart flutter again, but not so rustily this time. There was something definitely enticing about the way his eyes were twinkling at her. But just when she thought she'd swoon into her French toast, Grant appeared to be distracted by something outside. His pallor took on the color of old hard cheese.

Mitzi, who wasn't facing the windows, looked at him

in concern. "Is something wrong?" she asked, about to whip around to see for herself.

"No!" Grant yelled, nearly upsetting his juice glass in his effort to distract her from turning.

Of all the people to show up at this particular restaurant, Grant thought wildly. Ted! What was he doing here? He was supposed to be charming Mona and Uncle Truman.

He turned back to Mitzi, stiffly, and tried to smile. "I, uh, just saw someone I recognized, that's all. No big deal."

Mitzi smiled back. He wasn't sure whether it was her beaming face or the idea of his brother being mere yards away that made his heart keep thumping like a rodent's. "Would you like to say hello?"

"No," he answered quickly. "I'd like to hear more about advertising." He asked her a few questions about her work, but out of the corner of his eye he kept seeing Ted.

Once he could even hear Ted laughing, which was the last straw. "Mitzi, would you mind if I ran and made a quick phone call?"

She gave him a look of mock worry, as if she'd somehow offended him. "It's me, right? I've criticized your advertising and now you've had it up to here with me. In fact, you probably wish you'd never heard the word *bridesmaid*."

Grant chuckled. "Really, I just need to make a quick one. To my...stepmother. It's her birthday."

Mitzi sighed and sent him a warm gooey smile that stabbed him with guilt. "How sweet. Go right ahead."

Silently vowing to actually be more sweet in the future, Grant got up and dashed past the phones, ducked through the kitchen and exited through the employees' entrance.

Then he doubled back around the side of the restaurant and picked his way through the dining hordes and planted himself behind a potted ficus next to where his brother was sitting with a female friend. A very beautiful female friend.

"What are you doing here, Ted?" he asked with a huff.

Confused, Ted straightened and pivoted in all directions in his chair, trying to pin the source of the disembodied voice.

His companion, a very tall, very buxom blonde who looked vaguely familiar, nudged him. "Teddy, I think that tree is talking to you."

Ted finally spotted Grant. "Grant! What are you doing?"

"That's what I asked you! You're supposed to be at Mona's!"

Ted shrugged sheepishly. "You know Mona, she played right into my rich-boy guilt. The minute I mentioned the sale, she started talking about having been a poor waitress. Maybe I should have done like you and worked through college so I could stand up to people like that."

"Couldn't you have stayed and tried to talk to her some more?"

"I would have, but I was running out of gas. That woman eats like a bird. Cantaloupe wedges! You can't begrudge me a few crumbs of food after all I've done for you."

After all he'd done? What had he done? "All I asked was one little favor, and you couldn't even stay put for thirty minutes."

"Hey," Ted said in his own defense, "I charmed them

in record time. In fact, I charmed them more as you than you ever did as you. And then I got hungry."

"But did you have to come here?"

"What's the big deal?"

"Mitzi's inside."

"Oh, no!" Suddenly alert, Ted shuddered as he glanced through the glass window.

"Who's Mitzi?" the blonde asked. Now that she was used to it, she didn't seem to think it at all strange that her breakfast date was talking to a plant.

"I don't want her to see you," Grant said.

"Well, I don't want to see her either, so we're even," Ted said, buttering a piece of toast.

Grant searched for a way to coax his brother out of the restaurant. What if Mitzi looked up from her paper and saw Ted out here? "I can't let Mitzi know we're identical twins, or she might realize that we switched places at the wedding rehearsal."

"Why would she care?"

"Because there are two things she hates, and one of them is dishonesty."

Ted looked shocked. "You're as honest as a judge."

That's what Grant used to believe. "She might think I was dishonest if she happened to find out I sent you in my place when I was supposed to be best man at my nearest and dearest friends' wedding."

Ted nodded slowly. The problem was beginning to sink in. "So what's the other thing she doesn't like?"

"Workaholics."

Ted snorted. "You're screwed."

"I'm not a workaholic," Grant protested. "Well, you might think so, but you think everyone who sets their alarm clock in the morning is going overboard."

Ted puffed up proudly. "I'll have you know that I did

an important bit of work for you this morning. You were about to muck up the whole works, but I rescued you.''

Oh no. Grant's heart sank. Ted to the rescue had a definitely ominous ring. ''What did you do?''

''You were about to blow off that Joy Moreland chick Mona's so hot about,'' Ted gloated, ''so I set you up with her for Thursday night.''

A horrified yelp escaped Grant's lips, so that half the restaurant turned to stare at the ficus. More quietly, he said, ''You did what?''

''I set you up on a play date, bro,'' Ted explained. ''Thursday night. Don't forget to ask me for Joy's number.''

Mitzi was here for less than a week, and now he was going to spend one precious night squiring around some dimwit department-store heiress? No way. He would have to think of some way to call off the date by Thursday. Of course, by Thursday Mitzi might want to have nothing to do with him, especially if he didn't hightail it back to their table.

''Could you please just get a take-out box for that breakfast?'' He reached into his wallet and pulled out forty bucks. ''Here, it's on me.''

Ted had a healthy appreciation for money. ''Thanks, bro. Veronique and I'll be out of here in two shakes.''

Veronique?

Grant quickly retraced his steps to Mitzi. When he approached their table, she was putting something in that huge bag she toted with her everywhere. Probably a lipstick or something.

''Sorry about that.'' He looked into Mitzi's eyes and forced himself to relax. Ted was gone. Nothing else could go wrong now. ''Where were we?''

His cell phone jangled. Grant froze.

"Isn't that you?" Mitzi stared at the jacket hanging on the back of his chair.

It took the control of every muscle in his body not to pounce on the call immediately, as was his custom. What had Mitzi been complaining about yesterday? *The kind of man who couldn't make it through a meal without checking his messages.* Would she think he was one of those pathetic creatures?

Was he?

"Aren't you going to answer that?" she asked.

That was all the permission he needed. He whipped his hand into his jacket pocket and pulled out the phone. "Hello?"

"Whiting!" The booming voice of Horace Moreland bellowed tinnily through the little handset. "Where have you been? I've been trying you at the store all morning."

Grant sent Mitzi a long-suffering smile, then replied, "It is Sunday morning. You know, the day of rest?"

"Rest!" the man shouted in disgust. "I've never known you to rest before. That how you intend to make your millions, son?" Earlier in life, Horace had made a bumpy transition from United States marine to retail magnate, and hadn't worked out the chinks yet. "You can't capture a beachhead by sleeping in!"

"I'm not sleeping, I'm eating."

The older man grumbled. Meanwhile, Grant could see Mitzi glancing surreptitiously at her watch.

"I tried to get you all day yesterday, too," Horace complained.

Grant paled. The phone calls! After the brouhaha he and Mitzi had created at the wedding reception, he'd completely forgotten about business. "Dinner Wednesday sounds fine," he told Horace. "I'll make the reservations."

"I say, wait just a second there, son," the man barked.

Who did he think he was, Foghorn Leghorn? "I don't have time to chat right now," Grant said, noting that Mitzi's plate was empty, while his was still heaped with food. At this rate, it would be lunch before he had a chance to eat breakfast, and meanwhile, Mitzi looked ready to bolt. "In fact, I have to go."

"But you were going to send over a prospectus—"

Damn! He'd meant to do that yesterday. "I'll get it to you ASAP," he promised, then disconnected Moreland before he could receive any more orders.

He smiled at Mitzi. "Imagine, calling someone at a restaurant." He couldn't count the number of times he'd done the same thing.

"Are you always distracted like this while you're trying to eat?" There was a hint of disapproval in her tone.

He shouldn't have picked up that phone. He knew it. "Not at all." Which wasn't completely a lie. Usually he took meals at his desk at work, in which case he had his secretary hold his calls. He forced a smile and changed the subject. "Well, what should we do today?"

Mitzi grinned at him. "I'm going fishing."

Grant blinked, momentarily perplexed. "Fishing?"

"With Brewster."

Grant felt his facial muscles go slack. "Fishing with Brewster," he exclaimed. "What would you want to do that for?"

She thought for a moment. "For fun?"

As soon as he could recover from the shock, he leaned across the table toward her. "But I thought we would do something together. I thought you had the whole afternoon free."

"Nope," she answered. "That's why I suggested

brunch. Brewster asked me out yesterday during the reception. I've never been bass fishing before.''

"Oh, it's very dull,'' Grant said quickly. Maybe he could manage to change her mind. "Just sitting and waiting, mostly. I can't imagine what Brewster was thinking.''

Mitzi laughed. "I think he was thinking he had a little crush on me.''

Great. He couldn't believe he was being bumped off Mitzi's dance card by a rich fishing aficionado. "He'll swamp you with fishing stories. Believe me, I've heard them.''

Unmoved by his dire tone, Mitzi smiled. Fishing wasn't exactly her cup of tea, but she was glad to have some reason to get out of town and away from Grant. It might not hurt him to be forced to take a back seat to Brewster, either.

It was just as well that she bail out on Grant before those blue eyes charmed her into something she'd regret. There was still something about him she couldn't quite trust, like that mysterious phone call he jumped up to make. She hadn't been annoyed at first. Luckily she had her camera and could occupy herself taking pictures of the view from the restaurant. But then to discover that all the while he'd had a cell phone in his jacket pocket back at the table!

Where had he run off to, and why had he found it necessary to fib about it? His stepmother's birthday, for heaven's sakes. And did he always make dinner dates at the table when he was out with other women?

"I wouldn't worry, Grant. I've had men tell me fishy stories before.''

5

"DOES THIS MEAN we lose our benefits?" April Jones from handbags asked.

"What about our dental plan?" Harry Burns echoed nervously. "My daughter just got braces."

The group of anxious employees huddled around Grant's desk just made him more frazzled, and he was already pretty shaky. He'd barely slept at all last night, thanks, in part, to the fact that Mitzi hadn't been home all evening. Of course, considering that her date was Brewster, a bachelor who thought the ultimate conquest was a twenty-pound largemouth, he shouldn't have been too worried.

He shouldn't even be interested in her anyway. Ted was right. Women were the source of most of life's woes. Hadn't his own marriage fiasco proved that? The next time he saw her he was going to play it cool. Absolutely cool. Of course, after a day with Brewster, she would probably be dying to go out with someone else. But that didn't mean Grant had to drop everything and oblige her. After all, he had important work to tend to this week.

This very hectic week. Wednesday he had dinner scheduled with Moreland and his cronies. Friday night Mona was throwing a big shindig, no doubt hoping to celebrate the sale of Whiting's. And now Ted had obligated him to take out that Moreland woman on Thursday. Joy! The name rang in his head with a sarcastic twist.

He wanted to strangle Ted.

Instead of pondering the penalties of attempted fratricide, however, he forced himself to focus on Harry's daughter's braces. "You don't have to worry, Harry. None of you do. This store is not being bought."

Not if he could keep his mind on the sale and off sex.

The group in front of him breathed a collective sigh of relief. "Those men in the black suits downstairs aren't from Moreland's then?" April asked.

Men in black? Grant pictured Will Smith and Tommy Lee Jones as department-store goons, stalking through Whiting's cosmetics counters with dark sunglasses and ridiculously oversize weapons. Preposterous. He smiled, but felt an uneasy twinge nevertheless. "I wasn't aware of any men in black suits."

Harry nervously stepped forward. The man was normally jittery, today he looked like panic on legs. "One of them told me he was a security man for Moreland's, and that they had been instructed to study the store's layout."

Casing the joint. This was too much. Grant bolted to his feet, almost sending poor Harry into a swoon. "The Moreland Corporation is only attempting to buy our stores." He didn't add that half his family was jubilant at the prospect. Moreland had no business scoping out the lay of the land as if it were all a done deal. "You all just go about your business," Grant instructed the group. "And if one of these security men asks you a question, direct him to my office."

He led the employees out and to the elevators, then turned and took the stairs down two flights to the main floor. Security men. Already trying to decide where to put in hidden cameras, no doubt. This is what happened when he allowed himself to get sidetracked by a beautiful woman with green eyes. The barbarians barged right through the gates.

He stopped, took a deep calming breath, then scoped out the area for the pesky intruders. The aroma of perfume on the air, the sparkling tile floors, the high ceilings with chandeliers that gave the old flagship building a gracious feel that no mall store could ever achieve, comforted him a little.

He spotted one of the black-suited men in hosiery and made a beeline for him until he caught sight of something that stopped him in his tracks—*Mitzi in ladies' swimwear!* The private and the professional impulses warred inside him for a split second before the private declared victory. Grant hotfooted it over to the swimwear department, all the while reminding himself of his vow to keep cool.

As he approached her, Mitzi was lost in the process of picking out a bathing suit. The one she held up was a classic black one-piece, little more than a tiny black spandex strip. As he imagined just what that tiny black sheath would look like on Mitzi's tall leggy body, he felt himself getting as worked up as Harry had been at the prospect of losing his dental plan.

Stay cool, he reminded himself.

He leaned against the next rack and cleared his throat. The resulting sound was about an octave higher than normal.

Mitzi looked over, and flashed him her million-watt smile. "Hey!"

A day with Brewster had probably driven her out of her mind. That's why she was here—to see him. The bathing suits were only a flimsy excuse. Grant smiled back at her with self-assurance. "You should have told me you were coming here to shop. I can get you a discount."

His nonchalance did him proud. Especially since he'd noticed that in Mitzi's other hand, she held a bikini.

"Really?" she said, pleased. "I was going to call you this morning. I got your messages."

"Oh?"

"All twelve of them."

Grant frowned. He should have kept count of how many times he'd called her.

She continued to leaf through the hangers. "I would have called you back last night, but I didn't get in till late."

No kidding! "How late?"

She shrugged her thin shoulders. "Oh, around midnight."

"Midnight," he exclaimed. "I thought you two were going fishing."

She laughed gaily. "Oh, we made quite a day of it."

Quite a night of it, too. "What happened?"

"We went to dinner."

Dinner. Oh. That was no big deal.

Or was it? "Till midnight? On a Sunday night?"

"Grant, I'm on vacation, and Brewster..."

She didn't have to finish. Brewster, the son of one of the richest ranchers in Texas, was independently wealthy. No reason for him to get up early on a Monday morning. He didn't have to worry his head about little things like employee benefits and hostile takeovers.

Mitzi turned her attention to another rack. "Anyway, Brewster brought me home and we talked for a while..."

"You mean, Brewster stayed around to talk? What the hell were you talking about?"

Cool, stay cool, a little voice reminded him as soon as the heated words were out.

If Mitzi detected his nerves unraveling, she didn't let on. "We had to plan our trip."

"Trip," Grant repeated numbly. "Where are you going?"

"To Brewster's lake cabin. Doesn't that sound neat?"

Neat! It sounded way too intimate, was what it sounded like. And Brewster's cabin was hours away. "You'll have to be there overnight."

She nodded eagerly. "I haven't spent a night out in the wilderness since I was a Girl Scout."

"Is that why you're here, buying bathing suits for your expedition out to the middle of nowhere with Brewster?" He glared at the scrappy little bikini with new antagonism.

Mitzi sighed in exasperation. "Yes, but I hate buying them." She held up a little green number that gave about as much coverage as pasties and a G-string. "It's sheer torture."

He felt like the thumbscrews were on right now, just picturing Mitzi in that little thing, and then remembering it was Brewster who was actually going to see her in it.

Brewster! Grant wanted to howl at the injustice of it.

"Here, maybe I can help out." He turned to a rack of more modest styles and rifled through the suits there. "It's always best to stick with the tried-and-true. Like this one." He held up a navy blue suit with a little red anchor embroidered on its high, high neckline. The bottom was a modest skirt in blue-and-white stripes.

Mitzi laughed. "I think I had one like that once. When I was five."

"That's what I mean. It's a classic." Better still, it was about as sexy as a heart attack.

"No kidding. My grandmother probably would have loved it, too."

Grant frowned. "But you can't go out to Brewster's cabin with a bikini."

"Why not?"

"Because you hardly know him."

She giggled dismissively. "Oh, Brewster's harmless."

"Don't be too sure," Grant warned. "You're not a Girl Scout anymore. Brewster might seem harmless now, at a restaurant or at Kay's, but just when you're in that remote cabin in your bikini—"

Mitzi stopped him. "I'll only wear the swimsuit while I'm swimming."

"Even so, once you get back to that cabin at night, you'll have been fishing all day with him," Grant argued. "Maybe even have a piscine odor clinging to your hair. Something like that's bound to drive Brewster over the edge. What if the man turns wolfish?"

She laughed. "Brewster? That's ridiculous. He's a kind, sensitive, family-oriented man. Has he told you that he belongs to the Big Brother program? He just got back from taking the boy he mentors out to Lake Travis. He's very sweet."

Family-oriented? No one was more family-oriented than Grant. Wasn't he trying to save the family business? And he loved kids. A dozen wouldn't have been too many for his taste. As for sweet—hell, he was sweet!

Mitzi tilted a concerned glance in Grant's direction. He was tearing through the rack of bathing suits like a man possessed. More odd behavior.

She refused to believe that Grant could be jealous of Brewster. That was too preposterous. Like Tom Cruise envying Drew Carey. And it would make even less sense because Brewster's one topic of conversation, apart from fish, seemed to be their mutual friend, Grant. Brewster had assured her that Grant was a hell of a guy. Not nutty at all. And yet, he was acting so strange.

"Grant? Are you telling me you think I shouldn't go?"

Grant blinked. Maybe he was being a tad overbearing. "Of course not," he replied stiffly. "It's just odd that you're dropping everything and running off with him. What about..." He strained to find some reason for her to stay in Austin. Besides the fact that he wanted her there. "…Chester?"

"He's coming, too," Mitzi assured him. Then she laid a hand on his arm and beamed a calming smile at him that had the opposite effect. "Don't worry, Grant. I'm just following the advice you gave me—for once in my life, I'm loosening up."

Had he mentioned he wanted to strangle Ted? "That wasn't such great advice. In fact, it was terrible."

Mitzi shook her head. "Last night when Brewster proposed the overnight trip, I hesitated. Then I thought, heck, why not follow Grant's advice? I'm only going around once, so to speak. Why not cut loose?"

Cut loose. God, that sounded good. How wonderful it would be to leave Ted, Mona, Truman and the Morelands behind and run away. Especially if he was cutting loose with Mitzi. When he looked into her green eyes, it all seemed so easy. Something about Mitzi made him see his whole life differently. Before, he'd been the serious-minded one, the drone. Janice had always complained that he never did anything unexpected.

So why, whenever he was around Mitzi, was he pulling down buffet tables and being hauled out of bushes by policemen? Why did her green eyes make his feet, which had always been firmly rooted to the ground, instinctively want to do a little tap dance? Just one smile from Mitzi seemed to unleash a reservoir of goofiness inside him he never guessed existed. Before, he'd never known jealousy, either. Not even when Janice had run off with her prince. Oh, sure, he'd been angry, and felt betrayed, but he couldn't say he envied Omar. But with Mitzi, he was a miser. He wanted to hoard her every smile, her tinkling laughter, her funny comments, all to himself.

Why should Brewster be the lucky dog cutting loose

with her? he thought, feeling some last thread of sanity inside him snapping.

In a swift motion that took them both by surprise, he pulled Mitzi to him and brought his lips down just as hers parted in astonishment.

Mitzi could barely believe what was happening, and yet, when their mouths met, the kiss was exactly as she'd dreamed it would be, seemingly a thousand times. Grant's lips were possessive and strong, yet with a hint of tenderness that caught her off guard. She felt completely enveloped by muscle and male brawn, but fully free to exercise her own feminine curiosity by tasting her fill. Which she did with pleasure. She wasn't kissing Mr. Hyde, that was for sure.

More like Mr. Right. Because while she stood under the fluorescent lights of the swimwear department, with heaven knows how many people looking on, her belief in Mr. Right, so long extinguished in her mind, flickered back to life in the heat of Grant's embrace. Niggling doubts vanished as romantic optimism reconstituted itself in the flood of desire he sent swirling through her, from her fingertips that kneaded softly the corded muscles of his neck, right down to her curled toes.

She wasn't thinking anymore, just feeling. Just reveling in the first horns-blowing, fireworks-exploding, confetti-flying kiss she'd ever received. She'd thought things like this only happened in movies, to gorgeous women like Grace Kelly. But as Grant began dipping her back, Rudolph Valentino-style, she felt as if she could be on a movie set, or in a quiet hideaway all their own.

Grant hadn't meant to do it, hadn't planned it. But this kiss seemed so obvious, so natural. Mitzi's lips were warm and soft and giving, her scent an intoxicating mixture of perfumed soap and toothpaste that made him dizzier than the strongest, sexiest French perfume would have.

Suddenly, he realized this was exactly what he'd wanted to do since that morning when he'd first laid eyes on her in her lime-green dress. Before he'd messed things up. And as he held her in his arms, luxuriating in the soft pliant feel of her body against his, he vowed not to foul things up again.

As that determination crossed his mind, he felt Mitzi lean backward, then back some more.

He opened his eyes in time to see Mitzi's green eyes widen in a shock that mirrored his own. They were moving through space, as in a dream, still attached at the lips, each reaching out but finding nothing to cling to but each other. In the next second, they were splat on the floor, landing against the bathing-suit rack they had toppled over. Nylon and spandex rained down on and around them as the rack collapsed.

Yet as he untangled himself from the sea of plastic hangers, helped Mitzi to her feet and reassembled the rack, he didn't feel awkward, even when he saw Leanne Cummings, the sportswear clerk, come running over. Instead, he felt liberated.

"Oh, my," Mitzi breathed, tearing her gaze away from his to start picking up stray swimsuits. Then she looked back at him, her green eyes heartbreakingly liquid and beautiful.

Which made it all the more surprising when her eyebrows knit together and she suddenly barked out at him, "Are you nuts? What was that for?"

He grinned. "You have to ask?"

Leanne joined them, two red blotches in her cheeks indicating that she'd caught most of their spontaneous romantic moment. "Oh, Mr. Whiting! I'll pick these up."

Grant nodded his appreciation as he quickly helped

tidy things. "And when Miss Campion finishes shopping," he instructed Leanne, helping to move the rack to just the right spot, "please give her a fifty percent discount."

Then, before another glance into Mitzi's eyes could tempt him to take her in his arms again until they'd overturned every clothes rack in the store, Grant pivoted on his heel and headed back to his office, waving to a Moreland man in a black suit as he passed.

The grim-faced fellow made him laugh. "Security's terrible here," Grant informed the fellow blithely. "We call it shoplifter heaven."

Grant strolled on, feeling as if he were walking on air. Even discovering the person he least wanted to see, sneaking through the back employee entrance, failed to dampen his spirits. Just the opposite. A plan began to formulate in his head the minute he saw his brother.

He greeted Ted with a clap on the back as they went up the rear stairs. "Imagine running into you here."

Ted stiffened. "Okay, I know it's a little past ten, but I had to take my truck in for an oil change. You can't put things like that off, you know."

Grant nodded. "Of course not. Anyway, don't worry about it. You got here just in time."

Ted eyed him suspiciously. "In time for what?"

Automatically, Grant began ordering his thoughts. "I have four things I need from you, Ted."

His brother began to speed his pace. "If you really need me, I'll be in my office."

Before Ted could scamper away, Grant launched into his plan. "First, write up a memo telling all employees that there will be no layoffs, and that no change in the benefits package is in the works."

Ted looked doubtful. "I haven't written a memo since—"

"It's like riding a bicycle," Grant assured him. "Second, there is a prospectus on my desk. I wrote it up to make our store look subtly unattractive to the Morelands. I need your opinion."

"Oh, sure," Ted said, brightening a little. He was always glad to give an opinion. "Anything to help out."

"The next thing is to tell Herman Little to start handing around his union petitions. Tell him he can walk around the store with a sandwich board if he wants."

Ted's eyebrows drew together. "Whoa! Are you sure?" Grant laughed, which only made his brother look more confused. "What's the fourth thing you want?"

"Your boat."

Ted froze. "My...?"

As Grant stared into his brother's eyes, he realized he hadn't witnessed such an expression of horror since watching Janet Leigh in the shower scene from *Psycho*.

THE TROUBLE WITH FISHING, Mitzi decided as she sat with her legs flopped over the edge of Brewster's bass boat, a forgotten fishing rod perched in her hands, was that it gave people way too much time to talk. Apparently, Brewster had spilled all his fish stories, along with more than she ever wanted to know about chunking and winding, and now his topic of choice seemed to be Grant.

"Grant's mother died when he was little—about five, I think—and his father passed away while he was in college. He's been the bulwark of the Whiting clan ever since."

Imagine. She'd been kissed by a bulwark.

The trouble was, Mitzi couldn't let this intriguing subject drop, either. "To me he seems rather unpredictable."

The kind of man who would meet a woman and tell her she was brittle and devious, and then two days later take that same woman into his arms and kiss her silly right in the middle of a department store. Every time she relived the moment his warm lips captured hers, liquid heat surged through her.

"Grant? Unpredictable?" Brewster chuckled. "He's as reliable as an almanac."

She'd never had a reference book sweep her off her feet before. Nor had she imagined that the mere touch of skin against skin could create such a furor of sensations. Cut loose? Since that kiss, she wondered if perhaps she hadn't been cut loose from the land of reason. Her emotions were as hard to straighten out as a Rubik's Cube. Foremost in the jumble of feelings was her desire for another of those kisses. Then there was an equally strong dose of distrust. After all, he was still Grant Whiting, the bridesmaid's nemesis. And how could she feel so giddy over a man who couldn't even speak to her in public without causing some kind of scene? Who, even though their every encounter ended in calamity, kept turning up in her thoughts? The man was more annoying and harder to shake than a Bee Gees tune.

And now Brewster's information about Grant's family tugged her in a whole new direction. Mitzi was no stranger to tragedy. Both her parents had died while she was in her twenties, and it had taken years before she felt she was on an even keel. But to have lost both parents, and then have to go through a painful divorce...

Next to her, Chester, who was lying on his back, sunning his naked pink belly in the afternoon sun, shifted and let out a satisfied snort. At least he was enjoying their lake cabin getaway. Maybe because he wasn't focused on the sexy department store proprietor they'd left behind. Chester, apparently, was more interested in his tan.

"Did I tell you Grant was third in his class in college?" Brewster asked. Then he went on to add that

Grant was also on the boards of several prominent Austin charities. A pillar of the community.

She supposed she should be glad that they were discussing Grant and not, say, cleaning out fish guts, which had been the topic of their conversation earlier. But the more Brewster sang Grant's praises, the more Mitzi wondered what she was doing out here in the middle of nowhere with nothing but a bass freak and a dachshund for company, when Grant and his expert lips were back in the city.

In fact, she was contemplating diving into the water and making a frantic swim for shore when Brewster looked up. "Uh-oh," he breathed. "Boat motor."

Mitzi squinted into the distance.

"Well, I'll be," Brewster said. "Look who it is—one of the Whiting boys! Ted, I guess."

Mitzi looked, and couldn't believe it when she saw the familiar blond hair and blue eyes come into view. "No, it's Grant," she said, leaning forward. You'd think after blathering about his friend all afternoon, Brewster would at least be able to tell him from his brother. "Grant!" She practically hopped off the end of the boat as the sleek vessel pulled close.

Brewster was even more surprised. "Grant? I can't believe you pulled yourself away from the store on a weekday."

"Why not?" Grant asked as he slid up beside them. "It's a beautiful day, and I happened to hear that you and Mitzi were out here."

"But you're such a workhorse," Brewster said.

Grant looked wounded. "Me? Why, there's nothing I like better than to pick up and leave my troubles on the doorstep."

How refreshing.

Unbidden, the memory of their kiss popped into

Mitzi's head, and she glanced up at Grant to find his blue eyes burning into hers. Obviously he was thinking the same thing.

"You're in time to chunk for smallmouths with my new grubs," Brewster told him excitedly. "Bring your rod?"

Grant tried to appear as if he hated to disappoint Brewster. "Darn it, I forgot my rod and reel. I was hoping just to get in a little swimming and relaxation." He turned back to Mitzi, who, even standing in the middle of a breathtaking lake, had not the slightest difficulty putting Mother Nature to shame. "Would you be interested in going over to Miller's Hole for a dip? It's very close to here."

Mitzi was already prepared to heave Chester onto Grant's boat when she remembered Brewster. He was, after all, her host. "I might enjoy a break," she said to Brewster, as if fishing had exhausted her. "Wouldn't you like to go, too?"

"To Miller's Hole?" Brewster asked disdainfully. "There's nothing but perch over there."

"Oh, but—"

She was about to tell him that he could swim, or just sit and talk to them, but Brewster was having none of it. "I like to save all my energy for that wily competitor, Mr. Bass," he said gravely.

Mitzi felt a rush of warmth as Grant hoisted her and Chester onto his boat. As they roared away, with Chester rigidly nosing his pointy snout off the bow like a proud figurehead, she tried to tell herself that she was so glad to see Grant because she was tired of hearing about jigs, spoons and spinnerbaits. Not because she had the hots for him.

But who was she kidding?

"Bring your suit?" he asked, looking her up and down.

"Of course." She was wearing it under the oversize T-shirt and jean shorts she'd also bought today. "Thanks for the discount, by the way."

He sent her one of his heart-stopping grins. "Knocked over any clothes racks lately?"

"A true gentleman wouldn't bring up that subject."

"A true gentleman wouldn't have ravished you in a department store." He waggled his eyebrows rakishly.

"The Don Juan of retail," she joked.

They dropped anchor in a small cove that formed a beautiful clear blue swimming hole. The water looked so cool and inviting Mitzi almost stripped off her clothes as willingly as Gypsy Rose Lee. Then she remembered Grant. She wasn't overly modest, but usually she was hesitant to appear in a bathing suit in front of strangers, so she held back as Grant quickly doffed his T-shirt and dived into the water. She hadn't been able to tell his swimming trunks weren't shorts. In swimming attire, as in most everything else, men had it easy.

She took off her shorts and left her T-shirt on, dangled her legs over the side of the boat and enjoyed the view. And she wasn't talking about the scenery. Forget clear blue water and towering pines. Her eyes were helplessly drawn to watch Grant's glistening, muscled torso doing an easy backstroke.

He stopped, treading water, and aimed his dazzling grin at her. "Don't tell me you're afraid of sharks," he teased.

Funny, there was a time when she'd thought *he* resembled a shark, but now that she knew him better she couldn't imagine anything more preposterous. More like a cuddly harp seal.

He swam closer. "Is anything wrong?"

When she looked into his eyes, there was no sharklike or wolfish intent; it was something else entirely, and she racked her brain trying to find the right word to describe his look. He was looking at her as if he had wooing on his mind. He had taken an entire day off of work to woo her.

The realization made her feel as flustered as a teenager. "I was just thinking that maybe we should be wearing life jackets."

"Can't you swim?"

"Yes, but considering our track record of disaster, it might be wise to take a few precautions around the water."

"I was a lifeguard in high school," he told her.

It wasn't difficult to imagine him as the Greek god of the public pool, breaking the hearts of scores of sunburned schoolgirls. "You already saved me," she told him.

"From what?"

"Boredom," she replied. "Next time, remind me not to cut loose with a man immersed in a love affair with lures."

Grant's laughter was interrupted by the high jangle of his cell phone on the boat deck. Mitzi looked over at the handset, then turned to Grant. He was so frozen she was afraid he'd sink. "Don't you want to answer that?"

Grant's lips turned up in a limp grin. He'd never not answered his cell phone before. But he was here to romance Mitzi, not to conduct business. This would prove he wasn't really a workaholic, or a slave to technology. Besides, the call was probably Moreland, who he didn't want to talk to anyway.

But what if it wasn't? What if it was Ted? There might be some emergency at the store. What if Herman Little had actually unionized the employees in five hours?

He tensed as the phone rang again.

"Maybe it's something important," Mitzi said, unknowingly torturing him. Even Chester looked concerned. "Or business."

Grant forced his shoulders to lift in a stiff shrug. "Business be damned! I've declared this a vacation."

His tone might have lacked the enthusiasm his words called for, but Mitzi brimmed with admiration. Not many people could resist the call of the wireless. When the handset stopped ringing, she stood, feeling the sudden urge to frolic in the water with Grant. She decided he had unknowingly discovered a powerful aphrodisiac—not answering the telephone!

She looked into his eyes and saw a healthy male anticipation in them. "Would you stop leering? You're making me self-conscious."

"Just curious to see which of those suits you finally chose," he said, wriggling those eyebrows again.

She laughed. "It won't be much of a surprise. You picked it out!"

She tore off her T-shirt to reveal the cute navy blue bathing suit with the high neck and the modest skirt. She'd thought it was grannyish in the store, but now she was grateful for his good taste. "What do you think?" she asked, striking a model pose for him.

His face fell. "I think the next time I see a woman shopping for bathing suits, I should keep my trap shut."

Mitzi dived in the water and swam toward Grant, trying very hard to present the grace of Esther Williams, which was difficult given that her only stroke was a refined dog paddle. "This is wonderful!" Even though she felt like a waterlogged landlubber, it was the truth. "I never get the chance to swim at home."

"I thought New York City was surrounded by water."

"But most of it's not the type of stuff you'd want to

take a morning dip in," she said. "Unless you groove on the sewage experience."

Grant laughed. He'd been treading water forever, and he wasn't out of breath, whereas she already felt as if she'd just swum the English Channel. In fact, he appeared completely at home, with beads of water in his golden hair and his bronzed skin glistening in the sun. The lake god. He made her heart pump double time.

Or maybe the dog-paddling was doing that to her.

"Here," he said, reaching out for her. She grabbed on to his shoulders as if they were a life buoy. Swimming backward, he tugged her gently through the water, so that she really did feel like Esther Williams in one of those crazy old water musicals.

Only, even Esther had never had such a sexy partner.

He stopped suddenly, his eyes darkening with sensual intent. She'd seen that look before, back in the swimwear department. Mitzi felt the bottom of her stomach drop like an out-of-control elevator.

"I don't think this is such a good idea."

"Why not?" he asked, reaching forward to nibble at her ear.

The temperature in the water shot up ten degrees. "It's like that one summer when I was seventeen," she said between nibbles. "Some friends and I went to the beach."

"Mmm," he murmured in her ear. "What happened?"

"I was swimming with this boy I really liked, Lou Herkimer." His hand swept across her breast, making her shiver with desire.

At least, she hoped it was his hand. "See, there were jellyfish..."

His lips brushed lightly against hers. "And?"

It was as if she'd died and gone to a very wet heaven. "Lou was allergic," she practically gasped out as he continued to tease her lips. "It was terrible...we had to go...to...to the...emergency room...and they gave him this shot...of..."

"Mitzi?"

Her eyes opened and she stared into mesmerizing blue eyes darkened by unmasked desire. "Yes?"

"Will you please just shut up about Lou Herkimer and the jellyfish and let me kiss you?"

She did. Gladly.

6

She felt as if she were walking on air. Never mind that she'd eaten nothing but bass for twenty-four hours straight. Never mind that she barely got a wink of sleep and had spent the entire night blinking up at scaly fish carcasses eyeballing her from the walls. Never mind that she was half-crazy in lust with Grant. She was happy.

For the first time in her life, she'd found a man who didn't want to keep her at arm's length. Far from it. It seemed she and Grant couldn't stop flirting, touching, kissing. In one short day, they'd become addicted to each other. But with Brewster as affable host and chaperon, kissing had been as far as matters had gone. They were still perched on the edge of flingdom. Mitzi felt jubilant, and a little frightened, as if she stood on the edge of a high rocky precipice, and was about to hurl herself over the edge.

As she skipped down the path to the lake, she noticed Chester sniffing something behind a very large pine tree. She approached quietly, and discovered Grant, crouching with his back to her and whispering into his cell phone.

Looking at him, she felt a now-familiar tightening in her chest. He was so gorgeous. And those arms—she loved the snuggly feeling of having them wrapped around her. *Crave* was too weak a word for what she felt for this man.

She frowned, reining in her galloping lust. Why was Grant talking on the phone behind a tree?

She cleared her throat, sending him whirling around in surprise. He looked like a deer caught in headlights. "I'll call you later, Ted," he said, disconnecting the person at the other end. Then he sent Mitzi a bright smile. Overly bright. "I didn't see you."

She arched an eyebrow. "What were you doing?"

Grant laughed. A little nervously, she thought. A wave of foreboding shivered through her.

"Just thought I'd check in at the office," he said.

"Ted, that was your brother, wasn't it?" Without discussing it, they fell into step together toward the lake, with Chester padding happily in the lead. "Brewster mentioned him."

Grant winced. It was bad enough to have Mitzi catch him sneaking a business call, now he worried that she might have figured out that Ted and he were identical twins. Not that he wanted to keep it a secret from her forever, especially now that they were growing so close.

Memories of last night temporarily blocked his senses. They'd necked by the light of the moon like two kids at summer camp, and he was ready for more. Much more. But he felt a gnawing discomfort around her, and he knew why. He hadn't been completely honest.

He wondered whether she would forgive him for having pulled the switch at the wedding. But then, why wouldn't she? Certainly he had to come clean at some point. The trick was finding the right moment.

Of course, there was no time like the present. Grant took her hand. "Mitzi, there's something I have to tell you."

Mitzi froze as she stared into Grant's dead-serious eyes. Here it comes! The big letdown. For some stupid reason, she'd relaxed her guard, and had forgotten that all good things came to a speedy end. "Don't tell me, I think I can guess."

Grant's eyebrows arched dramatically. "You can?"

She sighed. "You have another girlfriend hidden away somewhere."

He looked surprised. "No."

"A model, maybe," she guessed, hoping to cut the bad news off at the pass.

"Of course not."

"You're quitting your job and running off to the Himalayas to join a monastery."

"No." He laughed, completely perplexed. "Excuse me, but what are you talking about?"

At the risk of sounding like a neurotic, she confessed, "I'm talking about all the excuses men use to avoid commitment, at least to me."

His smile faded. "Those things happened to you?"

She nodded. "In the past three years."

"Good heavens," he exclaimed. Then he tilted his head and asked, "A monastery?"

She nodded miserably. "That was Tim. Brother Tim now. Yes, I drove a man to celibacy." It was a longer, more humiliating story than she cared to relate in detail, but in her defense, she felt compelled to add, "He never even mentioned India to me. Or Buddhism. He was a stockbroker! The only thing I ever saw him follow religiously was the NASDAQ."

Grant shook his head in commiseration. "Something like that could make you lose faith in men."

"Maybe you can understand now why I value honesty above everything else."

His gaze locked with hers. "Of course."

"There's nothing more contemptible than dishonesty, or leading a person on."

He gulped. "Well..."

Mitzi gathered her courage. "Whatever you had to confess, Grant, I'd rather you just spit it out now than when I'm stepping on the plane back to New York."

His blue eyes were full of doubt, and for a moment Mitzi knew it was all over. Another one bites the dust, she thought, trying to hold on to some shred of humor. "You can be absolutely brutal," she assured him. "If nothing else, my dismal romantic past has served as an inoculation against real heartbreak."

Grant did feel heartened by her pleas for honesty. After all, what was a little twin switching when the woman had been abandoned three times in three years?

Then again, maybe his and Ted's deception would be the straw that broke the camel's back. "You must have had one romantic triumph," he said. "Nobody's that unlucky."

Mitzi thought for a moment. "I almost pulled off a romantic coup in high school. Barry Delaney, captain of the basketball team and all-around heartthrob, asked me to the prom. I thought I'd died and gone to heaven."

Grant was so accustomed now to her tales of woe that he was on the figurative edge of his seat, waiting for the custard pie to be lobbed.

The wait wasn't long. "But halfway through the prom, as we were dancing to my favorite Boy George song, I realized that I wasn't dancing with Barry Delaney, heartthrob, but Larry Delaney, head case."

Grant stopped in midstride. All the blood rushed toward his sneakers.

"They were twins," she said.

He felt sick.

"Larry was just out of juvenile detention, where he'd served three months for causing a disturbance during a pep rally."

"Wasn't that sentence a bit severe?"

"He'd caused it by using concentrated hydrochloric acid from the chemistry lab, and a torpedo."

"Oh."

She sighed. "After he was released back into society, he developed a fixation on me, and his brother—I guess he was trying to help in his twin's rehabilitation—helped set it up so that I went to the prom with him. After that, Barry didn't seem any more of a heartthrob than Larry."

Grant swallowed past the boulder-size lump in his throat.

"Well, so much for another stroll down memory lane." Mitzi laughed and turned to him. "Now, what was it you wanted to tell me?"

Mitzi obviously found telling these disaster stories a purging experience. But Grant's confession remained firmly lodged in his throat. How could he possibly come out with his tale of twin deception now? Chances were, the moment he even mentioned having a twin she would start flashing back to prom trauma and gymnasiums in flames.

Her eyebrows came together in an anxious bridge. "Is something wrong?"

There was. Mitzi could tell. She looked into Grant's troubled blue eyes and steeled herself for the worst.

But instead of coming out with some sordid confession of being secretly married or wanting to devote his life to beekeeping, he smiled at her reassuringly. "I don't know why we're getting all serious. I was just going to confess to you that I…"

Barry and Larry...Barry and Larry...Barry and Larry...

He swallowed, then looked into her adorable green eyes and felt his anxious thoughts melt away. Why borrow trouble? "I never cared so deeply for anyone before, Mitzi," he confessed.

She frowned. "What?"

He stumbled on, "I know how you feel about dates—about stepping into doom, and all that. But I want us to go out when we return to Austin. You know, for a real date—dinner clothes, a fancy restaurant, candlelight, the whole bit."

As what Grant was telling her sank through her thick skull, Mitzi wanted to kick herself for being such a paranoid. Not to mention such a blabbermouth.

"Of course, I'd love to," she said, joy quickly overtaking chagrin at having spilled out the most embarrassing moments of her love history. Someday, she would have to tell him about the good things about herself, like that she was valedictorian of her kindergarten and a very competent canasta partner. But for now, she decided to keep quiet. She didn't want to overwhelm the man, after all.

He smiled and took her in his arms for a long, searing kiss.

GRANT DANCED into his office humming "Call Me Irresponsible" and reached for the phone. The first thing he did was order a dozen pink roses to be delivered to Mitzi's. Romance, once you got the hang of it, was a cinch. All you had to do was what he'd avoided his entire life—go with the flow.

Last night after getting home from the lake, he and Mitzi had ordered out pizza and rented a silly action movie that had featured about thirty car chases and twice that many exploding buildings. Never mind that the pizza tasted like cardboard and he hated mind-numbing movies with explosions. The real pyrotechnics had been going off in his heart.

In fact, he could swear he was falling in love. Love! In less than four days, his whole life had been turned on its ear. The thought made him laugh out loud as he hung up the phone.

Ted appeared in the doorway, scowling, his arms crossed. "So! You're back!"

Grant grinned. "Don't worry about that beautiful boat of yours, brother. I left you with a full tank of gas."

"Beautiful boat? Good grief!" His brother crossed to the leather captain's chair across the desk, sat down and leveled a stern gaze at him. "Grant, are you feeling all right?"

"Never better!"

"Then do you have any idea how important this week is?"

"You're telling me," he said. "Did you know what Mitzi's favorite book is?"

Ted's eyebrows knit in confusion at the mental leap he was being asked to make. "No…"

Grant laughed. "*To Kill a Mockingbird.* Same as mine. Isn't that amazing?"

"Incredible." Ted cleared his throat officiously. "I don't know if you've forgotten, but we've got a problem on our hands here."

Grant lifted his palm to stop him. "Wait, let me show you something." He opened the top drawer of his desk and pulled out a little velvet jewelry box that contained a gold camera charm to go on the dangly bracelet Mitzi always wore. She said it had been her grandmother's. "I bought this yesterday."

Ted covered the box with his big hand before Grant could open it. "You've lost your marbles, Grant. You have responsibilities here that you've been completely ignoring," he lectured. It was given in the same *how-can-you-be-so-irresponsible?* tone that Grant had used on him a million times.

He even looked a little like Grant. The old Grant. Today, Ted was wearing a somber dark brown suit, while Grant had shown up in a pair of jeans and a pale-blue polo shirt.

Grant laughed. "Amazing, the place hasn't fallen apart in my absence." For years, he thought the old stone building would collapse in a heap of rubble without his presence.

Ted tapped his fingers impatiently. "Do you realize that while you've been running amok with that bridesmaid, Mona's been out to dinner twice with Moreland and that daughter of his? Mona's ready to sign on the dotted line, Grant, and the Moreland people have taken Uncle Truman to every golf course within a hundred-mile radius."

Grant chuckled.

"This is no laughing matter," Ted huffed. "We've got to start doing some sharp maneuvering here. Yesterday, in your absence I circulated a memo informing the staff of casual day."

Grant blinked. They had never had casual day before. "When is that?"

"Every day until further notice, i.e., until the Morelands leave. I thought you'd found out, considering that hobo getup you've got on."

Grant shrugged. "I just felt like being comfortable."

Ted looked at him accusingly. "And you didn't notice Fred the doorman was wearing cutoffs and a ZZ Top T-shirt?"

In fact, Grant did remember that everyone looked a little out of the ordinary, but his mind had been elsewhere. But he saw where Ted was going with the idea. Moreland, with his military love of spit-and-polish, would be as repulsed by employees in shorts as he would by Herman Little's one-man picket line next to valet parking.

"Casual day. Very clever," he said.

Ted basked in fraternal praise only for a moment. "These gimmicks will only carry us so far. It's time to let the man know we're going to hang tough. It's time for the big dinner."

"You're telling me," Grant agreed, his memory jarred pleasantly by the phrase. "Mitzi and I have a date tonight."

Ted looked as if he might have a heart attack. "Tonight? But tonight you're supposed to have dinner with Moreland and his people at the Sunset Grill!"

Grant shot him a level glance. "Or you could."

Ted's eyes widened, and his voice ratcheted up a full octave. "Me? Oh, no!"

"Come on, Ted, it's just this once."

His brother shook his head emphatically. "That's what you said the last time, and the time before that."

"You don't know what tonight means to me," Grant pleaded.

Ted looked down at that little square velvet box and squirmed uncomfortably. "What about what tonight means to the store, and our future?"

Grant crossed his arms and aimed his most desperate glance at his brother. "I'm talking about the future. You remember what kind of shape I was in before I met Mitzi. I was sleepwalking, living on caffeine and Zantac. This past year, the future was something I didn't like to think about, and when I did, it just seemed like a grim parade of work and duty stretching ahead as far as I could see. But now that I've met Mitzi, I feel like I've come back to life again.''

As he listened, the lines in Ted's face collapsed, and his blue eyes began to go suspiciously watery.

"For the first time since Janice left, I feel like I'm on solid ground again."

As always, mention of the name Janice caused Ted's jaw to work back and forth. His face darkened, and a fierce protectiveness shone in his eyes. "I'm sorry, little bro. I didn't realize how serious this had all become." He stared at the jewelry box, then looked pityingly at Grant. "All right. I'll do it."

Grant stood and walked him to the door. "I really appreciate it, Ted."

Ted shrugged and let out a sharp laugh. "Hey, I've got a news flash for you. I'm not all that bad at running this place myself. Did I tell you that yesterday I handled four phone calls?"

"You're someone I can really rely on, Ted," he told him, sending him off to his office with a light push.

He went back to his desk and started sifting through the mail in his in-box. When a sharp knock sounded at the door, he didn't even look up. "Come in," he said, expecting his secretary, Georgia, or Ted again.

It was long seconds until he noticed no one replied, and before he could look up, a now-familiar hand slapped a photograph on the desk blotter in front of him.

The picture was clearly taken at the restaurant he and Mitzi had gone to for brunch last Sunday. Sun shimmered off the lake, obscuring the left side of the picture with a sunburst reflection off the glass of the window. But in the corner of the frame was Ted, out of reach of the sunburst, leaning back in his lounge chair, smiling, with his blond friend sitting next to him, leaning close. It was a beautiful photo. Mitzi's talent with a lens was obvious.

So was the fact that Grant was now, officially and undeniably, in a pickle.

He took a gulp of air before looking into Mitzi's face. Her dark hair cascaded down her shoulders in dramatic waves, framing the anger in her beautiful green eyes. "I just got back from the developers," she told him in a clipped voice. "Imagine my surprise when I found that in the roll!"

"Mitzi, I can explain." But he stopped, wondering exactly how he should begin. *Remember your prom night?* would be one way.

"Don't!" she said, the hurt evident in her eyes. "I don't want you to explain in detail how I was fooled."

"It's not how it looks," he told her, but the words had a flaccid thud to them.

She began pacing furiously. "I thought it was strange that you arrived so late, and out of breath. Now I get it— too many women were running you ragged! You probably had a whole harem hidden away in that restaurant."

"Don't be absurd," he said. "It was just that woman, and—"

"Who was she?"

Grant's mind raced, trying to remember. "Veronique?"

Her face fell, and she let out a squeak of dismay. "Veronique? The supermodel?"

Grant had wondered why the woman looked familiar, but he hadn't given the matter much thought. "I guess."

Mitzi slapped her cheek with one hand and shook her head in disbelief. "Well! At least that's a step up from the Sears catalog."

Grant shook his head, trying to keep up with her. "It's not what you're thinking, Mitzi." He rose from his chair and crossed to her, but she darted away from him, toward the door.

"I thought you were different, Grant. For one day I dared to think that you were the man who was going to turn my luck around. But now I'd just as soon not see you again!"

She ran out and down the hall, leaving Grant so stunned, and his emotions so disordered, that he felt as if a tornado had just torn through his office and his heart. He wanted to sprint after her, but one thought stopped him. She was right. He had been dishonest with her from the start. He could have told her the truth, many times, but he'd been afraid of losing her. And now, the very thing he'd been afraid of had happened anyway.

Ted ducked his head inside the door. "Was that streak of human being I saw running down the hall who I think it was?"

Grant sighed. "That was Mitzi."

"Yeah, that's about how I remember her."

Grant sank into his chair again and tossed the picture across his desk to Ted. "She brought me this. She thought you were me."

Ted pointed to the tree behind his table. "But there you are, see? That's your elbow sticking out behind the ficus. Couldn't you have pointed that out to her?"

"Somehow, I doubt she would have been comforted by the sight of an elbow behind a bush." Grant buried his head in his hands. "She was too sidetracked by the blonde you were sitting with. You never told me she was a model.''

"Look on the bright side," Ted said. "If she'd snapped the picture fifteen seconds later, she might have caught you necking with the blond model."

For a bright side, it was pretty gloomy. Grant gathered a breath and looked up at his brother. "Well. This solves one problem."

"What's that?"

"Dinner. I guess I'll be able to make it, after all."

Ted shook his head. "Grant, don't be a dope. Go after her and explain. She'd have to be pretty unreasonable not to accept that it was me."

"She doesn't know about you," Grant said.

Two blond eyebrows poked up in surprise. "You never told her you have a brother?"

"Worse. I didn't tell her I have a twin. I couldn't."

Ted was shocked. "Why not, for heaven's sake? You were with her for two whole days. What happened?"

Grant groaned. "Barry and Larry."

Ted shot him a dubious look and picked up the jewelry box from his desk. He tossed it in his palm and watched his brother wallow in despair. He felt terrible. After all, it was his big mouth that had made Mitzi so mad to begin with. Then he'd shown up at the restaurant when he should have stayed around longer with Mona and Truman. He wished he could do something to make it up to Grant.

And then it occurred to him. He *could* make it up to him.

Strange, last week he never would have attempted it. But the past few days had taught him something. Namely, that Grant wasn't the only can-do type in the Whiting clan. Casual day had been his own idea. Imagine! He'd never had an idea before, especially one that would be essential to saving the family business.

And if he could save the business, how much trouble could saving a romance be?

He pocketed the little box and headed out the door.

MITZI DIDN'T START calming down until she got home. And the flowers arrived.

See you tonight! was the perky message attached to the gorgeous arrangement of pink roses. Her favorite color.

But did the man really think she would still go out to dinner with him tonight?

Would she?

She felt tears building in her eyes and dashed them away. "No!" She wasn't going to be an idiot about this. She wasn't going to weep over a man she'd known for barely five full days. It was too ridiculous.

So he'd lied to her. Worse things had happened. She tried to concentrate on something really unpleasant, like Tim running off to the Himalayas. That had been mortifying. A true disaster. In a few weeks, this would barely register as a bleep on the romance Richter scale.

But somehow, she'd never felt as devastated as she did at just this moment. She'd trusted Grant, even when all the evidence pointed toward him being about as trustworthy as a rattlesnake. Why?

What really hurt was that he hadn't offered her any explanation. He'd just stood there.

Of course, a niggling voice reminded her, *you didn't let him speak.*

But he'd let her run away, making no attempt to follow.

In the backyard, Chester started barking up a storm.

At first, the sound barely registered. Then, in the next moment, the doorbell rang. Working on raw nerves, Mitzi ran over and threw the door open. On the other side stood Grant, in a dark brown suit, holding a huge bouquet of roses—red ones, this time.

"I'm sorry," he said. His arms jutted forward, holding the bouquet out to her stiffly. Mitzi felt her glacierlike heart begin to melt. Just a little.

But when she looked into his eyes, she didn't see even as much remorse as she'd seen in his office. In fact, there was a steeliness in his eyes that sobered her immediately. She took the flowers gingerly, as if they might be booby-trapped.

"I suppose you're going to say that there's a logical explanation," she said.

"Well, there's an explanation," he agreed. "I don't know how logical it is."

She pursed her lips. "I'd like to hear it anyway."

"Then come to dinner with me tonight," he said. Apparently he'd managed to change clothes but not work up an alibi. "Once we've cooled off, everything will seem less dramatic."

She'd promised herself she wasn't going to be an idiot. And she wasn't. But could it hurt to hear what the man had to say for himself?

"I'll pick you up at seven," he said. Rather presumptuously, she thought.

She lifted her chin. "I'll meet you at seven."

7

HORACE MORELAND MARCHED into the Sunset Grill ahead of four of his subordinates and Grant, carrying himself like a four-star general. Patton came to mind. He was stocky and leathery, with a helmet of spiky white hair, and looked as if he'd spent half his life in a sweaty foxhole somewhere. Probably he had. And now, even though he was in Austin, Texas, and wearing a dark-blue suit instead of fatigues, it was obvious he intended to conduct dinner like a basic-training maneuver.

"Table for six!" he bellowed as the hostess greeted them.

Grant stepped up to the startled woman and clarified, "We have a reservation under the name of Whiting."

Behind him, Horace harrumphed disgustedly. Apparently, he didn't believe in mollycoddling food workers.

"Ah, yes. Whiting for six," she said as if the place were simply teeming with Whiting parties. "Right this way, sir."

Horace grumbled. "You sure the service at this place is all right? Seems a little lax to me."

"Tip-top, sir." Grant suppressed the urge to click his heels.

The Sunset Grill occupied the first floor of a Victorian house in the oldest section of downtown Austin. As the hostess led them through the hallway connecting the maze of intimate dining rooms done in rustic decor, Grant absently peeked into each, trying to train his mind off the cheerless evening ahead. Much as he willed himself to concentrate, however, his head just wasn't in business right now.

How different this evening should have been. He and Mitzi, all alone at a cozy corner table, the whole evening stretching ahead of them like a promise.

So absorbed was his mind in the picture that for a moment he actually could see them—himself and Mitzi—at a table. She was decked out in a plum-colored dress cut low in back, and all her gorgeous hair was gathered at her nape, revealing tantalizing creamy skin covering her delicate spine. Across the table, Grant was looking at a menu.

The vision was so real Grant thought he might be going a little batty. Then it hit him. This wasn't his imagination. Ted was sitting at a table with Mitzi!

He stopped in the open door, gaping at the couple. *What the hell did Ted think he was doing?* He was on the verge of confronting his brother when a machine-gun bark fired in his ears.

"Whiting!"

At the sound of their shared name, Ted glanced up. He saw Grant, smiled and sent him a wave. Then Mitzi glanced up at Ted, and just before she could follow his gaze to the door, Grant ducked out of sight, breathing hard.

What was he going to do?

Suddenly, Moreland's Sam the Eagle beak was in his face. "Is something wrong with you, son?"

Grant peeled himself away from the wall. "No, sir."

His body moved in a trance toward the business dinner, while his mind lollygagged back at that cozy table for two. What was Ted up to? Damage control? Girlfriend snatching? It didn't seem likely that Ted would suddenly view the maid of horrors as good dating material. But why else on earth would Ted have brought her out, and here of all places?

"Whiting!" Horace shouted from the head of the table. "Good Lord, man, are you with us?"

Grant tried to clear his head and focus on Mr. Moreland. At least he'd managed to sit down at the right table without thinking. "I'm sorry. What were you saying?"

The man puffed up impatiently. "I said it was time we got down to brass tacks, son. We need to hammer out a few things about that business of yours. First off, there's the matter of your employee situation."

Grant squinted in confusion at his menu, then looked around and noted that none of his blue-suited companions had opened theirs. "Excuse me, but shouldn't we order our food first?"

"I always order the same thing," Horace replied gruffly. "Steak, rare. Same as all my employees! No sense wasting valuable time fussing with our food."

Grant swallowed and pushed his menu away. "How efficient," he muttered. As Moreland burst into song again about employees wearing shorts, Grant struggled to focus his mind on his dinner companion.

But What had Mitzi ordered? was the unbidden thought that jumped to his mind. And what was she saying to Ted? More important still, what was Ted saying to her?

Unexpectedly, even to himself, Grant rocketed out of his chair. "I'll be right back."

Without explaining further, he whipped out of the room and sprinted the short distance down the hallway. Halting in the door of Mitzi and Ted's dining room, he waved his arms until he finally captured his brother's attention. For the first time really appreciating that interminable evening he'd spent with Janice watching Marcel Marceau, he gesticulated for Ted to join him by the phones.

Ted was all cocky grins when he met him in the little hallway, where a five-prong deer head was mounted above the pay phone. "Am I handling it or am I?"

"Handling what?" Grant asked, furious.

"I asked Mitzi here so you could talk to her and you two could patch things up."

Grant rolled his eyes. "And how are we supposed to do that when I'm stuck two rooms away?"

"Will you calm down?" Ted began fiddling with his tie to take it off. "Remember when I asked you what you were wearing tonight? This is why. We've both got on blue suits and white shirts. Now all we have to do is switch ties."

Grant frowned skeptically.

"Just do it, Grant," his brother said. "Believe me, after tonight, you'll see I'm right."

"I think you're touched in the head. This isn't even remotely like a stunt you'd pull." Normally, Ted's m.o. was to extricate Grant from relationships.

"I'm a changed man, Grant. Really. In fact, once this night's over, I predict you'll be calling me Mr. Love."

Mr. Love? "Mr. Chowderhead, maybe."

"It's for your own good," Ted said. "I've already done the initial apologies. Now you just have to explain the truth."

There was a slim chance they could get away with it. Harebrained as Ted's plan was, this did give him a chance to try to come clean and smooth things over with Mitzi.

"All right," he agreed, ripping off his own tasteful

striped tie and exchanging it for Ted's, which was done in a loud floral pattern. "I wish Mr. Love had better fashion sense."

"That tie's very *GQ*."

"Which doesn't necessarily correlate with IQ," Grant noted.

Ted's lips thinned and his expression turned funereal as he contemplated his role in this charade. "Okay, where's Herr Moreland?"

Grant poked him in the right direction and, taking a deep breath, went to meet Mitzi, his heart hammering as nervously as if he were about to step onto a Broadway stage.

He sat down at the candlelit table where everything was just as he had hoped it would be before his world had kissed the dust this afternoon. The lights were low, Mitzi's green eyes looked sultry across the table. Sultry and solemn. Apparently, Ted hadn't done a stellar job making those initial apologies.

"I'm sorry, I didn't mean to leave you sitting at the table alone for so long," he told her, watching for signs that she was on to the switch. So far so good.

"That's all right." She cleared her throat. "You can go ahead now."

Grant tried not to look befuddled. Ted had omitted something. "Go ahead with what?"

Her eyes had an almost gleefully skeptical glint. "You were about to explain why you were talking to Veronique when you were supposed to be making a phone call."

"Oh." He swallowed. This was a hell of a place to pick up a conversation. "The truth is, Mitzi..."

She smiled patiently. "Don't sweat it, Grant. Remember, I was born with a heart-shaped rain cloud over my head."

"The truth is…" Larry and Barry loomed large in his mind. What if she guessed that it was his brother, not himself, who had instigated this reunion tonight. What would she think of him then?

She sighed and put down her napkin as if she was about to get up and leave. "I knew this dinner was a bad idea."

"No, wait," he said, reaching across the table to take her hand in his. She sank into her seat again like a patient waiting to hear an unpleasant diagnosis. "Mitzi, listen. That woman, she's just a model who was doing some print ads for the store. I saw her through the window and didn't want you to think I was trying to ditch you. It was stupid of me, juvenile, but the truth is really that she means zip to me. I don't know why I behaved so foolishly. I'm sorry."

Her cheeks reddened as she stared at their hands intertwined against the starched white tablecloth. "Honestly, I don't know why I flew off the handle like I did," she admitted. "By this afternoon, I felt a little silly. I guess it just seemed we were so close at the lake, and after last night, watching movies and cuddling on the couch.…"

He nodded, feeling his groin stiffen at the very thought of cuddling. He wanted her so fiercely he could hardly wait for dinner to end.

She smiled, blissfully unaware of his physical agony. "It didn't really occur to me until after I had stormed out of your office that at the time that picture was taken, we barely knew each other. And there I was behaving as if I had some exclusive rights to you even then."

He frowned. The thing was, he wanted her to have exclusive rights to him. How could he explain it? She was the first woman he'd ever felt he truly wanted to belong to. Even after being married once, the feeling was a shocker. For the first time, he understood the reasoning behind all those ultra-PC New Age guys—the Alan Alda types who took their wives' names after marriage and wore matching T-shirts and insisted on being the ones to wash the dirty diapers. That was how he felt about Mitzi.

Okay, maybe he wouldn't change his name, but...

She frowned at him. "Did I say something wrong?"

"No," he exclaimed. "Everything's perfect."

"Oh, good, the food," she said, looking up as a waiter brought along a tray laden with their feast. Grant watched in approval as grilled chicken smelling of rosemary sizzled on a plate in front of Mitzi. His stomach rumbled. Then, the waiter placed Grant's plate down.

"Your venison, sir." Grant's stomach rumbled again, this time unhappily, as the waiter handed him a note. "A man down the hall asked me to give you this."

"Something wrong?" Mitzi asked.

She meant the note, but Grant focused his gaze on the plate as his hands unwrapped the message. "Eating venison never has been the same since I saw *Bambi*."

She frowned. "Then why did you order it?"

Good question. Grant frowned as he looked down at Ted's note. *Help! What is this guy talking about? Could you please meet me by the deer head? T.*

Grant's stomach sank in dread. No telling what Ted was doing in there. He'd thought his brother was catching on to the business, but what if he fouled up at this late date? Then the store would be lost.

Beads of sweat popped out on his temples. Grant folded the note and stood. "Will you excuse me again? Something's come up at the store."

"I hope it's nothing serious," Mitzi said, her forehead puckering in concern.

This time when Grant met Ted by the phones, his brother was agitated, and his tie was already off. "You've got to go back in there. He's talking about five-year inventory and position statements and all sorts of stuff I have no idea about."

Grant reluctantly removed his own tie. "Couldn't you have changed the subject? I was just smoothing things over."

Ted looked frazzled. "I'm drowning, man!"

It seemed strange to Ted that Grant wasn't just a teensy bit more grateful, considering all he'd done for him. But as he strode back to Mitzi's table, he tried to be big-hearted and not let it bother him. Even having to deal with nutso Mitzi was better than being baffled by a to-talitarian businessman like Moreland.

"Is everything all right?" Mitzi asked.

Ted nodded. "Oh, sure." At least the food was better here. He couldn't believe Grant had left all this beautiful deer meat untouched.

Mitzi blinked as she watched him scarfing down his dinner. "What was the emergency at the store?"

"Emergency?" he asked, then gulped down a piece of meat. Grant must have told her there was something wrong at Whiting's. He shrugged casually as his mind scrambled for an excuse. "Oh…it was just a…a fire."

"Fire!" She gasped. "Goodness! Shouldn't you—"

"It's out now," Ted assured her. That taken care of, he dug into his venison with more gusto.

Mitzi was watching him like an anthropologist who had just been teleported back to Cro-Magnon days. In fact, she wore a vaguely disgusted look, as if he were eating Bambi. City people!

He wished she would say something. Anything. They

just kept chewing and avoiding each other's eyes. Didn't she and Grant ever talk?

Something had to be done to break the ice. Feeling inspired, Ted finally remembered—the little jewelry box. He'd forgotten to hand it to Grant when they exchanged ties. Maybe that wasn't such a bad thing, though. Grant seemed a bit slow at getting the job done here, whereas Ted, the old football hero, could take the ball and run with it.

He finished swallowing a piece of meat, took a slug of wine and winked at Mitzi. "I got you something, doll-face."

She frowned. "I beg your pardon?"

Smiling big, he took the ring box out of his jacket pocket and shoved it across the table toward her. At least this would give them something to do. "For you."

Her mouth dropped open.

He laughed impatiently. "Well, don't just sit there gawking. Pop the thing open!"

Tentatively, she reached across and cradled the small velvet box. "You shouldn't have," she told him. "If this gift is just because of what happened this afternoon...."

Ted rolled his eyes. "Nah, I'd already shelled out the bucks by the time you broke into your Joan Crawford-shrew routine."

She flinched, then slammed the box down. "Look, you don't seem to believe I'm sorry for what I said this afternoon."

God, how annoying. Didn't the woman have a sense of humor? "I believe you, I believe you. Go ahead and open it."

She pursed her lips and took up the box again, touching it gingerly as if it might be rigged with an explosive device. Ted rolled his eyes.

Then, just as she was opening the thing, panic set in. He hadn't looked in the box. He'd assumed it contained some kind of pin or something. But what if it was something else?

Like an engagement ring!

"Wait," he shouted, waving his hands frantically. "Don't open that!"

Startled, Mitzi looked up at him. "What's wrong?"

If it was an engagement ring, what should he do? He couldn't ask the woman to marry him just because the conversation was lagging. But if Grant had bought the engagement ring, surely he wouldn't mind. Of course, some people liked to handle things like that for themselves.

But he couldn't take the little box back from her now, after the big buildup. He sighed. "Oh, never mind. Go ahead."

She bridled impatiently. "Grant, is there something wrong?"

Yes! If this was an engagement ring, shouldn't he be on his knees? Or was it just one knee? He knew there was something in proposal protocol about knees. Of course, if it wasn't an engagement ring, he'd look pretty damn silly on the floor.

He compromised by subtly dropping his napkin. Once he was on one knee, groping for the cloth, he shook his head. "No, everything's fine. Go ahead and open it," he said, adding, "Quick." His knee creaked from an old football injury.

With a grunt of aggravation, she took the box and flipped the top open. She gasped, and Ted smiled. Mission accomplished.

Really, he decided, he was getting fairly adept at all this romance stuff. And he had to admit, watching his brother's sufferings over Mitzi had given him a little curiosity about the whole true-love equation. Maybe there was something to it. In fact, when Mitzi's eyes teared up, he felt his heart swell in a way it hadn't since the last time the Cowboys had won the Super Bowl.

In fact, the whole thing made him wonder, and he didn't wonder very often. But he'd never felt so moved by the idea of a wedding ring. Could it be that he'd been missing something? Maybe that all his sneering at marriage was only skin-deep? Maybe *he* was really easy pickin's for some wily female. And why didn't that idea scare him the way it should?

The whole thing was blowing his mind.

Then Mitzi held up the little gold piece, and he nearly lost it. It wasn't a ring at all, just a lousy little charm shaped like a camera. He got off his knees, fast, feeling something like a letdown. After all, this was supposed to have been the first time he'd ever proposed to a woman.

For a moment, Mitzi felt as if her heart just might break. But in a good way. "Oh, how beautiful! How thoughtful! How..."

"Cheesy," Ted muttered.

She shot a questioning frown at him. "What?"

"Do you mean you like it? Really?"

"Oh, yes!" She lifted her bracelet toward him. "Here, put it on."

His eyes rounded in horror. "You want me to wear your bracelet?"

She laughed. "No, silly. Put the charm on the bracelet."

The lines etched in his face relaxed. "Oh!"

Funny, but she wondered if she would ever be used to Grant and his moods. He could be so caring and kind at times, yet so distant and tough at others. Even when he was doing something incredibly sweet, like now, an unexpected coldness could surface in his manner that was downright offputting.

A wave of guilt washed over her as she watched his large fingers fumble with the tiny charm. How could she be so critical when she was obviously nuts about him? After how heartbroken she'd been this afternoon, she should have been jumping for joy.

"Oh, Grant," she said when he was done. "I'm so—"

A waiter approached, note in hand, and Grant held his palm out to her. "Hold that thought, sweetheart." He jumped up from the table.

Mitzi recoiled, stunned. She'd thought they were having a tender moment, but her Romeo was making like Speedy Gonzales out to the hallway. She was floored by the way he could turn her off and on. Certainly she understood work emergencies. She wasn't completely unreasonable. But the man was a department store owner, not a brain surgeon. Which was probably a good thing, considering that he had the attention span of a flea.

And where did he get off calling her sweetheart and dollface?

By the time Grant slipped back into the seat across from her, she had worked up a head of steam again. "More about the fire?"

He sent her a smile that remained disconnected from his eyes. "Fire?"

"The one at the store," she reminded him.

"Oh, that," he exclaimed, understanding. He waved a hand at her dismissively. "Turns out it was a false alarm."

"Strange that it took two phone calls to confirm a fire that didn't exist." She slanted a glance at him, trying not to be too accusatory. "You don't happen to have anyone hidden away in another part of the restaurant, do you?"

He practically jumped out of his skin. "What do you mean?"

She laughed. "Say, a spare supermodel?"

His blue-eyed stare took a moment to register the joke. "Good heavens, no!" He reached across the table and took her hand. "I'm sorry, Mitzi. I promise, the rest of the meal, I'm all yours."

As if on cue, a guitarist wandered up to the table and bowed to Mitzi. "By request," he said, then started playing a sentimental instrumental rendition of "Angel Eyes" as she and Grant held hands and looked into each other's eyes. She felt her heart swell to bursting for him all over again. Some men were shy about doing the romantic, corny things that meant so much. With her eyes dangerously close to tears, she jangled her little camera charm at him.

His eyes zoomed in on the charm and widened in surprise. "Well, I'll be damned." He grabbed her wrist and examined it more closely. "Where did you get that?"

She yanked her arm away from him. "Grant, you're crazy!"

"You didn't have that at the lake." The words were almost a reproach.

"Of course not."

The ubiquitous waiter leaned down to Grant's ear and he shot out of his chair and looked back at Mitzi apologetically. "I'm sorry," he said quickly. "You understand..." Flustered, he pulled a wad of bills out of his pockets and stuffed them in the minstrel's breast pocket. "Keep playing till I get back."

Then he ran out.

Mitzi fumed. What the heck was going on?

By the time Grant came back to the table in a flurry, his tie askew, she was in no mood to hear any excuses about phone calls or fires. The guitarist was finished with ''Angel Eyes'' and was now halfway through a slow, Latin tune that sounded like music to tie one on by. Mitzi poured herself another glass of wine and slugged it down.

Grant watched her, then flicked the musician an annoyed gaze. ''I'm with you,'' he muttered in a stage whisper. ''That guitar noise would drive anyone to drink.''

Despite the bills Grant had stuffed in his pockets, the musician didn't take the insult lightly, and moved his trade elsewhere. Grant didn't seem to mind. He glanced apologetically at Mitzi. ''Sorry, but this is Austin. You just can't get away from those penny-ante musician types.''

Mitzi tossed down her napkin. ''I've had enough!''

Grant looked shocked. ''Hey, chill.''

She sent him her most quelling gaze. ''A chill is what you've given me at least several times tonight. What's the matter with you?''

He sputtered in amazement at her outburst. ''What the hell's the matter with you?''

This was the limit. ''You're driving me crazy, that's what's wrong!'' she shouted, drawing curious gazes from nearby tables. No doubt they were wondering how two people who were just holding hands and looking into each other's eyes could erupt in anger so quickly, but no one could be more confused by the schizophrenic romantic atmosphere than she was. ''You're either a compulsive liar or a split personality. What is your favorite book, Grant?''

He didn't bat an eye. *''To Kill a Mockingbird.''*

''And what happens in that book?''

He blinked. "What is this, a pop quiz? A lot happens."

"Who's the main character?"

He sent her a withering yet vaguely uncomfortable gaze. "Don't be a dope. Gregory Peck."

She let out a muffled howl. "I knew it! I knew I was being a chump!"

He tried to shush her, which only made her quiver with ire. "Would you stop making a scene?"

He wished! "I'll bet you don't even sing."

"Sing?" he repeated as if she'd gone loco.

She crossed her arms. "Sing a hymn, Grant. Any hymn."

He shot her a cold, stony gaze. "Lady, are you on some kind of medication that you've forgotten to take?"

She sprang out of her chair and turned on him in such a fury that not only did the people in the intimate room stare, but waitresses gathered at the door to gape. "You've never told me the truth, not from day one. I'll bet you've never stepped foot in a church."

"Don't be a nitwit, of course I have. I went…several Easters ago."

She released a howl of frustration. "There! See?" Tears gathered in her eyes. She had to get out of here. Fast. "And I bet you've never even seen *Bambi!*"

She whirled on her heel and stomped out of the room and the restaurant, leaving Ted stunned. *What the heck was that about?* He got up and scurried from the room to hunt down Grant.

That blowhard Moreland was carrying on about catalog sales when Ted interrupted them. For a moment, he endured another round of gaping stares from this bunch. Then Grant jumped up.

"What the hell is going on here?" Moreland demanded, likewise shooting up from his chair. "All night long we've been interrupted. Is there something wrong?"

Ignoring the older man, who looked about as irritated as Mitzi had been, Ted pulled his brother into the hallway. "Mitzi left," he told him.

Grant's face fell. "Why?"

Ted shrugged. "It's like I've always said—the woman's a basket case. A real Prozac princess. I told her I didn't like musicians singing at me while I'm trying to eat, and she just went berserk."

"Oh, no," Grant moaned, slapping his forehead.

Ted frowned. "Does she have a musician in her family or something?"

Grant rolled his eyes. "Stay here, will you? I have to go after her."

Ted watched his brother dash out of the room, then he turned back to the infuriated Mr. Moreland and felt a stab of dread pierce his heart. Why was he always left with the dirty work?

And now it occurred to him that Grant hadn't allowed him to explain all the stuff Mitzi had been saying about churches and singing. And *Bambi*. He needed to make sure his brother was prepared to handle what he was running into.

"I'm sorry, Mr. Moreland," he said, scuttling forward to shake the man's hand, "but as you can see, we're having a sort of family crisis."

Horace's face burned fire-engine red. "I've never witnessed such erratic behavior in all my born days!"

Ted laughed nervously. "Yes, well, I'm sure you'll understand. Just sit down and finish your dinner, and I'm certain I'll be able to hear what you have to say about catalogs on the putting green tomorrow. It's been a real pleasure. Really. The best raw meat I've ever had.''

Ted turned and ran out of there as fast as he could.

BACK AT HOME, Mitzi was still fuming. How could she have been so gullible, so stupid? Before coming to Texas she'd sworn off romance, kissed expectations goodbye, lashed her heart into stable condition. Never again, she'd sworn solemnly to herself. It was spinsterhood or bust. She'd begun looking into intricate needlework projects and small talkative parrots.

And then Grant had come along.

''I don't want to think about it,'' she moaned aloud to Chester, who bounced joyfully at her ankles, oblivious to her despair. She grabbed his leash, snapped it onto his collar and let all her thoughts focus on being tugged down a sidewalk by a twenty-pound, half-bald bundle of canine exuberance. But before she'd walked half a block from the house, she spotted a white truck racing toward her, the same white truck Grant had been driving the night of the rehearsal dinner. The hulking vehicle squealed to a halt mere feet from her.

Grant sprang from the driver's seat and then skidded to a stop, frowning. ''Oh, it's just you.''

''Who were you expecting? Uma Thurman?''

He didn't crack a smile. ''Are you alone?''

Did he think she had men in reserve hovering by in case their date went sour? She was about to tell him off in no uncertain terms, but surprisingly, Chester took one look at Grant and went rigid. He bared his teeth and let out a warning growl, going from dachshund to Doberman in nothing flat.

Grant scowled at him. ''What's the matter with you, you little mutt?''

Mitzi gasped. She'd always thought Grant liked Chester. "How dare you talk to him that way."

"Give me a break." Grant scowled at the growling pup on the end of the taut leash. "That little hairball and I go way back."

At that moment, Mitzi took great pleasure in letting the dog's leash accidentally slip out of her hands.

Chester lunged at Grant like a little red bullet, snarling and snapping, and Grant turned and ran like hell for the nearest tree. He grabbed a low branch of a live oak and had swung one leg up when Chester, with the grace of Baryshnikov and the ferocity of Mike Tyson, jumped and sank his teeth into a pant leg.

The air exploded with rips, shouts, growls and curses.

"Get that mangy little cur off me!" Grant yelled.

Mitzi stood half stunned by and half enjoying the scene. She'd never known Chester was so ferocious, but then she'd never heard Grant call him a mangy cur before, either.

"Hmm, maybe I should call for help," she mused aloud.

Behind her, another car squealed up to the curb. She turned just in time to see Grant hopping out of his BMW. Her lips tilted up in an automatic smile—then froze.

In fact, her whole body froze, from her toes right up to her brain, which seemed to stop working. She was staring at Grant—that much she knew. He was standing right next to her, breathing hard. But not fifteen feet away, Chester was attempting to make hamburger of Grant's leg.

Now, how could that be?

8

MITZI GAPED at Grant. Grant Number Two, that is. "What the hell is going on?"

Grim-faced, he held up a hand, then attempted to pry Chester away from his double's leg. Chester, catching sight of the new arrival, immediately stopped growling and started groveling, whimpering and licking the second Grant. That Grant held the dog in his arms while Grant Number One, still cursing, fell out of the tree. He stood, stamping his feet and grumbling, and began slapping oak leaves and dirt off himself.

All three of them, the two Grants and the dog, looked up at Mitzi expectantly.

In that moment, she understood. Everything. If it had been physically possible, she would have given herself a swift kick in the pants. Instead, she settled for a sharp mental slap. How could she have been such a dummy when the evidence was there in front of her all the time? It's not like this was the first time this had happened to her. Grant wasn't a split personality. Or Dr. Jekyll and Mr. Hyde. He was *twins!*

Anger surged through her. And fury. And extreme, extreme relief.

"Mitzi?"

Grant wished he could sink into the ground. He wanted to take her into his arms and murmur every apology known to man.

Gathering his courage, he stepped forward, as close to her as he dared, remembering the punch in the jaw Ted had received. "I don't know where to begin."

"Maybe at the beginning," she said, tapping her foot impatiently.

The wedding. "Kay and Marty are my best friends, so I agreed to be Marty's best man. But as the wedding drew closer, I started obsessing about what a failure my own marriage had been."

"And you were worried because Kay was matchmaking."

Grant drew a breath of surprise. "How did you know?"

She lifted her shoulders. "Go on."

"So I sent my brother Ted in my place, and then things started snowballing."

Her lip quirked cynically. "Mistakes were made, as the politicians say," she said finishing for him.

"*I* made mistakes," he said. "Incredible ones. You threw me for a loop, Mitzi. I used to be honest, and responsible, and dependable. I had a certain amount of dignity. But since you came along, I've made a public spectacle of myself on several occasions. I've lied shamelessly, and ignored my work, and behaved in a way that even has shocked my brother. I've almost topped Janice in the dishonesty department. In short, I've joined the human race. And the reason is you, Mitzi. I'm crazy about you."

After his speech, she looked down at her feet and buried her face in her hands. Grant turned to his brother.

Ted was glaring at him in quizzical disgust. "That was an apology?"

Apparently, Mitzi didn't call it one. Her shoulders began to tremble.

Heedless of her notorious right hook, Grant ran forward. "Mitzi, I'm sorry. If I apologized a thousand times, it wouldn't be enough. If I ran a full-page apology in the *New York Times* for a solid year, it wouldn't even begin to explain how sorry I am. If I hired a skywriting plane and...Mitzi?"

A tear streaked down her cheek, piercing him to the core. Her whole body began to shake. Grant shifted Chester and reached out a hand to one of hers, pushing it away so he could see her eyes. When he'd moved her hands away, he got the shock of his life.

She wasn't crying at all. She was laughing! She let out a hoot and doubled over, pointing at him and his brother.

Grant was stunned. He turned to Ted, who was gaping at her with equal confusion. "I don't see what's so funny, do you?"

Ted swept a leaf away from his nose and shook his head. "I told you all along she was a loon."

To which Mitzi responded with another peal of laughter.

"OUCH!" Ted howled. "You're enjoying this!"

"Don't be silly," Mitzi replied soothingly. But of course she didn't exactly mind pouring rubbing alcohol onto the open wounds on Ted's hands, which had been scraped on tree bark during his attempted escape from the jaws of a crazed dachshund.

Ted made a hissing sound through his teeth. "None of this was my fault. Grant was the one who started everything."

They looked up into the bathroom mirror at the reflection of his brother, who was standing behind them. Grant lifted his shoulders innocently as she began to wrap Ted's hands in gauze.

"This is revenge for that itty-bitty bandage you wore on your cheek at the wedding," she told Ted.

Ted shook his head. "That wasn't me."

She looked into the mirror, where Grant lifted his hand to confess culpability. Would she ever sort this all out?

"Please tell me you were at least bruised," she asked Ted.

He scowled. "I drank out of a straw all day."

Mitzi grinned. What a relief. For the first time, she was really beginning to suspect she would be able to forgive them both. At first she'd been spitting mad, but as Grant had sputtered out his weird apology, her mood had shifted. It was all so ridiculous, and it was gratifying to know that Grant really was Grant, and not that other creature.

She finished her gauze handiwork with a flourish and herded the Bobbsey twins out of the bathroom. "There's one thing I'm still unclear about." She glanced from brother to brother. "When we kissed at the lake…"

Ted waved his hands frantically. "I was in Austin the whole time!"

Mitzi laughed at Ted's horrified reaction. They were like oil and water, but she was beginning to appreciate him. For not being Grant.

Speaking of whom… She turned to him and found him grinning at her, and felt her own lips hitch up in response. "Why didn't you tell me that you had such an emergency at work? I would have understood."

"You kept talking about how you hated workaholic men. Then, when I was about to tell you that Ted and I had changed places at the rehearsal dinner, you told me the Barry-Larry story."

She put her hands on her hips. "But the whole point

of that sad tale was that I got stuck with the icky brother. In this case it's reversed."

Laughing, the two of them glanced over at Ted, who raised his wrapped hands in surrender. "Hey, a man's ego can only take so much."

Mitzi ushered Ted out the front door and returned to Grant who was sprawled on the couch, his arm flung over his face. She giggled. "What are you doing?"

He peeked at her and sat up a little. "Just wondering how I can ever win back your trust." He shook his head sadly, but his arch tone made her question how seriously she should be taking him. She perched on the edge of the couch. "I heard the doubts in your voice when you were wondering which of us was at the lake with you, kissing you."

She nodded, catching his drift. "It is difficult to tell you two apart. The resemblance is uncanny."

He raised an eyebrow. "But what if I swore to you that I was the only one who had ever kissed you?"

She leaned closer. "I guess that would be one way to make sure I had the correct brother. Of course, I would have to be absolutely familiar with every aspect of a Grant Whiting kiss."

He frowned dramatically. "It wouldn't be easy."

She answered with a somber nod. "It would take a lot of research."

"And practice. You'd have to know every facet of what our kisses could be like, so that in the end, a peck on the lips would be like a PIN code between us."

"Or a lock combination," she agreed.

"Or like the magnetic strip on the back of a credit card—one swipe of the lips and you'd know I was the right guy." He pulled her achingly close, until their lips were practically touching.

"I'm pretty sure you're the right guy already." Just being in his arms felt undeniably right.

He looked up at her through dark-blue hooded eyes, and his voice grew gritty and husky. "Why don't we make it definite?"

Their lips touched and Mitzi felt an explosion of sensation inside her. Hard to believe that just seconds before she'd been laughing and joking. This kiss didn't feel like teasing, or flirtation. It wasn't a mere touch of lips. Instead, it was almost as if they were memorizing each texture and touch. Every turn of the head and movement of lips and tongue. The usual awkward bumping of noses didn't bring a giggle out of either one of them. Right away, this was a kiss that meant business.

She sank against him, not certain at first whether he had steered her that way or not. They were both respectably clothed, but there was nothing modest about the way they were touching each other. There was something irresistible about the rich fabric of his jacket that made her want to run her hands underneath it, feeling the outlines of his chest as the silky lining of the jacket caressed her hand. She couldn't help noticing that he seemed likewise intrigued by the sueded silk of her dress. As they feasted on each other's lips, the air was thick with the sounds of whispers and rustles of fabric. Each movement of his hands as they caressed her arms, raced up and down her spine or made lazy circles around the perimeter of her low-backed dress sent spears of desire darting through her.

After the stress of an overly dramatic day, Mitzi found release in doing no thinking at all, just feeling. The taste of him, the fading scent of his aftershave, the warm strength of his lips—reveling in these sensations could have occupied her for hours. When he ran a hand expertly over her hip and down her leg, however, she let out a low moan, causing him to look up.

"Too much?" he asked.

Not nearly enough, she thought, letting the words remain unspoken as she looked into his handsome face. His blue eyes were as dark as a midnight sky. Thank heavens for the autonomic nervous system. She couldn't think of any other way she would have been able to breathe.

"In school, I was always terrible at remembering locker combinations," she told him. "I had to practice it over and over."

He smiled, then reached up and idly replaced a stray lock of her hair behind her ear. "It's terrible to be locked out," he said, giving her chin a little nibble.

Her heart started beating an erratic, insistent rhythm, like the tom-toms of an exotic jungle tribe. "And those little magnetic strips on the backs of credit cards..."

He bestowed her neck with a series of pecks and kisses. She shivered.

"...they're not very reliable. You have to keep testing to make sure they're functioning properly."

"Mmm," he agreed, touching that little hollow at the base of her throat with his lips. "You can never be too careful."

The tom-toms were thumping away like crazy now, and when he experimentally undid the top button of her dress, she felt as if a whole tribe was doing a fire dance in her stomach. She looked down at Grant and maneuvered a hand over his. "Grant," she said. Everything was happening so fast.

Then again, sometimes fast was good.

He lifted her hand to his lips and kissed it. "Something incredible has happened to me."

Something incredible was happening to her, too.

Namely, her blood felt as if it were transforming into molten lava. "What?" she managed to croak.

"I think I love you, Mitzi."

Suddenly, her doubts shattered. Her inhibitions, too. And her good sense, but that had taken a hike the first time she'd looked into Grant's blue eyes—*really* looked into his eyes, that day at the wedding.

She was on the verge of telling him that she loved him, too. That she'd loved him ever since the night he'd walked her around the neighborhood and told her about how he'd had to move out of the house where he'd harbored so many dreams of raising a family.

But he captured her lips again, making words superfluous. All that she would have had such a hard time saying aloud, she could now express in their kiss. And when the vocabulary of their lips seemed to fall short of what she wanted to communicate, she moved her body needfully against his, and perfectly expressed her mounting desire by boldly pushing off his coat and undoing his tie and the buttons of his dress shirt. She longed to feel his bare skin against her palms.

He caught her hand again and smiled. "I don't want to make love to you on a couch, Mitzi."

She drew back, smiling. "Whoever built this house was ingenious. There's a bedroom just steps away from here."

But when she looked toward the bedroom door, it seemed miles away. There was nothing more awkward than standing up, half-dressed, and stumbling for the nearest bed.

But she should have known that Grant would allow nothing about intimacy between them to be awkward. In one fast movement, he stood, gave her a hand up, then lifted her off her feet, carrying her against his chest into the bedroom. It was the first time a man had ever truly swept her off her feet.

He placed her lovingly on the bed and undressed her as carefully as if she were a treasured gift. Each time a new part of her was exposed, he stopped to examine and caress. His searing blue gaze made her feel beautiful, and cherished. And being the recipient of so much loving attention in turn gave her a confidence she'd never had before, so that when it was her turn to respond in kind, she didn't flinch. How could she? Her curiosity, her desire, was too great.

When they finally lay in each other's arms, both as naked as the day they were born, she felt that she had never been so close to another person before. But how could that be? They'd only known each other for such a short time. Maybe he did have some magical bewitching power that made her lose her good sense. Or, more wonderful still, maybe they were just meant to be.

She hoped it was true. She wanted to believe that when they made love, it would be the beginning of forever for both of them. That they would create a full life together, and a home, and children. Could it be? The jungle drums still beating insistently inside certainly felt that way. But what was left of her rational mind piped in with a memory.

I think I love you, Mitzi.

He thought he loved her. As usual, she was pondering forever, and the man was just agonizing over the moment-to-moment.

As last-minute doubts swirled in her mind, her eyes remained riveted on Grant, his eyes, his gorgeous body, his very aroused body. She blushed, the first hint of modesty she'd shown all night, then remembered how desperately she had waited for this moment. How unhappy she'd been when she'd thought, even for a short time, that she and Grant might never get their relationship off the ground. Now it was taking off like a rocket, and she wasn't about to complain.

He pulled her close, kissing her earlobe, and whispered, "Is something wrong?"

Too often in the past, she'd deep-sixed her romances by pushing for a commitment too soon. Not this time, she vowed to herself as she felt desire build from his caresses. This time, she would live in the here and now. If it killed her.

She nestled closer to him. "Everything's perfect."

And once their passion had played out and they lay together, sated and happy in each other's arms, she knew that she had spoken truly. Everything was perfect.

For now.

As GRANT'S EYES swept open, he was overcome with bliss. In his arms lay Mitzi, her hair tousled across the pillow. His fingers itched to comb through all that luxurious hair, but he didn't want to disturb her. Instead, he basked in the memory of all that had taken place last night. He'd never felt so much for anyone before. It was more than infatuation, that was for sure. The woman had turned his life upside down, and at a time when it seemed pretty wobbly already.

With the ink on his divorce papers barely dry, he'd found the woman he wanted to spend the rest of his life with. The trouble was, she wasn't even going to be in the same city after Saturday, and that was only two full days away. Long-distance romances being what they were, their fledgling relationship seemed destined to go the way of the dodo bird before it was barely off the ground.

As if sensing the tension his gloomy thoughts had spawned, Mitzi turned in his arms and looked up at him. Grant's heart did an elaborate flip in his chest. For a moment he was blinded as he remembered every touch, taste and sound. He swallowed, barely suppressing a groan. He thought his body would have been absolutely sated. Not so.

She smiled contentedly and stretched like some exotic feline after a particularly satisfying catnap. He couldn't stop looking at her. He wanted to make love to her again in the most desperate way.

Mitzi gazed back at him, and her smile slowly faded until dread registered in her eyes. "This is it, isn't it?"

He frowned. "This is what?"

"The end." Stoically, she sat up, careful to keep the floral sheet modestly over her bosom. "I should have known that after the most fantastic night of my life, I would wake up and discover I've been living in a fool's paradise."

He was having a hard time following her. "Last night was the most fantastic night of your life? Really?"

Mitzi groaned, collapsed, then flopped the bedsheet over her face. "Oh, how mortifying," her muffled voice exclaimed. "I thought you were at least enjoying yourself, too."

Grant shook his head, wondering how two people could make such a muddle of communication. "Are you kidding? It was wonderful!"

But he was talking to a bedsheet. He pried the sheet back down over her head and looked into her eyes. "Would you please come up for air and tell me what's wrong?"

Mitzi hesitated. Grant's confusion sounded genuine— a good sign. Last night she had let her guard down so completely; she'd never been so uninhibited with a man. Or so nervous come the dawn. But maybe for once the ax wasn't going to fall.

She shimmied up to a sitting position and eyed him doubtfully. "You tell me."

He looked perplexed. "The only thing wrong I can think of is that we're eventually going to have to get out of our love nest to forage for food."

Her assessing gaze remained pinned on him, until slowly the sincerity in his eyes telegraphed to her heart. "You mean you weren't about to tell me *bon voyage?*"

"Where did you get that idea?"

She smiled. Wonder of wonders! "You mean you aren't about to set off on your dream of exploring Antarctica?"

"Not in this lifetime."

Mitzi looked into those blue eyes of his and felt her fears fade away. "Oh, Grant," she exclaimed, melting against him. "I don't even want to think about lifetimes, or what might happen tomorrow. For once, I'm going to go with the flow and enjoy myself."

He looked down at her, confused. Was she still thinking that they were having a fling? "But?"

She covered his lips. This morning, she didn't want to hear any proclamations that might not hold water in another week. "No, Grant, let's take this one day at a time."

Grant frowned. "That shouldn't be difficult, since we only have two days." Personally, he was ready for two decades, two lifetimes, two centuries, but he didn't want to overplay his hand. If Mitzi wanted to take it one day at a time, he'd have to go along with her. After all, just five days ago he'd told his brother he wasn't ready to get married again.

There was only one problem. He didn't want her to leave.

"Why don't you stay?" he asked.

"In Austin?" She propped up on one elbow and studied his face. "I can't," she said regretfully. "I'm due back at the office on Monday."

Office!

Suddenly his work came rushing back to his love-fogged memory. It wasn't only Mitzi's timetable getting in their way. In an agony of dread, he slapped his palm over his forehead.

Mitzi hovered over him, concerned. "What's the matter?"

"The next two nights are a mess. Tomorrow my stepmother is having a big party for the people who want to buy Whiting's. I have to be there."

Mitzi smiled. "I've got the perfect party dress, Grant. It's lime-green, and has a few food stains on it, but I'm sure you won't be too embarrassed to be seen with me."

A party at Mona's wasn't how he wanted to spend his last night with Mitzi, but she did have a point. Grant grinned back at her, and for a moment as he looked into her sunny eyes, a weight fell off his shoulders. How could he worry about a stupid party when he was in bed with the most wonderful, whimsical woman in the world?

"Tell you what," he said. "Forget the party. We'll tag it, then we'll have one of our own—a party for two catered by yours truly, with thick steaks and champagne."

Mitzi's mouth watered in anticipation. "Steaks and champagne, and a bubble bath."

He raised an eyebrow. "Would that be as an appetizer, or dessert?"

"I always wanted to drink champagne in a bubble bath," she explained.

"But wouldn't a whole dinner get a little messy? I mean, the steak juice running into the bathwater."

Mitzi laughed. "Okay, forget the bubble bath."

Grant gazed at her adoringly, and in a moment she could tell that the bubble-bath idea had also taken root in his imagination. "Don't worry, we'll work around it."

In fact, a long bubble bath with Mitzi might be just the thing to top off this stressful week, Grant thought. Of course, he tried not to dwell on the fact that they were planning their private farewell wingding. He couldn't bear the thought of parting from her just now, when they were suddenly so close and so happy.

Two days. It was so little time. Tonight. Thursday night. He groaned.

"What is it?" Mitzi asked, looking primed for bad news.

He hesitated to bring up his date with Joy Moreland, but decided that honesty was the only policy to use with Mitzi from now on. "The real problem is tonight. Ted promised my stepmother that I would take out Mr. Moreland's daughter. I'd rather have a root canal, but I don't see a way out of it."

Mitzi nibbled her lower lip in thought. "There must be some way out."

They both lay flat on their backs, staring up at the ceiling, searching for an answer. So much was hanging in the balance. One night. It didn't sound like much, but when it came to Mitzi, Grant didn't want to sacrifice a single hour.

Mitzi bolted up. "Ted!"

Grant sat up, too, but quickly shook his head, catching her drift. "He wouldn't do it. I don't even feel comfortable asking him to."

"Why not?"

"He's already picked up so much of the slack."

There was no hiding Mitzi's disappointment. It shot like a spear through his heart. "But don't you see? Ted is your secret weapon. One date with him and Joy Moreland will pack her father's bags and they'll head back to wherever they came from."

Grant laughed. "You know, you might be on to something."

"I speak from experience. After one truck ride with your brother, I was ready to hop on the next plane out of Austin." She grinned. "And to make sure the plan's a success, I might try to find Joy Moreland ahead of time. Just to make sure she and Ted really hit it off. Maybe I'll suggest a long boat ride, and you could make sure they have an especially wonderful time by performing a little nautical sabotage."

Grant still hesitated. Even if Mr. Love had botched quite a bit of last night, in the final analysis his efforts were a sizzling success. He didn't want to pay Ted back by forcing him into doing another switch.

He felt Mitzi's hand on his thigh, and when he looked into her green eyes he didn't miss the sensual intent in them. Her hand began to work a slow path toward the part of him that was already burning with hunger for her. He swallowed.

A slow grin touched her lips. "It would just be this one last time," she whispered in a voice that was practically a coo.

When Mitzi's fingertips finally reached their ultimate destination, Grant closed his eyes and felt all thought of resistance fly from his mind.

Mitzi could be quite persuasive.

HAUTE HAIR, one of the more fashionable salons among the Generation X set, was in full swing that afternoon.

Every station was filled. Mitzi was lucky enough to maneuver herself into a chair next to Joy, whose whereabouts she had found out after a fib-filled call to the Morelands' hotel suite. Joy was a pretty, chipmunk-cheeked young woman still on the beer-and-peanuts side of twenty-five. Her perfectly sculpted body was tanned and fit without looking overly muscled up. And those cheeks of hers gave her the aura of being a soft little cuddlebug. A Sandra Dee for the nineties.

And, God bless her, she was a chatterbox, and luckily for Mitzi, the one topic she absolutely couldn't shut up about was Grant Whiting.

"His stepmother says he's just a doll," the young woman jabbered to her stylist, a green-haired woman in her thirties who looked bored by what Joy was saying. "And so sad—his wife just left him flat. Can you imagine? I know that if I ever get married, I'll never get a divorce. My parents were divorced, and I've always sworn that I'll never go through that. Or put my children through that. Once I get married, that's it, so it's got to be love. Love, and financial solvency. I don't know if I could give up my Bergdorf charge account!"

Beneath her silver plastic salon poncho, Joy's shoulders squared with determination at the thought of finding Mr. Right for the high-end shopper. Mitzi felt for her—little did Joy Moreland know that she was aiming at the wrong target.

"Of course, Daddy doesn't want me to get married right away," Joy said. "He's one of those strict old-fashioned dads. Still and all, I sometimes think it would be just so great to bust out on my own and get married. I majored in psychology in college, so I know it's really important for a young woman to establish her independence from her parents. Especially if a good-looking rich guy who can take care of her comes along.''

''Excuse me,'' Mitzi said, unable to hold back any longer. The whole situation was too beautiful. This girl and Ted were from warring tribes, personality-wise. She swiveled toward Joy. ''Did I hear you mention Grant Whiting?''

Joy's thick-lashed blue eyes widened in curiosity. ''Do you know him?''

She nodded, putting on her most sorrowful expression. ''I guess you could say we were practically an item for several months not too long after his wife left him.''

''What happened?''

''I made a terrible mistake with Grant. I kept him hanging. I was afraid of commitment.''

''Oh!'' Joy the psychology major blinked in astonishment. ''I know all about that. Usually it's men who are afraid to commit.''

''Not Grant,'' Mitzi said gravely. ''He's one of those men who are just meant to be married. Someone just needs to come along and snatch him, some lucky girl who would like to be married to a total dreamboat.''

As Joy stared at Mitzi, her stylist grabbed the younger woman by her slack jaws and faced her forward, forcing her and Mitzi to communicate through mirrors. ''But that's such a coincidence. *I* want to get married to a dreamboat!''

''Wow,'' Mitzi mouthed. ''That *is* a stroke of luck. But I hope you don't make the same mistakes that I made.''

The girl was practically quivering in anticipation. ''Do you think you could help me? I'm shy around strangers. It would be great if you could tell me a little about what Grant likes and what to talk about.''

Yeah, right…the tongue-tied type. "The first thing you should insist upon—absolutely insist upon—is going out in Grant's boat," Mitzi counseled. "The man loves his boat."

"I love boats," Joy exclaimed. "I was Kappa Kappa Gamma's water-ski champion my last spring break at Fort Lauderdale. Not that I like to brag, or anything."

"Get him to take you out on that boat, the farther away the better. Tell him you've always wanted to see the Atlantic Ocean, if you have to," Mitzi instructed. "Once you've dropped anchor, and the moonlight is shining on all that water, you can tell him about the real Joy Moreland—water-ski champ, shopper extraordinaire—and all about your aspirations for a home and a great big family."

Five minutes later, Joy practically had tears in her eyes as she thanked Mitzi for the advice. "Do you really think he'll like me? I really want this to work." She looked down at her silver poncho shyly. "See, I've had several bad experiences with men since leaving college."

At the sound of that last sentence, Mitzi knew she shouldn't have looked into Joy's mirror, because what she saw in those Sandra Dee blinkers, unbelievably, was the disappointed gaze of a fellow traveler on the bumpy road of singlehood. And Joy would just be starting out. Every protective instinct in Mitzi told her to put a stop to the ruse, to tell little Joy to run, flee, to go right out and buy herself a puppy, anything!

But she had to remember the short-term objective of getting the Morelands out of the Whitings' hair. She couldn't think of a better way. She forced a smile. "Like you? Honey, he'll eat you up."

9

"IN AND OUT," Grant assured Mitzi, squeezing her hand. "All we'll do is say hello to everyone and run."

Huddled against the light summer rain, they stood side by side staring at the brass cherub knocker on Mona's door. Mitzi couldn't wait to get this over with and begin their last-night wingding. It was going to be a bittersweet sensual feast.

As she watched him, Grant's forehead slowly creased with worry, and his eyes took on a vaguely familiar faraway look. "I hope our Joy ploy worked. If Moreland is still set on buying..."

Mitzi glanced at him nervously. *Please don't let me lose this one to his work tonight.* "Don't forget, there's champagne chilling at home, and steaks marinating, and a jasmine-scented bubble bath awaiting us."

His eyes darkened with anticipation and an expression of sexual possessiveness. Heat pooled in her. Immediately she wanted to skip the party, the steaks, everything, and just stay in bed until her plane took off the next day.

The next day! It wasn't nearly enough time. "Oh, Grant."

He looked as if he might bend down and kiss her, but in the next moment, the door was flung open with a dramatic flourish.

"Everything's a disaster!"

Grant and Mitzi sprang apart and gaped at Mona almost guiltily. Not that Grant's stepmother noticed. Aside from being flawlessly coiffed and groomed, the woman looked frazzled and desperate and jittery. But the most disturbing thing about the woman's appearance was that she was dressed in the same lime-green taffeta dress that Mitzi had on beneath her raincoat. Mitzi could hardly believe it. One person buying that dress was misguided but amusing. Two was a fashion cataclysm.

Grant and Mitzi exchanged nervous glances.

"Half my people have arrived and there's still no sign of the guest of honor!" Mona raved. She spoke of her people—her party guests—much as Evita Perón might have referred to the people of Argentina. As an afterthought, she glanced at Mitzi, who was huddled in the hallway in a long white rain slicker. "My, what a lovely thing," Mona said, her curling lip indicating disdain for the raincoat. "Would you like to take it off?"

"No, thank you," Mitzi answered politely, thinking the woman didn't appear emotionally strong enough to see the dress yet.

Mona shrugged her shoulders, then took her stepson's arm and fluttered dramatically toward the back stairs. "Oh, dear Grant! You just don't know what I've been through today! All my best-laid plans have gone awry!" Tears actually sprang to her eyes.

"What happened?" Grant asked as they went into Mona's bedroom suite. The two rooms and bath resembled a set from one of those old thirties art deco musicals—a suite done in gilt furniture, satin upholstery and thick white plush carpet that Ginger Rogers might have been at home in. "Did you say something to Mr. Moreland?"

"Me?" Mona sank onto a settee, her eyes widening in shock that he would even suggest such a ridiculous thing.

"I said absolutely nothing! The odious man simply called me out of the blue this morning, shouting at the top of his lungs about how his daughter was missing. How should I know where some spoiled little brat is?"

As she whipped out a long silk handkerchief to wipe her eyes, Grant and Mitzi gaped at each other. Ted hadn't shown up at work this morning, which hadn't seemed too unusual since he'd probably spent a terrible night with the Moreland woman. But having both of them missing painted a different picture entirely.

Mitzi grabbed Grant's arm and pulled him aside. "You don't think they killed each other, do you?"

Mona straightened from her swoon. "What are you two whispering about over there?" she asked sharply.

Grant pivoted. "Oh, we were just talking about Ted."

"Ted?" Mona repeated as if she had bigger fish to fry. "Never mind Ted, dear. Where is that tedious little Joy person? You must have taken her home last night."

"Actually, Mona, there's something I need to tell you."

Mona's black eyebrows rose like inky question marks on her forehead.

"It's about Ted."

"Ted? What has Ted got to do with any of this?" Grant was about to answer, when Mona flicked a distracted glance at Mitzi. "My dear, I don't know who you are, but I do wish you would take off that silly raincoat you have on. You look like a hobo, and besides, you're dripping on my carpet."

Mitzi looked anxiously down at herself, then stammered, "Oh, well, all right." With a long, grim glance at Grant, she pulled the coat off quickly and stood before Mona in her lime-green bridesmaid's dress—the same dress, in the same nauseating color, that Mona was wearing.

Grant's stepmother shot off the settee with a shriek, with the result that the two women stood side by side, as alike as lime-green Twinkies. Mona covered her eyes.

The effect was a little blinding.

"Where did you get that dress?" Mona still couldn't bear to look.

"A friend of mine ordered it, from a catalog, I think. She picked it as a bridesmaid's dress."

"A bridesmaid's dress!" Mona let out a choked sob, as if Mitzi had just added insult to injury.

"Well, I was maid of honor," Mitzi put in, hoping the elevated rank would appeal to Mona's sense of status.

It didn't. Mona shook a fist at the heavens or, rather, at the gaudy chandelier that hung down from her fifteen-foot ceiling. "Ruined, everything's ruined!"

Grant attempted to calm his stepmother. "There, there," he told her, sitting her back down. "You can put on another dress. You have so many beautiful clothes..."

Mona sniffed, still looking at Mitzi accusingly. "I bought this one especially," she said in the tone of a petulant child. Then she slapped her bejeweled hand against her knee. "Oh, that Horace Moreland," she exclaimed, as if Moreland and the dress had conspired to ruin her party. "What a horrid, horrid man."

Though Mona's words were music to his ears, Grant knew that Horace didn't deserve the brunt of her anger. "The thing I was going to tell you, Mona, was that I didn't see Joy Moreland last night," he confessed. "Ted did."

"Ted," Mona exclaimed. "But last Sunday you promised that you would take her out."

"Actually, that was Ted who promised."

Mona looked as if she was losing control of her mind as well as her party. "Oh, good grief! Ted had no business going out with that Moreland girl. The way he treats women? It's like throwing chum to a shark."

"I know," Grant admitted, feeling just the tiniest bit ashamed of himself.

"Oh, Grant! How could you do this to me? You know how I so wanted to impress that odious Horace Moreland." She shuddered, then straightened rigidly. "Of course, now I don't care. Not one itty-bitty bit I don't. If you could have heard the way he spoke to me!"

Suddenly, below them, the floor thumped from sounds of a small band playing on the floor below. "Oh, good, the musicians are here," Mona said, then, not missing a beat, she lit a cigarette, stepped out of her shoes and padded across the pristine white carpet to her enormous walk-in closet, which almost constituted another room. She disappeared, but like a burrowing mole tossing dirt out its den, she sent outfits of every shape and color flying toward the bed. "In fact," she yelled out at them as a silver lamé arced toward Grant, "I think it was from a Moreland's catalog that I bought this detestable green thing. Yes, I'm positive it was."

Grant strode across the room to the phone next to Mona's bed. He got thwacked with a scarf, but brushed it aside. He needed to find Ted. He picked up the white Princess phone and dialed his brother's home number. There was no answer. "Do you think I should call the police?" he asked Mitzi.

"Maybe they had a boating accident," she said. "Maybe they're stuck in the hospital emergency room."

"For twenty-four hours?" Grant worried more that they were both permanent residents of the hospital. But that didn't make sense. Ted was a responsible citizen, at least on the water. He didn't fool around with his boat, unless he'd dropped anchor for the night somewhere. But surely he wouldn't have dropped anchor with Joy last night!

Just as he was about to dial the first hospital, Uncle Truman stormed into the room, followed by Horace Moreland himself. The two red-faced, white-haired old men in suits looked as if they might be on the verge of coming to blows.

Truman caught sight of Grant and breathed an audible sigh of relief. "Grant! Thank heavens you're here!" He began pointing frantically at Mr. Moreland. "Will you please tell this lunatic that you didn't run off with his daughter?"

Grant looked up from the phone to Mr. Moreland and said politely and truthfully, "I didn't run off with your daughter."

"There!" Truman shouted. "You see? It's like I've been telling you."

"Ted ran off with your daughter."

The two men turned to him in unison. "Ted?"

Truman looked grave. "How could that be? You said you were going out with her."

Mona marched out of the closet with her hands on her hips. She glared up at Mr. Moreland, and seemed to dare anyone in the room to so much as utter a peep about her and Mitzi's matching outfits. "That was Ted who told us that, Truman."

Truman looked down his hawk nose through his spectacles in confusion. "Well then, Ted told us Grant was going out with her."

"But he didn't. Ted did," Mona explained.

Bewildered, Truman hunched in thought, but Horace

sprang forward. "Are you telling me that you don't even know which brother is out with my daughter?"

"Ted is," Mitzi finally put in. "Or was. We're not sure where he is, either. I've been worried sick!"

"I don't understand," Truman muttered, still in a daze.

"I can sympathize with your confusion," Mitzi told him.

"Who is she?" Moreland asked, pointing to Mitzi.

Truman squinted at her. "Heck if I know."

"I'll tell you who she is," Mona said, marching forward in her lime-green dress, the skirt of which she held out accusingly.

The number to the hospital was ringing interminably, and Grant held the handset away from his ear as the confrontation centered closer to Mitzi.

Mona stopped inches away from Horace. "That poor woman, like myself, is one of your retail victims!"

"Come again?" Horace asked.

"She ordered this dress from your catalog!" she said, poking her finger in his chest.

Horace looked dumbfounded. "I don't see what all this has to do with—"

Mona, in a fury, cut him off. "It has to do with the fact that if I had bought a dress at Whiting's for my party, one of the salesladies there would have been able to tell me exactly how many of these dresses had been sold and to whom, so that my guests would not show up at my house looking like their hostess!"

"Your dress is not my problem," Mr. Moreland answered back.

It was exactly the wrong thing to say. Mona looked as if she might throw a conniption fit, but to Grant's surprise, she didn't shriek or yell, but replied with icy calm. "You bet it's not your problem, buster. Because I will never, never, buy a dress from Moreland's again. Nor will I buy from your catalog. I will boycott Moreland's!''

Truman nearly choked. "Well now! Let's not speak in anger." He chuckled nervously. "Once we find out what happened to Ted and Jane, I'm sure we'll all feel much more rational."

"Her name is Joy," Moreland said, steaming. "And you'd better pray your nephew hasn't gotten them into a wreck somewhere. But even if they both come back safe and sound, I have serious reservations about doing business with this family. You're all a bunch of nuts! I should have packed my bags the night I had dinner with Grant, who seemed about as stable as a jack-in-the-box. Or the moment I saw that store's staff—doormen in cutoffs! Perfume-counter clerks in Birkenstocks! The United States Marines couldn't whip those hooligans into shape!''

The door banged open and a streak of white and blond shot across the room.

"Daddy!''

The next one through the door was Ted, smiling sheepishly. Grant, relieved the manhunt was over, hung up the phone.

"Oh, Joy, honey! My poor baby!'' Moreland gave his daughter a heartfelt hug and sent a stern glare Ted's way. "If that ruffian did anything to you…''

Joy tossed back her head, laughing, and walked backward until she was almost sandwiched between Ted and her father. "Guess what, Daddy? Grant Whiting and I just got married!''

Grant jumped up from the bed in shock. In fact, the whole room was staring at Joy as if she'd lost her mind.

Ted tugged on the sleeve of her dress. "My name's Ted, honey,'' he told her. "Remember? I explained it all to you.''

Joy giggled. "Oh, right! Ted Whiting and I got married!"

Grant was relieved to hear it, as relieved as he was stunned. He did a mental review of CPR, because Horace looked like a good bet to go into cardiac arrest.

"Good Lord, what happened?" Horace choked out.

Joy beamed a smile bright enough to absorb all the storm clouds outside, and a few in the room as well. "Teddy Bear and I fell in love!"

Mitzi and Grant exchanged amazed smirks. *Teddy Bear?*

"But not before we'd been adrift in the Gulf of Mexico all night long." Joy laughed. "We ran out of gas. Really! Teddy said he was sure he'd had a whole tank. But the Coast Guard had to come get us."

Mitzi stepped forward, amazed. Talk about a plan backfiring. "You mean, you two got along? The whole time?"

Joy's smile dissolved to a little pout, and she shuffled from her daddy's arms to Ted's. "Well, at first, Teddy was in a bad temper. Especially when we ran out of gas. Oh, we spent the first part of the night fighting like crazy. But I used my psychology expertise to explain to Teddy Bear that he's misplacing his anger at all women because of his mother's death when he was at such a tender age. And that what he really craves is a strong female in his life."

Ted lifted his chin, as if daring Grant to make fun of him. "Joy's very smart."

"Later, of course, when we were just concerned with our survival, we bonded," Joy said. "We didn't have enough food, and no radio. So Teddy and I built a fire on the deck of the boat and started trying to send smoke signals."

Grant frowned. "What did you burn?"

"Our clothes."

Mr. Moreland looked green.

Joy punched Ted playfully in the stomach. "Can you imagine? By the time that Coast Guard chopper saw us, we were both hopping up and down on the boat stark naked. And of course, by that time we were getting along a lot better. Especially after Ted had confided his nickname to me."

"What nickname?" Mona asked.

Joy sent an adoring look up at her new husband, whose chest was puffed up proudly. "Mr. Love." She emitted a breathy sigh. "This morning after we were rescued, we decided to run off to Louisiana to get married." Joy flashed her third finger, left hand, which bore a diamond ring. "See?"

Mona eyeballed the chunky stone appreciatively. "You did pretty well for yourself for a first date."

Joy nodded and laughed. "I've never been so happy! I've always said I'd only marry for love and for life, and this is it!"

Mitzi, still amazed, couldn't help feeling happy for her. And even for Ted. They both seemed absurdly, blissfully happy. In fact, the only one in the room not beaming with goodwill was the bride's father.

"This is the nuttiest thing I've ever heard of," Horace told his daughter. "You can't just run off and marry one of these irresponsible, lunatic Whiting men! I won't allow it!"

Mona tore her gaze from the diamond and turned on Horace, her face every bit as red as his. "And I won't allow you to talk about my sons that way in my house!"

"Sons!" Horace snapped. "Why would you stand up

for two lunatics when they aren't even your own flesh and blood?''

To Grant's surprise, Mona looked genuinely angry. "They might not be my own blood, Mr. Moreland, but Ted and Grant have been nothing but responsible and kind toward me ever since their father died. They could have left me out in the cold, forced me back to the cocktail lounge, and contested the fact that my husband left me a quarter interest in the store. But no, they were kind and understanding and even tried to reason with me when I foolishly wanted to sell the family's business to you.

"But now I wouldn't sell Whiting's if my life depended on it, which, thanks to the stewardship of these two men you call lunatics—" she gestured proudly to Grant and Ted "—it doesn't. So you can just take your money and skedaddle back to Saint Louis, Mr. Moreland. We're not selling!''

Even Truman, who had been looking rather startled up to this point, was roused by Mona's words. "Hear! Hear!''

Grant, besides feeling overwhelmed by Mona's defense of him, felt almost weak with relief that the ordeal was over. He hugged Mitzi to his side and smiled at Ted, who gave him a thumbs-up.

Horace smashed his hat on his head and glared at them all. "Before I go back to Saint Louis I'm going to the best lawyer in town to see about an annulment. And then, once that's done, I'll call in my board of directors and ask them what they think about hostile takeovers!''

Then he stomped out of the room, leaving a loaded silence in his wake. For a moment, the six people left behind merely gaped at the closed door.

Joy glanced a little apologetically at all of them. "I think secretly he's really very happy for me. Don't you?''

Everyone hastened to assure her that this was probably the case. But Grant felt nervous. "What he said about a hostile takeover, would he really?"

Joy shrugged. "Daddy can be sort of mule-headed at times."

That was putting it mildly. Grant sighed, and looked at Ted. His brother grinned. "Hey, don't worry so much. We're all family now."

But given the fact that Mr. Moreland had just stomped out screaming that he would have the marriage annulled, Ted's assurance didn't have a full-bodied ring to it.

"I'll take care of it tonight," Grant said, turning to pick up his coat from under the pile of clothes on Mona's bed. It would be best to work on Mr. Moreland now, while the shock was wearing off. Maybe he could make the man believe that a hostile takeover at this point would be traumatic for the newlyweds. Horace doted on Joy; he was bound to see that busting up her marriage wouldn't endear him to her.

"Grant?"

At the sound of Mona's voice, he turned back to his four relatives watching him expectantly. A chill swept through him. Someone was missing. "Where's Mitzi?"

"Gone," Ted said. "She ducked out a second ago."

Mona nodded. "She was muttering something about steaks and bubble baths." A black eyebrow raised questioningly.

Joy blinked. "Why, she's the same woman I saw at the hairdresser's yesterday!" She frowned in utter confusion. "But she said she and Grant Whiting were finished."

Finished was right, he feared. For a moment, he'd forgotten completely about their private party, forgotten that this was Mitzi's last night. Forgotten about Mitzi, period.

Grant scurried out the door and down the stairs just in time to catch a glimpse of her raincoat-clad back heading through the crowded hallway toward the living room. He began to weave his way through the milling, dancing crowd in the living room.

He was stopped halfway through the room when a hand clamped down on his shoulder. "Grant! Where are you running off to?"

It was Brewster. "Have you seen Mitzi?"

Brewster nodded. "She just ran through here looking as if piranhas were nipping at her heels."

Leave it to Brewster to fit a fish into the picture somehow. Grant frowned.

"I offered to drive her but she said something about swimming toward a bus."

She would have to swim on a night like this. At just that moment, a bolt of lightning struck outside, punctuating the rhythm of the band's rendition of "Mona Lisa."

"I've got to find her," Grant said, leaving Brewster in his dust. He didn't know how he was going to square his business obligations with Mitzi's last night, but he feared he wouldn't have to worry about it. He had the terrible feeling that he'd already blown it.

THE ROOM WAS SO THICK with revelers Mitzi could barely get through. It didn't help that her eyes were pooled with tears and she had a hard time seeing. How had it happened? How had she managed to travel a thousand miles and get herself involved with yet another workaholic? A man who would punt their last romantic evening together over a hypothetical takeover.

She finally reached the sliding glass door that let out onto the back patio and yanked it open. The landscaped area would have been stunning on a clear day. Huge trees created a canopy around the large pool, which was an elaborate affair with tile splashes and several mermaid fountains feeding into it. The Roman-bath effect suited Mona's old-Hollywood taste.

Picking her way across the slick pebbled surface of the deck, she had almost cleared the pool when she heard the door slide open behind her. Grant came running toward her, his shirtsleeves still rolled up as they had been when he had been anxiously calling hospitals, and his raincoat on his arm.

"Mitzi!" His voice competed with a clap of thunder. She spun on her heel to face him.

He looked flabbergasted. "Where are you going?"

"Home."

A wounded expression appeared in his eyes. "Please don't be unreasonable about this."

A fat raindrop plopped onto her nose as she stood gaping at him, stunned beyond belief. She had expected him to come out with any number of things—an apology would have been nice, for starters. The man hadn't even introduced her to his family, and then he'd forgotten all about her in his hurry to find Mr. Moreland. She also had expected him to cajole her into complacency. Workaholics were good at that. *I'll be there as soon as I can,* they always said. Meanwhile, the ice around the champagne would turn to a lukewarm puddle, and the steaks would char to a crisp. Mitzi wouldn't even have been surprised if Grant had asked her to come along while he spoke to Moreland, which was another suave tactic. The old work-as-date approach.

But once again, Grant had surprised her.

"This tops them all," she exclaimed. "You think I'm being unreasonable?"

Lightning brightened the sky, illuminating the hint of

doubt in Grant's eyes. "Moreland was talking hostile takeover," he said, sticking to his guns.

Mitzi rolled her eyes. "He was just angry. He didn't mean it."

"How do you know?"

"Because he was mad about his daughter getting married. Before Joy and Ted came in, he'd already said he didn't want to have anything more to do with Whiting's."

"But that doesn't rule out a hostile takeover."

Mitzi sighed. It was hopeless. Grant would always put the store first, and she would be left hanging.

He came closer. "Look, I'm sincerely sorry I blanked out for a minute. I completely forgot about our plans. I know we were going to have that thing back at Kay's place."

She snorted in offense to hear their last-night party, which she had been breathlessly anticipating, reduced to a "thing."

"I'll be there just as soon as I can," he promised.

Mitzi grinned, but shook her head as the familiar, expected words tumbled from his mouth as if they'd been scripted in advance. And maybe they had. From the way he sounded, he could have been any one of the big three who had preceded him. Except that her heart ached more to hear the words coming from him.

"What is it?" he asked.

"I expected better from you, Grant," she said, her voice coming out shaky. She tried without success to still the tremble. "I thought we were working toward something special."

She turned to walk away before she could make an idiot of herself, but she was stopped by his hand on her arm. Even now, his touch had the power to send an electric current zipping through her.

"Mitzi, wait," he said, obviously searching for words to smooth things over. Silently she prayed he would find them. "Would you like to come along with me while I talk to Moreland?"

He could have slapped her and she would have taken it better. "Oh, Grant!"

He tossed his hands in the air. "What? What did I say?"

She hadn't thought it possible to fall in love with a man in a week. She had laughed when Kay had forecast that she would. But in spite of it all, she had. But now it turned out the man she'd fallen in love with so recklessly was just like all the others.

"Now this thing with Moreland has come up," Grant explained, "and I have to deal with it."

"Ted could deal with it," she said. "It's his in-law."

Grant shook his head. "Ted can't handle a situation like this. It requires finesse."

"I think you're avoiding the issue, Grant."

His hand squeezed on her arm. "What issue?"

"Us."

It was only then that Mitzi realized they were drawing a crowd. About twenty guests had gathered under the eave of the patio, watching the lovers' spat. Worse, another group stood inside, peeking at the scene through the glass door.

Mitzi edged away from Grant, as close to the pool as she could safely get. "Don't come a step closer," she warned him, "or I'll jump."

He rolled his eyes. "I just want us to talk this through—quickly."

Of course, so he could find Mr. Moreland and continue his one-man crusade to save his store.

"There's nothing more to say," she said.

He tightened his grasp on her arm and she squirmed to get away. "Mitzi, I—"

True to her word, she inched closer to the water, but Grant wasn't letting go. They scuffled for a moment, wrenching this way and that as onlookers shouted encouragement. Just when Mitzi thought she might finally wrestle her way free, Grant got the upper hand—and no wonder. He had a five-inch, sixty-pound advantage. But she was more wiry. As she attempted to duck under his arm, her heels slipped on one of the tiles and she felt herself losing her balance.

As her arms looped in circles, and Grant grabbed at her desperately, either hoping to steady himself or her or both, Mitzi was overcome with a sense of déjà vu. And as they both hit the cold water in their best clothes, her mind finally found the perfect words to describe their relationship.

All washed up.

10

TED LEANED against the bedroom door, a sage expression on his face. "You know, I think everyone should be married."

Bundled up in one of Mona's thick pink terry-cloth bathrobes, Grant scowled up at his brother. His dunking in the pool had left him soaked, cold and without clothes. Not to mention without Mitzi, who Brewster had gallantly offered a ride home. His brother's happily wedded bliss was giving him a headache.

"What's the matter?" Ted asked him.

"I'm worried about the store," he said automatically.

But it wasn't true at all. He was worried about Mitzi.

Mona and Joy were off hunting down some of his father's old clothes from the attic for him. The trouble was, once he was dressed again, Grant didn't know who he should run after—Mr. Moreland, or Mitzi. He had a sinking feeling that both would welcome his arrival as enthusiastically as the onset of the flu.

"You can't live for business, bro," Ted said philosophically. "That's what the past day has taught me."

Grant gawked at his brother in open amazement. "When have you ever lived for business?"

Ted shrugged. "Hey, what was that boat ride you sent me on about? And while we're on the subject, what happened to all that gas you said you'd put in the tank?"

Grant squirmed with guilt. "I'm sorry."

"Hey, I don't care. It brought me Joy." Ted cackled at the unintentional play on words. "Brought me joy, get it?"

Grant's lips turned up limply in a half effort of a smile. Ted really was happy. He couldn't believe it. The dyed-in-the-wool bachelor was really just a fluffy little lamb willingly following Joy. And he, Grant, had brought this romance about by forcing Ted out on that boat. He'd managed to set Ted up with a wife while his own romance had capsized. Suddenly, he felt a surge of pure envy.

"Why don't you go after her?" Ted asked.

Grant shook his head. "My relationship with Mitzi has been a disaster from start to finish, from a punch in the jaw to a splash in the pool. Nothing's gone right."

Nothing except the two days when they impossibly, blissfully and undeniably fell in love. And now it was really over. Kay and Marty had flown in tonight, and Mitzi would be flying back to New York tomorrow morning. Grant stared grimly at his bare toes buried in the thick white pile carpet. "Do you think Mona has any aspirin?"

Ted laughed. "Why don't you call Mitzi?"

"That wouldn't help. You should have seen her. Every time I opened my mouth, she just got madder."

His brother nodded. "And no doubt you were probably explaining how important it was to you to save the store."

Ted sank onto the bed next to him and steepled his fingers, mulling over the problem. He gave Grant an intense stare. One day with Joy the psychology major, and suddenly the man was Leo Buscaglia. "What's really the problem with you two, Grant?"

Grant sighed. "There is no problem. It's just that

Mitzi's been through so many bad relationships, she's positively love-a-phobic, so she won't believe anything I say at this point. She thinks I'm a workaholic, like all the other men she's gone out with.''

Ted looked as though he'd have to think that one over. ''So what you have, as the man said, is a failure to communicate.''

''Yes.''

Ted smiled thoughtfully. ''Let me ask you this. Did you tell her that you love her?''

''Of course,'' Grant exclaimed.

Then he frowned.

Had he? Before they'd made love, he had wanted to give her a clear indication of the depth of his feeling for her. *''I think I love you.''* There. That was pretty darn clear.

Wasn't it?

He sank a little lower. ''Well, okay, not in so many words, but I think it was implied.''

Ted clucked his tongue. ''Grant, Grant. What's the matter with you? Don't you know anything about women? They have to have these things spelled out. You can't just imply love.''

He couldn't believe he was to the point where his brother was giving him romance tips. ''I know how to conduct my own affairs, thank you.''

''Is that what you want from Mitzi? An affair?''

''No!'' Why was he having such a hard time making himself clear?

''Then what do you want?''

Grant rolled his eyes, fearing he might explode. ''I want to get married!'' he screeched at his brother. But when he heard the words come out of his mouth, he was amazed.

Maybe his experience with Janice had made him reticent to say the words that needed to be said. Maybe he had been just the tiniest bit hesitant to make that commitment. But now that the proverbial cat was out of the bag, everything became crystal clear in his mind. "I want to get married again. To Mitzi. I want Mitzi to be my wife."

It was so clear to him now. Why hadn't he told her last night? Or, for that matter, the first time he'd ever clapped eyes on her?

Maybe because it had taken what he felt for Mitzi to make him understand spontaneity, and romance. And letting loose. Kay had been right. He had fallen loopy in love. At last!

As Grant had his revelation, Ted beamed him a satisfied grin. "You know, I sometimes think I am Mr. Love."

Grant jumped up and began pacing. "How am I going to get Mitzi back and deal with Mr. Moreland, though?"

Ted stood up and reached into his pocket. "Here," he said, tossing a small metal object to Grant.

Grant caught the key and frowned. "What's this for?"

"My boat."

Grant took the key slowly, as understanding dawned. "But Moreland..."

Ted grinned. "Is my headache now. Don't worry, bro. Joy and I will convince the man to lay off Whiting's. Joy's got a lot of pull with her dad, and she knows how much the store means to all of us."

Grant stood, tossing the key in his palm. Maybe it was crazy to trust Ted to handle things, but sometime in the past week he'd become comfortable with crazy. It was the idea of going back to his old plodding life that frightened him. He wasn't just riding off to rescue his relationship, but also the person he'd become with Mitzi. "Thanks, bro—I owe you one."

Ted shrugged casually. "Just chalk it up as another freebie from Mr. Love."

Grant dashed toward the door but was stopped by his brother hitching his throat. He turned.

Ted grinned as he nodded toward Grant's pink terry bathrobe. "I know you're eager, but shouldn't you wait for some clothes?"

MITZI BURROWED DOWN in the tubful of bubbles and polished off her third glass of champagne. No sense letting the stuff go to waste. "You were completely wrong about Grant," she announced to Kay, who was standing in the doorway, tanned and disgustingly happy-looking, despite the worried frown on her face. A true friend, Kay had pulled herself away from her new hubby and her new home at Mitzi's hysterical call. "He's completely wrong for me. A total workaholic."

"Except that you're in love with him," Kay guessed.

"So? I was in love with the others, too." She sighed. But when Tim had become a monk, she hadn't felt this heartsick. Nor when Mike had married his model. When Jeff had eloped with a jockey, she hadn't experienced the same sense of betrayal as when Grant announced his intention to run after Mr. Moreland.

She was in love with Grant.

"Maybe he was so stunned by Ted's getting married that he wasn't thinking straight," Kay said. "Heaven knows, I'm stunned."

Mitzi frowned, trying not to give the plausible argument any credence. But Grant had been perfectly attentive before Ted and Joy's disappearance came up. She shook her head. "This time, I'm not going to be the dumpee. For the first time in my life, I'll be the dumper, thank you."

"What difference does that make?" Kay asked.

"None, really, except that I won't have egg on my face. That's got to be some consolation." Unfortunately, she didn't think the pain she would suffer from the breakup would be any less for her taking the initiative in its demise. And the end result was the same. It was back to needlework and parrots for her.

"Grant wouldn't lead you on, Mitzi. I don't know what's come between you."

"A department store," she said.

Her friend raised a golden eyebrow curiously. "Are you sure it was Whiting's, and not Jeff and Mike and Tim?"

As the question sank in, a flush of understanding heated Mitzi's cheeks. It was true. The moment Grant's mind had turned to business, a switch had flipped in her brain. Grant had been wrong, but she'd been overly defensive. All she could see was that he was putting something ahead of her, and their plans, like all the others. All she'd been able to feel was her own disappointment, and anger, and heartache. And instead of telling Grant her concerns, she'd tossed him into a pool.

"Oh, no!" she groaned, suddenly flooded with regret. What had she done? How differently the evening might have ended had she kept her temper and tried to understand the family turmoil he was going through, and not jumped to the conclusion that Grant would always put her second.

The doorbell rang, and Kay smiled. "Hold that thought, Mitz." She disappeared through the bedroom and to the living room, probably to open the door for

Marty, who was no doubt wondering what had become of his bride.

"'The thought' is that I'm such a dope!" Mitzi moaned to herself. In frustration, she slapped the now-lukewarm water next to her, sending a spray of bubbles into the air, some of which landed splat on her face. She attempted to wipe them off, resulting in more suds on her face, and worse, in her eyes. She blinked several times to clear the stinging.

Footsteps approached via the bedroom, and she asked Kay, her voice in despair both from her soapy eyes and her soap opera life, "How on earth am I ever going to apologize to him now?"

A deep chuckle—not Kay's—rumbled from the doorway. Mitzi froze.

"I don't expect an apology."

She blinked double time to try to focus on Grant, who stood in the doorway in a dark suit and tie, looking devilishly handsome. Her heart did handsprings, though her tongue remained firmly tied.

Grant grinned, then from behind his back brought out a glass. "May I join you?"

"Oh, I..." She stammered, then finally came up with, "Sure."

He perched on the side of the tub. Even though he'd already seen all of her there was to see, Mitzi felt self-conscious being covered only by jasmine-scented foam.

"I'm sorry, Mitzi. I shouldn't have run off half-cocked like that."

"I was the one who ran off," she protested, sitting up, nearly throwing modesty to the wind. She hoped those bubbles held up for a few more minutes.

"But you were right."

"I was wrong."

They laughed. "Maybe we were both wrong," Mitzi admitted.

"You would be wrong if you thought I would put anything ahead of you and me again," he said, leaning close to her. "I love you, Mitzi."

She gasped. "Say that again?"

"I love you," he repeated happily. "I want you to marry me."

"I love you, too," she said, but the words caught in her throat. Had she heard him correctly?

He came so close their lips were almost touching. "Will you marry me, Mitzi?"

Would she? "Yes!" she cried, not stopping to think that just five minutes before she'd been espousing a dump-or-be-dumped philosophy. The rocky road of singlehood and her years as the Typhoid Mary of romance were far behind her already.

She looked into Grant's eyes and felt waves of emotion connecting them. People could fall in love in a week. She had. There were men who wanted the same things out of life that she did. Out of the millions and millions of people on the planet, she had found one. The unlikely odds, and the luck she'd found, brought tears of gratitude to her eyes. She'd never been so happy as she was right this moment.

"I love you, Grant," she said, realizing suddenly that this was the first time she'd ever told him the words she had so yearned to hear herself. "Will you forgive me for being such a dope?"

He chuckled, then bent down and brushed his lips against hers. "Forgive me," he said. The moment they kissed again, they were lost. Heat swirled through Mitzi's body, and building desire, as they thoroughly indulged in what would surely become one of their favorite pastimes for the next few decades.

Grant pulled away reluctantly, barely noticing that the front of his suit was soaked with suds. He did notice that Mitzi's soapy cover was quickly disappearing. With effort, he drew his gaze away from her flawless breasts. "I've got news. For the second time in one week, Ted's offered to step in as best man for me."

Mitzi grinned. "You'd better take him up on it."

Grant brought out a key. "And even more remarkably, he's offered us the use of his boat. We could go down to the coast and celebrate our engagement in the water," he suggested.

Mitzi tilted her head and stared at him with green eyes warm with desire. She twined her fingers around the nape of his neck. "Then again, I know a way we could get plenty wet right here."

With only the slightest of tugs, Grant joined her in the soapy water in a tidal wave of arms, legs, bubbles, laughter and long, lingering kisses.

Epilogue

Two months later

THE STRING QUARTET had played the most beautiful rendition of the wedding march Mitzi had ever heard, and now the bespectacled minister was halfway through the incredibly moving ceremony. Mitzi and Grant stood facing him, flanked by Ted on his side and Kay on hers, in the bower set up at the bottom of the sloping backyard behind Kay's house, which Mitzi had been renting for the past two months.

She had moved to Texas almost immediately after their engagement, and for the past months, she had wasted no time plunging into her new life. She and Grant had bought a house, one with plenty of room to start that family they'd both always wanted. She had taken over the advertising for Whiting's, and the first print-ad campaigns had been a rousing success. Meanwhile, she was pursuing her dream of becoming a portrait photographer by setting up her own studio in Kay's spare room.

When Grant had driven up with the boat at the airport two months ago, she'd never been so happy. But she'd repeated that phrase to herself every morning since then. There were no limits, she'd discovered, to how happy a person could be. Her own happiness meter had gone off the charts.

And now, on this day for which she'd waited so long,

she seemed to be in nirvana. The words of the wedding ceremony rushed by her too fast. She wanted to capture each one and savor it. *To love and to cherish, till death us do part.*

Grant's husky "I do" was like a caress. And then it was her turn.

She listened to the same vow, smiling. It was hard to take her eyes off Grant, but when it came time for her answer, she forced herself. Mitzi turned, looking toward Kay's house where Brewster stood guarding the back door, and gave him a nod.

Brewster fumbled with a latch, opening the back door, and out shot Chester, a liver-colored bullet snapping and snarling his way down the grassy aisle created between the two groups of folding chairs. People gasped at the sight of the little dog run amok.

Both Ted and Grant had turned to see the little brown tornado that Brewster had loosed on the crowd, but only the best man's eyes widened in horror, then turned to scope out the nearest tree. He made a mad dash for a low limb. Within seconds, all of Ted that was visible to the gathered guests was a pair of tuxedo pants, socks and black shoes dangling from the foliage, taunting poor Chester as he jumped and yipped and snarled.

Grant turned to Mitzi, eyebrows raised in understanding. "Afraid that we might have been pulling another switch on you?"

Mitzi laughed. "I just wanted to make sure before I said 'I do.'" She turned to the minister and added, "Oh, and by the way, I do."

Grant barely waited for the minister to pronounce them husband and wife to take his new bride into his arms. He had never expected to feel so happy, so complete. "There was another way to tell us apart, remember?"

She nodded eagerly, and he gave her very vivid proof with a soul-searching kiss that went on minutes longer than necessary.

"I love you, Grant." She'd discovered she could never say it enough.

She couldn't hear it enough, either.

"I love you, too." Her husband touched her lips again, then grinned as Chester's barks rose in frantic intensity. He pulled away reluctantly. "But now I think we'd better rescue my best man from that tree."

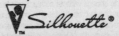

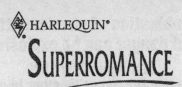

The combination of physical attraction and danger can be explosive!

Coming in July 1999
three steamy romances together in one book

HOT PURSUIT

by bestselling authors

JOAN JOHNSTON

ANNE STUART

MALLORY RUSH

Joan Johnston—A WOLF IN SHEEP'S CLOTHING
The Hazards and the Alistairs had been feuding for generations, so when Harriet Alistair laid claim to her great-uncle's ranch, Nathan Hazard was at his ornery worst. But then he saw her and figured it was time to turn on the charm, forgive, forget…and seduce?

Anne Stuart—THE SOLDIER & THE BABY
What could possibly bring together a hard-living, bare-chested soldier and a devout novice? At first, it was an innocent baby…and then it was a passion hotter than the simmering jungle they had to escape from.

Mallory Rush—LOVE SLAVE
Rand Slick hired Rachel Tinsdale to infiltrate the dark business of white slavery. It was a risky assignment, Rachel knew. But even more dangerous was her aching desire for her sexy, shadowy client….

Available at your favorite retail outlet.

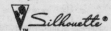

COMING NEXT MONTH

HARLEQUIN
Duets™

#7

ANNIE, GET YOUR GROOM by Kristin Gabriel

Private eye Cole Rafferty is a happily single man—despite the efforts of his matchmaking father. When Annie Bonacci turned to him for help, he made her a deal. If she played his fiancée-from-hell, he'd take her case for free. Little did he know he'd become fiancé number *three* for Annie...only soon he wanted to become husband number *one*.

TAMING LUKE by Jennifer Drew

Jane Grant's directive was simple: Transform Luke Stanton from Tarzan to tycoon...or her job was toast. So, no matter how desirable she found the enigmatic wildman, she had to make him a CEO worth his salt. Trouble was, Luke fought her every step of the way...and made her fall in love with the man it was her mission to change.

#8

THE BRIDE WORE GYM SHOES by Jacqueline Diamond

Marriage counselor Krista Lund doesn't believe in visions—especially when the prediction involved her sexy but annoying neighbor, Connor Fallon, and her wearing a wedding dress and red gym shoes! But, when Connor invited Krista on a romantic weekend to Vegas, she began to wonder if marrying this drop-dead gorgeous man *was* such a crazy idea after all....

MADDIE'S MILLIONAIRE by Tracy South

Maddie Randall was new to Ravens Gap, so how was she supposed to know that Keller Lowry was the most eligible bachelor this side of the Smokies? But after she wrecked his kitchen, renamed his dog and generally turned his life upside down, Maddie couldn't leave Keller alone until she'd set everything straight. Or lost her heart trying....

C